DEFICIT OF DILIGENCE

make no assumptions

PETER ROWLANDS

Topham

PUBLISHING

The Mike Stanhope series

Deficit of Diligence can be read as a free-standing novel, but in fact it's the second book in a series about the leading character, Mike Stanhope, and it contains revelations that might spoil your enjoyment of the first book, *Alternative Outcome*. If you haven't already read that book, you might prefer to start there and experience the story from the beginning.

To Fleur.
Ever supportive and encouraging

Chapter 1

I was wrenched out of sleep by my phone. As I groped for it I lifted the edge of the bedroom curtain. A brilliant summer's morning splashed in. I could feel the warmth in it. Blinking, I let the curtain fall. After six months I still found the quality of Cornish light extraordinary. It really did seem more intense than the London daylight I was accustomed to.

I held the phone to my ear. "You're still in bed!" Ashley's mirthful accusation instantly made me smile. Could she somehow see me from her hotel in London?

"No I'm not."

"Freelancers. You should try working a full day for once like the rest of us."

Nine to five was exactly what I was avoiding. I'd already done that in my previous existence. Ashley's employer, Latimer Logistics, had suggested more than once that I start working for them full time, instead of charging them fees for the writing jobs I did for them. I wasn't ready.

"You've got a letter. I meant to tell you when I called you last night."

She meant she'd retrieved it from my house in south London. I'd forgotten to renew the redirection mandate, so mail was stacking up there. I'd put the place on the market after moving to Truro late last year, and had recently agreed a sale, but I still had the keys. Ashley had volunteered to go and check it over while she was at her marketing conference in the West End.

Receiving a letter was hardly momentous news, but from her tone I sensed that it might be more than just a bill. I said, "What sort of letter?"

"It's from a firm of solicitors, according to the envelope. Green and Bavistock. Ring any bells?"

"Not that I know of."

"Want me to open it?"

"Please."

There was a pause. "Dear Mr Stanhope, we have been trying to reach you in connection with the estate of the late Miss Elizabeth Sanderson, etcetera etcetera." Another pause. "Would you kindly contact the undersigned at your earliest convenience." She broke off. "Did you know a Miss Elizabeth Sanderson?"

"I don't think so."

"Well, sounds as if she knew you. Do you think she remembered you in her will?"

"That kind of luck doesn't happen to me."

"Maybe your luck has changed."

* * *

It was a strange reversal, Ashley being in London and me being in Cornwall. We'd met the previous year through our mutual involvement in the world of logistics – in her case through her job as marketing executive with a transport and warehousing company near Truro, in mine as a journalist in London. We gradually got together, but it was plain that she had little inclination to leave the West Country. Instead, I decided to sell my house, leave London and rent a flat in Truro – nearly three hundred miles to the west, and just a few minutes' drive from Ashley's own tiny flat. It seemed radical, yet the way I saw it I had nothing to lose and plenty to gain.

Half a year later our relationship still felt fresh and new. By contrast, my marriage and previous life seemed drab and directionless. Back then I was on the road to nowhere. Now I was definitely on the road to somewhere, although I wasn't sure exactly where.

That uncertainty was brought home to me as I lifted the lid of my laptop. Three activities were still on the screen from yesterday evening, and they seemed to sum up my current state of indecision. One was a draft of a routine press release I'd written on behalf of Latimer Logistics: workmanlike but pedestrian. Another was the first six paragraphs of a freelance article I was writing for a forklift truck magazine. Even I found this boring.

The third window on screen was the beginning of my new novel, but this was very much an outside bet. My first novel, which I'd self-published as an e-book the year before, hadn't yet sold even a hundred copies, but I still nurtured hopes of pushing it to a wider audience. The problem was finding the right way to market it. Self-publishing, I now knew, was a minefield of conflicting advice and relentless online graft. The web seemed rife with forums where would-be writers took delight in warning of the pitfalls. Yet the hassle hadn't curbed my desire to write a second book. It might still be the way to turn the corner to recognition.

I shrugged. I would think about this some other time. More pressing was the question of whether or not I was still fundamentally a journalist. I felt I was being drawn ever deeper into the Latimer fold, but how far was I prepared to let that go? It was certainly tempting: more money, much more security, and a sense of belonging. But I wasn't quite ready to stop being a journalist yet, despite a recent lack of substantial commissions. It felt too much like compromise. And I certainly wasn't about to give up on my idea of becoming a novelist.

I was still debating which of the three activities should take priority today when my phone rang again.

"Mike, it's Bob Latimer. Is today one of your days for coming into the office?"

The company's headquarters were in St Austell, fifteen miles away. A tiny room had been allocated to me in the main office building, but I tried to limit my visits. I didn't want the staff to see me as a permanent fixture, and I wasn't really comfortable working there. It felt wrong somehow to spend time on any activity that wasn't related to Latimers.

I answered, "Not strictly speaking."

"Ah. Well would you be free to come over anyway? I wanted to run something past you."

It was a request that couldn't be denied. Bob, the chief executive and grandson of the founder, had been strongly supportive when I moved to Truro, increasing the amount of freelance work his firm gave me and making the room available when I wanted it. His tone was nearly always genial, but I'd learned that this shouldn't be confused with mildness of manner or lack of purpose. Invitations from him were almost instructions, and I felt I owed him enough to take this one as such.

I told him, "I'm on my way."

* * *

On a good day I enjoyed the drive to St Austell. Despite being the main route out of Truro towards Plymouth and points east, it was mostly just a busy single-carriageway road, flanked for much of the way by hedgerows and fields. Today it all looked gleaming and picture-postcard perfect, and reminded me why I was glad to be in Cornwall.

Bob Latimer closed his office door behind me and ushered me into a visitor's chair, taking a seat behind his desk.

"It's about Mellings," he said, unusually diffident. He was slim in build, somewhere in his mid-forties but perennially boyish in appearance. He brushed his slightly overlong dark hair back through his fingers.

I nodded expectantly, wondering where this was heading. Bob's company, Latimer Logistics, was a substantial family-owned business with headquarters in Cornwall and depots in various other cities. Its core business was storing and delivering goods, and it had hundreds of thousands of square feet of warehousing in St Austell and elsewhere, along with a sizeable fleet of trucks. I'd cut my teeth writing articles about such companies, and these days I was using that experience to write for, rather than about, this one.

Melling Logistics was a smaller but well-established business in north-east England, and Bob's company had just taken it over, gaining a presence in a new area. I'd had to prepare several press releases about the acquisition. Bob himself had been shuttling up and down the country for several months to seal the deal, usually taking various colleagues with him.

I said, "Things are all going to plan, are they?"

"So far so good. It's an exciting time." He smiled, still with that diffident air, then cleared his throat. "How would you feel about spending a week or two up there?"

I gave him what I hoped was a willing but slightly puzzled smile. "Doing what?"

"Good question." He glanced briefly out of the window at the forecourt of the office block, perhaps seeking inspiration in the bays where staff and visitors parked. Turning back to me he said, "I suppose you could call it liaison."

Clearly there was more. I waited.

"Where we're at with all this is that Mellings have signed a letter of intent, and we're waiting for due diligence to complete. Our lawyers are busy doing their stuff. In other words, the deal has gone through in principle, but we haven't signed our names on the dotted line yet."

I nodded. I had a vague idea what "due diligence" meant – something to do with lawyers and accountants checking that the acquired asset was really worth what the sellers claimed, and was free of undisclosed debts and obligations.

"So while that's all going on, I'm sending Jamie and Andrea up there to maintain an on-the-spot presence. They'll be able to get a handle on how Mellings run things at a practical level – operational management, customer account handling, that sort of thing. Eventually we'll need to integrate all that with what we do here."

Jamie worked in Latimers' operations department, which meant he was involved in the day-to-day running of the company. Andrea was in accounts. I knew them both slightly. I gave Bob a quizzical look.

"They're both quite young," he said, "and more to the point, they're in a mutual relationship. I don't think I'm breaking any confidences in telling you that."

I could hardly express any negative views about this. Ashley and I were in a similar situation.

He continued, "So basically, I don't want them to think I'm sending them on an expenses-paid holiday to the party capital of the North East." He gave me an ironic smile. "Ostensibly you would be there to progress the press and marketing aspects, but actually you would be keeping an eye on them as well."

"Why me?

"Ah, well." He sat back and stretched, clasping his hands behind his head. "Brian is on sick leave and Charles's wife has just had given birth. I can't expect him to travel. And I can't ask Gareth to go again either. He's already done three trips." Brian Wells and Charles Cornish were two of Bob's co-directors, and Gareth Hobbs was the recently-appointed sales manager. I'd only seen him briefly on a couple of occasions; up to now he seemed to have spent more time on the Melling project than in the office.

"Besides," Bob said, "you have exactly the right range of qualities for this. I don't know why I didn't think of you before."

I resisted asking what those qualities were. "But I'm not even on Latimers' staff."

He waved this away with a generous sweep of the hand. "I think you've earned your place on our team in the past half-year, Mike. People here respect you. Obviously I'll pay you a proper daily rate and all expenses, and if you have freelance work to do, you can keep on doing it while you're up there."

I caught him in an inscrutable smile, and smiled back at him, curious. "And there's something else?"

He leaned forward slightly. "Well, being an outsider has its advantages. You're not in the management hierarchy. You're an unknown quantity. That could help when it comes to interacting with Mellings."

"You have reservations about them?"

"No, not at all. You'll enjoy working with Chris Melling. I just want to make it clear to him and his team that the rules have changed. They're no longer calling all the shots. That's really what this whole visit is about – having an ongoing presence there on the ground."

"He might be a bit guarded with me. We know each other vaguely, and he already knows I have a separate life as a journalist."

"So be it." Another smile. "I see this as a bit of practical psychology." He sat back. "So what do you think?"

Chapter 2

"You should go." Ashley was uncompromisingly positive when she phoned me that evening from her conference hotel in Bloomsbury. "You'll earn brownie points with Bob, and you'll enjoy it. It'll be a good experience."

"But he wants me to leave on Thursday. I won't see you before you get back from London."

I could hear the plangent tone in my voice, but after half a year in Cornwall I still didn't like being separated from Ashley. I could hardly believe my luck in getting together with her in the first place, or work out what she saw in me. The spark between us had been obvious from the moment we met, but it was still a wonder to me that she'd chosen me over her fiancé. She brought so many things to our relationship that had been missing from my marriage.

"How long does he want you to spend up there?"

"It's a bit open-ended. Maybe a couple of weeks, to start with."

"But surely you can come back at weekends?"

"I suppose so, but it'll be hell of a long journey. Anyway, not this first weekend. He wants me to go to some social event that the company is putting on."

"It'll be fun. Newcastle is a place with a real buzz these days – that's what I hear."

"I don't think I'm very good with enforced exile."

"Maybe I could come and visit you."

"Ha! You'd have to ask Bob Latimer about that. One of the reasons he's sending me is to make sure Jamie and Andrea don't treat the whole trip as an expenses-paid sex binge."

She chuckled softly. "Listen to you. When did you get to be so old?"

Ashley was nearly eight years younger than me, but I didn't like being reminded of it. I said, "This is Bob talking, not me."

"Yeah yeah."

There was a pause, then she said, "What about those solicitors – the ones who wrote to you?"

"What about them?"

"Well, I think they were based somewhere in the north. You could actually go and see them. Let me get the letter." I could hear her rummaging around. "Ha! It's St Mary's Place, Newcastle upon Tyne. There you go. Couldn't be more appropriate."

* * *

So come next morning I was poring over maps on my laptop, trying to get a sense of the distance from Truro to Newcastle. As I'd thought, by UK standards Newcastle seemed impossibly far away: more than four hundred and fifty miles by road. The route was fast and relatively straightforward, but you could never rule out traffic delays and road works. According to the computer, it would take well over seven hours to drive it.

I phoned Sally Meadows, Bob Latimer's personal assistant. "How does Bob normally get to Newcastle from here?"

"Sometimes he flies. Sometimes he gets the train. There's no quick solution, unfortunately."

"Are there any direct flights from Newquay?" This was my favoured option. Newquay was not far from Truro.

"Possibly, but if so they're very infrequent. Bob's never tried it."

"Oh. Where does he fly from then?"

"Exeter."

"But that must be a hundred miles away!"

She laughed. "It's about ninety from where you are, Mike. Welcome to the realities of living in Cornwall."

When I said nothing, she added, "Take my advice, Mike – go by train and rent a car when you get there. Far less hassle than doing it any other way."

My next call was to the firm of solicitors in Newcastle. Ashley had read out the phone number from their letter, and I soon found myself talking to one of the partners.

"I can't tell you much on the phone," he said. I was aware of the refined but unmistakable Geordie accent – something that would become very familiar to me in the following weeks. "In essence, Elizabeth Sanderson lived alone in Harrogate. She had a house there. She wasn't very old – early seventies, I think – but I believe she was suffering from a long-term disease."

"Harrogate? But you're in Newcastle. Not exactly just round the corner."

"No doubt that aspect is buried in the history."

"But what's the connection? Why did you need to make contact with me?"

"You're mentioned in her will. I think I can safely tell you that much."

Confirmation, then, of Ashley's assumption. I wondered how far I could push my luck. "Is this a substantial bequest that we're talking about?"

"That's something I really can't get into on the phone."

"So how does this work? Will there be an official reading?"

"Oh no, nothing like that. Once we get the formalities out of the way I'll be able to put you in the picture. Coming here in person is a good idea – it should save on some of the correspondence. You'll need to bring various bits of identification with you. I'll email you the details."

Last on my list of calls was Chris Melling, who had founded Melling Logistics twenty-five years before. I'd interviewed him once for an article about his company, and found him relaxed and personable. But that was when he was calling the shots – telling me only what he wanted me to hear. How would he feel, knowing I represented the acquisition team, and might report anything I picked up directly back to Bob Latimer?

"Mike, I understand you're going to grace us with your presence." Wry and smoothly affable.

"I hope that's all right with you?"

"Of course. Delighted to have you with us. We've already found you and your colleagues a room to work in while you're here."

"I appreciate it."

"And we've got you booked into the hotel we normally use. It's a nice little place. I think you'll like it."

"Great, thank you." I hesitated. "Bob thought we could come to your event on Saturday night. Is that all right, or is it going to cause any problems? It seems a bit of a cheek, inviting ourselves along."

"Of course it's all right. I told Bob that. You'll all be very welcome." His Newcastle accent was more pronounced than the solicitor's had been, and also subtly different, even to my untutored ear.

"I'll look forward to seeing you on Friday."

* * *

In the afternoon I drove over to St Austell again. I wanted to strike the right note with Jamie Andrews and Andrea Smith before we all embarked on this expedition.

Jamie seemed relaxed about my involvement. He waved me to a chair next to his desk in the operations room and offered me a coffee. There was a subdued buzz in the open-plan office. Half a dozen people sat at computers, many talking on the phone with suppressed urgency, while others wandered in and out or chatted in earnest tones. Through the windows, the corrugated metal wall of one of the company's vast grey warehouses loomed.

Jamie was in his late twenties, with a smooth olive complexion and dark eyes. It was almost a Mediterranean look, though his accent seemed slightly Scottish. He asked me, "What will you be doing up at Mellings, actually?"

Was he expecting me to say "babysitting you", or was he genuinely curious? I thought I'd better seem frank. "I'm not quite sure, to be honest. I'm planning on playing it by ear."

"Lucky you. I thought I was getting a holiday, but it sounds as if you really are." He gave me a quick smile to show he wasn't serious about the holiday: a neat double bluff in view of what Bob Latimer had said.

"Don't count on it. I've got plenty of work to keep up with, quite apart from researching what makes Mellings tick."

Andrea was less forgiving when I wandered through to the accounts department. She asked me, "Do you really know enough about Latimers yet to lead a team like this?"

"I'm not leading anything. I'm just tagging along."

"That's not what Bob Latimer said. He told us you're in charge."

I wasn't going to contradict Bob, but I didn't want her to feel resentful either. "I think we'll all need to keep an open mind."

She nodded briskly. She seemed about the same age as Jamie, and was also dark-complexioned. They looked quite alike.

"I'm not planning on cramping your style, honestly."

She flushed slightly at this. Clearly I was treading on dangerous ground. Hastily I said, "I'm looking forward to it."

"Good. Me too." She sat down at her computer with a curt smile and started clicking at something with her mouse. Evidently the conversation was closed.

* * *

Ashley took a robust view of all this when I spoke to her on the phone again that evening. "Just ignore Andrea," she advised.

"I suppose I can try."

"I've never really got on with her. Brittle personality, inclined to be moody. I don't understand what Jamie sees in her."

"She's attractive. That might have something to do with it."

"Oh yes? Says who?"

I laughed. "I'm beginning to wonder what I've let myself in for."

"Jamie's all right. I think you'll like him."

There was a pause, then Ashley said, "I'm sorry you'll have left by the time I get back there." She wasn't given to frequent professions of fondness, so I took this to heart.

"Me too. But I'll see you soon."

What I didn't know was the tangle I'd be stepping into by the time that happened.

Chapter 3

"So, Mike. Good trip?" Chris Melling smiled amiably at me.

He had a bright, airy office on the second floor of his company's office block, with windows on two sides overlooking a service road flanked by neat lawns. Mellings was by far the largest occupant in the modest business park, which was on the western fringe of Newcastle, about a mile north of the River Tyne.

I shifted in my chair. "Not bad." In fact, the journey to Newcastle the previous day had been long and frustrating; delays had expanded the eight hours on the train to a door-to-door time of well over ten.

"The train's pretty slow, from what I hear," Chris said. "I've never done the whole journey by rail."

"It seems to crawl on the cross-country section."

Chris was somewhere in his late fifties, with a lined face and a good head of light-coloured hair tinged with grey. He was wearing a pale suit and an improbable lime green tie. He smoothed it down a little self-consciously, assessing me.

"You've changed horses, Mike." Another smile, this time accompanied by a slightly puzzled look. "The last I heard, you were a journalist writing feature articles in the weekly trade press. Now you're working for Latimers and living in the West Country. A bit of switch for you, no?"

"Long story." I wasn't sure what he knew and what he was expecting. "I'm not actually employed by Latimers, I just handle their editorial work. Bob probably told you that." I thought some more. "For present purposes I also seem to be some sort of emissary." I gave him what I hoped was a self-deprecating smile. "I still have a separate life as a journalist."

"A hotbed of transport interest, is it, Cornwall?" He managed to give that sentence a peculiarly Geordie lilt, especially the "is it", injected as a parenthetic throw-away.

"You've probably heard of the internet. Allows you to work anywhere you like."

He laughed. "Until you have to travel in the real world."

"Touché."

He leaned forward. "So if you pick up any interesting titbits of information about Mellings while you're here, should I expect to be reading about them online before the day is out?" He was still smiling, but I could feel an edge to his words.

"Of course not. I'm here on behalf of Latimers. That should be understood."

"Just so long as I know how the land lies." He stood up. "I'll come and find you later on and give you a guided tour."

*   *   *

I wandered through to the room we'd been allocated. It was in the executive corridor, a couple of doors down from Chris's office. Ostensibly this gave it some status, but I suspected the choice had been made primarily so that Chris could keep an eye on us. There was certainly nothing impressive about room itself; it was quite small and spartan, containing just three desks and a table.

Jamie and Andrea hadn't arrived in Newcastle yet. Bob Latimer had kept them back a day while Andrea's team completed an urgent forecasting project. They were planning on driving the whole way together in Jamie's car, which they reckoned would give them more freedom of movement while we were all here. Latimers were only prepared to stump up for one shared rental car, and I'd claimed that.

I sat down at the desk I'd chosen for myself, next to the window. My first self-imposed task of the day was to contact the firm of solicitors who had written to me about the unexpected bequest.

"I'm glad you called, Mr Stanhope. There's been a development that I need to talk to you about." I detected a slightly ominous tone.

"Development?"

"I'll put you in the picture when we meet. Would Monday morning suit you?"

My second task was to contact the Newcastle-based public relations firm used by Melling Logistics. My two previous phone conversations with their boss, Hugh Collins, had been awkward. He probably thought Latimers planned to fire him and give Mellings' PR work to me, but equally I was aware that he could put in a bid to handle all the expanded Latimer group's PR work, including mine.

Hugh picked up on the first ring, and cautiously agreed to meet me later on Monday morning at his office in Jesmond, a suburb north of the city centre. Slightly relieved, I disconnected and opened my laptop. My unfinished forklift truck article beckoned.

* * *

Chris Melling thrust his head round my door at midday. "Ready for the guided tour?"

In fact I'd had a similar tour four or five years ago, when I'd come here to write an article about the company, so it was familiar ground. I had to admit to myself, however, that I remembered few of the staff and none of the details.

Mellings' offices adjoined the main warehouse. The complex included not only extensive and cavernous areas of racked goods, but also a high-ceilinged assembly and re-working area. Chris and I stood on a balcony, looking down on the conveyors and workstations arrayed on the concrete floor. We watched people assembling cartons, inserting goods in them and feeding them through shrink-wrapping machines.

"It gets much busier than this at peak," Chris said. "This is our quiet time." I knew from experience that peak meant the peak season – the long run-up to Christmas.

He led me down a clanging metal stair to meet the section leader, a capable-looking woman called Mary. As we spoke she kept glancing over my shoulder at the activity beyond me, presumably reluctant to be distracted. I tried to pitch in a few informed questions about her job, and eventually felt I'd convinced her I actually knew something about the business.

"I hope you enjoy your stay with us, Mike," she said in the end, giving me an unexpectedly warm smile.

Greg Atkins, one of Chris's co-directors, proved a harder nut to crack. When Chris took me through to his office adjacent to the packing floor, his handshake was perfunctory. "I've seen your articles," he said with a hint of disdain, and if a mere nodding acquaintance with them had somehow tainted him. It was a surprisingly confrontational greeting, and I glanced at Chris, bemused.

Chris merely smiled blandly. "Mike has promised he's off duty while he's here with us."

I turned to Greg, a tall, well-built man with a roundish face and slightly receding curly hair. He said, "Very glad to hear it." Unlike Chris, he had a southern accent – perhaps from the West Midlands. "So what will you be getting up to while you're here, Mike?"

The question itself was mild enough, but the tone held an edge of sarcasm. Why was he trying to intimidate me? Fighting a sense of indignation, I met his gaze as squarely as I could. "What would you like me to be doing?"

He gave an exaggerated shrug. "It's your show. I'm sure you have your agenda."

Chris chipped in, "It's a fact-finding and liaison visit, isn't that right, Mike?"

"On the nail." Turning to Greg, I said a little recklessly, "It's already proving quite illuminating." If he wanted to be hostile, I couldn't resist giving him something to think about. He looked ready to say more, but merely nodded as if he'd expected no less.

* * *

"Greg is a good man," Chris said as we headed back towards his office. "He's inclined to be a bit protective of what we do here."

"But surely Bob Latimer has made it clear that he wants to keep all your key staff on the payroll? No one will be out of a job."

"Of course. But you know what people are like. Loyalty can be a commendable quality."

As we parted company in the corridor I asked him, "Your event tomorrow night – what's the format?"

"It's just a dinner in a nice hotel. It's a thank-you to the staff for their work through the year. We're always too busy to do it at Christmas. And we usually have a bit of dancing afterwards, for anyone who wants it." He turned to me and swivelled his hips in a parody of a dance move. It looked slightly absurd, but he accompanied it with a winning smile.

"Any dress code?"

"Well, some of us like to put on our best frocks, but just come as you are."

Chapter 4

Chris had placed me next to him at the dinner. It was either a mark of honour or a ruse to prevent me fraternising too freely with anyone who might bad-mouth the company after their fourth glass of Pinot Noir.

I looked round at the other circular tables, each of which seated a dozen people. There seemed to be a director or manager on many of them: very egalitarian. Subdued pop music trickled from a disco that had been set up at the end of the room: presumably a taster of something more animated to come.

I turned to Chris. "This must be costing you a fortune."

He grinned. "Not really – not for the good will it engenders. Surely Bob Latimer must do something like this down at St Austell, doesn't he?"

"I don't know, to be honest. Not since I've been there."

"If not, he should take a leaf out of our book."

At the end of the meal Chris called for silence by rattling a spoon against a glass, then rose and gave a short speech. There was little of substance in it, but he talked enthusiastically about the takeover by Latimers, and introduced me by name. Jamie and Andrea were merely described as "Mike's colleagues".

People started moving around, gathering themselves into new ad hoc groupings. I made my way over to Jamie and Andrea's table. They'd arrived in Newcastle late the previous evening, but had kept a low profile all day, so we'd barely spoken until we piled into a taxi from our small country hotel.

"I like the way Chris Melling gave you the name check," Andrea greeted me, making it clear that she didn't. "We do the grafting, but Mr Public Relations gets the credit." She gave me a wide-eyed smile to take some of the sting out of her words.

"You can't blame Mike for that," Jamie said quickly. "He didn't write Chris Melling's script."

"No, but it's so predictable, isn't it?"

I shrugged. The pair had barely spoken to each other on the journey over here, and Andrea's animosity apparently extended to anyone who came within her range. I'd eventually worked out that Jamie had taken a wrong turn somewhere en route from Cornwall, adding half an hour to their journey time, and she hadn't yet forgiven him. Nothing like that had happened between me and Ashley so far, but even if it had, I couldn't envisage her reacting like this, or imagine how I would have responded if she had. Not with Jamie's tolerant smile, I suspected.

I sat down at the table. "I suppose we ought to have a meeting on Monday morning, to work out what we're all doing."

"Jamie and I already know what we're doing," Andrea said. "No need to discuss anything."

Patiently, I said, "Well, I don't, so it's still worth coordinating, don't you think?"

Jamie quickly said, "Good idea. Then we'll all be singing off the same hymn sheet."

"Something like that."

Before the conversation could go any further the volume of the disco rose abruptly. Chris Melling emerged into a clear area of floor with his wife Sheila and they started dancing. It was a restrained jive, and they were good at it. We watched for a while, then one or two other couples joined them. Andrea grabbed Jamie's hand. "Come on then," she said brightly. "Let's show them how it's done."

Now alone at the table, I continued to watch the dancing. You never knew who would be good at it until you saw them doing it. Andrea was instinctively rhythmical and inventive, and Jamie's performance was passable. They worked well as a couple. Mellings also had its crop of local talent. I could see now why the event was so popular. I felt out of place, and wished Ashley were here.

* * *

"Not dancing then, Mike?" It was female voice, speaking loudly in order to be heard over the music. I was aware of a slightly exaggerated Geordie accent. I turned to find a blonde woman smiling down at me with a challenge in her eyes. She looked about thirty, and had straight shoulder-length hair that curled slightly inwards: a considered period style. She was wearing a short cream-coloured jacket and an aquamarine skirt.

I raised my arms. "Evidently not."

"Shove up then." She pulled out the chair next to mine and sat down, holding out her hand for me to shake. "Jenna Melling."

"Melling. That can't be a coincidence."

"Afraid not. Chris Melling is my dad." She smiled in mock chagrin. "Never let it be said that nepotism is dead."

"You work at the firm then?" I didn't recall hearing any mention of her until now.

"I did once. Then I saw the error of me ways and went freelance. Now I just offer them the benefit of my wisdom for a fee." More of the exaggerated Geordie.

I looked at her. The expression I saw was mischievous, but I also sensed calculation behind her eyes. I said, "Freelance what?"

"Marketing consultant. But most of my work now is for Ashurst Concepts."

I raised my eyebrows. Clearly I was supposed to recognise the name.

She said, "Your wife doesn't have a spiralizer, then?"

"I don't have a wife or a spiralizer."

"It was last year's big culinary sensation – or was it the year before's? Anyway, Ashurst imports electrical goods, and Mellings do their distribution."

"Very fitting."

"It is, isn't it?" She seemed about to say more, but at that moment a new record started playing and she changed her mind. "Do you fancy a twirl?"

We managed to acquit ourselves adequately on the dance floor in a classic disconnected bop, then the music slowed and we moved into a more dancerly hold. Jenna was the first woman I'd taken into any sort of embrace since meeting Ashley more than a year ago – and probably since long before that. Oddly, however, my familiarity with Ashley seemed to give me confidence with this woman. That strange piece of logic made me uncomfortable, yet it didn't stop me experiencing a momentary frisson as we were pressed together by other dancers.

It seemed like time to quit. As soon as I decently could, I told her I was ready to sit down. "Chicken!" she complained, casting around for a replacement partner. Greg Atkins happened to be passing, and she pounced on him. "Come on Greg, let's show them what this dance should really look like."

I watched them for a while from the table. Greg danced with his eyes closed, while Jenna's darted around the room, animated and inscrutable.

* * *

The event broke up some time after eleven o'clock, and I shared a taxi again with Andrea and Jamie, who seemed to be on good terms at last. The three of us made it back at our small hotel by half past midnight – not too late for me to phone Ashley, who had returned from her marketing conference late the previous day.

"How's Cornwall?"

"It seems to have survived without me. What about Geordie Land?"

"I haven't seen much of it yet, except for a logistics depot, and they all look more or less the same."

"Nice people?"

"They seem to be. But I still don't really know what I'm doing here."

"You'll probably work it out eventually."

"I suppose so."

"How was the dinner?"

"OK." I reflected for a moment. "I met a temptress while I was there. Chris Melling's daughter Jenna."

"Ha. She used to run their marketing department years ago, but she was too young really. I met her at one or two trade shows, but then I lost track of her. I suppose she's grown up a bit now, but temptress is right.

You could see that in her even then. You need to steer clear of that woman, Mr Stanhope."

"I wish you'd been there."

"Sounds as if I should have been."

Chapter 5

Green & Bavistock, solicitors, were based in St Mary's Place, not far from the Haymarket in Newcastle's city centre. Most of the other premises in the elegant Georgian terrace seemed to be taken up incongruously by fast food outlets or accommodation agencies. Across the road, an elaborate coronet topping the 1960s civic centre loomed from amid trees and lawns.

"There used to be solicitors or professional firms all the way along this stretch of road," David Smythe told me from behind his mahogany desk. "Now there are only a few of us left. All the rest is geared up for council workers and students."

He looked about sixty, and had a fleshy, reddish face and brushed-back grey hair. He pulled a manila file towards him on the desk without opening it. "You were not acquainted with Elizabeth Sanderson, I gather?"

"I'd never even heard of her until you wrote to me."

"*Ah*-ha," he acknowledged absently, placing the accent on the initial "Ah". I was gradually getting used to this Geordie expression of assent, though in situations like this it still came over as oddly informal. "That's what I thought."

He opened the file, then closed it again. "Elizabeth Sanderson died a few weeks ago. We are her executors, and you are named in her will." He scratched his head. "In fact you are the prime beneficiary. In a nutshell, she wanted you to have almost everything."

I flashed him a look of surprise. He merely smiled noncommittally, so I said, "What in fact is 'everything'?"

"Well, there's a freehold house in Harrogate – quite a substantial property – plus all the furniture and effects in it, and quite a bit of money in savings and investments. Some of the antique furniture could be quite valuable. The house is mortgage-free." He opened the file once again, pulled out a thin sheaf of pages and slid them over to me. "It's all detailed here."

I sat back, inwardly reeling. This had to mean several hundred thousand pounds in value at the least. In my world that was a life-changing windfall. It was certainly enough to have a significant impact on my day-to-day existence. It would mean for instance that Ashley and I could set our sights much higher when it came to looking for somewhere in Cornwall to live together. Or I could give myself more breathing space in deciding what to do with my life.

I'd already handed over various bits of documentation to confirm that I was the right Michael Stanhope. But who was Elizabeth Sanderson? I said, "Is it usual for people to leave their worldly goods to someone who has never heard of them?"

"It's not unknown, but I wouldn't say it's common."

"And you have no idea why she picked me out of the air?"

"I think you can safely assume she didn't pick you out of the air, but no, we don't know what did prompt her to name you. I daresay some detailed research would provide an explanation, but that goes beyond our remit."

I sensed a qualification, and looked at him questioningly. "You said there had been a development?"

"Yes. I'm afraid I have to tell you that the will is being contested."

Despite the fact that I'd never expected this bounty, I immediately felt indignant. "Contested? Who by?"

"His name is Philip Crabtree. He's Elizabeth Sanderson's nephew."

A relative. It was hardly surprising. Why should a total stranger inherit this woman's estate instead of fairly close relative? However, I heard myself saying, "Does he have any grounds?"

"That remains to be seen. All we know so far is that he has submitted a caveat. It's a technical term. It will delay the granting of probate, and if the findings go his way, it could eventually change the way the estate is disposed of."

I looked carefully at him, sensing that perhaps he knew more than he was telling me. "Does he have to state the basis on which he's objecting?"

He smiled briefly. "I gather he is alleging that Miss Sanderson was not of sound mind when she changed her will, and was subjected to undue pressure." He sniffed. "Actually that's two different objections. Mr Crabtree is evidently trying to cover all bases."

"So you're telling me she changed her will?"

"Oh yes. Just in the last few months. Up to that point the Crabtrees would have been the sole beneficiaries."

"I see. And do we know why she did that?"

"That's something nobody knows. Her final will is perfectly legitimate in itself, but unfortunately for you, the law allows this legal challenge."

I sat for a moment, thinking. "What did Elizabeth Sanderson die of?"

"It was from an overdose of medications for her condition. Cancer. It was ruled misadventure."

"But if she was subjected to undue pressure, who is supposed to have been exerting it? I didn't even know her, so it could hardly have been me."

"I can't answer that. It's one of the aspects that has to be considered."

"So what happens next? What should I do?"

"Well, if Mr Crabtree insists on pursuing his claim, a court will eventually consider its validity, and will then make a determination."

I said, "Do you think I should approach these Crabtree people myself? Perhaps we could come to some sort of accommodation. I don't want to disinherit them if this is something they've been expecting all their lives."

"Well, there's nothing to stop you reaching a settlement out of court. It's often the best way to resolve disputes like this." He gave me a curt smile. "It's not really my place to advise you. If you want advice, you should consider appointing a solicitor of your own. However, off the record I would say don't be in a rush to dilute your claim on the estate. After all, a will expresses the last intentions of the deceased. Who are we to dispute it?"

"Tell that to Mr Crabtree."

He smiled. "But you understand what I'm saying."

"Do the Crabtrees live in Harrogate?"

"Philip and Angela," he said. "No, they live here in Newcastle."

I would have liked to ask for their address, but felt it would be inappropriate somehow to provide any further indication of my intentions. Besides, I felt he'd already offered me a coded clue by naming Philip Crabtree's wife. If I went looking for them, that should allow me to find them easily enough.

I did however ask him for Elizabeth Sanderson's address in Harrogate, which he readily gave me. I could Streetview the house later. As I left he told me, "Keep in touch, and we'll advise you of any further developments."

* * *

On advice from David Smythe I caught a bus from outside his office to nearby Jesmond, which I'd discovered was a fashionable inner suburb of Newcastle. Imposing Victorian terraces offered a mix of hotels, flats, upmarket houses, bedsits and small businesses. Mellings' public relations firm, Ashby Collins, had its offices in a tree-lined street just off Osborne Road, the spine road through the area.

Hugh Collins, co-founder and head of the firm, was more affable in person than he'd sounded in our conversations on the phone over recent weeks, and seemed resigned to the possibility of losing his work for Mellings. "We've had five years with them. It's been a good run."

"Latimers won't be in a hurry to change things," I assured him. "St Austell is at the other end of the country. We can't expect to have a finger on the pulse of what's happening up here in the North East all the time. We're going to need people on the ground, and you have a good track record."

He nodded his acknowledgement. "I know you, don't I, Mike? Didn't you used to be a journalist? I think you're on our mailing list."

I cringed inwardly. Yes, I used to be a journalist, though I'd always had a love-hate relationship with the job. Yet it saddened me to think it might soon be in the past tense. "Jack of all trades, that's me."

"Well, at least you'll know what the press is after. It's more than can be said for a lot of our clients."

Chapter 6

Working in the same room as Jamie and Andrea wasn't as difficult as I'd feared. For much of the time at least one of them was out and about, liasing with people in various departments at Mellings. When we were all in the office together they mostly kept their heads down, apart from exchanging occasional knowing glances.

My main problem was that I didn't really know what I was supposed to be doing there myself. Unlike them, I didn't have a clearly defined function. When I got the chance I chatted to Chris Melling and his fellow-directors, and was able to report our conversations to Bob Latimer, who had already phoned me twice at my hotel. But what I told him seemed anecdotal and unstructured.

Ashley told me I should take advantage of being in the area and go off sightseeing around the North East. "Bob never said you had to be in the office all the time," she pointed out. "You're a free agent. Enjoy it." She laughed. "In fact, if you really do inherit that house, you'll soon be able to retire and swan around as much as you like. Maybe you should get in some practice."

She'd expressed amazement when I told her the extent of Elizabeth Sanderson's bequest, and cautioned me not to take anything for granted. Not that she needed to; the whole thing still seemed to have an air of unreality about it, especially since the will was being contested.

At any rate, for the time being I felt I should show at least some semblance of having a working role. I called Jason Bright, my contact in London at one of the weekly logistics publications. "Do you need an article about the logistics market in Tyne and Wear? Maybe an interview with a major player?"

"We just did a regional roundup of the area last month," he said. "Can't really revisit the subject for a while."

"That's a shame."

"If you pick up any news leads while you're up there, by all means bang over the odd story. We're always on the lookout for those."

"I'll keep my eye out."

So the week started to unfold, and I battled on with my article about forklift trucks.

* * *

On Wednesday morning Andrea looked up abruptly. "That's very odd."

Jamie and I stared across at her. She was poring over a sheaf of paperwork on her desk, glancing up and down at her screen at the same time.

"CJ Melling Holdings Northern," she said. "That's Chris Melling's private holding company, isn't it?"

We waited.

"They just recently transferred most of their assets to Melling Logistics."

Jamie said, "Chris owns both companies, so he's perfectly entitled to do that, isn't he?"

"But it's a bit odd, don't you think?"

"What are you getting at?"

"I don't know. It's just that the company isn't mentioned in the schedule of acquired assets in the Latimer takeover."

"Maybe it all happened too recently. They'll show up eventually."

"I suppose."

I asked, "What assets are we talking about exactly?"

She glanced down for a moment. "Mostly it's small shareholdings in some of the companies that Melling Logistics works for. Chris must have spotted potential in them. But there's a majority shareholding in one of them, Ashurst Concepts."

I'd recently heard that name. It was the company Chris Melling's daughter had told me she worked for – the one selling consumer electrical goods. I said, "So after the takeover, Latimer Logistics will have a majority holding in Ashurst Concepts?"

"Correct. The point is, Ashursts hasn't been audited from the point of view of the acquisition, so far as I know."

I said, "But presumably this will all come up in the due diligence process. It's just a matter of time, isn't it?"

"That's what you'd expect."

"Ashurst made a mint after championing the spiralizer, didn't it?" I was pleased with myself for being able to demonstrate this apparent insight.

She nodded. "They won awards for being one of the fastest-growing companies in their field." She grimaced. "It just seemed like a passing fad to me."

"So now Latimers will get the kudos."

"Maybe." She flicked her pen with her hand. "But if so, I wonder why Chris Melling decided to dump his holding?"

* * *

I decided to raise the Ashurst issue directly with Chris Melling, and caught him at lunchtime in the company's small canteen, buying a sandwich from one of the vending machines in the corner.

"My daughter Jenna persuaded me to buy into Ashurst," he told me, taking a seat and peeling open his sandwich wrapper. "She was right. Astronomic growth for a start-up company in the first couple of years."

"Why are you selling your stake, then?"

He shrugged. "I'm scaling back all my investments. That's just one. I thought Latimers might as well get the benefits. Bob knows all about it. In any case, I get a stake in the enlarged Latimer group as part of the deal. Presumably you knew that."

Did I know that? I didn't think Bob had mentioned it. However, I nodded, adding, "I've heard that Ashursts' growth rate is levelling out."

"Inevitable, after such a good start. But they've got critical mass now." He looked at me for a moment, assessing, then seemed to come to a decision. "I suppose you reported the hijacking, did you?"

"Hijacking?"

"Ah, you didn't then." He looked a little regretful over having brought it up, but was now committed. "It was a few weeks ago. A container-load of product was hijacked on the way from Southampton docks to Ashursts' headquarters in Leeds."

"What happened?"

"Someone drove the artic out of a lorry park, and it disappeared off the face of the earth. You wouldn't think it was possible in this day and age, but they obviously knew how to avoid surveillance cameras."

"Was it ever recovered?"

"The truck was found next day in Bradford, but the load was gone forever."

"But surely if someone starts selling the stuff to consumers, it can be tracked by product codes and all that?"

"You'd think so, wouldn't you? But obviously that didn't deter the thieves. I suppose they'll feed it into the market bit by bit. Or maybe they've re-exported it."

"Presumably it was covered by insurance."

"Oh yes. The claim is going through as we speak."

He rose to head off to his office, then turned back to me. "I wonder if you'd care to join me and my wife for dinner tomorrow night? With your two colleagues, I mean. Sheila loves entertaining, and you'll make a good target for her latest ideas on Mediterranean cuisine."

"That would be great, thank you."

"If you don't know the North East very well, I've got something that I think will fascinate you. A little film show." He pronounced it "fillum" – another exaggerated Geordie-ism.

"A film show?"

He grinned. "No, it's not soft porn, if that's what you're thinking, and it's not what we did on our holidays. Much more interesting. It's always popular with our guests."

"I'll look forward to it."

* * *

I thought about the coming weekend. Should I make the marathon trek back to Cornwall? I wanted to see Ashley, but it seemed a very long way to go for such a short visit. I was conscious that thousands of people flew regularly between Scotland and London, which involved a journey nearly as long as this, but getting to Cornwall from Newcastle and back seemed a challenge of a different order of magnitude.

Ashley settled the matter when I phoned her that night. "Stephanie's coming down for the weekend from Bishop's Stortford, so maybe you'd prefer to leave it?"

Stephanie was a friend of hers from college in Bristol. I'd met her on a previous visit, and we'd soon realised we had virtually nothing in common. If I went back while she was there, I would be forcing Ashley to divide herself between us, which seemed unfair and unsatisfactory.

"Let's save it for the next weekend," I suggested. "Either I could come down to you, or maybe you could come up here."

"Sounds good to me."

Chapter 7

Chris and Sheila Melling lived on a mature estate of well-to-do houses on the edge of a village a few miles north of Newcastle. I drove Jamie and Andrea there in our hire car, and we soon found ourselves drinking cocktails on Chris's ample lawn. The sprawling redbrick house was built in arts and crafts style with steeply pitched roofs and tall gables, though Chris told us it only dated back to the 1950s, forty or more years after that fashion had come and gone.

"Back then Newcastle wasn't the trendy place it is now. Industry was on the wane. Some areas were still pretty deprived. Your typical senior executive wanted a bucolic bolt hole where the world seemed a prettier place. This estate fitted the bill nicely."

"It can't have been that bad in the city."

"Well, I didn't think so. I grew up in Fenham, and I loved Newcastle." He pronounced it "New-*cassle*", in contrast to my southern inclination to put the accent on the "New". "Still, this place suits us very well."

I said, "Fenham?"

"It's a suburb on the west side."

We moved into the dining room, and Sheila unveiled her latest culinary experiment – an elaborate paella containing a variety of different seafood types. It seemed to go down well, and I could see she was pleased.

At one point she turned to Andrea. "So how long have you two been a couple?"

"About a year," Andrea said, looking slightly uncomfortable.

"And is marriage on the horizon?"

Andrea and Jamie seemed unperturbed at the question itself. However, she cast him a sullen look, saying nothing. He cleared his throat. "I'm waiting for my divorce to come through."

I glanced at him in surprise. I'd never given any thought to their personal circumstances, but perhaps it explained a lot.

Sheila was unfazed. "What about you, Mike? Bob Latimer says your other half is a lynchpin at the company."

I found myself smiling. "Ashley, yes. You'll have to meet her. You'll really like her." Why did I have to say that? Was I trying to contrast her with Andrea?

Sheila smiled indulgently. "I'm sure we will."

* * *

After the meal Chris led us through to a lounge that was set up as a viewing room. Two rows of comfortable upright chairs had been arranged to face a large white screen. Behind them, a projector sat on a tall table, with metal film reels attached on one side.

"Bell & Howell sixteen millimetre sound projector," Chris said reverentially. "They're not made any more."

I said, "Is it very rare?"

He smiled wryly. "Not really." He ushered us into the seats and dimmed the lights. "You have my great-uncle Frank to thank for this," he said, fiddling with the projector. "Frank Giardini, cinematographer supremo. He grew up in Gateshead."

A series of white count-down numbers flashed on the screen in descending sequence, and then we were launched into a travelogue film about Newcastle and its environs, apparently made in the 1950s. The colours were brash, the commentary was anodyne, the music was irritatingly jaunty. Nevertheless, the insight into a vanished world was fascinating. We saw ships passing under the arching Tyne Bridge, horse racing at Gosforth Park, children playing in Jesmond Dene, a royal visit to the city.

It lasted about ten minutes. When it finished, Chris turned up the lights and explained, "Frank was the lead cameraman on that film. I inherited his film archive. It's become a bit of a hobby with me."

I said, "He didn't work just in Newcastle, presumably?"

"Oh, no, his camera work was used in all sorts of films – whatever the film companies wanted. Then he went independent – set up a little company of his own. They worked on contract to the bigger filmmakers – people like Pathé, British Transport Films, that kind of thing."

He showed us a couple more short films, then we broke for coffee. I asked, "Do you have any more films about Newcastle?"

"Not complete films with sound, no, but there are plenty of fragments – speculative stuff that he took, positioning shots for slotting into big studio films, that kind of thing."

"Could we see some more?"

Andrea shot me a reproachful glance. Evidently she'd had enough. I ignored it. Anyway, Chris didn't need asking twice. "I've spliced some of it together. I thought I might add a soundtrack one of these days."

He changed reels and dimmed the lights again, and immediately we were travelling along one of Newcastle's main shopping streets on a sunny summer's day. Again, the film was in full colour. "This dates from the late nineteen forties," Chris said.

We watched as shoppers hurried silently out of our way and policemen on point duty waved us stiffly through junctions. The quality seemed extraordinarily good for its day: perhaps not on a par with high-definition television, but sharp and clear all the same. I'd seen similar material online, but it had always looked blurred and vague. On Chris's film you could make out small text on shop fronts, number plates of cars and buses, even the faces of pedestrians. It was a remarkable pictorial record.

As if hearing my thoughts, Chris commented, "There's a lot of stuff like this on the internet. People were just beginning to wake up to the opportunities that cine film offered. But of course it was an expensive hobby for amateurs, so most footage was shot on eight millimetre. It wasn't always very sharp in the first place, and footage that's been digitised for the web has often been done badly. Frank's sixteen millimetre film is much cleaner, and some of it was originally shot on thirty-five millimetre, which is better still. It looks good even when it's converted down."

"Have you put any of his archives online?"

"Not so far. The copyright ownership is a bit of a grey area, to be honest."

The scenes in Chris's composite reel jumped between different occasions and different parts of the city, and this time there was no connecting logic. Nevertheless, I was entranced. The fashions reflected a bygone age – men with trilbys or flat caps, women with elaborate hats and smart dresses. There was little indication of post-war austerity in their turnout, which seemed altogether more considered and formal than would be the case today. That said, many of the cars and vans looked old and rather shabby.

At the end of the short reel Chris turned up the lights again and the others retreated to another room. I asked if he would show the last reel again.

It was on the second run-through that I spotted something. As we progressed along one of the city's main streets, the straight-ahead view had been intercut with shots of bystanders, and a young couple caught my attention. Again I was impressed with the sharpness of the images; you could make out the couple's features with striking clarity. They were standing arm in arm, smiling at the camera as it passed. The woman wore a floral dress and had shortish curly hair. The rather gaunt-faced man was wearing a dark jacket and trousers. The woman seemed strangely familiar.

"Can you go back over the last ten seconds?"

Chris fiddled with the projector, then re-started it. I peered more closely. It felt almost as if I'd known in advance that this woman would be there. "I said, "Can you freeze-frame on that couple?"

"Not really," Chris said. "This isn't a video, it's film. I always worry that if I stop it I might blow the frame." He turned to me, apparently feeling the need to elaborate. "I don't want to run the risk that the heat from the projector bulb would damage the film."

"Oh." I pondered this. "But it must be possible to extract a still image somehow?"

"Of course. Best if I give it to my technical man in town."

"Maybe I could take a couple of photographs off the screen?"

"Be my guest." Obligingly he ran the scene a third time, and I fired off a couple of shots with my phone. I wasn't sure how well they worked, but at a glance they looked reasonable on the phone's small screen.

He stopped the film and turned up the lights. "I'd be more than happy to get a some stills made if you like. You want an image showing that young couple?"

I nodded. "If you wouldn't mind. I'll pay you for it. Don't ask me how, but I feel as if I know those people. The woman, anyway. I'd love to follow it up."

"Do you have roots in Newcastle then?"

"No, not at all. But maybe they were visiting or something."

"But you don't actually know them?"

"I don't think so, but maybe I can work out who they are."

He smiled a little sceptically. "Good luck with that."

Chapter 8

On Saturday I caught the train into Newcastle. Several of the people at Mellings had expressed amusement at the way I favoured trains and buses over driving. It was hard to convey how this was an ingrained way of life in London, so I'd given up trying. There was a station just across the river from the village where I was staying, and I was looking forward to the journey along the Tyne valley.

I wasn't disappointed. There were sweeping views across the sides of the valley, increasingly populated and industrialised as we approached the city centre, and the high-level Tyne crossing was dramatic. A multi-layered skyline of civic and commercial buildings lowered in front of us and stretched away to both sides.

This was my first full exposure to Newcastle city centre, which I'd largely ignored on my brief visit on Monday. It was more extensive than I expected. I marvelled at the Georgian sandstone terraces around Grey Street and Grainger Street, and eventually decided I'd found the street where I'd spotted the young couple in Chris Melling's film. It was Northumberland Street, a kind of mini-Oxford Street at the heart of the shopping area. No doubt a lot of the buildings had been replaced since that film was made, but the atmosphere seemed the same.

At Chris Melling's insistence I wandered along until I found the Tyneside Cinema, which he'd told me was the country's oldest active newsreel theatre. Two of its latter-day patrons, he said, were responsible for probably the most famous feature films set in Newcastle – *Get Carter* and *Stormy Monday*.

"They're both gangster movies," he'd pointed out. "Beautiful films, but they probably didn't do much to improve the image of the North East. It's not really like that around here."

"I'll take your word for it."

I had a snack lunch in the cinema's trendy café, then went in search of the castle that gave the city its name. However, it turned out to be a little underwhelming; all that seemed to be left was the monumental rectangular keep, which admittedly had been impressively restored. The cathedral, too, seemed somewhat apologetic, but its outsized main tower was undeniably striking.

I found myself near the High Level Bridge, which carried both a road and a railway over the Tyne. At this point the terrain on both sides of the river rose sharply, so Newcastle and Gateshead faced each other from elevated positions across the river valley. The High Level Bridge and the Tyne Bridge crossed the river at this upper level, while down below lay the Victorian Swing Bridge and further downstream, the more recent Millennium Bridge.

I decided to go down to the Quayside area, and made my way there via a series of ancient stone steps and passageways. I whiled away part of the afternoon outside a riverside pub, marvelling at the dramatic backdrop of high and low bridges against the sharply rising cityscape on both sides of the river. Sitting in the sun reading a guide book, I looked up periodically across the river at Gateshead's Baltic arts centre – formerly a flour mill.

* * *

"Mike Stanhope, by all that's holy."

I looked up in surprise. It was Jenna Melling, wearing dark blue jeans and a crimson jacket and carrying a couple of colourful paper shopping bags adorned with fashion brands. With her was Greg Atkins. I hadn't thought of them as a couple.

I shuffled round in my chair. "I'm just taking in some of the sights."

She grinned. "My dad told me he'd sent you to pick up some culture, but I didn't think I'd actually find you."

I indicated the spare chairs round my table. "Join me?"

I was hoping Greg wouldn't give me a repeat performance of the hostile welcome he'd offered when Chris Melling introduced us. In fact he seemed affable but reserved. He said, "I did the sightseeing thing when I moved here a couple of years ago. It's an impressive place."

I glanced up at the two giant bridges – the High Level to our right and the arching Tyne Bridge to our left. "I can't disagree."

At her insistence Jenna went to the bar to buy us all afternoon tea. When we were settled at the table again she turned to me. "So, Mike, what are you getting up to at the office? Are you busy raking through our murky past?"

"Sorry?"

"Well, you're part of the due diligence team, am I right? Making sure that Mellings is a good buy for Bob Latimer and his crew."

"Ah. No, not at all. That kind of stuff is done by lawyers and accountants – people who actually know what they're looking for."

"And you don't."

"Not in that way, no."

She nodded to herself as if satisfied on a point. After a moment she said, "So what *are* you doing up here in the North East?"

I looked into her eyes. "Getting in a bit of free sightseeing, courtesy of my generous boss."

Greg said, "I thought so," smiling to show he was entering into the spirit of this.

Jenna sat back, squinting at me against the afternoon sun. "It's a nice little business, Mellings. Bob Latimer has done all right for himself."

Greg raised his eyebrows. "Not so little these days – especially if we clinch the Franchi contract." He pronounced the name to rhyme with "lanky".

Jenna immediately frowned at him. "I don't think that's general knowledge yet, Greg."

He gave her an embarrassed look and said, "Right. Sorry."

She turned to me. "You didn't hear that, did you Mike?"

"Hear what?"

* * *

Although Jenna's rebuke had seemed mild, Greg fell into near silence. Nevertheless, Jenna kept the conversation going in her animated and slightly ironic style, and even persuaded Greg to fetch us some more tea.

Finally she turned to me. "Have you checked out the Newcastle night life yet, Mike? I think we should give you a taster."

Greg said, "Mike probably wants to get back, don't you Mike?"

I shrugged, unsure whose lead to follow. "I should probably head off."

"Why no! At least let's get ourselves up to Bigg Market and see what's happening."

Greg sat back, immediately defeated, so in due course off we went on the steep climb up to the city centre.

Bigg Market, a short but wide street, was the hub of Newcastle's night life, providing a home to numerous pubs and bars. Even though this was only early evening and it was still broad daylight, hefty-looking bouncers in semi-formal attire loitered outside some of the entrances like reluctant ushers at a wedding. A few young people dressed up for the occasion had already clustered in small groups in the pedestrianised area.

"This street was named after Mr Bigg, a famous gangster," Jenna said. I said, "No it wasn't."

She laughed. She picked a bar apparently at random, exchanging a word of banter with the bouncer as we entered. The volume of music inside had already been ratcheted up, but was still just about low enough for normal conversation. I volunteered to head for the bar.

As I stood waiting to be served I glanced at Jenna and Greg, who were silhouetted in front of the window. They seemed to be engaged in an angry exchange of words. By the time I returned with three glasses of white wine, Greg had disappeared.

"I never thought he'd just sod off," she grumbled. "Not very gentlemanly."

I looked at her questioningly. She simply said, "Don't ask."

I held up the three glasses. "One too many, I think."

She grabbed one of them. "All the more for me." She drank down half of it defiantly.

Jenna was a toucher. I was aware of a strange implied intimacy as she put her hand on my arm, pulling me towards the window. A small bench seat had miraculously come available, and we quickly sat down. There was barely enough room for two, and our thighs pressed together.

"I suppose I take advantage of Greg," she said with a sigh. "I know I shouldn't."

"How long have you been together?"

"Oh, we're not really together. I've only just broken up with my ex."

"Do I know him?"

"I doubt it. He's Piers Ashurst, the founder of Ashurst Concepts. We were at college together."

* * *

Jenna drank the whole of the first glass of wine in short order and made rapid inroads into the second. We chatted about nothing much for a while, and I became increasingly aware of the pressure of Jenna's body against mine. I couldn't escape it without ungallantly standing up to separate myself from her, but it was hard to know how not to enjoy it. Finally she said, "I'd better get going. I'm supposed to be meeting some friends later on."

"Will you be all right?"

"Course I will, man." She was back in defiant mood. "I'll grab a taxi to my flat." We both stood up, suddenly finding ourselves very close together. Smiling, she said, "I think I could get to like you, Mike Stanhope."

I smiled blandly as Ashley's words rang in my ears: Jenna was a temptress. The trouble was, she *was* tempting. Maybe it was a result of the wine I'd drunk too quickly, but when she leaned forward abruptly to kiss me, I didn't pull away.

What was the matter with me? I hadn't sought out this connection. It felt like an instant betrayal of my settled relationship with Ashley, and I wanted to deny it even as it was happening. Yet for some reason, for a moment at least, I allowed myself to be carried along by it.

It was fleeting and inconsequential, but that was all it took. As I straightened, over her shoulder I saw Jamie and Andrea, who had just walked in from the street. And they saw me.

Chapter 9

Elizabeth Sanderson's house in Harrogate looked impressive. I stared at it on my laptop screen the following morning, sitting in my hotel's modest lounge bar. It was a double-fronted detached property in a street of upmarket Victorian terraced houses. My estimation of its value crept up.

I opened a couple of property websites to get a feel for house prices in Elizabeth's area. They weren't as high as I expected by London standards, but it was clear that I was looking at a value of at least half a million pounds. That was before inheritance tax, of course. Still, it looked like being a truly remarkable windfall – assuming it came my way after the legal challenge to the will.

I then tried searching for Elizabeth Sanderson herself. This took more time, but eventually I learned that she had been an English teacher at a college in Harrogate, and had retired a few years before. The house seemed big for an unmarried woman living on her own, but that was something I couldn't explain.

The next task on my list was to search for Philip Crabtree, the man who was challenging the will. He proved easier to find. He was a businessman working at a company in the Newcastle area, and he lived with his wife Angela in Hexham, a small town fifteen miles to the west.

I was tempted to make contact with him. Although the solicitor had advised caution, I couldn't see any real problem. Meeting him surely wouldn't make matters any worse, would it? If anything, we might come to some compromise over the will.

More to the point, I felt that if I spoke to him I might discover some clue about why Elizabeth had included me in her will at all.

Then I remembered the woman I'd spotted in Chris Melling's film. Could there be some clue here? It seemed pretty tenuous, yet I really had felt a distant connection to her. Could it mean that I had some hitherto unknown roots in the North East?

I picked up my phone and looked at the two pictures I'd taken by pointing the lens at Chris's screen. I couldn't really make out the woman's features, so I copied the images to my laptop and looked at them on that.

I still couldn't see her features very clearly. Both images were dim and quite blurred, either through camera shake or because they were photographed from a screen. The faces were much less defined than I remembered from Chris's film.

I zoomed in on the woman anyway and studied her. She seemed to have a warm expression, and was smiling curiously at the camera. Presumably the cameraman had been in plain view, perhaps travelling in an open vehicle and wielding his camera conspicuously. She was definitely familiar, but I couldn't place her. Also, of course, I was aware that she had a classic look. I could be recognising a *type* of face, not an individual.

Unconvinced, I closed the images. Perhaps when I saw the blow-up Chris had promised me, all would become clearer.

Finally I allowed my mind to play over my encounter with Andrea and Jamie last night. Had they seen me kissing Jenna – or rather, Jenna kissing me? That was the central question, and I suspected the answer was yes. But did it matter? Well, there was no reason to think they would do anything about it, other than perhaps feel badly towards me over my disloyalty to Ashley. No, the concern in my mind was that their awareness made the incident into something real. They had prevented me from dismissing it as if it had never happened.

I sat back in my easy chair, staring moodily out into the leafy hotel garden. Did I want to have a relationship with Jenna Melling? Of course not. In that case, had the kiss meant anything? Not in my mind, and almost certainly not in hers either. So did it even matter? Well, apparently it mattered to me. The fact was that in a corner of my mind, for a brief moment anyway, I'd enjoyed it. What I felt now was chiefly a sense of surprise and self-dislike, but this wasn't enough to prevent a cloud of guilt from blowing up in my mind, and I didn't know how to dispel it.

* * *

I glanced at my watch. Eleven o'clock on a Sunday morning. What was Ashley doing now? Suddenly I felt an urgent need to speak to her. I picked up my phone.

She answered promptly. "Mr Stanhope!"

Immediately I was smiling. "What's happening?"

"Stephanie and I are having coffee, and in a minute we're going off to St Ives."

"That's nice."

"There'll be a lot of tourists, but she says she doesn't care."

I told her briefly about the woman in Chris's film, and the fact that I felt I recognised her. She said, "Don't tell me you're off on another of your obsessions. Look what happened last time."

She was talking about a series of events the previous year, when I'd embarked on a mission to track down a girl I'd met in my childhood. It was through that search that I'd met Ashley in the first place, and it had also revealed that the girl I was searching for was Ashley's half-sister.

"Be careful what you wish for – is that what you're saying?"

She laughed. "Well, it ended up all right for us, but you never know, do you? And I know what you're like when you get a bee in your bonnet about something. You just won't let go."

I took a deep breath. "So are you up for a visit to the north next weekend? I know it's a hell of a trek, but it could be fun."

"I might be. What's the plan?"

In fact I had no specific plan in mind, but as she spoke an idea came to me. "What if you came north as far as Leeds and we stayed somewhere in that area? It would cut an hour or two off your journey, and we could go over to Harrogate to scope out my new house. It's quite near there."

"Your new house? Getting a bit ahead of ourselves, aren't we? Or are you planning to migrate to Yorkshire?"

"Ha. No, I just thought it would be interesting. I looked up the house online, and it definitely could be worth quite a lot."

"I see." She paused. "I'd have to square it with Bob Latimer to take a day or two off, but I bet he'll say yes."

I disconnected with a sense of relief. The prospect of seeing Ashley should put all thoughts of Jenna out of my mind. It wasn't that I was seriously tempted to get involved with her. In the four or five years between my marriage break-up and meeting Ashley I'd survived with little enough female company. Casual relationships didn't seem to be in my DNA. Yet for some reason Jenna's teasing advances were proving unnerving. Hopefully Ashley's visit would help me put a stop to them.

Chapter 10

Philip and Angela Crabtree's landline number was listed in the local phone book. I tapped it into my phone, then sat staring at it. Was I really going to contact these people? Would it help the cause of my inheritance or merely muddy the waters?

I glanced out into the hotel garden. Although this was midsummer, today was dull and overcast. The prospect of a blank Sunday afternoon held little appeal. Almost for want of a better idea I pressed the green button.

"Angela Crabtree." It was a pleasant, mellifluous voice. I felt encouraged.

"Ah, hi. This is Mike Stanhope here. We don't know each other, but I'm mentioned in Elizabeth Sanderson's will. I believe we have a mutual interest in it."

"Oh, hello Mike. What can I do for you?" Her tone was immediately reserved, but still pleasant enough.

"Well, it so happens that I'm visiting the North East, and I was wondering if it would help for us all to meet."

"I see. Well, yes, I suppose that might be useful. What did you have in mind? My husband is out at the moment, but he should be back some time this afternoon."

I hadn't held out much hope that they would be willing to see me today, but since she appeared to be suggesting it, I was ready to jump on the idea. "What if I came over at about three o'clock?

* * *

Hexham, where the Crabtrees lived, was less than half an hour's drive from my village: a pretty country town on the south bank of the Tyne, with a period market square.

The Crabtrees lived on slightly higher ground on the outskirts. Between the large modern houses I glimpsed views across rolling tracts of Northumbrian countryside. I parked and walked down a short but steep driveway to the front door.

Angela Crabtree looked to be in her late thirties. She was dressed in jeans and a sweater and had dark hair tied in a bunch.

"I'm afraid Philip isn't back yet, but come in anyway."

She led me into a lounge with an impressive view across open countryside. Two young children were playing a game on the floor, and paid me little attention. Angela disappeared to make coffee, and I looked out through the floor-to-ceiling window at the garden and the landscape beyond it. The sun kept breaking through the clouds, illuminating parts of the patchwork of fields in brighter, differentiated colours – yellows, russets, greens, browns.

"What a wonderful place to live," I said as Angela returned.

"It is, isn't it?" Her speech had that light, engaging Geordie musicality. She indicated that I should sit down and she took a seat facing me. "We haven't been here long. We used to have a much smaller place in Newcastle." She gazed at the view for a moment, then turned to me. "So tell me, Mike, what exactly was your connection with Elizabeth?"

"Ha! I have absolutely no idea. Until I was contacted about her will, I'd never even heard of her."

She looked puzzled. "You didn't know her? I must have got the wrong end of the stick then."

For the first time it struck me that I could be talking myself into a hole here. If the will was going to be discussed in a court, perhaps anything I said could be given in evidence – and here I was, already casting doubt on my connection with Elizabeth Sanderson. Maybe visiting these people hadn't been such a clever idea after all. But it was too late now to back out.

I said, "No, the news about the will came completely out of the blue."

"That's very peculiar, isn't it?"

I smiled in complicit bafflement. "What was she like, if you don't mind me asking?"

"She was a nice lady. Very wise. Very self-contained. She just got on with her life."

"Were you close to her? I mean, did she figure much in your daily lives? I don't really have any feel for your family history."

She shrugged. "We exchanged Christmas cards, that sort of thing. We didn't actually see her much from one year to the next. But then she fell ill, and Philip started visiting her regularly in Harrogate. He was really supportive when things got harder for her. He put himself out for her."

Uncharitably, I immediately wondered if his visits had been prompted by altruism or by an urge to remind Elizabeth of her family ties. I admonished myself inwardly. For all I knew, Philip Crabtree might be the kindest man in Hexham.

If so, he showed little sign of it when he arrived a few minutes later. He thrust the lounge door open dramatically, a powerful presence that seemed to make the large room shrink.

Angela said, "Phil, this is Mike Stanhope."

He stared a me with a hard expression in his eyes: a striking man with a square jaw and head of fine dark hair. For a Sunday afternoon he seemed overdressed in suit trousers and a shirt and tie.

"Who invited you here?" Out of the corner of my eye I saw the two children stop what they were doing and stare over at us.

Angela quickly said, "I did, Phil. Mike thought it would be helpful if we all met up. Did I do wrong?" I thought I detected an undertone of fear in her voice.

"We shouldn't be in contact while this matter is *sub judice*," he said firmly.

Whilst this sounded plausible, it seemed to contradict what the solicitor had told me. He'd suggested we might be able to settle the matter by discussion. I said, "I don't think there's any rule against interested parties conferring if they choose to."

"Is that so? Well we don't choose to. Frankly you've got a cheek coming here while I'm out."

Angela gave him a reproachful look. "Phil, I told him you'd be back by three o'clock. That's what you said. Anyway, he's not doing any harm."

"He certainly isn't, because he's leaving now. Isn't that right, Mr Stanhope?"

I stood up, my pulse racing, and said, "I'm sorry you feel it necessary to be so hostile. I just thought we might be able to clear the air."

He took a small but menacing step towards me. "Well this isn't the way to do it."

I raised my hands in submission. "Point taken. My apologies if I've upset you."

He ushered me into the hall and towards the front door. "Goodbye, Mr Stanhope. Don't call again."

Chapter 11

An idea occurred to me on Monday morning, and I wandered along to Chris Melling's office to try it out on him. His door was half-open and he beckoned me in.

"I was wondering about Ashurst Concepts. I'm going down to Leeds this Friday to meet up with my girlfriend, and I thought maybe I could drop in on the company while I'm in the area."

He looked at me doubtfully for a moment. "What would be the objective?"

I hadn't expected any need to give a reason. I considered the question. "Just to get a feel for the operation, I suppose. To make the trip more worthwhile. And to be able to tell Bob Latimer from first-hand knowledge what he's bought into."

He frowned as he pondered this, and I had a sense that he might be about to veto the idea – a reaction I certainly hadn't anticipated. However, finally his expression cleared and he nodded. "Fair enough. I'll give Piers Ashurst a call." He grabbed his desk phone and pressed a short-dial code. In Chris's world as in Bob Latimer's, intent and action seemed to blend seamlessly together.

He chatted briefly on the phone, then turned to me. "Piers can see you on Friday afternoon. Will that suit?"

"Great, thanks."

He relayed this on the phone, then put the receiver down. "You'll be impressed with Piers. He's done well for himself."

"Will he be staying on under the new regime?"

I was expecting him to say yes, but he merely said, "For the time being, but I'm not sure about his long-term plans. We've got a tight team down there now – it's not a one-man band any longer."

As I started to leave the office Chris said, "I got Danny to take that film to my technical man in Westgate Road. He'll pull a few stills off it for you. He knows what you're looking for." Danny, I'd discovered, was the company's ad hoc driver and odd-job man.

"That's really good of you, thanks."

"They should be ready in a day or two. I'll let you know."

* * *

Jamie and Andrea seemed to be progressing well with their respective tasks. Jamie had made friends with Mellings' operations manager, a man called Simon, and was spending a lot of time with him in the planning office, working out how Latimers' operations and Mellings' could be dovetailed to cut costs.

Andrea had drawn up a list of Mellings' key clients, and was reviewing everything from billing cycles to warehouse picking prices. Such details made my head hurt; I was comfortable writing articles about the principles of logistics, but the minutiae tended to leave me floundering.

This morning, however, I felt a need to engage Andrea in conversation – mainly to check on whether she was nurturing some deeply-felt indignation over my behaviour with Jenna in the bar on Saturday evening. It wouldn't have surprised me.

"How's it going?"

She gave me what looked like a genuine smile. "Not badly."

"How long do you think you'll need to be here before you've got your head round everything you need to know?"

"Three weeks should do it, I think. That's the time span Bob Latimer put on it, so that's what I'm aiming for. Bob'll want us to get back, so that he can send an information technology team up here. He needs them to discuss ways of integrating the two companies' computer systems."

This was news to me. As far as I was concerned our visit was open-ended. Still, Andrea seemed to be showing me no hostility, which was a relief. Then my mobile rang.

"Mike Stanhope, how are you on this fine Monday morning?" Of all people, it was Jenna.

I didn't want to arouse Andrea's suspicions by sounding furtive, so I said, "Hi Jenna, what can I do for you?"

Andrea quickly looked down.

Jenna noticed my clipped tone. "Brisk and businesslike, eh? Well, no need. This is a social call."

"Oh yes?"

I could feel myself radiating reserve, yet she was clearly disposed to ignore it. She said, "The thing is, what are you doing on Thursday night?"

"Thursday? Um, I might be going out for a drink with Andrea and Jamie."

It was all I could think of, but Andrea quickly and loudly said, "No, that's all right Mike. Don't let us cramp your style."

Concluding that Jenna had heard this, I said to her, "Apparently I'm not going out with Andrea and Jamie."

"Great. So you're coming to the theatre with me."

"Am I?"

"I've got two tickets, but Greg is washing his hair that night."

"Clearly he's a man who plans ahead."

Ignoring this, she said, "It's the People's Theatre on the Coast Road. I'll meet you in the foyer at seven o'clock."

*   *   *

Working in the office with only Andrea for company was getting me down, so when Thursday came round I decided to stay back at the hotel and work in the lounge instead. There was no one except staff around during the day, and there was a good Wi-Fi connection.

I also had an ulterior motive for steering clear of the office. I'd been mulling over Greg Atkins' apparent gaffe on the Quayside, when he'd mentioned an upcoming logistics contract with an organisation called Franchi. Jenna had quickly jumped on him, clearly not wanting me to know about it.

So who or what was Franchi, and why was it a secret? I wanted to research it, but I didn't want Andrea or Jamie catching me doing it.

A quick trawl of the internet soon informed me that Franchi was a

upmarket online women's fashion retailer, which also had a small chain
of retail outlets. I felt I should have known this; I could already hear
Ashley's cry of disbelief when she found out I didn't. A further, more
intricate trawl eventually seemed to indicate that they currently used a
big national logistics company to distribute their products. If Mellings
were about to take over the contract, it would be a significant coup.

There was a news story in this, and I was loath to ignore it. Writing
technical feature articles about forklift trucks might bring me some
useful income, but there was more kudos in being seen to be on the ball
over current industry developments. The question was, how could I
report this one without breaking any confidences? The first requirement
was corroboration. I rang Mellings' office and asked for Chris Melling.

"I was just wondering about Franchi, the retailer. I picked up from
somewhere that Mellings might be in line to take over their logistics
operation. Is that right?"

He hesitated for a moment. "Well, it's something we've looked at,
but I wouldn't put it any more strongly than that."

"It sounded more like a done deal, from what I was told."

"You shouldn't believe all you hear."

In theory I now had almost enough information for a short news or
gossip piece. Speculative reports of this kind were commonplace in the
trade press. Such rumours could be denied or dismissed, and usually
meant little in the scheme of things, but they kept readers interested. All
the same, I'd picked this one up through my privileged position as an
agent of Latimer Logistics, which put me in an invidious position. Where
should my loyalties lie?

I picked up my phone and called Jason at the magazine. "I might
have a short news item for you," I told him. "Just a speculative piece.
But it would be on condition that you didn't by-line it. It would need to
be anonymous."

"OK, bang it over and we'll have a look."

I opened a new document on my laptop and started drafting
the piece.

Chapter 12

I'd been trying all week to think of an excuse to duck out of the theatre visit with Jenna, but as it had approached, my inspiration had dwindled. Now that Thursday had arrived I'd concluded that I had to go. Early in the evening I drove from my hotel to the local railway station, which was on the other side of a footbridge over the Tyne, and took the train into Newcastle. However, when I reached the Central Station I realised that the theatre was some way out of the city centre on the main road to Tynemouth. I had to take a taxi, which proved surprisingly expensive. My insistence on using public transport had its drawbacks.

Jenna was looking elegant in a cream jacket and black skirt. She explained that this was one of the country's longest-established amateur theatres, and was famous for staging avant garde productions. I tried to enjoy the play, an intense modern three-hander, but for much of the time I was preoccupied with trying to avoid brushing arms too often with Jenna.

As we left at the end she exclaimed, "Damn! I forgot your photos."

I looked at her.

"I was in the office today, and I told my dad that I was seeing you tonight. He said he had some pictures to give you, so I brought them with me. But I've left them at home."

"It doesn't matter, honestly."

"No, you must have them. Tell you what, we can go and collect them. It's only a few minutes' walk."

"You live around here?"

"In Jesmond, yes. Did I not tell you?"

I looked at her, trying to decide if this was a setup to get me to come home with her. She smiled guilelessly at me. "Come on man, a little walk won't hurt you." She took my arm in comradely fashion.

We crossed the busy dual carriageway that ran past the theatre and headed down the footpath on the opposite side, then forked right along a narrow road lined with trees. Before long we emerged on a viaduct over a natural dip in the landscape. "This is Armstrong Bridge," she told me. "Built by a famous industrialist in the nineteenth century. It used to be part of the coast road, but they closed it to traffic years ago because it was too weak." She pointed towards the high latticed sides. "Down there is one of Newcastle's nicest parks – Jesmond Dene. But don't look if you're afraid of heights."

The walk seemed to take longer than she'd implied, but finally we arrived at a redbrick Victorian apartment building and she led me up to her flat on the second floor.

"You'll have a drink." It was a statement, not a question. She fetched a chilled bottle of white wine from the fridge and poured two glasses, then sat down on the leather sofa and patted the position beside her. When I didn't respond immediately she said, "I won't bite, honest." I sat down, feeling slightly foolish.

We chatted about the play for a while, then she reached over to a table and picked up a large brown envelope. "Your pictures."

"Excellent." I opened the flap and slid out three ten by eight colour prints, all showing the couple who had caught my attention at Chris's house.

Jenna leaned over. "Are these from one of my dad's films?" She pronounced it "fillums", like him.

I nodded. "I thought I recognised that woman, but I don't really know how I could have. They were taken in the nineteen forties."

She peered down at them. "She's pretty."

The couple were much clearer in these prints than they had been on my phone. The woman still seemed familiar. I glanced at the man who had his arm round her. "He's wearing some kind of uniform, isn't he? Could he be a security guard or something?"

She looked more closely, then straightened triumphantly. "I know what that is! It's a bus driver's uniform. Or maybe a bus conductor's. Obviously they don't look like that these days, but I'm sure I'm right."

"How come you're so well informed?"

"When you've seen as many of Frank Giardini's films as I have, you become a bit of an expert."

* * *

I glanced at my watch. "Shit – I've missed my last train. They stop running quite early." I stood up abruptly.

Jenna immediately stood up beside me, and suddenly we were very close to each other, just as we had been in that bar in Bigg Market.

"You can stop here if you like." She accompanied the comment with a wicked smile, tilting her head slightly to one side. Her blonde hair brushed against her cheek. She wore more makeup than I was used to seeing, but it was a very beguiling face. She added, "You have to admit it could be fun."

We looked at each other for a long moment. I said, "I think I'd better get going."

"There's always the couch."

I cleared my throat and reached down to gather up the photographs. "How do I order a taxi?"

She smiled in mock chagrin, but I could see this was the outcome she was expecting. Shaking herself into action, she said, "Why no, that'll cost you a fortune. I'll give you a lift."

"Really, don't worry about it."

"Well, I'll drop you in town. You can pick up a taxi there."

I tried to protest, but she was insistent. In the end she drove me all the way to my hotel. On the way I said, "I wonder if I could track down that man in the picture. Presumably the bus company might have records."

"But which bus company? You can be pretty sure there were loads of them in Newcastle back then, and it was so long ago. Anyway, how would you identify him to look him up?"

I looked down at the pictures as the street lights flickered past.

"Maybe he had a badge number or something." But I couldn't actually see one.

She reached over and touched my arm in her characteristic confiding way. "I'll tell you what to do. Leave one of those pictures with me. Mary Carpenter's dad used to be a bus driver. Did you meet Mary in the re-working department at Mellings? I'll give it to her, and she can ask him if he has any ideas."

Chapter 13

Leeds, one of Britain's biggest cities, was a hundred miles south of Newcastle, but it was an easy drive down the A1, much of which was built to motorway standard. I arrived at Ashurst Concepts' headquarters just after lunchtime on Friday.

I'd expected to find high-tech modern premises, but in fact the company was housed in a nondescript commercial building that looked as if it dated back to the 1960s. However, it had been smartly refurbished, and the reception area was elegantly decked out with soft furnishings and recessed lighting. Around the walls were illuminated glass cases displaying some of the company's keynote products – blenders, coffee makers and the famous spiralizer.

Piers Ashurst himself emerged to welcome me – a pleasant-looking man in his early thirties with straight fair hair and a pale complexion. He was dressed trendily in an open-neck white shirt and a loose light brown linen jacket. He ushered me through a door behind the reception desk, where the environment immediately changed to the starkly practical: buff-coloured walls and flecked grey floor tiles.

I followed him up a staircase and along a corridor to his office, a modest space with pictures of Yorkshire landscapes on the walls and an incongruously expensive-looking oak desk. He took a seat behind it and waved me to the visitor's chair.

"It's been a roller coaster ride," he told me. "We were doing pretty well even before the spiralizer came along, but then profits went through the roof. We were in the right place at the right time, and we took full advantage."

His tone was affable, but I sensed an underlying edginess. Perhaps he was annoyed at having been more or less forced to play host to me, instead of whatever else he'd planned for the afternoon. Well, so be it. I resolved to let the visit run its course.

"So how come you sold out your controlling interest so soon to Chris Melling?"

"Simple. Mellings were already doing our distribution, and Chris had money to spend. He's done very well for himself with his company. We were looking for new investment, so it was a marriage made in heaven."

"But now Chris has sold his company to Latimer Logistics. How do you feel about that?"

He gave me a cautious glance. "Well, Chris assures me it will be business as usual after the deal goes through – and I hope you've come here to tell me the same thing."

"So far as I know, yes."

Piers looked at me carefully. "I hope I can take that as a reassurance."

Actually I wasn't sure what I could safely tell him. I'd tried to sound out Bob Latimer on his attitude to Ashursts when we'd spoken on the phone a couple nights before, but he'd merely told me to keep my eyes open. "If Ashurst represents a sound investment, all well and good," he'd said. "We might have some fun expanding into a new sector. But at the end of the day Latimers are in logistics, not consumer appliances, so they've got to pay their way."

I now said, "Bob Latimer is a good guy. He won't want to rock the boat for no reason."

He nodded. "Good to hear."

It seemed time to change the subject. "I understand you know Jenna Melling pretty well."

"Yes, we were at Leeds University together. She's developed a real eye for marketing opportunities. We owe a lot of our success to her vision. She usually spends two or three days a week here in Leeds, working for us."

Apparently their personal rift hadn't interrupted her working involvement here, but I was aware that if I kept talking about her I could easily stray into awkward territory. Changing tack again, I asked, "Are you planning to stay with the company under the new regime, if you don't mind me asking?"

"Initially, yes. In the long run I'll be reviewing my options. I'm a bit of a serial entrepreneur – always on the lookout for the next big thing."

I smiled inwardly at this. Surely "serial entrepreneur" should be a status bestowed by others, not something self-proclaimed? I wondered what Piers felt he'd serially entrepreneured in the past.

* * *

I asked if I could see the factory. Piers glanced at his watch, then agreed to give me a quick tour – a little reluctantly, I thought. Actually the place seemed more like a glorified warehouse than a factory to me; there was no production activity as such, or even assembly work – just a bit of repackaging and short-term storage. Nearly all the items apparently came pre-assembled and boxed from the Far East. The processes I could see looked quite similar to those at Mellings and Latimers.

However, there was a small technical department, and I watched as an engineer seated at a bench poked at a small electronic circuit board with a tiny screwdriver. There was also a room equipped as a rudimentary kitchen, where two people in white coats were putting some of the products through their paces.

We walked through to a holding area, which was currently cluttered with pallets of goods awaiting shipping to Mellings' warehouse in Newcastle. "Most of the work we do here will be transferred to Mellings eventually," Piers said. "That way we'll cut out a stage."

"It seems odd, sending product north to Mellings for distribution when you're much more central here in Leeds."

"As a logistics man I thought you'd understand. The key is in the consolidation."

I laughed. "I'm just playing devil's advocate."

"As a matter of fact, according to Chris Melling, Latimers have just taken on some warehousing here in Leeds, so we might be able to hold our stock in this area in future."

A man in overalls approached us and asked Piers something about operational procedure. The two of them disappeared round the end of an aisle of racking, and I glanced around me. Most of the fairly basic shelving was packed with cartons from Ashursts' product range, and there were also pallets of cartons on the floor. It seemed altogether crowded.

It struck me that I should have been taking photographs. Normally it was an ingrained habit, but I hadn't been treating this visit as a journalistic exercise, so the idea hadn't occurred to me. Belatedly I took out my mobile phone and fired off a couple of shots of the pallets on the floor.

Piers came striding back round the corner. "What was that flash?"

"I just thought I'd take a couple of photographs. I hope I wasn't out of order?"

He frowned. "I'd rather you didn't. The place is a mess at the moment. It wouldn't reflect at all well on the company."

"Sorry, point taken."

"Will you delete the pictures you took, please?"

I stared at him. Suddenly there was an iciness between us. I said, "If you really want me to."

"Yes please." He continued to stare at me, and it dawned on me that he actually wanted to see me delete the images there and then. Instantly my belligerent streak took over. I said, "You're not seriously doubting that I'll do it if I say I will?"

He continued to stare at me for a moment without replying. It was a stand-off. Finally he gave in. Presumably he realised that he couldn't maintain a cordial front if he insisted on having his way. "OK, just so long as they don't get out into the public domain.

He ushered me away to the loading bay, where stacks of the company's spiralizers awaited palletising. In an attempt to lighten the tone, he said, "You can see the high volumes of product going through here. The initial excitement may have come and gone, but people still want this stuff."

* * *

Piers took me upstairs to a large open-plan office, and introduced me briefly to a couple of his colleagues – the production manager and the marketing assistant, a brisk woman in her mid-twenties. A colleague interrupted her mid-sentence to pass her a call from a local radio station, and we left her gesticulating with her arm and saying, "Not this month, darling. How many times do I have to say it?"

At the door out to the corridor we nearly collided with a short man in a grey pinstripe suit. He looked out of place in this world of open-neck shirts.

"Sorry, Nick," Piers told him. "I'll be finished here in a minute. I got side-tracked by this gentleman." He gestured towards me.

The man frowned at him, apparently only partially appeased. "We really do need to talk." He held up a sheaf of A4 printouts. "We need to get these figures aligned."

Piers nodded. "Give me five minutes." He turned to me. "Nick looks after our accounts."

Back in his own office he sat down behind his desk and gave me a quizzical look. "So did we pass the test?"

"Test?"

"I got the impression you were checking up on us to report back to Bob Latimer."

I wasn't sure how to answer this. A little awkwardly I said, "I just wanted to get the feel of the place. I'm not here to pass judgement."

"Good." He gave me a penetrating stare, and for the first time I sensed the power of the personality behind his sociable veneer. After a moment he said, "Well I hope you found your visit illuminating."

"Very."

He reverted abruptly to more affable mode as I stood up to leave. "Does your wife have a spiralizer?"

His question echoed one I'd been asked by Jenna the first time I met her. Again I resisted commenting on the gender assumptions behind it, and merely shrugged. "To be honest, I don't know."

He reached round to a glass-fronted cabinet behind him, then turned to me and presented me with a colourful cardboard box. "She does now."

Chapter 14

My heart gave a leap when I saw Ashley walking purposefully towards me at Leeds City Station. I grinned at her, but felt suddenly shy. Although we didn't live together, we normally saw each other every day and spent most nights together. We hadn't been apart this long since I'd moved to Truro.

"Hello," I said diffidently.

She smiled broadly. "You can kiss me if you like."

Laughing, I took her overnight bag from her and put it down, then put my hands on her shoulders and kissed her about ten times.

"You're pleased to see me, then?"

Ashley was thirty years old, slim with even features, and had shoulder-length dark hair. She had a serene self-possession about her, and a wry sense of humour. I'd never dared to imagine being paired with someone so all-round attractive.

I led her out to where I'd parked the hired car, which she duly admired. "A step up from your own battered heap."

I told her, "I booked us into a posh hotel in Harrogate. I think you'll like it."

"Are we going to take the waters, then?" Harrogate had risen to prominence in Victorian times as a spa town.

I shuddered. "Not if I can help it."

We drove out through the northern suburbs of Leeds, and I noticed that the route would take us near the industrial estate where Ashursts were based. I said to Ashley, "Do you know what a spiralizer is?"

"It shreds vegetables into strands, doesn't it? It's supposed to be the fresh food fanatic's answer to pasta."

"Nicely put. You ought to be in marketing."

She laughed.

"Melling Logistics have bought a stake one of the leading suppliers, Ashurst Concepts, and they're based near here. I'll show you."

I turned off the main road and headed into the industrial estate. It was mid-evening, and most of the employees' cars had disappeared from the street in front of the Ashurst building.

"Not a very prepossessing head office for such a high-profile company," Ashley commented.

"I suppose they started modestly and they're working their way to greater things."

I inched the car forward, and we paused outside the gateway to the loading area. There were no trucks in the yard, but a scruffy white panel van was backed up to the loading bay. Faded signwriting read "Black Cat Deliveries". We watched for a while as someone inside the van passed cartons to a man on the loading bank. I could just make out simplistic spiralizer graphics on the brown cardboard outers.

Ashley asked, "I wonder what they're doing?"

"It looks like a delivery, but it's a strange time of day for it, and a strange sort of van to be using. I think their stuff normally arrives in big container trucks, not like this."

As we watched, the man on the loading deck noticed us. He jumped down to ground level and strode rapidly over towards us, shouting, "What do you think you're doing?"

I got out of the car and leaned over the roof. "It's OK – I was visiting Piers Ashurst earlier on today. We happened to be passing again, and I'm showing my colleague the factory."

He eyed me with disbelief. "Well would you mind passing somewhere else? This is private property."

I resisted pointing out that we were on a public road. "OK, no offence intended."

He stood with his hands on his hips, waiting for us to leave, so I started the engine and pulled slowly away.

"Charming man," Ashley said. "I don't think I'll be buying one of their spiralizers any time soon."

"Too late. They gave me one to give you."

* * *

Ashley had never been to Harrogate before, and declared herself impressed with the swathes of manicured greensward that seemed to surround the town. "You've picked a nice place to inherit a house," she told me.

I'd booked us into a large period hotel in the central area, which nicely combined the modern touch with its air of timeless elegance. In the evening we walked around the town centre among other tourists, pausing to admire Bettys Tea Room and the extensive spa pump rooms.

Later we lingered in a cosy restaurant. "Bob Latimer sends his regards," Ashley said.

"He needn't have bothered. He phones me almost every day."

"I suppose he likes to keep in touch."

"How are things otherwise?"

"OK." She looked pensive. "Gareth Hobbs is a bit of a pain."

Gareth was a relative newcomer to the company. He'd joined as sales manager from a big logistics group – part of a drive by Bob Latimer to reinforce his company's fire power on the national scene.

"I wouldn't have thought he would have much involvement in your department."

"Nor would I, but he seems to think he does. He keeps coming in, basically telling me what to do."

Ashley's immediate boss had left some months ago, and her role was currently that of acting marketing manager. "I've got the job, but not the authority," she said with a scowl."

"I don't know why Bob doesn't just confirm your new position."

"I suppose I'll have to tough it out until he's convinced I'm ready for it."

"I'll put in a good word for you."

She laughed. "Oh yes? You and Uncle Bob? Since when did you have his ear, Mr Stanhope?"

I smiled. "Well, I would if I could."

Later, in our hotel room, I was reminded of our first time together. As I looked down at Ashley's face, an image of Jenna Melling jumped fleetingly into my head. No contest, I thought to myself. Life didn't get any better than this.

Chapter 15

Elizabeth Sanderson's house was in a district just north of Harrogate centre, on a road of assorted Victorian terraced properties. It didn't look quite as monumental in reality as it had on screen, but it was double-fronted and detached by a few feet from the houses on either side, and in its unassuming way it was impressive.

I parked diagonally opposite and we sat looking at it for a while.

"It's a big house for one person," Ashley said.

"Maybe the history will explain it."

"I suppose there's no way we can see inside?"

"Not unless you've brought your lock-picking kit with you."

At that moment the door of the next-door house opened and a middle-aged woman emerged. She walked along to Elizabeth's house, opened the gate and approached the front door. Taking out a key, she unlocked the door and disappeared inside.

Ashley and I looked at each other. I said, "It seems we've turned up at just the right time."

"What are you going to do?"

"See if we can talk our way in. Come on." I started to get out of the car, then reached round behind me and grabbed a case I'd brought with me. "Might as well take our credentials with us."

I pressed the bell push, and the woman quickly opened the front door.

I gave her my best friendly smile. "Hello. My name is Mike Stanhope, and this is Ashley. You won't know me, but I've just inherited this house from Elizabeth Sanderson. We were hoping to have a quick look round."

She looked at me guardedly – a round woman in her late sixties or early seventies. "Phil didn't tell me anything about this. I thought the house was going to him and his wife – Philip and Angela Crabtree. Who are you, if you don't mind me asking?"

"I'm a writer from London. I recently moved to Cornwall. Elizabeth evidently had a late change of heart, and decided to leave her house to me." I thought a blast of frankness might help, so I added, "To be honest, it was as much a surprise to me as it probably is to you. But we are where we are."

She shook her head. "I don't think I should let a total stranger into the house, even if what you say is true. I need proper authority."

"Oh." I tried a look of disappointment, and fumbled my case open. "I tell you what – have a look at this."

I handed her the original letter from the solicitors and the schedule of assets they'd given me in Newcastle. The woman pored over them for a moment, then looked up. "Well, that makes it plain enough, I suppose. But it's funny that Philip never said anything about this."

Chancing my arm, I said, "You could ring him if you have any doubts. He'll confirm who we are." Out of the corner of my eye I caught Ashley trying to suppress a look of amusement at this bluff.

Finally the woman relaxed. "Come on in then. I'm just watering the plants. We can have a cup of coffee if you like. But I'd better stay with you while you're here." She started into the house, then turned to us. "My name is Rosemary."

* * *

The house had a pleasant, lived-in feel. It was furnished in assorted styles – antique, sixties, nineties, contemporary. Some of the older furniture looked valuable, though it would have taken an expert to pronounce on it. Bookshelves lined one of the walls in the main living room, and there was a large desk pushed up against the back window. A mature garden stretched away behind the house. "Elizabeth used to do her work in this room," Rosemary said. "Research for the college, that kind of thing."

"Were you close friends or just nodding acquaintances?"

She considered this. "I suppose you could say we were good neighbours. That amounts to friends, doesn't it? We've both lived in this street for years."

"It must have been a shock for you then."

"Well, we knew it was coming, but we thought she had much longer. It was very sudden in the end."

"What was she like?"

"You didn't know her, then?"

I shook my head.

"She was energetic. Always busy. She'd retired from teaching, of course, but she was always working on some academic project."

She went through to the kitchen and made coffee rather than tea. "It'll have to be coffee whitener," she called. "There's no milk in the house."

When she returned I asked her how well she knew Philip Crabtree. "Not very," she said. "I saw him occasionally when he was visiting over the years, but then he started coming down from Newcastle regularly at the start of this year, when he heard about her illness. I think she really appreciated it. She didn't have much other family, or many close friends either."

"Was it Philip who asked you to look after the place, or the solicitors?"

"Oh, it was Philip. I've had nothing to do with solicitors. I already had the keys from Elizabeth, so he asked me to pop in every now and then, just to keep things ticking over."

Ashley asked if we could explore the rest of the house, and Rosemary waved her assent, apparently now at ease with us. "I think I should get back," she said. "I didn't lock my own house. Will you pull the front door shut when you leave, and give me a knock? I'll come over later and clear up."

*　*　*

"It's a friendly house," Ashley said. "It seems full of Elizabeth's personality."

I went over and looked at the desk. There was a computer keyboard and screen, but no computer in sight – just trailing wires that must once have been connected to one. I turned to Ashley. "Who has the authority to take things away in this situation?"

"I've no idea, but when my gran died, my parents just treated her house as if it was their own. They more or less did what they liked with anything that was lying around. Nobody objected."

I nodded. I'd done the same thing when my mother died. I had a sense that this was a grey area. During the early days after a death there would be no inventory to check against, so it would be hard for anyone to complain if they thought something had gone missing.

I said, "I bet Philip Crabtree took her computer. It might have given us more of a clue to what she was like, and why she left me the house."

There were small piles of academic magazines and jotted notes in an in-tray, presumably in Elizabeth's cursive handwriting, but we found nothing especially revealing.

Upstairs we inspected the main bedroom and several guest bedrooms, all tidy and well maintained. Ashley idly opened wardrobe doors, and presently commented, "There are some men's clothes here."

I went over. Several men's suits and jackets hung on the rail towards the side. They seemed stiff and unused, as if they'd been there a long time. Ashley and I exchanged meaningful glances.

Returning to the lounge, we sat down on the deeply upholstered sofa. Ashley said, "Well, it's a nice place, but I wouldn't want to keep much of the stuff in it, would you?"

"Not really, but according to the solicitors the antique pieces could be valuable. Until the will is sorted out it's not my call anyway. I might end up sharing it all with the Crabtrees, or losing any claim to it."

I felt something digging into my thigh, and shoved my hand down between the seat cushions. It was a tablet computer. "Ha! Looks as if Mr Crabtree missed this."

Abruptly we heard the sound of a key being thrust into the front door lock. We froze. Was this Rosemary returning to check up on us, or someone else? Instinctively I grabbed my case and shoved the tablet computer into it, closing the flap to hide it from view. Ashley watched me, wide-eyed.

We heard the front door open and close again, then the lounge door was thrust open and Philip Crabtree was staring at us with eyes blazing.

"What the hell do you think you're doing here?"

Chapter 16

"We just came to have a look at our bequest," I said.

Philip Crabtree continued to stare at me. "You have no right to be here. How did you get in? I'm going to have to ask you to leave." When we made no move, he added, "Now!"

I felt Ashley tensing in readiness to stand up, but I put my hand on her arm. She sat back dubiously. I said, "Elizabeth Sanderson left me this house in her will. You know that. Surely I have a right to take a look at it?"

"You don't have any rights at all, mate. That will is crap. It'll soon be overturned."

My pulse was racing. I wasn't used to hostile confrontations like this, and my instinct was to back off. Yet a wave of irritation was running through me, and somehow I found the resource to argue. I said, "But the will hasn't been overturned so far. I could just as easily ask you what right *you* have to be here."

"What right *I* have?" This seemed to anger him even more. "Why should I have to explain myself to you? Elizabeth was family. She was part of our lives. I've been in and out of here constantly for the last six months. I helped nurse her through her illness. I don't know how you even have the nerve to ask."

Ashley said, "Those aren't rights. They're just matters of circumstance."

He switched his gaze to her. "What the hell would you know about it?"

She merely glared at him. I said, "Were you a dependant of Elizabeth Sanderson's?"

He looked quickly back at me. "Of course not."

"Is this your place of residence?"

"You know damned well it's not."

I knew from my limited internet research that these were key factors people could invoke if they were asserting special rights to a share in a contested legacy. I said, "So you don't have any special claim on Elizabeth's estate."

"Oh yes I do. She left it to me – until she put her name to that bogus will."

I said nothing and he continued to stare at me angrily. Finally he said, "So are you leaving, or will I call the police?"

I stood up slowly, anxious to avoid showing him any kind of threat. Ashley stood up beside me. I said, "Look, we don't have to be in dispute over this. I never expected to be left this house. It was news to me when I heard about it. If we could discuss it calmly, maybe we could resolve the whole thing in a friendly way."

"I'm not discussing anything with you, mate." He pronounced the word as "meert" in true Geordie style. "Are you leaving, or do you want to explain yourself to the police?" He pulled out his phone and started tapping digits into it.

"They'll probably throw you out as well, and then none of us will have access."

"We'll see about that." He stared at us defiantly, making a show of holding his finger over the Send button. "Well?"

I said, "Where is Elizabeth's computer?"

"What?"

I didn't repeat the question – I just stared at him.

He lowered the phone. "I don't have to answer to you."

"Fair enough, but it's something I might raise with the police when they get here."

I could see him tighten his fist. "Do you want to get a kicking, mate?"

I heard Ashley draw in breath sharply. It seemed like time for a tactical withdrawal. I said, "OK, we'll go." I picked up my bag and glanced around in case we'd left anything else. I took Ashley's hand and forced myself to walk past Philip Crabtree at close quarters, drawing her behind me. He merely watched us. At the hall door I turned. "I have to say I find your attitude very strange. Why do you need to be so hostile? Surely you can see we're trying to be reasonable?"

"That's not what it looks like from where I'm standing. Now get going, and don't expect to be let in here again."

* * *

In the car, Ashley said, "Jesus! What's the matter with that man?"

"He's been disinherited, and he's not very happy about it."

"But god almighty, what's the point of him threatening you?"

My pulse was still racing. I said, "I don't know. Maybe it wasn't such a clever idea to talk our way in there."

"All the same."

I started the car and drove us back towards the hotel, but Ashley said she wanted some fresh air. I drove on down to The Stray, the broad area of greensward outside the town centre, and we struck out on foot across the grass.

Ashley said, "Do you even want to inherit this woman's estate?"

"I must say it's leaving a bitter taste at the moment. No one turns down half a million lightly, but if it leads to a load of acrimony, I'm not so sure."

She stopped and turned to me. "You wouldn't really give up on it that easily, would you?"

"I don't know. It's not a situation I've ever been in before. What would you do?"

"Huh! Don't put it on me. I'd be inclined to say take the money and run, but then I'm not the one having to fend off the irate Mr Crabtree."

"Thanks for your support!"

She laughed. "Don't worry, we're in this together."

"I knew you only wanted me for my money."

We walked on. I said, "What I'd like to know is who Elizabeth Sanderson was to me, and how come she picked my name out of a hat."

"She can't have done that. There must be some logic to it."

"And I've got to find out what it is. If I can, maybe I can appease Philip Crabtree, and we can all move on."

We spent the afternoon exploring the town again. In the early evening we returned to our room at the hotel, and I remembered the tablet computer I'd taken from Elizabeth's house. Maybe she'd used it for email. I tried switching it on, but the battery was flat. I fetched out my phone charger and plugged it in. The charging graph read zero per cent. Its secrets would have to wait.

Chapter 17

Sunday morning brought sunshine, and we headed out in the car to explore the North Yorkshire Moors. We found a country pub for lunch, and did some modest fell walking in the afternoon. It was a relief to forget the world of Melling Logistics for a day, as well as Elizabeth Sanderson's strange bequest.

However, when we got back to the hotel in the evening I remembered her tablet computer, which was now fully charged. I switched it on, and as I'd hoped, she'd used it for at least some of her emailing.

I scrolled through her messages, looking for anything significant. There were predictable notes to friends and colleagues, and there was some ongoing correspondence with her college.

There was nothing obviously relevant to me, and I was about to give up for the day when an idea struck me, and I ran an email search for "Mike Stanhope". I watched the hourglass icon without much hope, but then a single find appeared among Sent Items – a message Elizabeth had written the previous year to someone called Howard.

There was nothing about me in the main text, but I found it in a postscript: "BTW, have you heard of an author called Mike Stanhope?" Just that – no elaboration. Quickly I switched to the inbox, looking for messages to Elizabeth from Howard. There were a few, but I could find no mention of my name. I turned to Ashley, who was lying on the bed browsing through a guide book. "Elizabeth Sanderson definitely knew me. She asked about me in an email she wrote to someone called Howard."

She looked up. "Well obviously she knew about you. She left you the house."

"But this is corroboration."

"So what did this Howard person have to say?"

"Nothing, apparently."

She leaned over and looked at the tablet screen. "She probably used her laptop for day-to-day emailing, and just used this tablet as a backup."

"I wish we had the laptop."

"Have you searched for just plain 'Stanhope'?"

"Doing it now."

Remarkably, this brought another result – again a single find, this time in an email I'd missed from Howard. I read it out to Ashley. "I'd not heard of that writer, Stanhope, but I think I've tracked him down. Bit of a coincidence, actually. I'll tell you about it later. He recently published an electronic book – some kind of thriller. But you probably know that already. What's this about, Lizzie? Does it have something to do with the distaff thing?"

I looked up. "Distaff thing? What can that mean?"

"Something to do with the maternal side of her family."

"Yes, but I wonder what?"

I scrolled through other emails to and from Howard, trying to find out who he might be. There was no surname in sight, and the email address was merely 'howard' plus a string of digits.

I turned to Ashley. "I like the way she describes me as an author. She's got her priorities right."

* * *

I dropped Ashley at Leeds in the morning to catch her train to Truro.

"Don't go baiting that Crabtree man," she warned. "He looked as if he could be really nasty."

"I won't."

I told her I might make the trip down to Cornwall the following weekend. "That's if this stint in Newcastle carries on. According to Andrea it was only supposed to last three weeks, but when I asked Bob Latimer he just said 'Stick with it'."

"I might come up to Newcastle in a week or two if you're still here. Then I can find out what all the fuss is about."

"That would be great."

Walking out through the station concourse I felt suddenly alone. I returned to the car and drove off through the suburbs towards the A1 and Newcastle, but then an idea struck me, and I followed the signs to Harrogate instead.

Fifteen miles later I arrived in Elizabeth Sanderson's street for a second time, and knocked somewhat nervously on Rosemary's front door. She answered promptly, but looked disconcerted when she saw me. "I'm sorry, but I don't have anything to say to you. Philip Crabtree told me I did wrong to let you into the house on Saturday. I don't want to get involved in a dispute between the two of you."

She started to close the door. Quickly I said, "Please – I'm sorry if he was heavy-handed with you. I don't want to get you into trouble. I just wondered if you could tell me something."

"Tell you what?" she asked warily

"Elizabeth Sanderson had a friend called Howard. I wondered if you knew who he was, or where he lived."

"Howard." She pondered. "I think he might be Derek's brother."

"Derek?"

"Elizabeth's partner. He lived here with her when they moved in. I didn't really know Elizabeth then, so I never got to know him properly. He died of a heart attack, poor man."

"Do you know his surname, or where Howard lives now?"

"Derek Salmon, I think. So that's probably Howard's surname. I never met him, and I don't remember him being at her funeral. I don't think he lives around here." She put her hand on the door, preparing to close it. "I think that's all I can tell you."

* * *

Just over two hours later I was back at Mellings. I booted up my laptop and scanned through my draft of the news piece I'd written about the Franchi contract the previous week. It seemed to read all right, but both Jamie and Andrea were working in our little office today, and I was worried that one of them would see it. Hastily I typed out a short email to Jason at the magazine and attached the document to it. Barely hesitating, I hit the Send button.

"Nice weekend?"

I looked up with a start to see Jenna Melling leaning round the door grinning at me.

"Not bad."

"You'll be wanting this back, I imagine." She held up a light jacket that I'd taken with me to the theatre on Thursday night. I hadn't even missed it. "You left it at my place." I had to lunge from my chair to catch it as she tossed it over towards me.

If she'd wanted to imply that something untoward had passed between us she couldn't have done it more effectively. I could see Andrea glancing meaningfully between us, drawing her own conclusions.

"Thanks," I said, adding "and thanks for the lift home." I hoped this would dispel any misunderstanding, but when Jenna said, "My pleasure," her arch tone seemed reinforce the original inference. I couldn't decide whether she was doing this guilefully or merely out of habit.

She came over to my desk, letting the door swing shut behind her. "I've just been talking to Mary Carpenter downstairs. I gave her that photograph of yours, and she says she'll show it to her dad. She sees him most evenings. Have a word with her tomorrow, and she'll probably be able to tell you what he says."

"Great."

She seemed to notice the other two for the first time. "Hi guys," she said with a little wave of the hand. "I hope you're having a good time in Newcastle?"

"It's a great place," Jamie said.

"I'm glad you think so." And she was gone.

Chapter 18

The following morning I made my way down to the packing floor and approached Mary. "I don't suppose your dad has had a chance yet to look at the picture that Jenna gave you?"

She beamed at me. "As a matter of fact he has."

"Aha! So any luck? Did he recognise which bus company that man worked for?"

"Better than that – he knew the man himself!"

I looked at her in amazement. "Seriously?"

"That's what he said. Come through to the back for a minute."

I followed her into a cramped office, where she picked up a bag and rummaged inside it, seating herself on the corner of a desk. She pulled out a piece of paper and studied it.

"Len Roberts – that's who he thinks the man is in the picture. He was a traffic manager when my dad first worked at the bus company, but he could have started out as a driver."

"That's absolutely brilliant."

She gave me a quick smile. "Glad we could help."

"What was the name of the bus company?"

"Aitken Services. It was a small independent company, not one of the big ones."

"So did your dad actually know this man personally?"

"Not well, from what he said. I think he just saw him around, and maybe took orders from him. This guy would have been much older."

She pulled the picture itself from her bag and held it out to me. "You'll want this."

I glanced down at it, then up at her. "What about the woman he's with? Did your dad recognise her?"

"Sorry, no. She might have been his wife I suppose, or a girlfriend."

"And he didn't know where this man lived, or anything else about him?"

"I don't think so. He was just part of the company management."

She started to get up, but I was reluctant to let her go without exploring all angles. I said, "How sure is your dad that this man really is Len Roberts?"

She smiled. "He said if you asked me that, I should say ninety per cent positive."

I laughed. "That's pretty definite then."

* * *

Returning to my office I found Jamie and Andrea tidying up, apparently preparing to leave for the day. I glanced at my watch. It was only mid-morning.

"You're off then," I said teasingly.

Andrea stopped what she was doing and stared defiantly at me. "We're going to the races, if you want to know. At Gosforth Park. They only run them on certain days of the week, and in the summer the programme is reduced. I think we've earned the right to a break."

Jamie shrugged, perhaps less enthusiastic than his partner, but evidently willing to go along with her. I said, "Don't mind me. I hope you enjoy it."

I watched as they closed their computers, gathered up their belongings and started to head out. It struck me that this was the very kind of activity Bob Latimer had intended me to prevent, but when it came to the crunch I couldn't see what I could reasonably do to stop it. I didn't have it in me to act the indignant boss.

I said, "Have a nice day."

Jamie shot me a slightly embarrassed smile as he passed. Then at the door they nearly collided with Jenna Melling. Andrea turned to me and said pointedly, "Visitor for you, Mike."

Jenna watched as they disappeared down the corridor, then turned to me. "Spikey lady. What did you do to upset her?"

"Don't ask me."

"So how did you get on with our Mary?"

"Brilliantly. Her father actually knew the man in that picture. He was a manager at the bus company where he worked when he was young."

"That's great! I knew he would help if he could."

"I owe you one."

"So does this help you to track down the girl in the film?"

"Maybe, although I'm not sure how. I know his name now, but unless she was his wife or fiancée, I suspect the chances of identifying her are pretty slim."

"Well, you never know." She turned to leave, then swivelled round on her heel. "Fancy a pie and a pint at lunchtime? I could do with getting out of this place for an hour." She gave me a facetious smile. "Greg's still washing his hair."

* * *

After she left I thought over what I'd learned about the people in my picture. Was it a breakthrough? If so, a breakthrough to what? I now knew the probable name of the man in the film, but I didn't know who the woman was, or why she had caught my attention in the first place.

I looked at the picture again, and had that same sense that I recognised her. Well, I would keep on trying to work out why, and at the same time I could consider tracking down Len Roberts.

As a first step I Googled the name, but predictably got half a million finds. I added "Newcastle" to the search parameters, but this still produced more than four hundred thousand results. I would have to think of a more specific approach.

Instead, I tried Aitken Services, the bus company. There weren't many finds for this, but eventually I discovered that it had gone out of business in the 1980s. Some of the assets had been acquired by a bigger rival, but the company itself had simply faded away – which probably meant its records had faded with it.

I tried Len Roberts in combination with Aitken Services, and got nothing. Then I tried Aitken Services on its own again, and this time I spotted a reference to a recent book, *Vanished Buses of the North East*. I was reluctant to buy it without even seeing it, but perhaps I could look at it in a bookshop.

Chris Melling's office door was open – which I now knew was a sign that he was willing to be approached. I asked him about bookshops in Newcastle, and he recommended two. In my own office I phoned one of them to find out if they had the book in stock. The answer was yes, so I decided I'd go and check it out. Andrea and Jamie weren't the only ones who could award themselves an afternoon off.

Chapter 19

At lunchtime Jenna drove me to the pub that Mellings' management team favoured. It was only five minutes from the office, but the village environment made it seem a world away. The low-ceilinged bar was decked out with horse tackle, ploughshares and similar rustic paraphernalia.

I was annoyed with myself for being cornered in yet another social encounter with Jenna, but she seemed to have a knack of making her proposals impossible to refuse. Once we'd settled at a table I said, "You seem to spend quite a bit of time at Mellings."

"It's supposed to be just a day a week – that's what I agreed. But that's not really enough to run the marketing properly. You might think it's a sinecure, but actually it's a lot of work – company literature, the website, all that good stuff. Mellings' PR firm, Ashby Collins, do most of the grafting, but I have to keep them on track."

"Sinecure isn't a word that often comes to my mind."

She laughed dryly, then added, "To be honest, I need to keep up all my income streams. I'm not sure how long I'll carry on working for Ashursts."

"You mean, because of breaking off with Piers Ashurst?"

"Well, that's part of it." She leaned forward, switching to confidential mode. "They're a funny company. I'm not sure half the time what they're up to."

"How do you mean?"

"Well, look at that lorry hijacking. What was all that about?"

"Surely you can't blame them for that?"

"Maybe not, but it came at a strange time – just as their sales were levelling off." She shrugged. "It's not just that. Piers is a difficult guy. Don't get me wrong – I've always liked him, and I don't want to talk him down. But you never really know what he's thinking. You always feel that whatever he's doing, he has some other plan going on at the same time."

We continued to chat about this for a while, but I felt I had to address a point that was troubling me. I said, "I don't know if you realise, but my girlfriend Ashley runs the marketing at Latimer Logistics. When this merger goes through she'll probably have overall responsibility. You might find yourself working for her."

I couldn't tell if this intelligence worried Jenna or not. She merely said, "Isn't that charming? Nothing like keeping things in the family, I always say."

"I was just thinking that if you're pinning your hopes on future work at Mellings, the circumstances might change."

"You mean I could be out on my ear? Might as well call a spade a spade."

"Well, that sounds a bit drastic."

"I'm just trying to be realistic." She narrowed her eyes. "There's an alternative scenario, of course. I might get the top marketing job."

I gave her a wide-eyed look, but her expression told me this wasn't really her plan. I was reminded of the calculating quality I'd sensed when I first met her at that dinner.

* * *

After lunch Chris Melling spotted me in the corridor and called me into his office.

"I meant to ask you, how did you get on at Ashurst Concepts last week?"

"Impressive operation. Piers seems a real achiever."

He gave me an indulgent smile pointed to the visitor's chair. "OK, so have a seat and tell me what you really think."

I sat down cautiously. "Well, they've hit a high spot with the spiralizer – that's obvious."

"But you're wondering if it's all a flash in the pan."

I shrugged. "I don't really know the market well enough to judge. I did feel that maybe it's a bit of a hand-to-mouth operation. I didn't see much sign of future product development."

He nodded. "That's pretty much what Jenna says."

"And there's a lot of spare stock lying around."

"That too."

"Forgive me, but I thought you regarded them as a really sound investment."

"Oh, I do, I do. But it's interesting to get an outside perspective."

"Fair enough."

He brightened. "I hear your friends are off to the races."

"You're very well informed."

He laughed. "Not a lot gets past me, sitting here. Anyway, there's nothing wrong with the occasional flutter. I've been known to indulge myself once in a while. Maybe they'll hit a winning streak."

* * *

In the afternoon I drove to my hotel and took the train into Newcastle. For access to the central area I still couldn't fault railway travel, even though it wasn't cheap. I enjoyed the bustle of the Central Station, and the classical frontage was irresistibly impressive, featuring a row of high arches in monumental style.

I made my way to the bookshop I'd telephoned and found the transport section. Sure enough, there was one copy of *Vanished Buses of the North East*. It consisted mostly of pictures, but the photo captions looked informative. I leafed through it.

There was just a single page on Aitken Services, which included a black and white picture of an old single-decker bus, with the driver and conductor posed in front of the radiator. I looked more closely. Surely one of them was the same man who featured in Chris's film? I took out my own picture and compared them. No question; it was him.

I glanced at the caption. "AEC Regal of Aitken Services, Ryton, with local men Leonard Roberts (left) and Tommy Barlow in charge." Not much, but it seemed to suggest that Len Roberts himself hailed from Ryton, wherever that was. It might be something I could follow up.

It seemed an amazing piece of luck, but as I studied the other captions on the page I realised that Aitken had been a very small company. Presumably this meant it had only a handful of drivers, so the chances of Len being featured in this photograph had probably been quite high.

I checked the price of the book, which was £20. I had to remind myself that I might be about to inherit half a million pounds. On that basis everything seemed cheap. I took the book to the pay point and opened my wallet.

Chapter 20

Next day everything started to fall apart.

It began in the middle of the morning with an unexpected call from Ashley. All three of us were working in the office, so I spoke to her in a low voice. "What's up?"

"That's what I was going to ask you. What's this about Jenna Melling?"

"What's what?" I wondered if this had something to do with Jenna's involvement in Mellings' marketing activity.

"You and her," Ashley said. "Spending the night together. Or have I got that wrong?"

Ashley had never spoken to me with such venom before. I felt utterly wrong-footed.

"What! You most certainly have got it wrong. Where are you getting this from?"

"So you didn't go to the theatre with her last week, and then on to her flat?"

"Well, yes, but – " I glanced over at Andrea and Jamie. I didn't want to start discussing my love life in front of them. Andrea seemed to be watching me attentively. I said, "Just a minute."

I stood up, hurried out into the corridor and strode down to the end of it, as far away from any doors as I could get. Lifting the phone again I said, "I went to Jenna's flat for half an hour. I didn't spend the night with her. What on earth made you think that?"

"Apparently it's all over Mellings. You should try listening to what people are saying about you up there."

"Rubbish. That's completely untrue."

"Don't 'rubbish' me, Mike. Tell me a straight story."

"I didn't mean you're talking rubbish, I meant what you've been told is rubbish." On the back foot again.

"I see. That makes a difference, does it?"

This was an Ashley I simply didn't know, forcing me into the wrong over every detail. Taking a deep breath, I said, "Look, I've given you a straight story. What you're thinking is complete fiction. Whoever told you this, they must have done it out of misguided loyalty or spite. Was it Andrea Smith?"

"So tell me you don't find Jenna attractive."

I hesitated. A lie wouldn't go down well at this point. "Of course she's attractive. No one in their right mind would say anything else. That doesn't mean I'm having an affair with her. Good grief!"

"I wish I believed you."

"Well why don't you? Can't you have a bit of faith? Tell me honestly, when we met up last weekend, did I seem like someone who was having an affair?"

"I can't tell what to think, Mike."

The whole conversation was running away with me, and I couldn't think how to regain control. Finally I said, "I tell you what – why not ask Jenna about this? She'll soon put you right."

"Ah, yes, I can really see that. That's bound to clarify things."

For a moment neither of us spoke, then she said, "So why didn't you mention your theatre trip to me last weekend?"

Now she had me. I hadn't wanted to talk to her about Jenna at all, but I now realised this had been a mistake. I said, "There's nothing mysterious about it. It didn't seem very important, that's all."

She made a tetching sound and said nothing. I said, "Look, am I right about where you're getting this from? It is Andrea, is it?"

"Does it make any difference? I know Andrea can be a silly cow, but either it's true or it's not."

"And it's not."

Abruptly she said, "I've got to go."

* * *

I strode back to the office and thrust the door open. I said to Andrea, "Have you been talking to Ashley about me?"

"What if I have?"

"And telling her outright lies about me? Where is that coming from?"

"I haven't told her any lies."

"No? What would you call it then?"

She said, "Sorry, Mike, I can't have this conversation." She looked down at her screen.

Floundering, I said, "Is that all you have to say about it?" I glanced over at Jamie, who was watching our exchange with a worried look on his face. Andrea still said nothing. I said, "At least I ought to get the chance to put my side of the story."

She looked up quickly. "It's not me you have to convince about anything, it's Ashley." She looked down again and started typing something.

I said, "This is ridiculous."

She glanced up and down at me a couple of times, then said, "I can't work if you're just going to stand there glowering at me." She grabbed her bag, thrust her chair back emphatically and strode out of the room.

I turned to Jamie. "What's got into her?"

He stopped what he was doing and leaned forward on his desk. "Bob Latimer was on the phone to her before you came in this morning. He knew about us taking the afternoon off the other day, and that upset her."

I looked at him in surprise. "It was hardly a sacking offence, I'd have thought. He can't have been that bothered, surely?"

"Maybe not, but Andrea blows these things up in her mind. She can't bear to be in the wrong, that's the thing. To her, being caught out is the worst thing ever."

"But what does this have to do with me?"

"Well, you told Bob about us going to the races, didn't you? That's partly why you're here in Newcastle, I assume. To keep an eye on the two of us."

"God, no! Bob might have had that idea originally, but it was never going to work. He knows that."

He looked perplexed. "So who did tell him?"

I shrugged. "Chris Melling, probably. He knew you went to the races." Jamie looked at me doubtfully, so I added, "*I* didn't tell him, I assure you. He seems perfectly capable of picking that kind of thing up on his own. He didn't think anything of it. He probably thought Bob would be amused."

Jamie said, "Jesus."

I looked at him for a long moment, piecing the logic together. "So, what – Andrea told Ashley this story about Jenna and me out of revenge?"

He gave me a disconsolate look. "It's not exactly that. She has a strong sense of loyalty."

"Good for her. But it's not bloody well true."

"You don't have to tell me."

"I think I do. Maybe then you'll tell Andrea."

"So there's absolutely nothing in it?"

I simply glared at him. He nodded. "I'm really sorry about this, Mike."

I smiled grimly. "I'm not blaming you."

The door swung open and Andrea strode in, frowning at me. She gathered up her laptop and a few items from her desk. "I'm going upstairs to work with Jackie in accounts."

I said to her, "I didn't tell Bob Latimer or Chris Melling anything about your day at the races. You've misjudged me."

She stared at me for a moment, then said, "Fine. Whatever you say." I watched as the door swung shut behind her.

Chapter 21

I sat staring at my computer screen, but I couldn't settle to any kind of work. I was too preoccupied by my conversation with Ashley. Phoning her straight back was my initial instinct, but somehow it seemed a bad idea. I could explain Andrea's motive for contacting her, but that wouldn't necessarily change her mind about what Andrea had said. It was too soon. I needed to let the dust settle.

Yet I couldn't put it out of my mind. I felt I was being punished for having normal male reactions to an attractive female. That was quite different from acting on them, wasn't it? If I was guilty of anything, surely it was simply of failing to fend off Jenna's advances more firmly. But was the mere thought as disloyal as the deed?

Before I could come to any conclusion about this, Chris Melling put his head round the door. "Could I have a quick word, Mike?"

It sounded ominous. I followed him into his office, where he picked up a magazine from his desk and handed it to me. It was the latest issue of the weekly publication I wrote for, folded open to an inside page. He said, "What's happening here, Mike?"

I didn't have to look very far. Towards the bottom of the page I spotted a small news item with the heading "Franchi to switch to Melling for national contract?" And under it, a by-line glared up at me: "Mike Stanhope reports."

Chris said, "I thought what went on at this company was supposed to be confidential. Isn't that what you told me?"

I lifted my hands helplessly. "Chris, I don't know what to say."

"So what else are you going to do? Announce the pick prices we charge our individual clients? Publish our customer hit list?"

"Of course not, no."

"Apparently that story has been on the web for the last three days."

"Has it prejudiced your dialogue with Franchi?" I hadn't wanted to ask that question, but felt I must.

"Well as I told you, discussions are just at a very early stage. Nothing has been decided yet." He gave a humourless laugh and sat down behind his desk. "Not that I know why I'm telling you this. The next thing I know, presumably I'll be reading it as a follow-up in this paper."

"No, no, absolutely not." They probably sounded like hollow words, but I couldn't think what else to say.

I stood in front of the desk, feeling like a schoolboy facing an irate headmaster. Chris said nothing. Finally I said, "Once a journalist, always a journalist. I suppose that's all I can tell you. But I promise you there will be no more of this."

"I should hope not. Anyway, it won't arise. You're due to be going home at the end of this week, aren't you? That will be my recommendation to Bob, anyway."

"I can't blame you."

Abruptly he leaned back in his chair with a glimmer of a smile. "Don't let it get you down, Mike. In your shoes I'd probably have written exactly that article. But I would have told them not to put my name on it."

I gave him a pained smile. "I did."

* * *

I returned to my office feeling punch drunk. First Ashley, now this. Jamie glanced over at me as I sat down, but I couldn't bring myself to recount the conversation I'd just had with Chris. I felt humiliated.

At least Chris seemed to have taken the article in good part; perhaps I should console myself with that. But even as this thought came to me my phone rang. "Bob Latimer here, Mike. We need a word."

"Hang on." I rose shakily and went out to the corridor again, taking up the position where I'd spoken to Ashley. "Is this about the article?"

"Of course it is. What did you think you were doing, Mike? We agreed when you started working for us that everything we told you would be kept within the four walls. Surely you knew that included Mellings?"

I stared through the window at the road leading out of the industrial estate. What could I conceivably say to appease him? I felt I had to choose my words with extreme care. Warily I said, "I suppose looking at it from up here in Newcastle, the connection to Latimers seemed remote. But I realise I should have known better."

He chose to ignore this. "What you don't know, Mike, is that Franchi have been talking to us at Latimers about taking over their logistics operation as well as Mellings. You only had half the story."

"What, you mean it's a two-pronged attack?"

"No, we started talking to them last year, before we knew the Mellings deal was going to happen. It's just a coincidence that Mellings and Latimers made an approach independently."

"God, Bob, I'm sorry."

"The thing is, it's not just the gossip element that's problematic. There's another angle. You say in your article that the Franchi people use a logistics company to do their fulfilment, but that's not strictly true. They do contract the work out, but only in the north. They do it themselves in the south. If we took it over, there could be redundancies among their staff. We didn't want to go public with that until the terms had been thrashed out. So this is pretty embarrassing for us."

I shook my head. This was going from bad to worse. Not only was my story awkward for Latimers, it was also incomplete – which was another word for wrong. Weakly I said, "I see."

"I think we're going to have to consider your position with us, Mike."

"Just tell me what I can do to make things right."

"That's not a conversation I can have at the moment. For now, I need you to finish at Mellings and come back south as soon as you can. I don't want to upset Chris Melling any further."

"I think he's cool with it now."

"Well, I'm glad to hear it, but he certainly didn't sound very cool when I spoke to him earlier this morning." I said nothing. He continued, "So will you wind things up please?"

* * *

I knew I shouldn't phone Jason Bright at the magazine until I'd calmed down, but by this point I couldn't stop myself. As soon as he picked up I said, "You put a by-line on that news story I sent you."

"Did we?" I could hear him leafing through the magazine to find it. "So we did. Sorry about that."

"But I specifically asked you not to."

"I was out the day your piece came in. It was handled by my deputy. Hang on, let me find your covering email." Another pause. "Yes, here it is. There's nothing in it about not running a by-line. He probably thought he was being helpful."

"But Christ, Jason, this has really dropped me in it. I get half my income from Latimer Logistics, and they're hopping mad about this." He knew I had an involvement with the company, so I was giving nothing away.

"I'm sorry, Mike, but you should have mentioned it in your email. You can't expect us to be mind readers."

"But I told *you*. Couldn't you have left a note out about it or something?" Yet even as I spoke, I could see that arguing was a lost cause. Jason didn't owe me a living, and I had no right to expect him to help me with something that would seem to him so trivial.

"Sorry Mike, it's just one of those things."

"Well thanks very much for your support." I regretted the anger in my voice as soon as I said this, but I couldn't take it back.

There was a pause, then Jason said, "Mike, I don't think that tone is helpful." And he cut me off before I had a chance to speak.

My future work options seemed to be dwindling by the minute.

Chapter 22

It was mid-evening by the time I walked into my flat in Truro. The train journey had seemed endless. I couldn't settle to work and I couldn't concentrate on reading. My mind kept running over the fact that I was returning to uncertainty, both on the personal front and at work. I spent most of the journey in a state of indeterminate dread.

The flat felt hot and airless. I threw my keys on the side table and stared moodily round the modern lounge, with its dark wood cupboards and its fashionable modern suite of easy chairs. It didn't feel much like home, but it was currently the nearest thing I had to one. I'd sold my house in London, so this was it: my bolt-hole. Yet currently my two reasons for having come here, my relationship with Ashley and my work with Latimer Logistics, were both under threat. Without them, what the hell was I even doing here?

I slumped down in one of the armchairs without switching on the light and stared out into the communal garden as the weak sun faded towards twilight. Ashley had only visited this flat a handful of times; most of the nights we spent together we spent at her flat, closer to the city centre. It was smaller than this, but it had more history and more personality.

What was she doing now? I called her mobile number, but it went to voicemail. I was unsurprised, and left a short message. "I've just got back. When can we get together?"

I poured myself a neat whisky, downed it in one and poured second glass. For most of my life I'd only been a moderate drinker, but my intake had risen sharply in the three or four years before I met Ashley. In present circumstances I could see it quickly rising again.

After the second whisky a wave of self-pity washed over me. I should have been returning to Ashley, not to this empty flat. I felt a fierce urge to drive round to her place, confront her over the Jenna issue, dispel the misunderstanding and take her in my arms. I could do that, couldn't I? I stood up, almost ready to stride out to my car, but a small cautionary voice told me to slow down, to think things through. Although by now I knew Ashley pretty well, I couldn't be sure how my imagined scene would play out. Trying to force the issue might simply make matters worse.

* * *

In the morning I phoned the Latimer office and asked for Bob. I was put through to his assistant Sally, who told me he was away for a few days.

I liked Sally, and felt she was an ally. Cautiously I said, "Can I speak to you frankly?"

"Course you can, Mike. What is it?"

"Well, you probably know I'm not Bob's favourite person at the moment. I just wondered … well to be honest I wondered if I'm permanently fucked at Latimers. Not to put too fine a point on it."

She laughed. "That sounds a bit extreme, Mike. Bob hasn't told me about any change in your status here, if that's any consolation."

"Any suggestions?"

She seemed to think for a moment. "Well I wouldn't push things, if I were you. Let the dust settle. Bob doesn't respond well if you put him on the spot."

"Fair enough. I appreciate that."

I asked her to connect me to Ashley's extension, but after a moment she told me Ashley wasn't answering. She didn't say whether she'd told Ashley it was me.

* * *

I spent the day fiddling with a couple of unfinished editorial jobs, but I couldn't put much enthusiasm into them. Then I glanced at the early chapters of my new book, to which I hadn't even given any thought while I was in Newcastle. I quickly closed the document; there was no way I could concentrate on that.

When I was sure Ashley would be home from work I drove round to her flat. There was no answer when I rang the bell, and I stood rather foolishly on the street, wondering what to do next. Then it occurred to me that she might be at her parents' house on the outskirts of Truro. If so, that could prove to be helpful neutral ground. I returned to my car and headed off on the short drive out there.

Mary, Ashley's mother, opened the door to me: a well-preserved but slightly heavier version of Ashley, thirty years hence. "Michael – what a surprise. Ashley didn't tell me you were coming over."

I looked at her carefully, trying to gauge what she knew. After more than half a year she still hadn't entirely forgiven me for coming between Ashley and her long-time fiancé Jack. She also blamed me for unearthing some aspects of her own family history that she'd have preferred to forget. Lately I'd thought she was relaxing a little in her attitude to me, but if Ashley had reported her recent suspicions about me, that might be a forlorn hope. I couldn't decide if she had.

She led me through to the lounge, where Ashley was sitting on the sofa, watching tennis on her parents' large-screen TV. Mary said, "Look who's here."

I couldn't read Ashley's expression when she glanced up. She merely said, "Hello Mike. Don't say anything – it's break point."

I watched obediently as two women players slogged it out on court. The break point was saved and the game went with serve. I said, "Do you think we could have a word?"

Mary was still hovering, and Ashley said, "I don't think this is really a good time, Mike."

"Well when would be a good time?"

Mary gave us each a meaningful glance, but must have realised neither of us was in any mood to elaborate. After a moment she said, "Don't mind me," and drifted out to the sun porch, making a show of closing the door behind her.

I perched on the arm of an easy chair, deciding to get straight to the point. "There's nothing in this Jenna stuff. Surely you know that?

It's meaningless."

"Don't let Mum see you sitting on her precious armchair like that."

"Oh for god's sake." I shuffled down into the chair. "I just want us back on an even keel."

"Perhaps you should have thought of that before swanning off with Jenna Melling."

"I didn't swan off with her."

She gave me a long look. "You thought about it, though."

"No I didn't. I thought she was attractive. I told you that. It's quite a different thing. You must meet people *you* think are attractive. You can't just shut off your reactions. It doesn't have to mean anything."

"No, it doesn't have to, but in some cases it plainly does."

I said nothing for a moment, then, "Why are you so determined that I'm in the wrong here?"

"I've seen this before, Mike. I know how it goes."

She was talking about her own first big relationship. She'd thrown in her job and risked the wrath of her family to go off and live with a man who had then betrayed her with at least two other women. This was long before I knew her, but she'd told me all about it.

I wasn't sure how to respond. I'd never met Kieron, the man in question, but I'd encountered plenty of people like him. I knew how plausible they could seem, and also how much harm they could cause. Finally I said, "I'm not like that. I'm not another Kieron."

"But you're going to be ogling other women every time my back is turned – is that what you're telling me?"

"Of course it isn't." I rubbed my face with my hands, lost for ideas about how to break out of this cycle of accusation. "Look, Andrea Smith is mean-spirited and vindictive. I had nothing but hostile vibes from her the whole time we were in Newcastle. Don't ask me why, but it was almost as if she was looking for a fight. I reckon she was over the moon when she finally found something she could really hit me with."

Ashley actually gave an ironic smile. "I must say I sometimes feel sorry for Jamie Andrews. She'll make his life a living hell."

"Well, it's his own lookout. He seems to know the score well enough."

"But this is getting off the point. The point is, how can we carry on if I can't trust you?"

"But you *can* trust me. That's what I'm telling you."

"I'm not so sure."

Impasse. We stared at each other for a long moment, then Mary came in from the sun porch. "I assume you're staying for dinner, Mike? There's more than enough for four."

I flashed a glance at Ashley. "No, I appreciate it Mary, but there's somewhere I have to be. I just wanted to touch base with Ashley first."

She gave me a look of surprise. "Well, if you're sure."

"Next time."

Even before I turned to leave, Ashley's eyes were back on the tennis.

Chapter 23

My first instinct was to appeal to people close to Ashley and persuade them to plead my case with her. For instance, I got on well with Celia, a school friend of hers who lived in Padstow. I was strongly tempted to phone her. Or there was Patrick, her brother, who had a cottage outside Truro. He'd been wary of me at first, but we seemed to have settled into an amicable relationship. Perhaps he would argue the male point of view with her. I even considered talking to her father, who seemed to have liked me from an early stage.

In the end I decided all this was ridiculous. I had to fight my own battles.

I still didn't know what to make of Ashley's hostile attitude. Until now she'd never been anything but warm, funny, supportive and unquestioningly loyal. How could all that crumble away so quickly?

I knew my so-called involvement with Jenna had upset her, but she must have realised by now that Andrea had built it up out of almost nothing. Why was Ashley so unwilling to rethink what had happened – or at least to give me the benefit of the doubt?

It was partly my fault, of course. I should have considered her feelings more carefully before allowing myself to become friendly with Jenna in the first place. It wouldn't have been any hardship to be more cautious.

I should have reflected that Ashley had lunged into an ill-judged relationship when she was much younger, and that it had predisposed her to suspect the worst of people. I thought she'd put this behind her, but it seemed she hadn't. I would never have described her as fragile, but perhaps some wounds never healed.

* * *

I was restless. I knew I should stay in Cornwall and continue trying to appease Ashley, but the environment felt claustrophobic. I wanted to get away again, to regroup. Maybe when I came back I would sound more convincing, and her attitude to me would have softened.

I reviewed my bank balance online the following morning. It wasn't bad, thanks to the regular work I'd been doing for Latimers in recent months. However, I could no longer assume I would be given any more work by them. My freelance programme had also more or less ground to a halt. I should be phoning Jason at the magazine, trying to rebuild bridges with him, but today I didn't have the stomach for it.

All in all, the only way my worldly wealth seemed likely to go at the moment was downwards. The one bright spot on the horizon was the sale of my house in London. When it was finalised my bank account would see a sudden injection of cash. But the notion of living off the proceeds didn't exactly have a lot to recommend it. After the mortgage was paid off, the net amount would hardly be a fortune, and in any case I needed to preserve it to buy a new place with Ashley. That was supposed to be the plan, anyway.

There was always the possibility that I might inherit the house in Harrogate, of course. If that happened it would give me more than enough breathing space to sort out my life. But currently it seemed little more than fantasy.

My mind was buzzing over all this when my phone rang.

"Mike, it's Tina. What's going on with you and Ashley?"

Tina was Ashley's half-sister, but they'd only met for the first time as adults the previous year. I'd remembered Tina from holidays I'd spent in Cornwall as a boy, and embarked on a campaign to track her down. My search had taken me to Cornwall, where I got to know Ashley, and eventually we found out that the two women were related. Happily, they'd immediately taken to each other, and were now in regular touch, but we didn't often see Tina because she lived in Doncaster, hundreds of miles north.

I said, "It's a ridiculous misunderstanding. She's got it into her head that I've been unfaithful."

"And you haven't."

"What do *you* think?"

"So why don't you just tell her that?"

"I've tried. She doesn't want to listen."

"She's a sensible girl. She will in the end. You've just got to hang in."

"That's what I keep telling myself."

"If you want to take a break from it all and give her some breathing space, you could always come and stay with us for a while."

It was a generous offer. She must have realised that if I accepted it, Ashley would think she was taking sides. I said, "That's really good of you, but Ashley might not be terribly impressed."

"If I can mediate, I'm happy to."

"I appreciate it."

* * *

After a restless night I woke on Sunday morning with a new plan. Instead of returning Tina's call, I phoned Joanna, a long-standing friend of mine in south London. I knew Ashley was fond of her and would never see her as a rival.

"I'm coming to visit," I told her. "Today. Is that all right?"

Without even pausing a beat she said, "What time are you arriving?"

So I packed my bags again and headed off on the long drive east. By lunchtime I was already approaching Bristol and the M4, and less than three hours later I'd arrived at Joanna's house.

"What's got into that silly girl's head?" Joanna demanded as I sat down in her lounge. She was married to one of my friends from college, but somehow I'd ended up closer to her than to him.

I sighed. My head still was ringing from the long drive. "I don't want to blame her. It was my own fault. I was spotted allegedly living it up with the siren of the North East, and misguided do-gooders drew the wrong conclusions. I should have seen it coming."

"So you weren't attracted to this woman?"

"Attracted?" I looked cautiously at Joanna. "What does that mean? Yes, I found her attractive, but if she'd been a man, there would have been nothing wrong with us spending time together. That's all it was with her – the same thing."

She shook her head. "It's never the same thing, Mike."

"Don't you start."

We talked about other things. I asked about her husband and her young son Jeremy. She'd lost a little weight since I last saw her, and her dark hair was longer.

"I miss these chats," I said to her suddenly.

"It's a shame they usually seem to happen when things are going wrong for you."

I looked at her sharply. Was that supposed to be a reproof? Yet I saw nothing but warmth in her eyes. I said, "I know I shouldn't take advantage of you."

"That's what I'm here for."

I laughed. "I hope I'd do the same thing for you, if it ever came to the crunch."

"But you can't have it all ways. You don't really need me, you need Ashley."

"I just have to work out how to get her back on side."

Later, in Joanna's spare bedroom, I thought back over the past few weeks. Somehow I'd taken my eye off the ball – or off several balls, to be more accurate. I'd been coasting along, taking far too much for granted, and the result was that everything had started to fall apart at the same time.

I stared round the room, which was nicely decorated and cheerful, despite the tidy piles of junk in several corners. Last time I'd slept here Ashley had been with me. We'd been clearing my house and deciding which items should go to Cornwall. I suddenly felt very alone.

Chapter 24

Either I could continue to feel sorry for myself or I could do something about it. My instinct for self-preservation kicked in, and I decided to do something.

I started next morning in a low key. I'd realised that being in London gave me an unexpected opportunity; I could follow up an idea that had been nagging at me in connection with the woman I'd spotted in Chris Melling's film.

I drove the few slow miles down to Croydon, where I'd put most of the contents of my house into storage. At the time, Ashley had asked me why I couldn't store my stuff in Cornwall, and I'd explained that this solution seemed quicker and easier. Now I wondered if somewhere in the back of my mind I'd had doubts that I would be living in Cornwall for very long.

Shoving this thought out of my mind, I parked my car and walked over to the glass-fronted self-storage building. At the door I tapped in the access code, then navigated my way along the warren of passageways to the unit I'd been allocated. But for a moment I could only stare in dismay at the task that confronted me. Buried somewhere amongst this stack of furniture, cardboard boxes and miscellaneous junk was a large carton of ancient photographs, and I had to unearth it.

I'd been spurred into this exercise by a sudden flash of memory, or perhaps of inspiration. Last night I'd been telling Joanna and her husband John about Chris Melling's film, explaining that I felt I recognised the woman in it. Suddenly I knew who it was that she reminded me of. I was here to put that idea to the test.

It took nearly twenty minutes of humping furniture and cases around to expose the stack of boxes I was looking for. Finally I was able to pull the one I wanted from the bottom, and I sat on an ancient footstool, rummaging through the pictures it contained. Last year, when this box was stored in my loft, I'd retrieved a picture from it of Tina aged about twelve, and that had helped spur me to track her down in the present day. I'd also glanced idly at some of the other pictures in the box – mostly taken by my parents and grandparents.

And here it was, half-way through a black leather-bound album: the photograph I'd had in mind. It was a black and white print, small but sharp and clear, showing a young woman in a garden. Underneath, a caption written in pencil read, "Emily at Wokingham, 1951."

Emily was my maternal grandmother. I didn't remember her, but I knew she came from the Berkshire area. It had been purely by chance that I'd noticed this picture last year, but I had, and I could instantly see the similarity to the woman in Chris's film: the same tight curls, the same open smile.

I'd brought Chris's stills with me, and I sat comparing them with the photo under the dim light of the storage unit. Was it the same person? I couldn't swear to it, but the similarities were striking.

I leafed through the album, finding several other pictures of Emily. Satisfied, I closed it and stood up. Now all I had to do was restore all this junk to some sort of order.

* * *

I spread the photographs from Newcastle on Joanna's table and compared them again with the pictures in the photograph album. I felt even more convinced that it was the same person. Joanna agreed, asking who the woman was. I told her I would explain when I knew more.

So could I be right? No one in my family had ever mentioned my grandmother having lived in the North East, although presumably she might have travelled there on a visit. But why would she be arm in arm with a bus driver from Ryton?

There could be any number of explanations, but none that I could think of seemed to fit in with the comfortable, relaxed look on the face of the woman in the film. This didn't seem like a special occasion; it was more of a vignette from the couple's daily lives. If she'd been on a formal date with that man, surely he would have been dressed up for the occasion, not wearing his workplace uniform? No, they seemed somehow to belong in the scene, to be part of the environment.

I shook my head, aware that this judgement was subjective and meaningless. The trouble was that I had no immediate family to ask about this. I was an only child, and my parents were both dead. I had cousins on my father's side, but not on my mother's.

If I wanted answers to this particular puzzle, I would need to look elsewhere.

* * *

The next phase of my new plan involved Dave Matthews, a long-standing friend who also happened to be a police inspector in south London. Over the years he'd helped me with background information on various cases I'd reported on, and last year, when I'd come up against some really unpleasant people in my quest to find Tina, he'd been especially supportive.

I phoned his mobile and persuaded him to meet me for a drink that night, and a few hours later we were sitting on bar stools at the pub where we used to meet when I lived in London.

Dave was a large, heavy-jowled man in his mid-forties with a lugubrious expression and a penchant for irony. He asked, "How are you liking life in Cornwall?"

"Life in Cornwall is great. Lovely environment, nice people. I honestly haven't missed London at all. The only drawback is that it's such a long way from everywhere else. Oh, and currently I have no work and no girlfriend."

"All going well then." He treated me to a sardonic grin.

I told him briefly about some of the things that had been happening to me. He shook his head dismissively. "It'll all come right. These things usually do."

We sat in amicable silence for a while, and I looked judiciously at him. He usually grumbled when I asked for his help, but nearly always came through for me if he could. I'd long ago given up wondering why.

At first I'd thought it was because I'd once done him a favour. While researching a story, I'd held back information that could have harmed a relative of his, and he seemed to see me in a new light after this. But I had the sense that his goodwill ran much deeper, and I'd concluded there was really no accounting for it. Some friendships needed no explanation.

Tentatively I said, "You probably feel you've done me enough favours over the years."

"But you want another one."

"Well, I know I shouldn't ask."

"You're going to anyway, so get on with it."

"Right." I smiled apologetically. "Well a couple of months ago a truck was hijacked on the way from Southampton docks to Leeds. I can give you the company name and the dates."

"And?"

"Well, these days a lot of trucks are tracked by GPS. People can't just hijack them unless they know how to disable the system."

"So?"

"So I was hoping maybe you could find out what happened – whether the tracking system failed, that kind of thing? Basically I'm wondering if the finger of suspicion was pointed at the company or the driver, or if it was just bad luck."

"But you don't know which police force handled the crime, or any other details? Boy, you do love to get me running around."

Despite his complaint, however, he seemed much more upbeat than last time we'd met. I said, "You seem very cheerful."

"Do I?" He gave me an unusually sheepish grin. "It might have something to do with the new lady in my life. Suzy. You'll have to meet her."

Chapter 25

Dave returned my call next morning. "You struck lucky. The officer in charge of that lorry theft reports to an old mate of mine in Sheffield. If it wasn't for him, I doubt if I would ever have found out anything."

"Fantastic. So what did he say?"

"Well, the first thing is that the truck did have a tracking system on it, but not covert tracking. That's the kind of tracking where no one knows exactly where the on-board equipment is fitted, not even the driver, so it's very hard to disable. This one didn't have that."

"So … ?"

"So it had a normal tracking system on it, but it wasn't working."

"Right. So was it sabotaged?"

"Not apparently. There was some kind of connectivity problem, but no one could tell how it was caused."

"Was there anything suspicious about the driver?"

"Apparently not. No criminal record, nothing like that. And no sudden spending spree to suggest he'd been paid off."

"What about the cargo? Any idea what happened to it?"

"Sorry, no. They reckoned it would probably just be filtered out to the grey market – popup shops and market stalls, that kind of thing.

"Can you remind me of the driver's name?"

"Civet – Roy Civet."

* * *

I wasn't sure whether to be relieved or disappointed by Dave's information. If, as he'd suggested, there had been nothing overtly suspicious about the hijacking, surely that meant there was little I could do about it? Yet Jenna had told me it had come just at the time when

Ashursts' sales were levelling off. The connection was slender, but perhaps the coincidence made it worth pursuing.

Clearly I had to think myself into investigative mode. In the early years of my journalistic career I'd written a lot of investigative articles – digging into exploitation and other kinds of wrong-doing in the world of transport and logistics. Something about that kind of article suited my enquiring temperament. But I'd found the work itself increasingly stressful, and in more recent years my output had been much more anodyne. Frankly I was out of practice.

Bracing myself, I phoned the transport company in Southampton where the truck driver worked, and asked to talk to the traffic office. When I was put through I said I was a journalist writing a follow-up to the hijacking episode. What was it like for the driver, having a valuable truck snatched in broad daylight? How did it affect his future work? Roy Civet, I said, was a case in point, so could I interview him?

It was a toss-up. In this situation some people would tell me to take a running jump, while others might be more accommodating. Apparently I'd remembered how to sound sufficiently persuasive, and this man seemed reasonably cooperative.

"He's driving down from Manchester today. He should be back at the depot some time this afternoon. You can try to catch him then if you like."

"Could you give me his mobile number so that I can arrange to meet him?"

"Sorry, it's against company policy to give out staff numbers."

I disconnected and considered this. It seemed that the only easy way to speak to this man would be to do it in person – and I now knew I could probably get hold of him this very day. But did I really want to drive the eighty miles to Southampton with so little prospect of coming up with anything useful? It sounded an expensive waste of time. Yet I had no other plan for the day. The idea of having an objective suddenly seemed surprisingly appealing.

Should I phone some of my editorial contacts and try to drum up some freelance work involving a visit somewhere along the way? No, there was no time, and in any case I had no inclination. I just wanted to get going.

The M3 was surprisingly clear and the sun was shining. I wished I was heading off on a holiday, not on what would probably turn out to be a wild goose chase. But at least I would get the trip over with quickly. Within a couple of hours I was approaching the south coast.

I skirted Southampton city centre on the M27, exulting as always in the broad and busy sweep of the motorway at this point, and headed for the docks area. The transport company turned out to be relatively small, which promised to make it easier to find the driver I wanted. I followed a corrugated iron fence to an open gateway and drove into a pocked and uneven yard, parking in a small row of other cars.

I walked over to the office, a modest single-storey building with a flat roof. At the reception desk I asked for the man I'd spoken to in the traffic office, and after a moment he emerged from within. He was younger than I'd imagined, but seemed unintimidated by talking to a journalist.

"Roy's not back yet. Give him an hour or two."

I asked if I could wait in the yard, and he nodded. "You're all right parked where you are."

"How will I know him?"

"Look out for red truck pulling an Evergreen container. But don't worry – I'll tell him you're here when he comes in." He looked judiciously at me. "I told him someone from the press might want to talk to him, and he sounded a bit iffy about it. Don't be surprised if he tells you to leg it."

"Fair enough."

As he was about to retreat I asked him, "Was it unusual, having a truck stolen like that? Has it happened to your firm in the past?"

"Not in the two years I've been here. But you'll need to talk to my boss if you want to know more about that sort of thing."

I decided I didn't, so I sat in my car in the scruffy parking bay for more than an hour, listening to the radio and watching trucks come and go. Finally a red DAF artic pulling a green container drove into the yard. The driver reversed it up to a low warehouse and brought it to a halt with a hiss of air brakes. A wiry man in his forties jumped down from the cab and headed over to the traffic office.

I waited. A couple of minutes later he reappeared and walked cautiously over towards my car. I got out and stood leaning against it, blinking in the sun.

"You wanted to see me, mate? What's it about?" He spoke with a Yorkshire accent.

I pulled out one of my business cards and held it towards him. "I'm a transport journalist. I'm writing a piece on lorry hijacking from the driver's point of view – what it's like, the aftermath, that kind of thing."

He glanced at the card without taking it and gave me a belligerent frown. His deeply lined face gave him a permanently aggrieved expression. He said, "My truck wasn't hijacked, it was stolen off a lorry park."

"Sorry, you know what I mean."

"Anyway, I've got nothing to say about it. I had enough fucking grief over it at the time. I'm not going through all that again."

He seemed about to walk away. It was a long journey for me to have made for nothing. Quickly I said, "Was that lorry park a regular stop for you?"

He stopped. "You're as bad as the bleeding police. No, it wasn't a regular stop. So what?"

"I was just curious about how the thieves targeted your truck."

"It was random. That's what the police said. If it hadn't been me it would have been somebody else."

"And is that what you think?"

"I don't have an opinion. All I know is it's been a right pain ever since." He started to turn away again, then thought the better of it and turned to me a second time. "Take my advice and drop this, mate. There's nothing in it for you." There was a definite threat in the look that accompanied this remark.

So far everything he'd said had rung true. I'd already decided he was an innocent victim. But now he was protesting too much. My interest was piqued.

"What makes you say that?"

He looked at me angrily for a moment. "Just drop it, all right? Leave me to get on with my life."

That last comment seemed to come from the heart, and the way I heard it, this man was talking about the entire hijacking episode, not just the aftermath. The way he spoke, it sounded like a heavy burden, not just a shock and an embarrassment.

"Sorry, it must have been a load of grief."

"You don't know the first thing about it." Giving me a final glower, he turned and strode away to the office.

Chapter 26

I stayed with John and Joanna three more days, working as best I could on their coffee table and playing computer games with their son Jeremy when he let me. In the evenings I watched TV with them and tried not to think about Ashley.

It didn't work too well. On the second evening I phoned her while Joanna was preparing a meal, and to my surprise she picked up. Her tone, however, didn't exactly fill me with optimism.

"So you've retreated to London. Is this how you normally deal with your problems?"

"I thought we could both do with some breathing space, that's all."

"But you've just had three weeks of breathing space. How much more do you need?"

"OK, I meant *you* could do with some breathing space. You didn't seem very keen to talk when I saw you on Friday."

"Well thank you for being so considerate."

Ignoring the sarcasm, I said, "So if I was having this conversation sitting in my flat in Truro, would you be saying anything different?"

"I don't know."

I took a deep breath. "Look, once and for all, this is not Kieron you're dealing with here. It's me. Completely different case."

"I know." She added nothing, and there was a pause.

I didn't know what to make of this. She no longer sounded hostile, but the defeat in her voice was almost worse. I said, "I realise this will sound trite, but you're the best thing that's ever happened to me. By far. You must know that. I'd be a complete fool to compromise that."

She said nothing, and there was a longer pause. Finally, in an effort to lighten the tone, I said, "Bob Latimer hasn't fired me yet. I'm hoping it's a good sign." I hadn't discussed my situation at Latimers with her, but I assumed it was now common knowledge.

"I wouldn't get your hopes up. He's preoccupied with problems over the leases on the new warehouses in Birmingham and Leeds. He probably doesn't want to be distracted."

"Oh. Well thanks for that reassurance." I couldn't keep the irony out of my voice.

"I'm only trying to be realistic."

"So shall I come back to Truro tomorrow? Can we sort this out?"

She gave a small sigh. "Come when you're ready, Mike. You'll just have to take things as you find them."

At least she was talking to me, but I wasn't exactly encouraged by her downbeat tone. The idea of returning to Truro seemed premature; not enough had changed.

* * *

When I phoned Bob Latimer next morning I was put through to Sally again.

"Bob says can you ring him one day next week."

I wasn't sure what this delaying tactic meant. It sounded faintly positive, but it could just be confirmation that he was preoccupied with more pressing matters. Either way, there was evidently no urgent need for me to go back to Cornwall. I wanted to clear the air with Ashley, but it still felt too soon to pick up the threads of that conversation. The irony was that if I couldn't make things up with her, there was little point in worrying about my involvement with Latimers – unless I decided to stay on in Cornwall even without her. I didn't want to think about that.

I decided I'd better phone Jason at the magazine and try to restore good relations with him, but his mobile went to voicemail, and when I rang his office landline I was told he was away on a course for three days.

My whole life seemed to have gone into suspended animation.

My laptop beckoned, challenging me to do something constructive, but I couldn't settle to anything. Although the welcome John and Joanna had given me was warm and uncompromising, I was beginning to feel an intruder. Spending time here seemed like an indulgence I hadn't earned.

Then I knew what I needed to do instead: go back north. If there was anything more to be learned about the lorry hijacking, that's where I would learn it. Maybe I could pick up more background on the house in Harrogate, too. And I might even find answers to the puzzle of my grandmother's photograph.

I had also a vague sense that if I made the trip north it would somehow help restore my relationship with Ashley. Wishful thinking, perhaps, but at least it gave me an added sense of purpose.

All the same, it was a long way to go on a whim. In the past, my enquiring spirit had helped me with a succession of probing press articles. Now I was all too aware that I might be inventing distractions merely to avoid confronting real problems.

To hell with it. I had to go somewhere. I had to do something. This plan would serve as well as any.

Tina answered my phone call on the first ring. She told me I was welcome to stay with her, and I could turn up that very day. It was all the encouragement I needed.

* * *

From south London the drive up the A1 to Doncaster took nearly four hours, but I was happy to be out and about again. The sunny weather had persisted, and the intense green of the landscape lifted my spirits.

I arrived in the middle of the afternoon. Tina would still be at work, so I parked in the central area and wandered around like a tourist. Doncaster, a medium-sized industrial town, was originally a market town, but had been bypassed in every direction and was not on many people's tourist itinerary, and I found the narrow streets unexpectedly quaint. Eventually I made my way to the modern flat on the outskirts where Tina lived with her partner Martin.

Tina and Ashley looked quite alike. Tina's father had had a brief affair with Ashley's mother a few years before I first encountered them all as a child, and Ashley was the result. Ashley's parents, however, had kept this a secret from her until recently.

My involvement with them had started while I was on holiday with my parents in Cornwall, by which time Ashley was about five years old. I'd yearned to embark on a relationship with Tina, who was closer to my own age than Ashley. Nothing had come of it, but in the course of trying to track her down last year I'd got to know Ashley, and the whole history had eventually been brought out into the open.

Over drinks that evening Tina asked me about my falling-out with Ashley, and I tried to give her an uncensored account of the reasons for it. At the end of it she commented, "I suppose you might be guilty of something, but nothing as bad as Ashley is making out."

I smiled gratefully. "I appreciate the support."

It was probably difficult for her to know how to judge the situation. Although she and Ashley seemed to like each other, they didn't know each other well, and had virtually no shared history. But blood seemed to be thicker than water.

"Don't forget," Tina pointed out, "Ashley's mother was unfaithful to her father, and from what she says, she had a bad experience with that guy Kieron. She's seen betrayal going on all round her. She's probably ultra-sensitive about it."

"Well, she has nothing to fear from me."

Martin, who was dipping in and out of the conversation whilst cooking a spaghetti bolognese, asked me, "Do you have any plans while you're here?"

I turned to Tina. "Well, you're in marketing. Have you come across a company called Ashurst Concepts?"

"The spiralizer people? Of course. A couple of years ago they were a pretty hot property. A lot of firms in my field were on the lookout for marketing and advertising work with them, but I think they kept most of it in-house."

"But they're not such a good prospect now?"

"Well, the word in the biz was that they were cutting back, so the interest waned. I haven't heard much chatter about them for a while."

I sat forward. "That's interesting. I was wondering if there was something suspicious about them. I thought I might do a bit of poking around."

"Suspicious how?"

"I don't really know." I gave her a self-deprecating smile. "I'm probably just groping in the dark."

"What's your connection with them, anyway?"

"Well, indirectly Latimer Logistics, the firm that Ashley and I work for in Truro, has just taken a controlling interest in the company. At least, it will if the acquisition goes through. I'm wondering if it's a shrewd buy."

"Ashursts did incredibly well in a very short time. You can't take that away from them."

"But was it all just a flash in the pan? That's the question."

She smiled. "If I hear anything more about them, I'll let you know."

Chapter 27

Tina and Martin were as welcoming as Joanna and John had been. Although we'd only met the previous year, they treated me like an old friend or family member. They took me out for a meal on the Saturday night, and the following day we visited a stately home outside the town. It felt like a holiday, but one I hadn't earned – and one from which a key member of the party was missing.

On the Monday morning they both went off to work, and I fetched out the tablet computer I'd taken from Elizabeth Sanderson's house. She'd corresponded regularly with someone at her college in Harrogate, and I wanted the name. I soon found it: Daniella Marsden. Without much optimism I phoned the college and asked for her. Remarkably she was available and willing to speak to me.

I explained to her that I'd been named unexpectedly as the prime beneficiary in Elizabeth Sanderson's will. "I didn't know her very well, and it would be an enormous help to be able to talk to someone who did."

She offered to meet me in her college canteen at lunchtime. "It's the summer vacation," she explained. "I'm not terribly busy." This was a much better result than I'd dared to expect. Harrogate was about an hour's drive from Doncaster, so by midday I was on the northbound A1 again.

Daniella was a friendly woman in her early fifties with a large bust, a prominent chin and intensely black shoulder-length hair that flicked out at the ends. As we sat down she explained that she'd worked with Elizabeth in the English faculty.

"It's a pity you didn't know her better. She was a lovely person. But very private. She never invited any of us home, for instance."

"I may as well be honest with you – I didn't know her at all. I'd never even heard of her until I was told she'd mentioned me in her will."

She stared at me for a moment, surprised but apparently unperturbed. "I wonder why she did that?"

"Me too."

She smiled. "So you're doing a bit of detective work, are you?"

"Something like that. I hope you're not offended."

"Not at all. In your shoes I'd probably be doing the same thing."

I asked her if she'd ever heard of Elizabeth's nephew Philip Crabtree and his wife Angela. She said no, "but there would have been no reason for her to talk about them to us here." Then I asked about her partner – the man her next-door neighbour Rosemary had named as Derek Salmon.

"I remember him vaguely. I think she brought him to a couple of events here years ago. But then he died. She was quieter after that. I had the impression that she retreated into herself."

"Do you remember what he did for a living?"

She reflected for a moment. "I have a feeling that maybe he owned an accountancy firm in Leeds."

"Apparently he had a brother called Howard. Did you ever hear anything about him?"

She shook her head. "As I say, she didn't talk much about her private life."

* * *

After lunch I sat in my car in the college car park, searching the internet on my phone for accountancy firms in Leeds with the name Salmon in their title. The company might not bear his name, of course, but it seemed a reasonable guess.

Within moments I was sure I'd found it: Salmon, Fischer & Partners. I smiled to myself. Salmon fisher? A nice piece of serendipity.

I wasn't sure how to approach them. Should I play my journalist's card or come clean and adopt a more personal line? I decided the personal approach was more likely to succeed. According to the internet, Anton Fischer was alive and still active at the firm. I tapped the number into my phone and asked to speak to him.

"Mr Fischer is not available. What's it concerning?"

"It's a private matter really. I have an interest in a house in Harrogate that was owned by Mr Fischer's late partner Derek Salmon. I wanted to discuss this with him."

This seemed to flummox the receptionist, who finally said, "Transferring you to Roy Bramble."

Roy Bramble sounded brisk but personable enough, so I repeated my story to him. However, he said, "Mr Fischer is out of the country at the moment, but in any case this is all a long time ago, and from what you say it's not strictly company business anyway."

"I can see that, but I'm really floundering here. This all came completely out of the blue, and I'm sure Mr Fischer could help me with the history."

He hesitated. I could tell he wanted to end the conversation, but some kind of compelling customer service ethic was preventing him. Finally he said, "I tell you what, I'll transfer you to Norah Stevenson, Mr Fischer's personal assistant. She used to work for Derek Salmon in the old days."

After some clicking and a long pause, a mature woman's voice came on the line and I told my story for a third time, on this occasion adding, "I could drop into your office for a chat about this if it would help."

"Well, if you like. Do you know where we are?"

Before she had time to change her mind I said, "I'll find you. See you later."

* * *

The fifteen-mile journey south from Harrogate to Leeds was becoming familiar, and by mid-afternoon I was parking in a multi-storey car park in the centre of Leeds.

Salmon, Fischer & Partners were based in a redbrick Georgian-style terrace in Park Place, a street in the business district. I was led up a carpeted staircase with gleaming white-painted wooden banisters to a large room on the top floor, where Norah Stevenson rose to welcome me – a slight grey-haired figure somewhere in her mid to late sixties. We shook hands and she pointed me to a visitor's chair.

"So you wanted to know more about Derek and Elizabeth?"

"Please. In a nutshell, I've inherited the house in Harrogate that they used to share. Until this happened I'd never even heard of him or Elizabeth. It came completely out of the blue. I'm trying to work out why."

"You didn't know Elizabeth at all?"

I shook my head.

She raised her eyebrows. "What a strange thing."

She glanced over to the window, presumably delving into her memories, then looked back at me. "Derek met Elizabeth about twenty years ago, after his wife died, and in due course she moved in with him. He lived in a village just outside Leeds then, but they wanted somewhere of their own, somewhere to make a fresh start, so they bought the house in Harrogate. It was very convenient for her work, of course."

"And they never married?"

"They didn't see the point. But Derek was a few years older than Elizabeth, so they bought the house in her name, to make sure she would be secure if he died before her." She gave a quick, regretful smile. "Then of course he did."

I waited respectfully for a moment, then tried out an idea that had been hovering in the back of my mind. "Derek didn't have any connection with Wokingham in Berkshire, did he? That's where I come from. I'm wondering if Elizabeth made the bequest in order to respect something in his past life."

She smiled at this. "Not that I know of, no. Derek was a Yorkshireman born and bred. He hated travelling anywhere."

"What about Newcastle? Any connection there?"

She shook her head. "No, the same thing applies. We once thought of opening a branch there, but it never came to anything."

"Did he have any children?"

"No, it never happened for him. His wife couldn't conceive, and it was never an option with Elizabeth." She smiled again. "And before you ask, he had just one brother, and he didn't have any children either."

This seemed fairly conclusive. Somehow I'd felt all along that the connection to me lay with Elizabeth herself, not in some obscure link on Derek's side that I'd failed to recognise. But I still needed to find someone who was in her confidence.

"Talking of Derek's brother, I believe Elizabeth was quite close to him. Her next-door neighbour told me that."

"Ah, Howard." She looked at me sadly. "Such a nice man."

"He hasn't died too?"

"No, but he had a stroke a few weeks ago. I don't think he's able to speak again yet, and they're not sure if he ever will."

I asked where he lived, and she told me it was Prince of Wales Drive, London – overlooking Battersea Park on the south bank of the Thames. She also told me the name of the hospital he was in. "But if you're thinking of visiting, I would call them first if I were you."

As I was descending the staircase to leave I nearly collided with a man coming up. We both stopped. I recognised him, though for a moment I couldn't think why. Then it came to me. He was the man who had appeared at the Ashurst Concepts office while Piers Ashurst was showing me round. Piers hadn't looked especially happy to see him.

He frowned. "Were you looking for me?"

"No, not at all. Complete coincidence."

He seemed unconvinced, and continued to give me a hostile stare. I said, "Well, if you'll excuse me I've got to go."

"Fine." He stepped aside with exaggerated courtesy, watching me as I passed him. I could still feel his eyes on me as I reached the bottom of the flight.

Chapter 28

I sat in a café in the centre of Leeds, thinking over what I'd learned during the day.

In some ways the sum total was not much. I'd heard nothing about Elizabeth or Derek to suggest any connection to me. The only new information I had was how to find Howard Salmon – and I now also knew he was gravely ill. Ironically, Howard seemed to be the one person who might be able to shed light on my unexpected bequest. He'd referred in an email to "the distaff thing", and I had to assume he knew what this meant. But according to what Norah had just told me, he was in no state to explain it.

Putting all this out of my mind, I thought again about the man I'd met on the staircase at the accountancy firm. He'd looked at me with real dislike, and there must be some cause. So how had I managed to antagonise him merely by my presence there?

I looked at my watch. It was around six o'clock. Ashursts would presumably be closing for the day soon, but I was wondering if they might be about to receive another of those mysterious evening deliveries. It seemed a shame to miss the opportunity to go and find out. I ordered some food, and when I'd finished it I headed out to the industrial estate.

* * *

As I'd expected, the Ashurst office was closed when I arrived, but several cars were parked along the frontage. I drove past and continued a hundred metres down the street, then turned into a narrow lane between tall redbrick warehouses and parked out of sight. Cautiously I walked back along the street as far as the gateway and peered into the yard.

There was no loading or unloading in progress, but a white panel van very similar to the one I'd seen on my visit with Ashley was backed up against the brick wall just inside the gateway. I glanced around to check that there was no one in sight, then slipped into the yard and approached the van.

There was no livery on this one, so it must be a different vehicle from the one I'd seen before. I checked the small white legal lettering low down on the left-hand side. It read "ARC (Leeds) Ltd, trading as Black Cat Deliveries".

I stepped into the yard and slipped between the brick wall and the rear doors of the van. What was in it? I placed a foot on the back bumper and pulled myself up high enough to see through one of the muddy rear windows. The van was empty.

The roller-shutter doors leading into the building from the loading bay were lowered, but there were lights on behind a row of windows on the ground floor, even though it wasn't yet dark. I checked again to ensure there was still no one in sight, then hurried over to the building and peered in cautiously through one of the windows.

I saw a packing area similar to the one at Mellings, partially lit on one side by a row of overhead lights. Two or three people were lifting coloured cardboard cartons off a rudimentary roller conveyor and placing them on a metal bench, then fiddling with them in some way and putting them into larger boxes. I couldn't tell what they were doing, but I would think about that later.

I pulled my phone out of my pocket. I might as well photograph whatever was going on. There might be nothing suspicious about it, but something told me there was. I lined up the phone and pressed the shutter icon.

The flash went off.

The workers all looked up, and one of them immediately broke away from the workbench and strode briskly across the packing floor, no doubt heading for a door out to the yard. I was half-way to the gateway by the time I heard him emerge, but not far enough away to avoid being seen.

"What the fuck do you think you're doing?" His shout echoed round the walls.

I glanced over my shoulder and saw that he was pursuing me across the yard. This time he wasn't prepared to let me retreat. My only two choices were to confront him or try to outrun him. While I was wondering what to do another figure appeared at the doorway and followed the first one towards me. I decided flight was the sensible option.

I glanced over my shoulder half-way to the lane where I'd left my car. My pursuers were already on the street, showing no signs of abandoning the chase. Urgently I reached into my pocket for my car keys, anxious to avoid any delay while I unlocked the doors.

Rounding the corner, I sprinted the last few yards to my car, blipped the remote, flung myself into the driver's seat and locked all the doors. Then I realised the lane was a dead end. The only way out was the way I'd come in, and my pursuers were already in view in the driving mirror, hovering at the corner of the lane.

I decided the best prospect of getting past them was to be resolute. Thankfully the engine fired at the first attempt. I revved emphatically, shoved the gear lever into reverse and backed directly towards the two men. One of them stood his ground, and a wave of panic ran through me at the thought that I might knock him down. However, at the last moment he stepped aside and I roared safely past him.

If there had been any traffic passing on the street at the end of the lane I would have backed straight into it. Thankfully there wasn't, and I came to a slithering halt facing along the street and away from the Ashurst factory. Glancing down the lane, I saw one of the two men already talking on a mobile phone.

I'd seen enough. I engaged first gear and pulled away.

Chapter 29

What would those two men have done to me if they'd caught me? That question kept interrupting my thoughts next day as I tried to work at Tina's kitchen table. An angry exchange I could have lived with. The people at Ashursts were quite entitled to wonder why someone had been nosing around their yard, taking photographs through the window. But the vehemence of their reaction told a different story. I sensed an underlying violence, and it seemed out of proportion to anything I'd done.

Yet would it really have come to that? Indirectly I was an associate of Piers Ashurst, the managing director of the company. In fact I could claim I represented the organisation that had just acquired it. Would he really have been a willing party to actions that could have done me physical harm?

Those men, of course, would have known nothing of this, and perhaps felt they were merely defending the interests of their employer. But what activity would be so sensitive that it demanded extreme measures to discourage enquiry?

I was tempted to return to Ashursts and confront Piers Ashurst in broad daylight, questioning the mysterious activity that I'd witnessed, but I couldn't be sure he would be willing to see me. Even if he did, an acrimonious exchange with him might damage relations with Mellings, and by association with Latimers. Bob Latimer would scarcely thank me for that.

So I muddled through the day, still uncertain what to do next, and then spent a lively evening with Tina and Martin, during which we demolished several bottles of red wine. My welcome didn't seem to have run out yet.

However, when I woke next morning I knew instinctively that I'd been staying there long enough. I lay in bed in the cramped spare bedroom, wondering what to do instead. If I couldn't usefully achieve anything else at Ashursts, maybe it was time to return to Cornwall. But matters turned in a very different direction when my phone buzzed on the bedside table. It was an unfamiliar number.

"Michael, it's Jenna Melling. You left without saying goodbye."

This was a development I didn't need. After a moment I said, "Huh! Things got a bit sticky. I decided I needed to beat a tactful retreat. In fact the decision was more or less made for me."

"So I understand. Giving away trade secrets – not very clever."

Surely she wasn't calling simply to reproach me? It seemed unlikely, yet it would be understandable, given that my article about the Franchi contract had been prompted by a conversation with her and Greg. I said, "Are you looking for an apology? I realise I owe you one."

"Why no. You were just doing your job. Water under the bridge."

"OK. So to what do I owe the pleasure?"

She waited a moment, perhaps collecting her thoughts, then said, "There's something funny going on at Ashursts. I thought you might want to know."

Immediately she had my attention. I said, "Funny in what way?"

"Well, their finances don't seem to stack up, unless I'm missing something."

Could this somehow tie in with what I'd seen last night? I couldn't think of any obvious connection, but it might be something worth pursuing. Yet I was loath to get drawn into anything involving Jenna. I said, "Why don't you talk to your dad about it? He's the one most affected, I'd have thought."

"Ah, well, I'm not his favourite person at the moment. Don't ask."

"What about Greg, or your other colleagues?"

"Listen, man, I'm telling this to you. You're the Latimer liaison man – or you were two weeks ago. Do you want to know about it or not?"

"OK, OK. Fire away."

"Well I can't really go into it on the phone." She waited a moment, perhaps considering her options, then said, "Are you likely to be up here in Newcastle again any time soon?"

I started to say no. If I really was ready to return to Truro, Newcastle was a hundred miles in the wrong direction, and I felt as if I'd done enough motorway driving in the past month to poleaxe the hardest-bitten truck driver. Yet I couldn't help being curious. I said, "I suppose I could be. As it happens I'm in Yorkshire at the moment. In fact I was at Ashursts the day before yesterday."

"You're joking! I was there too. Why didn't I see you?"

"Ah, well this was early evening. I was poking around, to be honest."

"You bugger! And what did you find?"

"I don't really know. We could talk about it."

"Listen, why don't you come over to my place tomorrow evening? Do you mind driving a bit further north? Come for a meal." She left a pregnant pause, then added, "I promise you your virtue will stay intact."

"OK. What time?"

* * *

Tina seemed genuinely sorry when I told her over breakfast that I was planning to leave, but her disappointment turned to faint suspicion when I admitted I was going to Newcastle again.

"Not to visit that woman, I presume?"

In fact that was precisely why I was going there, but I didn't want to tell a lie. I said, "Do you think I'm mad?" Not exactly the whole truth, but it did express my feelings pretty well.

"You realise Ashley might get the wrong idea?"

"There's something I have to do there. It has nothing to do with my relationship with Ashley. If you're talking to her, can you make that clear to her?"

She shook her head. "I'm staying out of this one, Mike."

"OK. Well I'll explain everything to her when I see her."

I couldn't afford the prices at the country hotel outside Newcastle where we'd all stayed before, but my instinct pointed me towards the same general area. An internet search turned up a motel on the main route out to the west of the city, and I booked myself in for two nights. Half an hour later I was back on the road, once again heading towards the North East.

By lunchtime I'd checked into the motel, but as I stared round at the characterless standard-issue bedroom furniture I regretted my hurried departure. I wasn't due to see Jenna until the following evening, so I could have stayed with Tina for another night.

Then my phone rang. It was the solicitors in Newcastle, calling me about Elizabeth Sanderson's will.

"There's been another development," David Smythe told me. "It might be helpful if you could come by the office. You're not still in Newcastle, by any chance?"

Chapter 30

There was no convenient railway near my motel, so I decided to use my car this time for the trip into Newcastle. I managed to find a space in an open-air car park not far from the solicitors' office.

I was about to press the door phone buzzer when the front door opened and a man in a blue suit and tie emerged: Philip Crabtree. He checked his stride, staring at me from half-way across the threshold.

"Stanhope – I might have known I'd see you here. You've come to gloat, I suppose?"

"I don't know what you're talking about."

"Of course you don't." He scowled at me. "Well don't let me hold you up." He made a point of letting the door slam shut behind him. "I wouldn't get too excited, if I were you." He stared at me a moment longer, then turned and walked away in the direction of the car park. I watched him briefly, then pressed the buzzer.

"I just met Philip Crabtree outside," I told David Smythe as he pulled up a chair for me.

"Ah, yes. He's not a happy man, I'm afraid."

"Why not?"

"Well, matters seem to have turned in your favour. It seems his solicitor is advising him to rescind the caveat. I've just been discussing the implications with him." I gave him an enquiring look, and he added, "In plain terms, he may be about to relinquish his claim on Elizabeth Sanderson's estate."

"So what do I have to do?"

"Well, as I told you before, it's not my place to advise you." He gave me a half-smile. "Should I assume you haven't yet appointed a solicitor of your own?"

"Correct."

"Well, ideally you should do that, but perhaps it won't be necessary."
He leaned forward. "Unofficially, you don't need to do anything, but it
might help if you were to draft an affidavit affirming that you had no
contact with Elizabeth Sanderson prior to learning that you were a
beneficiary. You didn't even know her, let alone know that you stood to
inherit, so you couldn't have been guilty of interference."

"Fine. I can certainly do that." I tried to read his expression. "Do you
think this means I really will inherit the house?"

"You can never be sure of these things, but it seems a bit more likely
now, yes."

As I was pulling out of my parking bay I happened to notice a blue-
grey Audi emerge from a few spaces along. I couldn't be sure, but I
thought I could make out Philip Crabtree behind the wheel.

I made my way round the periphery of the city centre, heading west
towards the A69. Whenever I checked my mirror, the Audi was still
behind me. Was he really following me? We climbed up Westgate Road,
a long straight urban ascent. The traffic was slow and dense, and the
journey seemed to take forever. I suspected that somehow I'd missed a
faster route, yet still the Audi was behind me.

The road broadened out where it crossed the A1, and I started to feel
slightly panicked. Then it occurred to me that this must also be Philip
Crabtree's route home to Hexham, so perhaps there was nothing
surprising about him coming this way. Then again, why had he taken so
long to get going? He must have waited the whole time I was in the
solicitor's office. Come to that, why had he taken the same tedious route
that I had? I slowed down a little, hoping to see if the Audi would to the
same. It did.

The entrance to my motel loomed on the left, and instinctively I
pulled into it. Too late, it occurred to me that I should have headed off
in some other direction. Now Philip Crabtree knew where I was staying.
But why did it matter?

* * *

With the rest of the afternoon and all the evening to fill, I opened my laptop. The Wi-Fi signal in the motel was good, so I decided to pick up the threads of my search for the man and woman in Chris Melling's film.

I now knew that the man was Len Roberts, and he'd worked as a bus driver in Ryton. I ran a search on Roberts and Ryton, wondering if any of his family still lived in the area. Predictably there were thousands of finds, so this told me nothing useful.

I checked to see where Ryton was, and found it was a village on the south bank of the Tyne, just west of Blaydon. In terms of crow-fly distance it was only a few miles from my motel on the north side. Moreover, Ryton appeared to be easily reachable by a bridge. For want of anything else to do, I decided to take a look at it.

The route to the river was easy enough to follow. Newburn Bridge, which was approached by a modest country lane, was a surprisingly apologetic affair – a single-lane Victorian structure with lattice girder sides. But it got me across to the south bank, where an unexpected tree-lined avenue took me past an area of indeterminate light industry. According to what I'd read, it was around here that the bus company had been based, but clearly no vestige of it now remained.

Ryton itself was a pleasantly unremarkable middle-class suburb of Gateshead, presumably once a free-standing village, made up mostly of Victorian terraced houses. I found my way to what seemed like the central area and pulled in near a tiny park. For a while I sat on a bench in the early evening sun, wondering what connection my grandmother could possibly have had with this place.

Chapter 31

The next day was one I wouldn't forget in a long time.

It started with a call from an unfamiliar number. A woman's voice said, "Michael, it's Angela Crabtree – Philip's wife. Do you have a moment?"

"Of course."

She seemed uncertain how to continue. Perhaps she'd expected a hostile response. Finally she said, "I'm sorry if Philip has been giving you a hard time. It was quite a shock when we realised we might not inherit Elizabeth's estate. He didn't take it well."

"It sounds as if this bequest must be very important to you."

"Well, yes." She sounded close to tears. "Money was already tight, and now Philip has lost his job. We're not sure if we'll be able to afford to stay here in this house."

"Can't he get another job?" I was aware that this was a harsh response, but I already felt resentful of the moral blackmail in her tone.

"It's not that easy. They're cutting back in his industry."

"I see."

There was another long pause, then she said, "To be perfectly honest, I was wondering if you would consider dividing the inheritance with us? I don't think Philip would argue with that. Surely it's the fairest outcome? It would get us out of a jam, and you would still have a windfall that you never expected."

It was a plea from the heart. I wasn't sure how to respond. Temporising, I said, "The solicitors told me yesterday that you were dropping your appeal against the will. They seem to think you've been advised that you have no grounds."

This seemed to throw her, and for a moment there was silence. Then she said, "I don't know about that. I still think my idea makes sense. If we came to an agreement, it would clear up all this uncertainty, and everyone would end up better off. Morally it has to be the right thing."

This made me uneasy. It was one thing for me to argue over this with people I hardly knew, but another to be reminded that real lives could be affected.

"I think I need to take advice on this. I'm sure you'll understand. I can't make any commitment standing here talking on the phone."

"No, no, I quite understand. If you could just give it some thought … " She broke off. "I think that's Phil coming in. I'll have to go."

* * *

Despite Angela Crabtree's appeal, I couldn't easily dismiss her husband's intimidating attitude, or ignore the fact that he appeared to have followed me to my motel last night. It was almost as if they were adopting a hard-cop soft-cop approach in their efforts to wear me down. Yet for all that, I couldn't help but feel some sympathy for her.

I would have loved to talk this situation over with Ashley. She would have been sure to offer a pragmatic view. Yet under the circumstances I felt it was a conversation I couldn't embark on.

If only I could work out *why* Elizabeth had left me the house in the first place, I might have a more definite view on what to do about it.

Sitting in the rather spartan reception area at the motel, I stared at my computer screen. Somewhere in there, on the internet, lay the answers to all my questions. I just had to work out where.

I thought again about my grandmother. If the woman in that film was her, she must have had some connection with the North East. And if so, then by association I had indirect links here too. Could she have been born here, as I'd felt when I last looked at the image taken from the film?

I trawled the internet for a while, examining genealogy web sites that claimed to help you construct a family tree. It looked easy enough to track down someone's place of birth, but in most cases you had to pay a premium, or else wait for your registration to be confirmed.

Then a much simpler solution struck me: a woman called Adele.

She'd been a close friend of my grandmother's, and had continued to send me Christmas cards for years after my grandmother died. Our contact had fallen by the wayside in recent years, but she'd been a lot younger than my grandmother, and might still be alive.

Holding my breath, I searched my laptop. Would her details be in here, or did they date back too far? I was in luck; I still had a phone number for her.

A woman too young to be Adele answered the phone and told me in a Polish accent that she was Adele's carer. "She is not ill, she is just a little frail. I will fetch her."

After a moment Adele's voice came on the line, familiar and stronger than I expected. "Michael, what a nice surprise! I can't remember the last time we spoke."

"You make me feel very guilty."

"Don't worry my love, life moves on. It's the same for all of us."

"So how are you?"

She chuckled. "Well, I'm still here. I seem to be in good hands."

We chatted about the past, but finally I said, "I might as well admit the reason I'm calling you. I wanted to ask you about Emily – my grandmother. I hope that's all right?"

"Or course. What did you want to know?"

"Mainly where she was born. I always thought it was Berkshire."

"Oh no, she originally came from Longbenton. That's a district of Newcastle. She grew up there, but I think she left when she was still in her teens, and she never went back. I only got to know her years later, when she was living here in Berkshire."

So I'd guessed right. I should have thought of contacting her long ago.

"Did she ever tell you anything about her life in the north?"

She thought for a moment. "Just childhood stories, I suppose – nothing special."

"And did she ever mention any men friends back there?"

"Oh no, nothing like that. Although … "

"What?"

"Well, when I first knew her she sometimes used to talk about someone she'd known a long time ago. The way it sounded, he must have been the love of her life. But she never said much about him. I think it made her sad. And she loved her husband, of course – your grandfather. She didn't want to keep living in the past."

"And was this man someone she knew in the north?"

"I never thought so at the time, but he could have been, couldn't he?"

"What was his name?"

She spent a long time thinking about this. "I'm so sorry, Michael, I can't remember."

Chapter 32

I was due at Jenna Melling's flat at eight o'clock that evening, but around five o'clock she sent me a text to say she was running late. Could I make it nine o'clock instead? "Bring your car this time," her message added. "Mine's off the road."

To kill time I sat in my motel room watching TV, but this proved to be a mistake. To begin with I paid it little attention, but gradually I found myself being drawn into a complicated film. When eventually I glanced at my watch I found I'd left it almost too late to get to Jenna's flat on time. I hurried out to my car, reproaching myself for my inattention, and drove off towards the city.

It was only when I reached Jesmond that I realised I didn't actually know Jenna's address. I'd been assuming I would recognise it from my previous visit, but that time we'd arrived from the theatre on foot. Seen from a car in the gathering dusk, the Victorian streets all looked the same to me, and I couldn't get my bearings.

I drove from one street to another in mounting frustration. This was ridiculous. I could feel myself breaking out in a sweat. I reached for my phone to call Jenna, then realised that in my panic to get under way I'd left it on my bed in the motel.

A wave of annoyance pulsed through me. I jammed on the brakes and brought the car to an abrupt halt. What now? After a moment's reflection I decided the best plan was to find the theatre we'd visited and retrace our pedestrian journey from there. Perhaps it wasn't the quickest solution, but it should work.

Grumbling to myself, I drove off and threaded my way to the main coast road, which I knew would take me to the theatre. By car the route was much longer than I expected, and included a broad road tunnel. At the theatre I turned off, hoping to work my way back along the side roads I'd taken with Jenna. It was only at that point that I remembered we'd crossed a Victorian viaduct that was closed to motor vehicles. Swearing out loud, I parked the car and struck off towards it on foot.

The bridge was just about wide enough to accommodate two lanes of traffic, which had evidently been its original purpose, but it was now laid out as a wide footpath. As I approached it a man and a woman came off it and strolled past me, deep in conversation. There was no one else in sight, and their voices quickly dwindled. Through gaps in the steel lattice sides, the steep-sided Jesmond Dene park snaked away to my right.

I'd only taken a few paces on to the bridge itself when I became aware that some new people had materialised from the trees behind me. I tried to pay them no attention, but quickly realised that although I was striding out in my haste to reach Jenna's flat, they were walking faster than me, and in moments would catch up with me.

I glanced over my shoulder. Two figures, both wearing grey hoodies and trainers, were now only a few paces behind me. Were they a threat, or should I ignore them? I was tempted to break into a run, but had a sense that it would be futile. If they wanted to catch me, they would.

They made their move quickly. As if acting on a silent signal they both accelerated at the same time, and before I could do anything to stop them they'd moved forward to either side of me and grabbed me by the arms.

I shouted, "What the fuck!"

They said nothing, and simply hustled me over towards the side of the bridge. I braced myself for them to start frisking me for valuables, then realised that as well as forgetting my phone, I'd also left my wallet at the motel. At least they couldn't steal that.

My relief was short-lived. They didn't seem inclined to steal anything – they evidently had a much more drastic plan in mind. As we reached the girders at the side of the bridge they started to lift me by the arms. They were going to throw me over the edge.

I thrashed around in wild panic, desperately trying to loosen their hold on me. I tried kicking at their shins. I tried to elbow them. At one point I freed my right arm and landed a hefty blow on one of the men's arms. It seemed to have no effect, and he'd soon grabbed my own arm again.

Within moments I could be dead. My whole life could have been leading to this single point of finality. I could feel the pressure of the cold metal girders as they tried to raise me to the top and bundle me over. I was yelling incoherently and struggling like a downed animal. Nothing I could do seemed likely to prevent the inevitable.

Then a shout. "What the fuck are you doing, mate?" It was accompanied by cries of indignation.

Instantly the two men relaxed their grip on me. There was a moment's pause as they assessed this new development, then they let go of me altogether and I slithered to my knees. By the time I looked up they were jogging away across the bridge.

I looked round for my liberators. Three young men were approaching, one of them carrying an open beer can. He called, "Are you OK, mate?"

I struggled to stand up. "I am now." I gave him a grim smile.

One of them leaned over to help me. "What the fuck was the matter with those two guys?"

I straightened shakily. "Don't ask me. They just appeared out of nowhere."

"Bloody maniacs."

My legs were trembling. I allowed myself to slide into a sitting position and squatted on my heels, leaning on the girders. "I thought they were going to kill me."

"They bloody nearly did."

I stayed in that position for a long moment, breathing deeply and rejoicing at still being alive. Gradually I focused on the youths, who were still standing around, uncertain what to do but evidently reluctant to leave me there. One was lighting a cigarette and another was taking a pull from a beer can. In any other circumstances I would have felt uneasy encountering them on my own on a dark night. There was a lesson here.

"You should go to the police," one of them said.

"I will, I will."

I waited a little longer, then said, "Do you mind if I tag along with you?"

"No problem. Where are you going to, mate?"

I gestured vaguely across the bridge. "That way."

"Right. When you're ready."

I wasn't sure if I would know where to go when we reached the other side of the bridge. In fact I remembered immediately. However, the youths were heading in another direction.

"Are you sure you'll be OK?" one of them said.

I looked around. The street was quiet but well lit, and not far away I could see a man walking a dog. I told them I would be fine, and thanked them for effectively saving my life. It was only after they'd walked off and I'd turned a corner that I realised I should have asked them for names and contact details. They might not have been keen to provide them, but the fact was that they were witnesses to the attack. Yet I'd simply let them go.

Too bad. What I wanted more than anything was the refuge of Jenna's flat. I was already imagining myself downing a double whisky.

I wasn't convinced I'd be able to follow the route I'd taken with her on that previous occasion, but thankfully my instinct took over, and at each turn I made the right choice. A few minutes later I was standing in front of her building, reflecting that when I'd been looking for it earlier I'd been looking in slightly the wrong place.

I stepped up to the front door and pressed the buzzer.

Chapter 33

No one answered. I buzzed again. Still nothing.

I took a couple of paces back and looked up at Jenna's windows on the top floor. The lights were on. If I'd had my phone with me I would have rung her to tell her I'd arrived. I stepped forward, about to press the buzzer again, but at that moment the front door opened and a middle-aged woman emerged with a dog on a lead.

Seizing the moment, I reached out and held the door for her as if I'd already been on my way in. It worked; she gave me a brief smile and left me with my hand on the partly-open door. I stepped inside and made my way upstairs.

There was no buzzer on the door to Jenna's flat, but there was a brass knocker. I rapped a couple of times. No result. Tentatively I turned the handle. It wasn't locked. A couple of seconds later I was inside the flat.

I called Jenna's name. No response. I walked through to the lounge. All the lights were on and everything looked normal, but no Jenna. I glanced round the room. Had she slipped out on some errand? Once again, I wished I had my phone with me.

I checked the kitchen, then stepped out into the corridor and glanced into the bedroom, then the bathroom. Nothing untoward; just no Jenna.

I wasn't sure what to do. Would she be offended if she returned to find me already in the flat and sitting on her sofa? I didn't know her well enough to judge. But what else was I supposed to do? My car was about half a mile away, on the other side of that terrifying viaduct. I wasn't prepared to make that journey yet, and I wasn't about to camp out on her doorstep or loiter on the landing either. I sat down on the sofa and leaned back cautiously.

Ten minutes passed. If she'd only gone out on a quick errand, surely she would have reappeared by now? She must know I was already late, and would probably have arrived by this point. How long should I wait?

The landline phone on the desk burst into life. I stared at it in shock. After four shrill tones an antiquated voicemail system kicked in. The device emitted a variety of mechanical clunks and electronic whistling sounds, then finally a man's voice spoke.

"Jen, it's Gary. What's happening? I could do with a status update. Is everything squared away with Greg? Give me a call when you get the chance." Clearly this had nothing to do with her absence. The phone clicked and whistled again, then finally fell silent.

I decided to give her a more few minutes. Still nothing. Gradually I became aware that my upper arms were throbbing where those two men had grabbed me. As a distraction, I picked up a glossy magazine from the coffee table. It focused on the Yorkshire area, and was folded open to an inside page. I looked at it without much interest, running my eye over a selection of colour photographs taken at a society event: everyone dressed up to the nines, chandeliers sparkling. The subjects had been caught chatting informally over wine and canapés.

Then among them I noticed Piers Ashurst. Perhaps his presence at the event was connected with Jenna's marketing efforts for his company. He seemed to be speaking with some vehemence to a man of about fifty with a thick neck and receding sandy-coloured hair. The other man appeared to be reacting with a stony expression.

I heard a car draw up in the street. Could this be Jenna? I tossed the magazine back on the table and stood up, ready to greet her. The car door closed, and after a moment a front door slammed somewhere along the street. No Jenna. Then I remembered she'd said in her text that she had car problems, so it couldn't have been her anyway.

I was now restless. If Jenna wasn't going to put in an appearance I should really be reporting my attack to the police. I found an envelope on a side table and wrote a short message to her on the back of it. I said I had no phone with me, but if there was still time I would return later, otherwise I would phone her tomorrow from my motel. I placed the envelope on top of the magazine on the coffee table.

Finding the location of a police station proved easy enough. There was a phone book on the side table, and I discovered there was one not far from where I'd left my car. Now all I had to do was make my way there without being attacked again.

I found my way to the footpath that led to the bridge, but glancing warily along it, decided there was no way I was going to cross it on my own. Instead, I set off on a parallel road that led down into the dene. I assumed there would be bright lights and plenty of traffic along here, and I would feel reasonably safe.

I was wrong on all counts. It was little more than a leafy side road, lacking either pedestrians or houses. In some ways I felt even more vulnerable than I had up on the bridge. Somewhere to my left and high above me I sensed the viaduct hanging against the sky, but it was more or less hidden in the dusk beyond a wall and undergrowth.

At the bottom, the road swerved right and passed underneath the broad modern dual carriageway I'd driven up earlier, and I peered around nervously, seeing potential assailants in every shadow. In the end, though, no one accosted me. I emerged in a road flanked on one side by pretty period houses, and made my way back up out of the gorge.

* * *

The police were helpful but seemed bemused by what I told them. Initially they were inclined to put the attack down to a failed robbery, but they were mystified when I insisted that the attackers had made no attempt to steal anything from me. "All they wanted to do was throw me over the side."

"Can you think of any enemies who would do this to you?"

I marvelled at the question. It was one that I'd encountered many times in books and films, but I'd never expected to hear it addressed to me in earnest. Did I have any enemies? Surely not of the kind who would want to murder me?

Then I thought of Philip Crabtree. He'd apparently followed me to my motel, so maybe he'd also followed me into Newcastle this evening. Certainly he had a deep grudge against me over Elizabeth's will, but would it really have provoked him to this extent? Would he stand to gain anything if I were killed?

I thought I'd better mention this to the police, but I emphasised that I had no evidence to suggest that he'd played any part in the attack. Neither of the two men had been him; even in the panic of the moment, I'd been aware that they were both slight, athletic figures. Philip's build was much taller and squarer.

The police were noncommittal. They seemed to believe me, but gave no indication of whether they intended to follow up my report. They asked where I was staying in case they wanted to contact me again, and in the end one of them drove me the short distance to my car. "I was coming this way anyway," he told me.

Alone in the car, I glanced at my watch. It was now well past eleven o'clock: too late, surely, for a social encounter with Jenna. Yet I felt I couldn't leave the area without checking her flat again. Driving back to it seemed far more complicated than it should have been, involving another trip through that road tunnel, but finally I found my way there.

The lights were still shining on the top floor, but again no one answered the buzzer. I didn't attempt to go in. With a slight shiver I returned to my car.

Chapter 34

I woke in a sweat at around 3am, back in the moment on that bridge when I thought I was going to be thrown over the side. My heart was racing. I switched the light on and stared round at the reassuringly unexciting walls of the motel room. There'd been a moment when I thought I'd never see these or any other walls again.

I switched the light off, but for about an hour I lay there wide awake, unable to stop myself reliving the whole episode repeatedly. Eventually I fell into a troubled sleep.

The first thing I did next morning was ring Jenna's mobile. The call went to voicemail. Something seemed wrong here, but I didn't know what to make of it.

After breakfast I phoned Jenna's number again. Still no answer. Then I phoned David Smythe, the solicitor handling Elizabeth Sanderson's will. I wanted to know if Philip Crabtree stood to gain anything from my death.

"Well, yes," he said almost reluctantly. "Theoretically if you were to die now, the estate would go to Philip and his wife. Did I not mention that to you?"

"You most certainly didn't."

He seemed unapologetic. "Ah, well, there's a survivorship clause in the will. They're quite common in wills involving husbands and wives. They're usually used to reduce tax liability – that sort of thing."

"But Elizabeth wasn't married."

"No," he said patiently, "but there's nothing to stop people putting qualifications in their wills for other reasons."

"What would be the point in this case?"

"Not a lot," he admitted. "Probably there was a similar clause in her own partner's will, or some other will that she was involved with, so she just made a similar stipulation in hers. People tend to go with what they know. It's human nature."

"But in theory this kind of clause would be a good reason for one beneficiary to do away with another. Is that right?"

He laughed. "Good lord, no. If something like that happened, the police would be on to it like a ton of bricks."

"But it sounds to me like a recipe for conflict."

"Well, personally I try to discourage these clauses unless there's an obvious benefit, and I can't honestly see any here, but in the end it's in the hands of the testator."

I put the phone down feeling barely reassured, and wondered what to do next. My upper arms were still aching from the attack on the bridge, making it impossible for me to put it out of my mind. Whether or not it had been orchestrated by Philip Crabtree, someone had set it up, and that someone might be planning a repeat performance.

Could I do anything to prevent it? Or should I choose what seemed the safest option, and simply head south? After all, if I couldn't get hold of Jenna Melling, there was no point in being here in Newcastle. Staying on would mean wasting money and using up potential working time – and perhaps putting myself in danger.

But I was uneasy about Jenna's unexplained disappearance. I couldn't imagine her simply hiding from me last night until I went away. It wasn't her style. So why else would she abandon her flat in the middle of the evening, leaving the lights on and the front door unlocked?

I stared round the bedroom, uncertain what to do. The idea of simply getting into my car and heading south was certainly tempting, yet it would seem like an admission of failure to leave without resolving the situation with Jenna. I sat down heavily on the bed, feeling trapped in a situation that was partly of my own making.

My phone rang and I snatched it up, thinking it might be Jenna. In fact it was Jamie Andrews of Latimers. I hadn't spoken to him since we all went back south to Cornwall. He started diffidently. "Mike, I realise I'm probably not your favourite person at the moment."

"It's OK. I'm not blaming you for anything."

"Well, I feel I owe you an apology all the same. Andrea can be a bit impulsive."

"Don't worry about it." I sensed that there was something else.

"In a way I'm phoning you on Andrea's behalf. She's embarrassed to talk to you herself."

I was tempted to retort that I wasn't surprised, but clearly that wouldn't help. I waited.

"You probably know the due diligence on the Mellings acquisition has gone through."

"No I didn't. So is the deal signed and sealed now?"

"Not quite. There are a couple more formalities to go through – or so I'm told. But it shouldn't take more than a few days."

"So … ?"

"Well, Andrea was looking again at Ashurst Concepts – trying to get a handle on their profit and loss, their cash flow, that kind of stuff. The due diligence process has apparently given them the green light, but she says it doesn't square with the figures she came up with." He interrupted himself. "She's very conscientious. She doesn't like to let go of these things."

I glanced around, wondering where this was going. He continued, "You went down to Leeds, didn't you? You saw the company for yourself. You met the founder. Andrea was wondering if you dug up anything while you were there that made you uneasy. If so, it might give her stronger grounds to take her concerns to Bob Latimer."

Now I was paying attention. I did have questions about what was going on at Ashursts, though I'd never have expected to be sharing them with Andrea Smith. Moreover, Jenna Melling had suggested on the phone that she too had found out something strange about Ashursts. I said, "They seem a rather odd company to me, but it's difficult to explain on the phone."

"Well, I would suggest meeting up in person, but I'm away from the office again. In fact I'm back in Newcastle for a few days."

"You're joking! I'm in Newcastle too. What are you doing here?"

"We've got a tender out for a big logistics contract, and I've been trying to work out how we could share the work between Latimers in the south and Mellings up here in the north. I'm going home to St Austell tomorrow." There was a pause. "So why are you in Newcastle?"

"Huh! Long story." I did some rapid recalculating. "Are you staying in the same hotel as last time? I'm stuck in some motel. Maybe I could come over for a drink this evening?"

* * *

I went down to the motel reception to book myself in for another night. As I was walking back along the corridor my phone sounded again, and a loud voice said, "Mike Stanhope? It's Greg Atkins at Melling Logistics. Is Jenna with you?"

Quite why he should think so was a question I could consider later. I closed my door and said cautiously, "Sorry, no."

"Can you tell me where she is then?"

"I have no idea. Why are you asking me?"

"You were having dinner with her last night. Did she leave with you?"

So Greg had known about my assignation with Jenna. I marvelled at how poorly I seemed to understand people. I said, "No, I just told you she's not with me. The dinner never happened. When I got there she wasn't around. I left without seeing her."

"Well she was at home when I talked to her at seven o'clock. Where else would she go? If she's not with you she's disappeared."

For a moment I said nothing. Despite Greg's hostile manner, I was relieved that someone apart from me was worrying about Jenna. It was no longer solely my problem. As calmly as I could, I said, "What makes you say that?"

"Her lights are all on and the door's open, but she's not here and she's not answering her phone."

"You're at her flat now? Are you checking up on her or something?"

I thought I had him on the back foot, but he quickly responded, "No, of course not. I live near here. I'm being a good neighbour." And with barely a pause he was on the offensive again. "Before you deny it, I know you were inside this flat last night yourself. I'm looking at the message you left. You say you'll be coming back later."

"I'm not denying anything. I wrote that message because she wasn't there. It confirms what I'm telling you."

"So what happened when you did come back?"

"I didn't – not into the flat. There was still no answer, so I decided to call it a day."

"So you say."

Exasperated, I said, "Well it's true."

For a moment neither of us spoke, then I said, "I suppose she's never disappeared like this before?"

"Of course not. Would you go off if you had guests coming, leaving all your lights on and your front door unlocked?"

"A family emergency? A friend in need?"

"So why isn't she answering her phone?"

I had no response to that. I said, "Have you talked to the police?"

"I'm talking to you."

Suddenly I'd had enough of his accusing manner. I said, "For god's sake, Greg, Jenna's not with me, and I didn't see her last night. There's no point in talking as if I've have spirited her away or something. Why would I do that? If you're really worried, go to the police. That's what I would do." In a surge of irritation I added, "And make sure you tell them about our dinner date. I'm sure they'll want to know about that." I disconnected before he had a chance to reply.

Chapter 35

After the excitement of the early morning the day proved uneventful. I took my laptop to the motel reception area, which was marginally less depressing than working in my room, and tried to focus on the one outstanding article I had to write.

At lunchtime I asked the woman at the reception desk where I could buy a sandwich, and she suggested a convenience store on the other side of the main road. I headed off on foot, looking for a place to cross the road, but when I found an underpass I was suddenly nervous. If those people from the bridge were still after me, this would be the ideal place for an ambush.

I stood indecisively in the sunshine, leaning on a metal fence and watching the traffic rushing past. I couldn't live my life like this, wondering if some danger was lurking round every corner, but how could I escape the threat when I didn't know the cause of it?

It felt like a test. Was I going to let that terrifying experience haunt me, or could I shake myself back to normality? I wasn't sure, but I felt I had to try. Glancing around, I satisfied myself that there were no other pedestrians anywhere in the vicinity, then walked cautiously down the ramp.

There was no one in sight. A dank smell and an array of graffiti greeted me. Taking a deep breath, I sprinted the full length of the underpass and arrived gasping at the other end.

So far so good. I found the shop, bought the sandwich, then gave a repeat performance on the way back. Object achieved, which perhaps was something, but this was no way to live.

In the afternoon I shifted out to the motel's tiny patio, sitting in the shade so that I could just about see my laptop screen. Behind a tall wooden fence I could hear the traffic on the A69 roaring past.

Every time I broke off from what I was doing my mind kept running over the same question: what on earth was I doing here in Newcastle, so far from home? In effect, I'd returned to the very place where things had started to go wrong for me – and now, with Jenna's apparent disappearance, they'd taken a definite turn for the worse.

On top of that, I was still thinking about the attack on that bridge. It was by far the most frightening thing that had ever happened to me. I kept reliving those moments when I really believed my life was about to end. How was I to know those people wouldn't attack me again? But if I left the North East, would I be leaving the danger behind or merely taking it with me?

Finally it was time to drive over to the village where Jamie Andrews was staying. He gave me a good-natured welcome and led me through to the hotel lounge. Over his shoulder he said, "I didn't tell anyone at Mellings that you were here. It seemed better not to."

"Probably wise."

"So what are you actually doing here?"

We sat down by the window. I said, "In a way, it's the same reason you phoned me. I had a vague idea there was something odd about Ashurst Concepts." I shrugged. "Maybe I thought that if I could prove a point, I might redeem myself in the eyes of Bob Latimer."

"Odd in what way?"

"Well, there was that lorry hijacking. Jenna Melling thought there was something strange about it. Too much of a coincidence." I broke off. "In fact it's because of Jenna that I'm here. She said she'd found out something else about Ashursts, and she wanted to tell me about it. I was supposed to meet her last night."

"I assume you don't want me to tell Andrea about that." He attempted an ironic smile.

I gave him a caustic look.

"So what did she tell you?"

"I don't know. She never turned up."

"Oh, I see. So will you reschedule?"

"I suppose so, if she's willing. I don't know yet why she pulled out."

He nodded, saying nothing, so I asked, "What was it that Andrea dug up?"

"Well she says that from her figures, Ashursts have been running at a loss for months. They have negative cash flow and no reserves."

"But Mellings can support them, can't they? Presumably they're in it for the long haul."

"Yes, but at the Melling end Ashursts appear to be in profit. It was only when Andrea talked to an accounts assistant at Ashursts that she got these other figures." He paused for dramatic effect. "This is where it gets a bit mysterious. When Andrea phoned the assistant back a few days later, she'd been fired, and their head of accounts told her those figures were a load of hogwash. According to him, everything was sweetness and light."

He opened his laptop on the coffee table and displayed two spreadsheet files. "These are the official figures … " He clicked the mouse. "And these are the ones Andrea came up with. They're not the figures she was given – they're just what she remembers."

"That's pretty weird." I looked at the screen for a moment. "So if this is true, how come it wasn't spotted in the due diligence process? That's what it's all about, isn't it?"

"I can't answer that one, but something I do know is that the people managing the due diligence were over-committed. Andrea picked that up. They're based in London, but they farmed out the Ashurst review to a local accountancy firm in Leeds. Maybe those people cocked up."

"What does Andrea think about that?"

"She doesn't know much about due diligence. It's a specialist activity – not her thing. But I suppose the people doing it can conduct it however they like."

"Maybe."

Jamie reflected on this for a moment, then said, "You mentioned that you were already suspicious about Ashursts. What did you mean?"

"Well, it's probably nothing, but when I was there they were receiving deliveries from a scruffy white van, and they seemed ultra-keen not to let me know what was going on. I tried to see what they were doing with the stuff that was being delivered, and basically they chased me away. They were quite aggressive."

"What did Piers Ashurst say they were doing?"

"Oh, this was after I left him. I sneaked back on my own. Twice, actually."

He looked at me with a what might have been a combination of admiration and disbelief. "You sure know how to get on the wrong side of people, don't you?"

I asked him about the logistics contract he was working on.

"It's the bid for the Franchi contract. The idea is to spread the load between Mellings and Latimers. I'm talking to Simon and Greg at Mellings to establish how it would work."

"Huh. That's the contract I reported in that article – the one that could get me fired from Latimers. So you're telling me it's still on?"

"Well, they're still talking to us. We think we can put in a pretty convincing bid." He gave me an ironic smile. "Off the record, that is."

"Very funny." The chances that I would report this in the press were less than zero. In fact, however, this was the one encouraging piece of news I'd heard today. If the contract was saved, Bob Latimer might be less inclined to dispense with my services. It was a straw to clutch at, anyway.

My eyes were drawn to a screen saver on Jamie's laptop. It was cycling through photographs of a race meeting. He glanced over at it himself, then said, "Those were taken when I went to Gosforth Park with Andrea."

We watched the slideshow in silence for a moment, then something caught my attention. It was a candid photograph of a throng of race-goers, most of them in animated conversation, and among them I recognised two people: Philip Crabtree and a man I couldn't immediately place. They were standing close to each other, though they didn't appear to be together.

"Can you go back and freeze the last image?"

Jamie leaned forward and restored the picture of the two men. I peered at it carefully, then remembered where I'd seen the other man. It was in the picture I'd seen last night in Jenna's magazine. He'd been talking to Piers Ashurst.

"Could you let me have a copy of that image?"

He leaned forward again, opening and closing various windows. "OK, I've sent the image to your email address."

Chapter 36

An abrupt triple knock on my motel room door next morning set my nerves jangling. It wasn't the usual discreet approach of the cleaning staff, and I realised I was still uneasy about being pursued by the two men from the bridge. I wasn't greatly reassured when I peered through the spy hole in the door and saw two men, but I realised quickly that they weren't my attackers. They were too smartly dressed, and were taller and older. All the same, I opened the door warily.

It was obvious even before they showed me their IDs that they were police officers.

"Michael Stanhope?"

I nodded.

"Are you acquainted with a Jenna Melling?"

Suddenly and irrationally fearful, I assented. There followed a brief sequence of questions and answers. When had I last seen her? Did I know where she was now?

They seemed unimpressed with my responses, and told me they would like me to come to the police station to talk further. I had the impression that this is what they'd intended from the moment they arrived. Presumably Gregg Atkins had alerted them to my existence, and they were predisposed to be suspicious of my involvement.

In the motel car park they asked if they could look at my car. I nodded and unlocked it, and they glanced inside and then checked the boot. Apparently satisfied, they took me to their car. They spoke little on the journey across Newcastle and answered none of my questions about Jenna. "We'll come to that." Finally we were all seated in an interview room at the same police station where I'd reported my attack on the bridge.

"You are here of your own free will," one of them told me – a thickset man in his forties. "You're free to leave at any time."

"Then why am I here?"

He considered this. "We're trying to trace Jenna Melling's whereabouts, and we believe you may be able to help."

"So she's really missing?"

"She hasn't been seen or been in contact with anyone for two days."

"Well if I can help I will."

"You had arranged to see her on Thursday night. Is that right?"

"Yes, but when I arrived she wasn't there."

"This was at about nine forty five in the evening?"

"Give or take."

"And you arrived at her flat on foot, not in your car. Why was that?"

"I couldn't remember the exact address. I decided the best way to find it was to walk from the place where I started the last time I went there."

His look of disbelief suggested that he thought this alone was suspicious. He let my answer hang in the air for a moment, then said, "You entered her flat. Did you have her permission to do that?"

I tried to give a dismissive shrug. In fact I'd been uneasy about going in uninvited, but I'd never expected I would have to explain myself in this sort of situation. I said, "She was a friend, and I was invited to dinner, so I assume the answer is yes. I had no phone to ring her, and I thought maybe she couldn't hear her front door buzzer for some reason. I thought I should go inside and check."

"Why didn't you have a phone with you?"

I was tempted to object that there was no law yet compelling people to carry a phone with them at all times. Instead I merely said, "I left it behind by mistake."

He gave me another sceptical look. "And what happened when you went into the flat?" He was looking at me attentively, but trying not to show it.

"Nothing. She wasn't there. I looked around in case she'd – I don't know, had a fall or something. But she hadn't."

"And then what?"

"I wrote her a note and left."

He glanced briefly at his colleague, a slightly younger man. "Later that evening you came to this police station and reported that someone had attacked you on Armstrong Bridge."

"Correct."

He looked at some notes on the table in front of him. "I understand there were no witnesses."

"What, you're doubting me now?"

"You said some young lads helped you, but you didn't take any particulars from them."

"I didn't think I'd need to!" I realised there was no future in sounding indignant, but I didn't like the way they were turning Jenna's disappearance round on me. More calmly I added, "I just thought I should let someone know there were two madmen on the loose."

He sat back. "You see, I'm wondering if you invented this supposed attack in order to deflect attention from whatever had happened at Jenna Melling's flat."

"Well I didn't. For god's sake! I thought I was going to die." I glared at him. He merely stared back. "In any case, I was attacked before I got to the flat, not after."

I waited for a response, but there was none. I added, "And for the record, nothing 'happened' when I did get to the flat. I went in, I waited, I left. End of story."

"So why didn't you report the assault immediately?"

I gave him a look of exasperation. "I was in shock. I just wanted to sit down somewhere and recover. I bet you'd feel the same in that situation. Anyway, I had no phone. Was I supposed to wander around looking for a police station while those bastards might still be watching me?"

He gave me a suspicious glance. I could see that he thought I was trying to outsmart him, and was unimpressed. He looked at his notes again. "These attackers took nothing from you – is that right? They didn't attempt to rob you. Why do you think that was?"

"I have absolutely no idea. Ask them."

"So two unknown people appear from the shadows, grab you and attempt to kill you by flinging you over the parapet from Armstrong Bridge into Jesmond Dene." He gave me an ironic look. "How did they know you would be crossing that bridge? Logically you would have driven directly to Jenna Melling's flat, so it wouldn't have been on your route."

I'd been wondering that myself, so I already had an answer. "That would only have been a problem for them if they'd been lying in wait. I don't think they were. I think they followed me from my motel. Attacking me on the bridge must have been purely opportunistic. They probably thought they could make it look like suicide or something."

"Very inventive."

"Well why not?"

Abruptly he said, "So where is Jenna now?"

"What? I keep telling you I have absolutely no idea." I stared defiantly at them. "I came all the way from Doncaster to see her. A hundred miles! As far as I'm concerned it's been a wasted trip."

"Why did you come to see her?"

"Because she invited me to dinner." I sat back in frustration.

"Were you in a relationship with her?"

"No I wasn't! Absolutely not. We were colleagues when I was in Newcastle a couple of weeks ago. I came to discuss something connected to our work."

"A long way to travel for a business meeting in the middle of the evening. Was that how Jenna Melling normally conducted her affairs?"

I glanced quickly at him. "Why are we talking in the past tense? She's not dead, is she?"

"We sincerely hope not. But we'd be happier if we were able to find her."

"So would I!"

He looked judiciously at me. "Can you explain why Jenna's mobile phone has been found in a grass verge adjacent to Jesmond Dene – on the walking route between her flat and your car?"

This information was a bit of a stunner. A lost phone was bad news. Suddenly it was much harder to dismiss the thought that something sinister had happened to Jenna.

"Of course I can't explain it. But it's concerning, isn't it?"

"That's precisely what we thought."

Eventually they'd finished with me. They asked me how long I would be in Newcastle, and I replied somewhat indignantly that I couldn't afford to stay in the North East indefinitely just for their convenience.

"Well please inform us if you're intending to leave, and where you will be going."

I nearly turned down their offer of a lift to the motel, then realised it would take me an age to get there on my own. We travelled back in silence, and I watched with relief from the car park as the cruiser pulled away.

Chapter 37

The rest of the day seemed to pass in a blur. I tried to summon up enthusiasm for my outstanding work projects, but didn't get far with them. I reached for my phone ten times to ring Ashley, but stopped myself each time.

I opened a browser window on a writing forum I'd joined when I was working on my book. Nothing doing; I couldn't see any posts by the handful of people I'd continued to follow. I'd had some lively exchanges there, but I seemed to be drifting away from that world, and apparently they were doing the same. The voices I'd most appreciated had gone quiet.

In the evening I ate in the adjoining roadside café. I knew how to live it up on a Saturday night.

I woke to an overcast Sunday morning. It was hard to contemplate spending yet another night in this motel, yet I didn't want to go home either, and I seemed to be running out of other options. So I sat in the motel reception area, staring out morosely through the glass doors into a light drizzle.

What the hell had happened to my life? Two months ago I was living in a beautiful part of the world, planning a future with the new woman in my life. I had plenty of work – some of it mundane, but all of it manageable – and although I didn't know it, I was about to be told I'd inherited a house worth half a million pounds.

Now I was in danger of losing large parts of my work, my relationship with my girlfriend was on the line, I'd been attacked by people who apparently wanted me dead, and the police seemed to view me as a murder suspect.

To cap it all, I was on my own, hundreds of miles from home. And lately my flat hadn't felt much like home anyway.

My points of reference were disintegrating one by one. The only thing that hadn't gone sour was Elizabeth Sanderson's legacy, but I still regarded this as largely fantasy. I was only going to believe I'd inherited that house when it happened, not before.

I thought back to a remark Jamie Andrews had made: "You know how to get on the wrong side of people." Was he on to something? Had I brought all these ills on myself? If I was honest, the answer had to be at least partly yes. Clearly I should have been more wary of Jenna Melling's flirtatious manner. I could blame Andrea for misleading Ashley about my involvement with her, but in reality the fallout was down to me.

It was also my fault that my work with Latimers was under threat. I should have thought twice before submitting that magazine article about the Franchi contract. I was too busy trying to prove I was still a journalist to think through the ethics of what I was doing. True, the by-line shouldn't have appeared on the article, but really the article shouldn't have appeared in the first place.

Ironically, far from gaining the kudos I'd expected from submitting that article, I'd found myself in a verbal wrangle with Jason Bright, my contact at the magazine, and I'd possibly compromised my future work for him. Yet again, I'd acted without thinking carefully enough about the consequences.

I glanced over at the reception desk. Should I book myself in here for yet another night? I didn't want to stay on in this soulless environment, and I certainly wasn't going to do it for the benefit of the Northumbria Police, but to leave would require a conscious plan, and I wasn't in the right frame of mind to make one. I felt I had no other option, so I walked over to the desk.

Set up for another day at least, I decided to go and see Longbenton, the district where Adele had told me my grandmother had been born. It was on the other side of Newcastle, on the route out towards the coast, but it was further north of the city centre than the area where Jenna lived.

The trip told me little. Longbenton was an area of mixed housing, offices and modern light industry – unremarkable as far as I was concerned. Geographically speaking it was diametrically opposite to

Ryton, the place where the bus driver hailed from. Perhaps they'd met in the middle.

* * *

Just after breakfast the following morning I was phoned by Don, Jason's editorial assistant at the logistics magazine: the very man who had put the by-line on that article and caused me a lot of this grief.

"Mike, Jason asked me to ring you. You were looking for editorial work in the North East. I don't suppose you'd be willing to go back up there, would you?"

I was tempted to remonstrate with him over the by-line episode, but I reminded myself that it wasn't his fault; he hadn't known I'd asked Jason for anonymity. In fact I should be rejoicing that the magazine was contacting me at all. It could be first step in mending relations.

"Well, believe it or not I'm already back in the area as we speak."

"Ah. That's great. A job has come up, and we hoped you could take it on." He explained that the magazine wanted an extensive feature article on a transport company in Sunderland, which was only a few miles from Newcastle. "But they can't see you until the end of the week. Will you still be up there in the north by then?"

I said, "I could be."

"Excellent. I'll email you the details."

I went down to the reception desk and re-booked my room for another five nights. I'd never voluntarily exiled myself from home for so long, but I couldn't think how else to play things. The distances were so large. Returning to Cornwall and then coming back here would have used up two of the five days I'd just committed to staying in the north. The driving would have been exhausting, and the journey would have cost nearly as much as the motel bill – probably a lot more if I'd taken the train. I could have thrown myself on Tina's mercy and returned to Doncaster, but I felt I'd used up my credit there, for the time being anyway.

Besides, in a corner of my mind I felt unexpectedly cheered. At least that article would cover some of this cost, and should help me restore good relations with the magazine. More important, it gave me an objective. Lack of purpose was one of the greatest enemies of peace of mind. Now I had a reason to stay on here while I tried to untangle what was happening to me, and hopefully also found out what had happened to Jenna.

Sitting down again, I started to think through the sequence of events that had led up to this point. I was getting the sense that Latimers' acquisition of Melling Logistics somehow lay behind a lot of it. There seemed to be some sort of issue over the due diligence process, and in particular, there could be flaws in Ashursts' accounting.

Jenna had noticed something odd, and she'd gone missing before she had a chance to pass on her concerns. Cause and effect? It was a melodramatic reading, but it seemed to fit. Meanwhile, I'd been poking around at the Ashurst factory, and now someone had tried to kill me. Hardly a coincidence, surely? If anything, it seemed to support Andrea's worries about Ashursts' accounts.

At the back of all this, someone seemed to be determined that Latimer Logistics' takeover of Mellings should go ahead at all costs – and the most likely suspect was Piers Ashurst.

I should take my concerns to someone in authority – but who should that be? I'd upset both Chris Melling and Bob Latimer, the two people who might be most affected, so I would need a strong case to persuade them to pay any attention to me. All I had to go on so far was suspicions.

I certainly had nothing concrete enough to take to the police, and even if I had, I wouldn't have known where to begin with them. They were already hostile to me, and it would be an uphill struggle to get them on my side.

No, I needed to follow all this up on my own until I'd found enough evidence to present a plausible case.

* * *

I went up to my room again and opened my laptop. The first thing that jumped out at me related to Elizabeth Sanderson's will. It was the picture Jamie Andrews had emailed to me – the one he'd taken at the racecourse. It showed both Philip Crabtree and the man I'd seen in that Yorkshire society magazine at Jenna's flat. Two questions: was Philip a regular race-goer, and who was the man?

I opened the magazine's website and trawled through its editorial archives, trying to find the picture – and hopefully a caption. But apparently the publishers limited the amount of past material that they posted online. This image wasn't there.

I took the easy option. I phoned Dave Matthews, the one policeman I could count on. Unusually he answered first time.

"I'm at home, watching my plumber repairing a leak in my kitchen."

"I'm sorry to hear that."

He gave a dismissive grunt.

"So if I emailed you a photograph, could you find out the identity of the person in it?"

Perhaps I'd caught him on a bad day. For once he seemed reluctant to help. "Mike, I know you don't mean any harm, but you can't keep on constantly asking me favours and expecting me to risk getting into trouble over them. One of these days I'll get a kick up the backside, and after that my boss will be watching me like a hawk. If that happens I won't be able help you with anything."

I was slightly taken aback. For a moment I couldn't think how to reply. I said, "Dave, I'm sorry I take advantage of you, but I'm having a bad time here. My life seems to be falling apart round me."

"What are you on about?"

I took a deep breath, and tried to condense the events of the past few days into a few succinct sentences. He listened without comment, then said, "You should have told me all this in the first place."

"None of it is your problem."

"I'm amazed you didn't contact me when the police took you in. Instead of that, you keep your head down, and now you're just asking me about some photograph."

"What could you have done? The police up here wouldn't have known you, and it could have worked against me. It would have looked like special pleading."

H grunted again. "So what's this photograph? Why do you think we would know this guy?"

"It might be nothing. Call it a hunch."

He sighed. "Bang it over, then."

"He probably lives in Yorkshire or the North East, if that's any help."

"That really narrows it down."

"Oh, and the picture was taken recently at Newcastle racecourse."

*   *   *

I had one other line of enquiry about the bequest. I rang Philip Crabtree's landline, hoping his wife would pick up. She did, but she immediately seemed to wish she hadn't.

"Mike, I'd rather you didn't phone me." She was speaking quickly and in a low voice. "I don't want Phil to find out I've been talking to you."

"Is he there now?"

"Yes, he's in the garden."

"All I wanted was to ask you something."

"He's coming in." There was a note of real panic in her voice. "Look, you could meet me in Hexham tomorrow if you want. I'll be there anyway." She named a café in the town centre. "Eleven o'clock?"

Chapter 38

That evening I phoned Ashley. She answered quickly, and seemed in surprisingly good spirits.

"Michael, how nice to hear from you. What are you up to on this dark and stormy night? And more to the point, *where* are you?"

"You sound very upbeat."

"Second glass of Chardonnay." She gave a self-indulgent laugh. "Or is it the third?"

It sounded to me like the third, but if it meant she was willing to drop the silent treatment I wasn't complaining. I said, "Does this mean you're talking to me?"

"Well obviously I'm talking to you. What does it sound like to you?"

"I'm very pleased to hear it."

"People are telling me various things," she said. "Mostly they're telling me I'm being a stupid cow." I thought I'd better not respond to this, and after a moment she added with irony, "This is the Mike Stanhope fan club, you understand." Another pause. "So tell me, Mike, is that what you think? Am I being stupid?"

"Of course not."

"Of course not." She cleared her throat. "Well, you have say that, I suppose. But it's probably what you think."

"I think I'm an idiot, if you want to know. But I'm not a bad person."

"I know you're not."

For a moment I said nothing. I was rejoicing inwardly, but I was also nervous. She sounded as if she was ready to move on, which I'd been waiting to hear for what seemed like weeks, but what I was about to tell her could take us straight back to square one.

I said, "I'm glad I phoned."

"So am I. For some strange reason I seem to miss you."

"Likewise."

Another pause, then she said, "So where are you? What have you been up to? The last I heard, you were in London at John and Joanna's."

I wandered over to the bedroom window and glanced out. Car headlights flickered at me from the A69. Telling my story to a hostile Ashley would almost have been easier than this. I couldn't think where to start.

"I'm back in Newcastle."

"Oh." A different tone. "I thought Bob Latimer wanted you to stay away from Mellings. Has he changed his mind?"

"No, I came here of my own accord. I haven't been to Mellings."

"What are you doing there, then?"

I thought carefully. "Basically I got it into my head that there was something weird going on with the due diligence process over Mellings. I thought if I could track down what was happening, I might be able to rebuild my good faith with Latimers."

"But god, Mike, what do you know about due diligence? Where would you even start?"

"I don't know anything about it. At least I thought I didn't. I'm letting other people do the digging for me."

"How do you mean?"

There was no way round this. Wincing inwardly, I said, "Jenna Melling contacted me. She said she'd found out something weird about Ashursts – the spiralizer people. She was going to explain it to me."

"Jenna." Her tone spoke volumes.

"Yes, she phoned me, and I arranged to meet her. And before you say anything, it was purely to talk about this, not for any other reason. But she never turned up."

"What a shame."

"Don't say that. It's quite weird. I went to her flat … "

"You went to her *flat*?"

"To talk. That's why I came to Newcastle in the first place."

"Oh, great."

"Look." I sat down on the bed. "I'm telling you this because I want you to know about it. I wouldn't even have brought it up if there was something furtive about it. I arranged to meet Jenna to find out what she wanted to tell me."

"Couldn't she have told you on the phone? You had to go all that way to talk to her in person?"

"Obviously she thought not."

"It's not obvious to me."

"Well, there you go. Anyway, I went to her flat, and she wasn't there. No show. And now the police are looking for her. She's a missing person."

For a moment she said nothing, then in a different tone, "How bizarre."

I swung my feet up on the bed and leaned on the headboard.

"You can say that again. The police hauled me in and questioned me about it this morning – because I was there on the night she disappeared."

"My god, Mike, that's horrible. And they still don't know what happened to her?"

"Nope."

"What do *you* think?"

"I have absolutely no idea."

Another pause, then Ashley said, "You shouldn't have arranged to meet her like that. Sometimes you're a fool to yourself, Mike." She sounded reflective rather than reproachful, but I wasn't off the hook yet. "Maybe you should come back to Cornwall. If you stay up there in the north you might just make things worse."

"Ah, well I have to stay here for the rest of the week now. I've agreed to do an interview for the magazine, and the people I have to see aren't available until Friday."

"Oh. OK."

"Does that mean you'd like me to come back?"

I shouldn't have asked that. She said, "You'll come when the time is right."

* * *

I lay on my bed, running through the losses and gains in the conversation I'd just had with Ashley. Then the phone buzzed in my hand.

"Mike, it's Dave. Were you having a laugh with that photograph you sent me?"

"What do you mean?"

"Well, the man in it is Ernest Bladen. That's B-L-A-D-E-N, not as in the Blaydon Races. Have you really never heard of him?"

I gave him a grudging, "No." The Blaydon Races were celebrated in a Geordie song of the same name: a coincidental irrelevance in the present circumstances. I said, "Who is he?"

"Ernie Bladen is the head of Bladen Building Supplies, among other things. I knew him straight away. I thought you would have recognised him yourself."

"Why would I?"

He chuckled ironically. "You're a strange one for a journalist. Don't you ever read the papers?"

I sighed. "Evidently not. So go on."

"He's a business magnate and racehorse owner. He's been in and out of the press for years. But he's really a ne'er -do-well made good. He used to have gangland connections – made his money from loan sharking, protection scams, that kind of thing – but he was never actually prosecuted for anything. He's too clever by half. He was notorious for never doing business with anybody unless he had some kind of leverage over them, so no one would ever testify against him. Now he runs a legitimate business empire. Part of it is a chain of hardware stores. And he married that actress – much younger than him – and then they divorced. That got him a load of coverage in the tabloids." He laughed ironically. "You obviously read the wrong kind of newspaper."

"So it would seem."

"How come you're interested in him? He's a nasty bit of work. You would be very well advised not to tangle with him. Not that you ever seem to take any notice of what I tell you."

"I appreciate the heads-up." I thought for a moment. "I don't actually know if he's involved in anything. He might not be. It's just a suspicion I have."

"Huh. I know about your suspicions."

"Look, since you've told me all this as a freebie, am I still in credit for a favour?"

He gave an ironic laugh. "What? You're never in credit, Stanhope. You're in my debt to your dying day."

"I just wondered if you could come up with an address for this man."

"He lives somewhere in the Newcastle area. You'll probably find him in the local directory."

"Just in case I don't … "

"Yeah, yeah. If I get the chance I'll call you tomorrow."

Chapter 39

The café in Hexham looked appropriate for afternoon teas: chintzy tablecloths, tea from china teapots. The target market appeared to be tourists. However, when I walked in the following morning it seemed to be patronised mostly by women with shopping baskets or baby buggies – in some cases both.

I looked around for Angela Crabtree. She was alone at a small table in the corner, sitting upright and facing outwards watchfully. She smiled briefly when she saw me. I sat down and asked her, "Aren't you worried that your husband might walk in here any minute?"

She shook her head dismissively. "You'll never see Philip wandering around in town. It's not his thing. He has much more important affairs to attend to. I doubt if he's ever even set foot in the square."

I couldn't decide whether she was speaking in ironic fondness, dislike or fear. I said, "But it's such a charming place."

"That's why we moved here. But he's always too busy to enjoy it."

A waitress came over and I ordered coffee. Angela said, "Did you have a chance to think any more about my suggestion? Splitting Elizabeth's bequest in half, I mean."

"I'm sorry, not really. I see where you're coming from, but I need to take proper advice, and I've been tied up ever since we spoke."

"Can't you just make your own mind up? I mean, dividing it would be fair, wouldn't it?"

I looked carefully at her. Her attractive features were drawn, and I fancied I could see a hint of bruising around one eye. Had Philip been hitting her? I couldn't be sure.

I said, "It'll be my decision in the end, but I don't want to rush into anything."

She nodded solemnly. "I'm sure you'll come to the right decision for everybody."

I said, "I was surprised to hear that Philip had retracted his claim on the estate. It seems to contradict what you're saying."

She shook her head. "He hasn't really retracted it. That's why I didn't know about it before. He's just told the executors he might have to. His solicitor has told him it could cost us a lot of money to pursue it in the courts, and if we lose, we'll have to pay the fees. We simply couldn't afford it." She gave me a pleading look. "That's why I thought a settlement between us would be the answer."

"Well I appreciate your frankness."

Suddenly there were tears in her eyes. "That legacy seemed like a lifeline to us. Then we suddenly found Elizabeth had cut Philip out of the will. It came as quite a shock."

"You have debts, then?"

She nodded.

Thinking about the photograph of Philip that Jamie Andrews had taken at the racecourse, I said, "Is Philip a gambler?"

She placed her hands on the table and tensed her arms, as if about to push herself away from this very notion. However, she merely said, "He likes an occasional flutter."

"So he has gambling debts."

She nodded fractionally, saying nothing, then she sat forward. "I'll be honest with you, Mike, we originally expected the house would be left to Maggie. Then Elizabeth changed her mind and told us she was leaving it to us. It probably doesn't speak well of us, but we were so relieved. We needed the money much more than she did."

"Maggie?"

"Philip's sister. She lives in Consett."

"I didn't know he had a sister."

She gave me a troubled look. "Maggie was wayward. She fell out with Philip before I knew him, and they haven't spoken for years. Elizabeth used to like her, and tried to help her, but she wouldn't be helped. Eventually I think Elizabeth lost patience with her. She could be quite a prickly lady."

"Why do you say Maggie needed the money?"

"She's had a hard life. She got in with the wrong crowd when she was in her teens – drugs, petty theft, that kind of thing. Now she's a single mother with a handicapped son." She looked close to tears again. "I know I probably sound hard-hearted, wanting to have the money for ourselves, but my own family comes first."

I moved the conversation on to my connection with Elizabeth Sanderson. "I'm still trying to understand why she named me in her will."

"You really never knew her then? And no one in your family knew her either?"

"Not that I know of. My parents died years ago, so I can't ask them."

"Well, she never mentioned anything about you to us, so I can't help you there. I asked Phil again about that."

Finally I came round to the question that had prompted me to contact Angela in the first place. "Elizabeth never married, did she? So was Sanderson the family name of her parents?"

"Funny that you should ask that. You're right that she never married, but Sanderson wasn't her original surname. She changed it when she was young. I don't know why." She smiled faintly. "It always seems a strange thing to do, but people have their reasons, I suppose."

"What was her real surname?"

She frowned as she thought. "Roberts. I'm pretty sure that's what it was. Elizabeth Roberts."

* * *

Angela said she had to leave to do some shopping. "If I stay here too long Phil will wonder what I've been up to."

I watched her thread her way past the tables to the door – a nervous but determined woman who seemed to be doing more in her quiet way to hold her family together than her belligerent husband.

I ordered a second coffee and sat watching other customers come and go, not really seeing them. My mind was elsewhere. Chiefly I was trying to make sense of what Angela had just told me about Elizabeth's original family name. Roberts was the surname of the bus driver in that photograph from Chris Melling's film: Len Roberts. And in the late 1940s my grandmother Emily, or someone who looked remarkably like her, had known Len Roberts. They'd been caught on camera in that unguarded moment, standing arm in arm in Northumberland Street, Newcastle.

So the Len Roberts in the picture, who apparently once knew my grandmother, could also be Len Roberts, the father of Elizabeth Sanderson. It was too much of a coincidence not to be true. This had to be my connection with her. But how? That was something I still didn't understand.

I thought back to what I'd learned from Adele, my grandmother's friend in Wokingham. She'd said my grandmother once used to talk of a man who had been the love of her life. Could that man have been Len Roberts?

I had no real evidence for it, but it seemed to fit. And if Len wasn't Elizabeth's father, some other member of his family must have been. It was something I could easily check.

So what did this mean? Well, although Len had apparently once known my grandmother, and perhaps had been in some sort of relationship with her, it couldn't have come to anything because my grandmother had moved away from the North East and never returned. Len had then presumably married someone else, and the connection had been broken.

However, if Elizabeth was indeed his daughter, perhaps she had somehow known about my grandmother, who would probably have seemed a mysterious woman from his past. Maybe he'd even reminisced about her. But why did this matter so much to Elizabeth? Why had her interest been so strong, in fact, that she'd ended up bequeathing her worldly wealth to me?

Chapter 40

I walked out of the café into a light drizzle, but the sun broke through the clouds as I made my way across the small town to my car, and there was a summer sultriness in the air. On the main road towards my motel the wet road surface gleamed. It felt good to be out and about.

The idea of returning to the motel depressed me. Although I knew I could probably do some useful internet trawling, I was coming to hate spending time there. The impermanence seemed to reflect the uncertain status of so much about my current life. At least out here on the road I felt more of a sense of normality.

On a whim, I drove on past the motel and turned off in the direction of the industrial estate where Melling Logistics was based. I'd been thinking I should take my concerns about Ashursts to someone in authority, but Bob Latimer seemed somehow out of reach. Chris Melling, on the other hand, could prove more approachable. I might not have learned much more than when I'd last considered talking to him, but I felt it could do no harm.

However, as I drove into Mellings' car park it dawned on me that Chris must be preoccupied with Jenna's disappearance, which presumably would take precedence over any concerns he might have over the Latimer acquisition. And if he knew the police had interviewed me about it, he might well not give me a particularly warm welcome. Coming here had been a stupid mistake.

It was too late. As I glanced over at the glass doors leading into the reception area I saw Chris Melling himself standing just inside, staring out towards my car. If I retreated now it would look bizarre, not to say suspicious. I had no choice but to go over and present myself.

"Mike," he greeted me as I pushed open the door. "What a surprise to see you here. I thought you were down in Cornwall." He didn't offer to shake my hand, but he didn't seem hostile either – just reserved. Presumably he didn't know I'd arranged to meet Jenna at her flat the night she disappeared.

I said, "I was in the area anyway, on another errand. I thought I would drop in."

"D'you want to have a seat?" He led me over to a cluster of black visitors' easy chairs. This was a coded message; it said he was willing to speak to me, but not to give me the privileges of entry to the inner sanctum. My status here had been downgraded.

He frowned as we sat down. "I don't know if you've heard, but my daughter Jenna has gone missing. The police are looking into it."

"Yes, I did pick that up. And no news yet?"

"Not so far. But it could be a storm in a teacup. Jenna is an impulsive person. She may have gone off of her own accord. I wouldn't put it past her."

"Let's hope so."

He gave me an assessing look. "So did you have a reason for dropping in on us, Mike? I assume you're not here on behalf of Bob Latimer."

"No, not at all." I smiled awkwardly. "I'm still trying to recover from the fallout over that article." He said nothing, so I added, "It was extremely ill judged. I should have known better."

"I won't argue with you on that."

I waited a moment, then said, "Actually I was hoping to sound you out about Ashurst Concepts. I know they've been given the green light in the due diligence process, but Andrea Smith at Latimers felt there were some inconsistencies in Ashursts' accounts. Had you picked up anything like that, by any chance?"

He gave me a strange look. "Inconsistencies? No, I wasn't aware of anything like that. And if you'll forgive my asking, Mike, with the best will in the world, what business is it of yours? You're not an accountant, are you? If Andrea had any real concerns, she would have voiced them herself. You're not even working on Latimers' behalf now, as far as I know. In a minute you're going to tell me you're writing another exposé for that logistics rag."

"God, no. No way. I'm just … I'm speaking as a concerned bystander, I suppose."

With a penetrating smile that was almost a glare, he said, "Are you trying to derail the Latimer acquisition, Mike?"

"No, of course not. Why would I want to do that? Anyway, I thought it had all gone through."

"All bar the shouting. We're just waiting to finalise things. So it's not a good time to be upsetting the applecart, is it?"

"No, I can see that."

He stood up. "Take my advice, Mike, and keep your head down. It's not going to help your career if you start rocking the boat, and it's certainly not going to help any of us here. I've got enough on my plate with Jenna going missing. I don't need any more headaches at the moment."

I stood up myself. Clearly I was dismissed. I said, "Please believe me when I say I'm only trying to be helpful. And I'm sure Jenna will turn up soon."

"I hope so."

Back in my car, I glanced over to the reception area. Chris had now disappeared inside. Had he just threatened me over my position with Latimers? That's what it had sounded like. If so, this wasn't the benign Chris Melling I thought I knew. Then again, perhaps it was no more than a logical reaction. His daughter had gone missing, and he was about to tie up what was probably the biggest deal of his career. He didn't need some ill-informed part-time journalist interfering.

As I was driving away through the industrial estate, Dave Matthews phoned me from London. I pulled in to the side of the road.

"I've got an address for Ernie Bladen," he told me, and read it out. "It's a place somewhere north of Newcastle. It used to be a mining village, but it's gone seriously up-market. It was in the press when he moved there. He said he was returning to his roots, something like that, but you'd have to be very gullible to see it that way."

I thanked him. He said, "He also has a cottage in the Yorkshire Dales, but I don't think he spends so much time there."

"OK, great."

"Enough favours for now?"

"Point taken."

I launched the navigation system on my phone to find the village. It was some miles from where I was now – to the north of Newcastle, whereas I was to the west. But the roads in this area were remarkably good. Why not go there now? It was another excuse to avoid that motel.

Chapter 41

Ernie Bladen's village exactly matched Dave's description. To reach it I had to drive several miles north on the main A1, then strike off east towards the coast. The older part of the village was made up of unremarkable inter-war semi-detached houses, part pebble-dashed in a style that was clearly impossible to keep smart. Ernie Bladen, however, lived at the far end of a new housing development. All the properties here were impressively lavish, but his was bordering on the palatial – a modern multi-wing mansion behind a high brick wall, with wrought iron gates across the entrance.

I pulled up fifty metres short of the gateway. I could make out three vehicles in the drive – a new-looking Rolls-Royce, a scruffy Transit van and a small white service van. Now I had to work out my objective. Did I want to meet the man himself? Hardly. He might well figure somewhere in recent events, but I had no idea yet how. Really I just wanted to get a better feel for the man and his lifestyle – and that objective had now been achieved.

I was about to start my car and drive away when a shadow loomed at my side window. I reached for the central locking button, but before I got to it the driver's door was snatched open and a man in a dark suit leaned down.

"Were you looking for Mr Bladen?" A strong Geordie accent.

I could see pinstripe trousers and a white open-neck shirt. The sudden intrusion seemed at odds with his businesslike appearance. I stared at him, my pulse suddenly racing. "No, I think I got lost. I was just leaving."

"You're all right. Mr Bladen's house is just over there." The words themselves might have been anodyne, but there was more than a hint of menace behind them.

"Fine. Well I'll know where he lives if I ever want to visit him."

"Now would be a good time."

I looked up sharply, hoping to banish this unmistakable threat. It didn't work. He simply stared implacably at me.

I didn't know what to do. He still had his hand on the door, so to escape I would have needed to snatch it away from him, then start the engine and drive away before he could prevent me. The car was facing the wrong way into a *cul de sac*, so the likelihood of turning round without being thwarted seemed remote. I was debating whether to attempt it anyway when I sensed jeans and a leather jacket at the front passenger window. I felt surrounded.

"When you're ready," the first man said. So I climbed cautiously out of the car and accompanied the two of them over to Bladen's house.

We came to a halt in an expansive tiled hallway, and the suited man said, "Give me your wallet." There seemed little point in arguing with this affront. I handed it over without speaking and he rifled quickly through it, pulling out one of my business cards. "Wait here." He handed the wallet back to me.

He disappeared into one of the rooms, then returned a few moments later. "This way." He led me into a wide lounge overlooking a large formal lawn. I vaguely took in a mismatch of modern furniture and Chinese rugs.

Ernie Bladen was standing in the middle of this, holding a mobile phone at arm's length and frowning down at the screen. My business card was in his other hand. He was shorter and stockier than I'd imagined from his photographs, and was wearing a white open-neck shirt, blue jeans and brown business shoes. He gave an impatient sigh, clicked the phone off and put it in his jeans pocket. He looked up at me for the first time.

"I don't like people nosing around my house without being invited." His Geordie accent was even stronger than his colleague's. "What do you think you're doing?"

I shrugged, hoping I looked suitably puzzled. "I took a wrong turn. I don't understand what's happening here."

"Don't treat me like an idiot. You're Michael Stanhope. You're a journalist." He glanced down at the business card, then tossed it contemptuously on a coffee table. "Are you looking for a scoop? You won't get one. Plenty of people have tried. I'm fed up with telling them they're wasting their time."

I had to think carefully what to say. I stared at him for a moment, wondering if he would add anything else. He simply glared back. Then I had a flash of inspiration.

"I wondered if you were an investor in Ashurst Concepts in Leeds?"

I sensed a suppressed double take, though if it was there it was very subtle. After a moment he said, "What business is that of yours?"

"It's just part of some research I'm doing."

"I have no comment on that or anything else. You have no right to come here bothering me about it. If you have any questions you should talk to our press office. You know the drill. This is completely out of order."

At that moment the other man I'd seen at my car appeared from beyond Bladen, perhaps from an adjacent room. He approached Bladen and muttered something to him. Bladen frowned at him. "I told you – don't let her soft-soap you. How many times to I have to say it? Jesus!"

The man muttered something else, and Bladen said, "Soon. Do you think you can manage that?"

The man retreated sullenly and Bladen turned to me again. I thought I might catch him in a moment of complicit man-to-man indignation – something on the lines of "You just can't get the staff these days" – but he wasn't having any of it. He merely resumed glowering at me.

I said, "So it's true then?"

"What is?" Suddenly he was alert. I had the impression that he thought I was talking about his exchange with the other man.

"That you invested in Ashurst Concepts."

"Oh." I could almost hear his thoughts racing as he stared at me, assessing. Finally he seemed to reach a conclusion. "I've already told you – read my lips. I don't do interviews. I don't answer questions."

"But you're not denying it?"

He cocked his head slightly to one side and gave me a "You must be joking" look.

I thought I'd try one more idea. I said, "Jenna Melling."

Was that another suppressed double take? He was hard to read, but I felt there was a tell in his eyes. However, he merely said, "What?"

I repeated, "Jenna Melling."

He stared at me for a moment, then said, "Have you lost the power of speech, mate?" He stared for a moment longer, then looked past me and shouted, "Harry!"

The man in the suit came into the room quickly. Bladen said, "Our guest is leaving. Make sure he understands that he isn't coming back." He turned to me. "Stay out of my affairs. I won't say it again."

Was it as easy as that? As the man led me out into the hall I felt a surge of relief. It was short-lived. With a deft movement he side-stepped towards me, tripping me over. I sprawled on the tiles in the middle of the hall, and before I could recover he kicked me hard, then again, and again, and again. The first blow caught me in the ribs, the second on my arm, the third and fourth on my shoulder. I curled up, cradling my head with my hands and shouting in pain and protest.

Was there more to come? I risked a glance up. He was standing by impassively. "Whoops," he said.

"What the hell was all that about?"

He raised his arms innocently. "Don't know what you mean. You weren't here. I never met you. And as Mr Bladen mentioned, you won't be coming back. Are we clear?"

He opened the front door as I struggled unsteadily to my feet, and thrust me out into the gravelled driveway and towards the gate. We passed the white service van, whose blue signwriting proclaimed "Bladen Building Supplies". Out of habit I glanced at the tiny strip of legal lettering painted low down on the left-hand side. It read "Melling Logistics (Contracts) Ltd".

Chapter 42

I drove painfully back to the motel, trembling the whole way. My shoulder was smarting and my ribs ached, but I had a feeling there was no long-term damage, except to my pride and my peace of mind. I'd only ever once before been subjected to calculated violence like this – if you discounted the attack on that bridge. It was humiliating, and just as last time I'd been left completely unnerved.

My instinct was to go to the police, but I couldn't decide it if was worth it. Presumably Bladen and his cohorts would simply deny that the incident had taken place. Basically they'd warned me off, and unless I had the strength of mind to ignore it, the warning would work.

But warned me off what? The violence they'd meted out might be the way they dealt with all unwelcome visitors, but I had a feeling that I'd inadvertently barged my way into something they were determined to keep hidden.

Back at the motel I ran myself a deep bath. This was one thing hotels and motels were good at. Lying there, I felt the pain from my bruises dissipating as I tried to reason through what had just happened.

The first conclusion I reached was that Bladen and his people couldn't have been responsible for the attack on the bridge. Although I was grasping for connections wherever I could find them, I could see none here. The two men on the bridge had apparently wanted to kill me: end of subject. Bladen had merely wanted to persuade me to back off. Quite a different mindset.

The next point I considered was the fact that the white van in Bladen's driveway belonged to Melling Logistics. Presumably Mellings provided services to Bladen's company – perhaps distributed his product around the country, or at least supplied vehicles. I hadn't been aware of anyone at Mellings mentioning the name, but I was all too aware that I sometimes suffered blind spots. This could be one of them.

This strongly suggested that Chris Melling must be personally acquainted with Ernie Bladen. I didn't know what significance this had, but it seemed important.

My last, and most revealing, discovery came half an hour later, when I was checking my emails. My phone bleeped to announce an incoming text – an unnecessary transaction update from my bank. As I clicked the Back button I noticed an unread text dating back several days. It was from Jenna Melling.

For a moment I thought it was a repeat of a text I'd already seen, but no, it was new to me. I sat up straight and scanned the message urgently. It had been sent on the evening she'd disappeared, and somehow I'd missed it. "If you want some homework to keep you busy before you come over, look up BBS. I think Piers is in trouble, and their boss is keeping him afloat."

BBS could mean Bladen Building Supplies – and this was a name I did recognise from Mellings.

* * *

I was out of my depth. I decided I had no option but to pass on my thoughts to the police. They might still treat me with suspicion, but I had a feeling they wouldn't recognise the possible Bladen connection unless I pointed it out to them.

I checked my watch. It was nearly five o'clock: not too late to drive into Newcastle if I had to. I phoned the number for the police station where I'd been taken, and asked for the detective who had led my interview. I was told he was out, but I might catch him on his return if I went straight over there. So I walked stiffly to my car and drove off to do battle with Newcastle's rush hour.

The detective I wanted still wasn't there when I arrived, and I was referred to a younger man who wasn't involved directly in Jenna's case. He took me to a small interview room and listened as I tried to explain my thoughts. But the complexities of Melling Logistics and its acquisition of Ashurst Concepts seemed to baffle him, and he kept trying to bring me back to the practicalities of her disappearance.

"You say Mr Bladen might have invested in this company in Leeds, but he was upset when Jenna Melling found out about it. And he was so determined to stop her sharing this information that he decided to abduct her from her flat in Jesmond. What evidence do you have for that? I don't quite see why you're putting Mr Bladen in the frame at all."

I showed him Jenna's text message on my mobile phone. He was sceptical. "This is scarcely evidence of anything."

I shrugged. "I'm just trying to offer you a potential lead. I might be wrong, but surely it would be mistake to discount it?"

He jotted a some brief notes on a sheet of paper, clearly unconvinced, then looked up at me. "Ernie Bladen is a leading figure in the local economy here. Are you suggesting he would go round to Jenna Melling's flat and drag her out of it against her will?"

"Not him personally. He has his people. He would know how to organise something like that if he wanted to. I understand he has a history."

He shook his head. "Before my time, but you're right about that. All the same … "

I told him about my visit to Ernie Bladen's house that afternoon, and the beating I'd been given. His eyes narrowed at this. "Going there was unwise," he said.

"But surely it proves he has something to hide?"

"Not really. He's had a lot of trouble with press harassment over the years. He's probably ultra-sensitive. If you go hanging around outside his gate, it's a red rag to a bull. I'm not saying we ever condone violence, but the press have a habit of antagonising public figures. You should know that, considering your job. You shouldn't be surprised if these people sometimes hit back."

"I was on a public road. I had a perfect right to be there."

He gave me a cynical smile. "Some rights are difficult to enforce."

He asked me if I wanted to press charges against Bladen and his right-hand man. I said, "There's no point, is there? I have no evidence. They would just deny it."

"Probably."

"So are you going to follow this up?"

"I'll talk to my colleagues in the morning."

I had a strong suspicion that this meant no.

Chapter 43

I had no phone number for Andrea Smith. I'd never expected I would want to contact her. However, I had one for Jamie Andrews, and I rang it from my room that evening. He'd returned from the North East to Cornwall, and was with her when he took the call. He passed the phone over to her.

"Mike, this is a surprise."

"Listen, I can't explain the whole story now, but I was hoping you could tell me a bit more about those inconsistent accounts that you dug up at Ashursts."

"Oh. OK. Well, a girl in their accounts department accidentally emailed me some incorrect figures. Or that's what she told me afterwards. They made it look as if Ashursts were barely breaking even. The implication was that they'd had to cut the unit price of some of their lines because of over-supply. Their cash reserves were at rock bottom."

"Do you still have the figures she sent?"

"No, I deleted them when she sent me the official figures."

"Oh."

Sounding defensive, she said, "I don't like untidiness." A pause. "I realise you probably think that sounds stupid. I should have kept them. But I tried to remember them."

"So how could her figures be so out of line with the official ones?"

"I don't know. Either they were complete fiction, or someone senior in Ashursts' accounts department faked the official figures, and it was those that were fiction."

"But no one at Mellings questioned them?"

"Not that I could see."

"Will that change when Latimers' takeover of Mellings goes through?"

"Well, we'll have full authority to examine their accounts properly. If there's anything untoward, it should come out."

"And if it turns out that Ashursts is a basket case?"

"I don't know really. A lot of questions will be asked, that's for sure. There could be accusations of fraud."

"And Piers Ashurst couldn't duck out of that."

"I don't see how."

I asked, "What actually happens when a deal like this goes through? Who gets paid what?"

"I've never been involved in a corporate takeover, but as far as I know, the money is transferred, just as if you'd sold your house. But in this case there's an added element. Part of the payment by Mellings for their stake in Ashursts was deferred, pending the takeover."

"Is that usual?"

"I don't think so, but it's probably not unknown."

"What does it mean in practice?"

"Well, there's a cascade. Latimers pay the acquisition fee to Mellings, and Mellings pay what they owe to Ashursts."

"And if Piers Ashurst had debts, he could pay his share on to his creditors."

"I suppose so. Obviously if it emerged that there was fraud involved, a lot of questions would be asked, but it could take ages for everything to be unpicked. Some payments might be impossible to recover – say if Piers used the money to pay off private loans, that kind of thing."

I said nothing, and she asked, "*Is* there some kind of fraud going on? Is that why you're raising all this?"

"That's what I'm wondering." I tried to think what else to ask her. "Who actually runs the Ashurst accounts department?"

"There's a finance director, but apparently he's a bit of an air-head – Piers Ashurst's uncle or something. The real work is done by a part-time consultant who dips in and out. I forget his name …" She broke off as she searched her memory banks. "I think it might be Nick somebody. I could probably find out."

"You're pretty well informed."

"I like to keep my ear to the ground."

There was an awkward pause. It probably dawned on us both at the same time that her propensity to interfere had led her to jump to wrong conclusions about me and Jenna. Forcing a laugh, she said, "Sometimes it gets me into trouble."

"I wouldn't worry about it."

There was one other thing to ask. "Do you know if a man called Ernie Bladen has any involvement with Ashursts?"

"You mean the head of BBS? Mellings' logistics client?"

"That's the man."

"Right. Well I don't know of any actual financial involvement with Ashursts, but I think he was an advisor to Piers Ashurst when he was building up his business. It was mentioned in an article I read in the finance press. In fact I think Chris Melling originally introduced them."

"That's interesting."

She said, "Look, I've been wondering about going to Bob Latimer to tell him about all this, but I couldn't decide if there was enough in it to make a fuss. I don't really have much to go on." Tentatively she added, "What do *you* think?"

Clearly it had taken her some effort to ask me for advice. I said, "I agree that there's something strange going on, but we don't have all the details yet. Maybe we could compare notes in a day or two. Once we've got a proper story, I definitely think he should know."

"All right, I'll be guided by you."

"Just one other thing. Jamie said the due diligence checks on Ashursts were done by a local firm in Leeds. Do you know the name of that firm?"

"No, but I might be able to find out."

* * *

I disconnected and phoned Ashley again. "Guess who my new best friend is. Andrea Smith. I've got her eating out of my hand."

Ashley chuckled – a warm, confiding tone that I hadn't heard in a long time. She said, "I saw her this morning, but she didn't have a lot to say for herself. I think she's embarrassed to speak to me."

"And guess why that is?"

"I know – she's having second thoughts about what she told me."

"Not just second thoughts, she's realised she was completely wrong. You should ask her about it."

"Perhaps it's best not to rake it all up again."

"But I want you to know the truth."

"I think I'm getting a sense of it."

I felt I'd better not push my luck too far, and said nothing. She said, "Still no sign of Jenna Melling, then?"

"Not as far as I've heard."

"But the police haven't bothered you any more about it?"

"Not so far. I'm hoping they've realised I'm not involved."

I felt a stab of pain from my bruised shoulder. I was on the point of telling her about the beating at Ernie Bladen's house, but I resisted at the last moment. It would feel like special pleading.

There was a pause, then she said, "I was thinking I might make a trip to the north again."

"That would be brilliant!"

"Only as far as Tina's in Doncaster. It seems ages since I last saw her."

It wasn't really ages – only a few months. I sensed an olive branch somewhere here. I said, "I suppose I could meet up with you while you're there … if you'd like me to."

"Well, it might be the only way we'll ever see each other again. You seem to be taking up residence in Newcastle."

Under the circumstances this represented massive progress in our relationship, but I was wary of pushing too hard. I said, "Let me know what you decide." I thought some more. "I've got an appointment in Sunderland on Friday morning, but I could head on down to Leeds from there." Then, despite my resolve, I heard myself saying, "If I've got everything tied up here in the north, I could even come back with you to Cornwall."

"Well, one thing at a time. Let's see how it goes."

Chapter 44

I'd never conducted a stake-out before, or imagined in my wildest dreams that I would want to. I'd seen them in films, read about them in books, but had no idea how they worked in practice.

Today was the day I was going to find out.

I rose early, skipped breakfast, bought some snacks, chocolate and bottled water at the local convenience store, packed my heavy outer jacket, and checked that my phone was fully charged. By seven thirty I was on my way.

I'd managed to convince myself that Ernie Bladen was involved in Jenna's disappearance. My evidence was painfully thin, but that was partly why I was doing this. I was sure the police would take no useful action to follow up my suspicions, so I felt the responsibility lay on my own shoulders. And I had nothing else to occupy my time.

My thinking was that if Bladen really had abducted Jenna, he wouldn't be foolish enough to keep her incarcerated in his own house. Someone might hear her or accidentally discover her, and she might encounter him while she was there. No, he would hide her somewhere else, and my hope was that one of his staff might lead me to her. It was a lot of assumptions to make, but I had the time to test them out, and nothing to lose.

I was still thinking of her disappearance in terms of abduction, not murder. I had to persuade myself of this. But quite *why* Bladen would have abducted Jenna, and how long he would keep her captive if he had, were issues I hadn't entirely resolved. Presumably his motivation must be to prevent her from revealing something or doing something: either something relating to Ashursts and what she'd learned there, or something else entirely.

I would have preferred to be in a different car, since Bladen's crew would no doubt recognise my battered brown Nissan from my visit yesterday, but I didn't feel flush enough to pay a car rental fee, and anyway there had been no time to arrange it. Besides, I had no intention of parading myself in front of Bladen's house. I'd realised that since his street was a dead end, anyone venturing out of it would be forced to drive through the minimal village centre. That's where I would station myself.

I parked in a side street next to a blank brick wall – the side of a small grocery shop set in a Victorian terrace on the village's main street. The road leading into Bladen's estate led off a modest village green opposite me.

I waited.

And waited.

Nothing happened. Pedestrians occasionally passed the end of my side street. Cars emerged from Bladen's estate from time to time, but none of them suggested any connection with the man himself. The day was overcast and not particularly warm for a British summer. I shuffled into my jacket, then decided after a while that I was too hot and shuffled out of it again. I listened to the radio. I ate some of the chocolate.

After a couple of hours I felt the stirrings of a call of nature. I'd noticed a public toilet set into an apologetic concrete structure on the corner of the green, so I made my way over to it. To my disappointment the door was padlocked and a very old notice on it read, "Closed until further notice". This was a setback, and my solution was awkward and potentially embarrassing. At least I was able to maintain my vigil.

My phone rang: a mechanical handling magazine, wanting to know if I could write another article about forklift trucks. I gritted my teeth. At least this was a further demonstration that my world hadn't entirely forgotten me. I said yes.

Then at around midday Ernie Bladen's Rolls-Royce emerged from his estate, driven by his assistant. I could just see Ernie himself in the back seat. My heart rate immediately shot up. But what should I do? He wasn't going to lead me obligingly to Jenna, was he? If anyone was likely to do that, it would be one of his minions. Keeping my head low, I watched as his car turned on to the main road and headed off towards the A1.

Time passed slowly. I flipped between music and talk on my car radio. I ate some more of the chocolate. I counted objects within my field of vision that started with the letter A. Then B. Then I got bored with that. I kept reminding myself to stretch and move around to avoid falling asleep.

The sun came out, and almost instantly the car interior was stifling. The chill of the early morning was a distant dream. I opened all the side windows and rolled up my sleeves.

By the time my watch had wound agonisingly round to 2pm I was beginning to lose my resolve. This had to be a monumental waste of time. I glanced over to Bladen's road. Should I forget about waiting here and try to stake out his house on foot? After all, I knew he wasn't around. But he might return, and others might still be there. It seemed too dangerous.

Just as I was debating giving up the project altogether, I spotted a white vehicle approaching me from the estate road. It was the battered Transit van I'd seen parked in Bladen's driveway. I felt a surge of excitement. This could be what I was waiting for. It could be my one chance.

Now I had a new challenge: how do you follow another vehicle without being spotted? As with stake-outs, I'd seen it done many times in films, but I had little idea how it worked in practice.

I watched as the van turned in the opposite direction to the one Bladen had taken. I made myself wait a moment, then started my engine, nosed cautiously out from my refuge and headed after it.

Minutes later I nearly missed a trick. Rounding a bend a couple of miles out of the village, I was just in time to spot the van pulling off to the left and disappearing through a gateway. I continued past it, then slithered to a halt on a muddy verge next to a hedge. I got out and walked a few paces towards the gateway.

Through the hedge I could make out a roughly gravelled car park with a scattering of cars in it, plus the white van. Glancing around, I realised it served a pub a hundred metres back down the road. So had the van driver merely come here for a late lunch? Then I caught sight of a figure in a blue anorak walking across the car park from the direction of the van. A car door slammed and an engine started, then I saw a grey car move across the car park and emerge from the entrance: an old Fiat with a square, boxy body. He'd swapped vehicles.

I tried to shrink into the hedge as he drove past me, and I turned my head away. All the same, if he was looking he couldn't have failed to notice me, standing incongruously on the verge of that country road. I just had to hope he hadn't.

I waited until he rounded the first bend, then ran to my car and set off after him.

Chapter 45

The Fiat was moving slowly, so it wasn't hard to follow. My main challenge was resisting the impulse to surge forward and overtake it. I had to keep reminding myself to hang back. Fortunately there were few turn-offs, so there was no need to keep close.

We continued for some miles along quiet country roads. The landscape around me was fairly flat and unremarkable – pasture and indeterminate crops, divided by hedgerows, fences and occasional stands of trees.

Suddenly I became aware that I could no longer see the car ahead of me. Instantly I broke out in a sweat. What had happened to it? Had I wasted most of my day, only to lose my target through a moment of carelessness? I accelerated to twice my previous speed and lunged forward for a mile or so, flinging my car round the bends.

No Fiat.

I lurched to a stop in a muddy gateway, cursing out loud. What should I do? I hadn't noticed any turn-off since I'd last seen the car, but had I missed one? Or had the other driver accelerated too – perhaps realising he was being followed?

I had to make a decision, and I decided to turn round. It seemed unlikely that he'd speeded up quickly enough to lose me. That meant he must have turned off somewhere further back.

I retraced my journey as swiftly as a dared, worried that I might pass a side road without seeing it. Then after a mile and a half I spotted a small road leading away to the right just before a bend. From the opposite direction it would have been hidden by the acute angle. This had to be the route he'd taken.

It was a single-track road threading between fields, properly surfaced but uneven in places. I drove as fast as I dared, crossing my fingers that

I would still catch up with the Fiat.

I continued for at least a mile, then another mile. Where the hell did this road lead? Then I came to a crossroads. Now where should I go? I had three possible choices. This was a lost cause.

I stared at a wooden signpost indicating unknown villages to the left and right. I might as well give up and go home. More out of sheer doggedness than with any great hope, I pulled off again, choosing the road in front of me.

This soon seemed a bad decision. The hard surface quickly deteriorated, and within a few hundred metres had turned into a cinder track. This plainly wasn't a public road, it was an access to a private property. But there was no space to turn round, so I pressed on, looking for a turning place. I increased my speed.

Rounding a bend, I suddenly came on the Fiat. It had pulled half off the track and into a gateway, and had been out of sight behind bushes. All I could think of was to keep going past it, hoping the driver would pay me no attention. Under the circumstances that seemed unlikely.

The lane continued for another few hundred metres, then opened into a farmyard. I braked to a halt and stared around. Could this be where the driver had been heading? If so, why had he stopped short? I got out of the car and glanced down the track. No Fiat in sight.

I studied the stone-built farmhouse. It had dilapidated, unoccupied feel. A few of the roof slates were missing, and there was a diagonal crack running down one of the upstairs windows. There were no vehicles in sight, and there was no sound. A five-bar gate into a field was collapsing, and the farmyard was empty, apart from tall weeds sprouting everywhere. I glanced along the track again. If the Fiat driver decided to block it, there was no way I could get past him. I was trapped here. Perhaps that had been his plan.

Checking again nervously over my shoulder, I went up to the front door and listened. No sound from the interior. There were cobwebs growing round the doorknob, and ancient leaf mush formed a natural seal across the doorstep. I glanced at the nearest window, which was coated with grime. I could see nothing inside.

I tried the door. Locked. I walked along the frontage and round the corner. More grimy windows; another locked door. I kept listening for the other car and glancing over my shoulder. No sound; no one in pursuit.

At the back I found a further door, also locked, but the small window next to it had a crack in it, and there was a small hole where part of the glass was missing. Bracing myself, I hit the pane with my elbow. More shards of glass broke away and fell inside. I reached in cautiously and groped for a door key.

There wasn't one.

Now what? The window was too small to crawl through even if I knocked all the glass out of it. In any case, by delving into the house I would be putting myself even more at risk than I was already. Instead, I made my way along the house to the far corner, and cautiously peered round it.

Which is when everything went black.

* * *

A woman's voice was speaking to me in a Geordie accent. I opened my eyes. The space around me was dimly lit. I made out a small window in a corner. Shapes swam in my peripheral vision. My head hurt.

"You stupid bugger! Where the hell did you come from?" It was Jenna Melling, speaking with a mix of warmth, bravado and disbelief.

I was lying on an uneven flagstone floor, and she was bending anxiously over me. I struggled to sit up. My head hurt more.

"What happened?"

"They dragged you in here. I thought you were dead at first, but then I realised you were breathing. I've been waiting for you to wake up." I could now see the concern on her face. "Are you all right?"

I winced. "I suppose so. Someone hit me over the head. Jesus!" I pushed myself back until I was leaning against a wall. "I feel as if they cracked my skull."

"You should get it checked."

I said, "Some hope while I'm in here." I shut my eyes as I fought against the throbbing in my head, then opened them again. "How long have I been here?"

She shrugged. "Twenty minutes? Maybe half an hour. I haven't been checking." Her voice softened. "I couldn't believe it when I saw it was you. Did you come looking for me?"

I nodded. "I was hoping – " I cleared my throat – "I was hoping I might find you here."

"Well I *am* here, but now you're in here as well."

As full consciousness flowed back I looked at Jenna more carefully. She was wearing a pale skirt and a dark top, as if ready for a social occasion. Even in the subdued light I could see that her skirt was dirty and scuffed. She straightened and sat down sideways on a rustic wooden chair next to a small table. She leaned round towards me with her arm on the back, silhouetted against the light from the corner window.

"Where is 'here'?" she said. "They won't tell me."

"It's a farmhouse in the middle of nowhere. I followed one of Ernie Bladen's men here."

"My hero," she said in her strongest Geordie accent. "Except that you're supposed to get me out, not get yourself in."

"Sorry. I should have been more careful." I sat up straighter. "I can't believe I've actually found you. It seemed such a long shot."

She gave an ironic laugh. "At least I've got someone to talk to now. It's been quite lonely here." She managed to give those simple words great weight.

"Nobody actually lives here, then?"

"I very much doubt it. A study in silence, this place. They turn up once or twice a day to check on me, that's all. I hear their car arriving."

For a moment I couldn't think of anything to say. I cleared my throat again, then asked, "So you've been here all this time?"

She seemed to revive. "Yeah. It seems like weeks. The bastards!" She pronounced it "*bass*tards", and spoke it with ferocity.

"I don't know how you've kept your sanity."

"It's the gourmet meals they serve us twice a day. You'll love them."

"Glad to hear it."

"Do you think you can get up?"

I managed to struggle to my feet, and sat down on a second chair next to the table. "What is this place?"

"It's some kind of storage room. There's just one window, and it's barred. Probably to keep thieving bastards out, but it works the other way too. Solid walls. And that door is three feet thick. But there's an ensuite loo." She pointed to another, smaller door. "All mod cons."

"I would have gone mad if it had been me."

"I nearly did. I bawled my head off for two days – much good that it did me. And I screamed loudly enough to bring the roof down ... but it didn't work." She laughed humourlessly. "Nobody heard."

"But they haven't ... attacked you, or molested you, or anything like that?"

"No, thank god. The guy who comes here never has anything to say for himself. I don't even see his face. He makes me look away."

"Well, that's something."

"Be thankful for small mercies, eh? It doesn't feel much like that from where I'm sitting.

I smiled at her suddenly. "I'm so pleased that you're alive and well."

"Huh! I'm quite pleased about it myself." She gave me a rueful smile. "I'm sorry about the dinner."

"It'll keep." I looked round the small room again. "So how do we get out of here?"

"I thought that was your department. I've tried everything."

I stood up carefully and walked over to the main door. Immediately my head resumed throbbing. There was an old metal latch, which I lifted. Experimentally I pulled the door towards me.

It came open without protest.

I could hear Jenna stumbling to her feet. "You must be *joking*!" Her tone conveyed a mix of relief and indignation. "Do you have magic hands or something? I've been trying that fucking door a hundred times a day, and it's always locked. Now Mr Wonderful waltzes in, and suddenly it's open. I don't sodding well believe it."

Chapter 46

The door led out into a dimly lit corridor, and from here we were able to work our way into the main house. It seemed frozen in time – fully furnished, but dust-laden and neglected. Clearly no one had lived here for years. The front door was now unlocked, and we peered out warily. There was no one in sight. My car still sat in the middle of the yard where I'd left it.

The bright afternoon sunshine accentuated the ordeal Jenna had suffered. Her blonde hair was dishevelled and her face had a gauntness about it, emphasised by her lack of makeup.

"I probably look a fright," she said with a hysterical laugh. "I've been trying to keep up appearances, but these hotels just don't have the facilities … "

"You look fine to me."

She touched my arm. "Oh, Michael, I can't tell you how glad I am to see a friendly face."

"I'm just glad you're OK."

"I would give you a hug, but I don't think you'd enjoy it very much. I must have been wearing these clothes for about a week."

"To hell with that. Come here." I pulled her towards me and held her for a moment, saying nothing.

"I don't know what the hell you did to these people, but whatever it was, it obviously did the trick."

I shook my head. "I didn't do anything. They caught me, didn't they? I wish I could take the credit for getting us out of there, but basically they've set us free. Whatever it was that made them keep you here, apparently it doesn't matter any longer."

"I suppose so."

"We should call the police. They need to see all this." I felt for my phone, but it wasn't in my pocket. Then I spotted it on the driver's seat of my car. The man I'd followed must have taken it from me, but then restored it to me when he'd decide to let us go. The people behind all this seemed to follow a strange code of politeness.

We sat in the car with the doors locked, waiting for the police to arrive and staying alert in case our captors decided to make a reappearance. They didn't. Jenna told me what had happened the night she'd disappeared.

"A man phoned me and said he was a policeman. He told me somebody had trashed my car, and they'd looked me up in their database to find out my address. They wanted me to go down and check out the damage. It sounded totally genuine."

"Then what happened?"

"I'm so stupid!" She stared through the windscreen at the house, reliving the moment. "I could have saved myself all this grief."

"How do you mean?"

"Well, when I got down to the street it dawned on me that my car was in the garage for repairs, so it couldn't have been trashed. But by then it was too late. These two guys suddenly appeared from nowhere. They grabbed my arms and shoved me into the back of a van. The bastards!" She shuddered. "It was so quick, Mike. I felt so powerless. It was like something from a gangster movie."

I nodded sympathetically. "Believe it or not, the same thing happened to me last year. It's a horrible experience."

"Really?" She looked at me with surprise. "I don't know how you dealt with it. I'll probably need six months of counselling after this." She gave a shaky laugh.

We sat in silence for a while, then I turned to her again.

"This must have something to do with the due diligence. What did you want to tell me about it?"

"Ah, fuck the due diligence. I just want to get to a bath."

"Yes, but it could explain all this. What were you going to say?"

She sighed wearily. "OK, let me think." She leaned back in the seat and took a deep breath. "When I was in Leeds the other day, at Ashursts,

I asked Piers about his future plans. How was he going to make his money when everyone got bored with spiralizers? Etcetera etcetera. I was only making polite chat, but obviously I hit a raw nerve."

"How do you mean?"

"Well, normally he's in control. He doesn't let the mask slip. But that day he seemed at the end of his tether. I think he'd been on the booze at lunchtime, and it loosened his tongue. He told me he was in deep debt to Ernie Bladen. Deep, deep debt. I think he almost forgot we'd broken up. He just wanted to confide in someone, and I was there."

"What did he say exactly?"

"He'd over-reached himself. He wasn't selling product fast enough. He had some kind of bail-out plan ready, but that had gone wrong as well. He'd only kept going this long through creative accounting – that's what he called it. But he said it should all come right when the Latimer takeover went through. Then there would be enough money to pay off his creditors."

"And he really thought he could make this happen? What about the due diligence process?"

"Ah, well I asked him about that, but he said it had been taken care of."

I laughed. "You ought to be a reporter."

"Huh! I don't know about that. If I'd been a reporter I would have kept my mouth shut till the right time. But no, I told him what he was doing was dishonest. He was defrauding my father and your people to save his own business. He didn't have any answer to that."

"So how did you leave it?"

"He said he'd told me all this in total confidence. He made me promise not to say anything about it. I said I would think about it."

"But in fact you decided to talk to me about it."

She nodded. "When I thought it through next day, I realised there was no way I could keep quiet. I know Piers and I were together for a while, and he's an old mate and all that, but I wasn't going to collude in theft. That's what it amounts to."

"But presumably this got back to Piers somehow."

"My fault. Fool that I am, I phoned him and gave him an

ultimatum." She laughed bitterly. "What was I doing, thinking I could bully Piers bloody Ashurst?"

"What did you tell him?"

"I said if he didn't do something to put a stop to all this by the end of the day you were coming, I would go to my father with it, and probably the police as well. What a dummy, eh?"

"So how come you phoned me about it if you were going to talk to your father?"

"Ah, well my dad's not best pleased with me at the moment. I wasn't sure he'd give me a hearing."

"What, even when it was about something as important as this?"

She shrugged. "We have our ups and downs. At the moment we're having a down. So you were going to be my backup."

"Great." I glanced at her, and she gave me an apologetic smile. I said, "So do you think Piers alerted this guy Bladen?"

"It looks like that, doesn't it? And he had me kidnapped to keep me quiet until the deal went through."

We sat in silence for a while, each no doubt reflecting on this strange sequence of events. Then I had a sudden thought.

"Christ! We must do something."

"What?"

"Well look, let's assume you really were kidnapped to prevent you from obstructing the Latimer takeover. Now the people who took you have set you free. What does that tell us?"

"The deal must have gone through!"

I grabbed my phone and called Bob Latimer's mobile. It went to voicemail, so I called the company's landline.

"Mr Latimer is in a meeting. Who's calling?"

"It's Mike Stanhope. Tell him it's a matter of life and death."

The receptionist's scepticism radiated from the phone. "The meeting is in London. I can't really reach him till he comes out."

"Shit." I thought fast. "Andrea Smith then, please."

There was a pause while we were connected, then, "Mike, I've been trying to call you. Why aren't you picking up? We might have left it too late for this due diligence thing."

"How do you mean?"

"The takeover was due to be confirmed this afternoon."

"Is it too late to stop it? There really could be possible fraud involved. I'm with Jenna Melling. She knows all about it."

"Let me go and talk to Brian Wells. I'll call you back."

Brian was one of Latimers' directors. I exchanged glances with Jenna. A couple of minutes passed, then my phone buzzed again.

"It's Andrea. We're too late. The deal has gone through."

Chapter 47

Two police cars turned up at the farm, and we did our best to explain what had happened and why we had called them out. The officers listened carefully as Jenna told her story, and asked her several times if she'd been assaulted in any way. They seemed surprised when she insisted she hadn't.

They were more sceptical when we tried to explain our theory about all this. They didn't want to hear about complex company takeovers or our speculation about Ernie Bladen's involvement. It was agreed in the end that we would make full statements the next day at the police station in Newcastle.

Eventually we were driven all the way into Newcastle and deposited at one of the main hospitals for medical checks. After a long wait I was finally given a provisional all clear and handed a leaflet on head injuries and what to do about them.

I met up with Jenna in the reception area just as her father was walking in. Clearly they'd made up their recent differences, for now at least. He smiled warmly at me. "Mike, I hear you saved the day."

"Not really, but it was good to be able to give Jenna some moral support at the end."

"Can we give you a lift to wherever you're staying?"

"It's OK, I'll get a taxi. But thanks."

Jenna said, "If you like I'll drive you out to that farm tomorrow to collect your car, assuming mine is back on the road."

"Do you think you'll feel up to it?"

"Course I bloody well will."

* * *

I rang Ashley from the motel.

"Guess what – I found Jenna Melling!"

"My god. Where was she?"

"Kidnapped, and held in a farmhouse somewhere in the wilds of Northumberland."

"Poor girl! And you found her yourself? How on earth did you do that?"

I explained how I'd taken a chance on Ernie Bladen being involved, and followed the car to the house, then been imprisoned myself. She was aghast when she heard I'd been hit over the head.

"Are you sure you're going to be all right? Head injuries can be really serious."

"Well, the hospital said I should be OK. I can only take their word for it."

"It's no trivial matter, Mike. You need to be careful."

"I know. I will be."

"So does anyone know why Jenna was kidnapped in the first place?"

"We think it was all part of a plot to stop her from derailing the Latimer takeover."

She was quiet for a moment, and I immediately understood why. I'd probably just implied a cosy complicity with Jenna. I added, "Anyway, that's what she reckons."

"Well, if so, it worked. The takeover was completed yesterday. We were all sent an internal memo."

"Right."

"So are you saying there really is something in suspicious about that company in Leeds? Everybody here seems really happy with the deal."

"That's probably because they don't know what's going on."

"And you do?"

"Hah! Not exactly. I'm working on it."

"Well don't work on it too hard if it's going to get someone kidnapped again. I mean that. Next time you might be seriously injured."

"I know.

* * *

I called the logistics company in Sunderland next morning. I was
supposed to go and interview the managing director, but I already knew
I wasn't going to make it. I felt battered, and wanted to save what energy
I had for dealing with the aftermath of the kidnapping. He agreed to
switch the arrangement to the following Tuesday.

Then I called a taxi to take me to the police station on the other side
of Newcastle. I was conscious that no one was going to reimburse me
for all this expense, but going by bus would have taken too long, and I
didn't have the patience.

At the police station I tried to pull my story together coherently, but
it proved harder than I expected. The detective who had first interviewed
me was now much less hostile, but he was sceptical.

"Did you take down the registration number of the white van or
the car?"

I shook my head, embarrassed. Some sleuth I was.

"Did you see the face of the driver?"

I hadn't.

"Was the Fiat driver definitely the same man as the van driver? Did
you actually see him get out of the van and into the car?"

Same answer again. I was beginning to realise what I was up against.

"Moving on to this corporate takeover, do you personally have any
evidence of corrupt accounting at this company in Leeds?"

I sighed. "No. I was just told about it."

"And you have no specific knowledge of any connection between
this company and Mr Ernie Bladen?"

"No, but why don't you ask Chris Melling about all this? He's the
head of Melling Logistics. If he's been ripped off, I'm sure he'll be the
first one to complain about it. Or you can ask my boss, Bob Latimer.
He'll take the same view."

"We'll follow up any relevant leads."

All in all, I was left feeling distinctly inadequate. I'd bodged most
aspects of the stakeout the day before, and then failed in my
objective of liberating Jenna. She'd been freed anyway, but not

through my doing. It was lucky for me that I wasn't still incarcerated with her.

I put the facts of yesterday's escapade in a written statement, and was then free to leave. As I walked through to the front desk Jenna and her father came in. She'd stayed the night with her parents, and I'd phoned her there earlier. She was looking smart again and outwardly unscathed by her experience.

I sat with the two of them for a few minutes in the waiting room, then Jenna was called in to give her statement. Chris turned to me. "What an awful experience for the poor girl."

"And no clue as to how long it would go on. She seems amazingly resilient."

"That's our Jenna for you."

Neither of us spoke for a moment, then Chris said, "At least she was treated well. She said the food they gave her wasn't bad. They even gave her books to keep her occupied." He smiled. "But can you imagine it – *Barchester Towers?*"

"Better than nothing, I suppose."

We sat in silence. I wondered if he was planning to give a statement of his own, but then he looked at his watch. "I need to be somewhere. Will you look after her when she comes out – see that she gets home safely?"

"Of course."

I sat for a long time in the small waiting room, then finally Jenna thrust the door open. "They want to put me into counselling. Bollocks to that. I keep telling them I don't need any. I was joking when I said that to you. It's not me, is it?"

It was another sunny morning, and we made our way to her flat on foot. She said, "I can't tell you how wonderful it is just to walk along the street whenever I like."

"I can't imagine how horrible it must have been."

"It was strange, though. I never got the impression that they wanted to harm me. All the time I was there, it felt … I don't know, temporary somehow. I never doubted I would get out in the end. The guy who brought my meals seemed almost apologetic."

When we reached Armstrong Bridge I looked at the lattice sides with a shiver, and found myself steering a course close to the centre line. I said, "Two men tried to throw me over the edge of this bridge on the night we were due to meet. It was horrendous."

"Bloody hell, Mike! Do you think it was the same people who kidnapped me?"

"I don't know. It might have been."

We stopped at a small café on a street near her flat, and sat in the sun over coffee and donuts. I told her more about my attack on the bridge, and she fleshed out some of the details of her days in captivity. "They gave me books to read. They must have found them in the house. Hardback copies of *Moby Dick*, *Barchester Towers*, *The Mill on the Floss*, that kind of thing." She grimaced. "Not exactly what I would have chosen for myself, but at least they made a bit of effort."

"Couldn't they find any modern paperbacks?"

"I don't think they looked very hard."

I asked about her sleeping arrangements. "There was a mattress. Did you not see it? Smelly old thing. I suppose that came from the house too. And some blankets. I wasn't cold or hungry." She chuckled dryly. "Once they even gave me a change of underwear. Very civilised. But Jesus, I thought it would never end."

"I'm amazed you haven't been put into some sort of recovery programme. They've just let you wander out here on your own."

"Ah, to hell with all that. I told them I wasn't having any of it. I want to get on with my life." She exaggerated her accent in that last comment, which came out "gerron with me laif".

I smiled broadly at her. "I hope you're ready for the nightmares."

"Huh! Don't you start."

I told her about Greg's concern for her. "He's the one who first got the police involved. I thought he would be with you today."

"I talked to him on the phone last night. I don't want him fussing around. He's cool with that."

"I'm glad you think so. I get the impression he's jealous of me, if you want to know."

This brought an ironic smile to her face. "Well, he has no reason to be, does he?" She stretched. "Anyway, me and Greg – can you really see it?"

I smiled. "Maybe not."

Jenna's car was at a back-street car repair company a couple of blocks away. "Personal service at practical prices," she commented, parroting the slogan over the door.

It took us a while to find the farm, which we'd approached from a different direction this time. When we did get there we found a police car and the remains of a forensic team, and we had to explain who we were. Jenna had lost a lot of her bluster, and refused to get out of the car. "The sooner we're out of here, the happier I'll be."

She asked me to follow her all the way to her flat. "I know nothing's going to happen to me, but it'll make me feel safer." I left her at her door and headed back to the motel.

Chapter 48

I didn't kiss Ashley ten times when I met her at the station in Leeds on Friday evening. I didn't even kiss her once. We both smiled nervously, dancing around each other like shy teenagers.

I asked her, "Good trip?"

"Long trip."

When we reached my car she commented, "No posh rental job this time?"

"Sorry, we're in economy class today.

"Cheapskate."

We steered clear of anything personal on the drive over to Doncaster. Neither of us seemed prepared to embark on any topic that might derail our good relations. Ashley said she thought Bob Latimer wanted to talk to me. "I had a long chat with Andrea Smith yesterday. She's told him you both reckon there's something weird going on at Ashurst Concepts. He wants to hear about it from you."

"I might give him a call, but he hasn't been picking up lately."

"I think he will now."

"Huh."

"By the way, Andrea gave me a message for you. The company that managed the due diligence at Ashurst Concepts was Salmon Fischer in Leeds." She smiled. "Easy name to remember."

So the accountancy firm running the due diligence audit at Ashursts was the same one that had once been headed by Elizabeth Sanderson's partner Derek. What a small world. I filed away this information to consider later.

I said a little warily, "I'm not sure if I'll be able to come back with you to Cornwall after all. I have to stay in the north for a few days more. I postponed that visit to Sunderland for the magazine, and I have to do it on Tuesday." It seemed wise to get this on the table from the start.

She gave me a cryptic look. "We'll have to see about that, won't we?"

It sounded encouraging. I decided not to press her on what she meant.

Tina and Martin gave us a warm welcome, and Ashley immediately disappeared into the kitchen with Tina for a catch-up chat. Martin handed me a beer. "I hear you've been getting into all kinds of trouble in Newcastle?"

"You could say that. I'm just hoping Ashley is ready to let me off the hook."

He studied his glass, then looked up judiciously. "I probably shouldn't be telling you this, but she's over the moon at meeting up with you here. That's what she told Tina. She thinks she's been giving you a hard time."

Exulting inwardly, I said, "Thanks. I'll pretend I didn't hear that."

Over our evening meal, Tina said, "You know that company you mentioned last time you were here? Ashurst Concepts? I said I would keep my ear to the ground in case I heard anything about them."

"Absolutely."

"Well, it's not strictly related to Ashursts, but apparently at one point the founder, Piers Ashurst, was getting very pally with Dan Wilson, the man behind the Spirit Spiralizer." She looked at me expectantly.

I said, "So …?"

"You haven't heard of them, then?"

"Nope."

"I thought you would have, being a journalist. Wilsons were pulled apart a few months ago by one of those TV consumer programmes. Their products were found to be unsafe. Didn't meet electrical standards, that kind of thing. It was a high-profile humiliation for the company."

"What happened?"

"I don't know the detail. Presumably the affected products were withdrawn from the market. The company told the press it would deal with the problems, but of course it must have been a public relations nightmare. There was talk that they might go bust. But of course pretty soon it was yesterday's news, so I don't know if they did."

"So what was this about Piers Ashurst getting pally with them?"

"Oh, there was speculation that he might be going to acquire Wilsons for Ashurst Concepts. Market consolidation, that kind of thing. But this was before the TV programme was broadcast. I assume it can't have happened, or else the world would know about it."

Half-way through the meal my phone buzzed. I glanced at it and saw that it was Bob Latimer. I went through to the lounge to take the call.

"Mike, I'm sorry I haven't been in touch lately." This was a typical piece of Bob Latimer diplomacy. He'd been avoiding my calls for weeks; now he was making this airy apology. But at least he was speaking to me, and apparently not addressing me as a pariah. Perhaps my bid to redeem myself was working.

"Not a problem."

"So what's all this about these Ashurst people?"

"Well, I suppose you know about the inconsistent accounts that Andrea dug up?"

"Yes, but according to the financial people we use in London, their accounts are perfectly shipshape."

"I don't know about that, but I've been getting a different story from Jenna Melling, Chris Melling's daughter. She works with Piers Ashurst on marketing."

"Is this the daughter who was kidnapped?"

"Yes, her. She also helps with Mellings' marketing."

"I think we met her one time when we were up there."

"You probably heard she was released unharmed."

"And you were in on this somehow – is that right?"

"Huh. Yes, in a way. Anyway, apparently Piers Ashurst told her confidentially the other day that he was in hock up to his ears. He'd had to indulge in 'creative accounting' to keep his books straight. Needless to say, he wasn't expecting her to pass this on to me."

I paused to give him a chance to take this in, then added, "The bottom line is that she may have been kidnapped to stop her spilling the beans until the takeover went through."

"Christ, Mike, this is serious stuff. What are the police saying?"

"Well, I know they're looking into the kidnapping, but I don't know if they're taking the Ashurst connection seriously. We told them what we know, but it's not much. It's down to them now."

I could almost hear his mind whirring. After a moment he said, "It's very hard to imagine anyone going to the lengths of actually kidnapping Chris's daughter. I mean, good god! Who would consider it so important to keep her quiet?"

"Presumably somebody who stood to gain a lot of money once the takeover went through. One candidate is Ernie Bladen, the head of Bladen Building Supplies. It looks as if he may have invested heavily in Ashursts."

"But that would be on the record, and I haven't seen anything about him being involved."

"Not if he invested via a private loan to Piers Ashurst. He might be a sleeping partner. The investment would be in Piers' name."

"Chris is running a logistics contract with Bladen," he said ruminatively.

"That's right, yes."

He thought some more. "It sounds as if I need to take myself up to Newcastle again. Are you still staying up there?"

"No, I've come down to Doncaster for the weekend. I might not go back north."

"OK, well let me know if you do." He seemed about to disconnect, but then added wearily, "I think I'll have to get our financial people to look again at Ashursts' accounts. I'll talk to Chris Melling."

"Well if you do, it would be worth making sure that your people actually do the job themselves this time. I've been told that they farmed it out last time to a local accountancy firm in Leeds."

"You're remarkably well informed."

"I got that one from Andrea."

Still he didn't disconnect. I waited a moment, then he said, "I know I don't have to say this to you, but all this is one hundred per cent confidential, and not for publication under any circumstances until I say so. That's understood, isn't it?"

Should I give in on this? My rebellious side said no, but I quickly realised that if I wanted to restore good relations with Bob I had no option but to swallow my pride. I said, "Trust me, I've learned my lesson. You have my word."

"Thank you, Mike."

This seemed the end of the conversation, but after a moment he said, "This is unreal, isn't it? It sounds like a plot for one of your novels."

"You know about my writing, then?"

"Of course. My wife read your first book."

I'd often heard this type of comment: "My wife would like your book, but it's not really my kind of thing." It was as if real men didn't indulge in anything as lightweight as mystery thrillers. But this was hardly the time to get into that debate.

I said, "Well, that's good to know, but I assure you this isn't fiction."

"That's what's worrying me."

* * *

Tina had put Ashley and me together in the spare bedroom without consulting us about it. Ashley was already in bed by the time I opened the door.

"Hello," she said.

"Hello yourself."

She was lying down, staring at the ceiling, but she glanced over at me and gave me a quick smile. I climbed into the bed and leaned on my elbow, facing her. I said, "Thank you for coming."

"I wanted to see Tina."

"Thank you for coming to see Tina."

I saw another quick smile flit across her face.

I said, "Tina is over the moon that you're here."

The smile came and remained.

"I'm not unhappy about it myself."

"Likewise." She turned her head to me, the residual smile still in place. "Let's not rush things, Mike. Is that all right?"

I lay down facing her, then reached over and rested my hand on her stomach. She didn't flinch. I said, "Fine by me."

Chapter 49

I'd taken three photographs at the Ashurst factory, but until now I'd more or less forgotten about them. Sitting in Tina's lounge after breakfast, I copied them on to my laptop. They might provide a new angle on what was going on.

Two of them were more or less the same, and showed a couple of pallet-loads of cartons in the Ashurst warehouse. I'd taken them during my guided tour with Piers Ashurst, and had told him I would delete them, but of course I hadn't. The third was the shot I'd taken through the window when I'd sneaked into the yard, and showed people working on an improvised production line.

I showed them to Ashley, who said, "That one with the conveyors in it looks as if it's showing people re-labelling spiralizer packs."

"Why would they do that?"

"I don't know. You should ask Jamie Andrews."

It sounded a useful idea, so I emailed the images to him at St Austell. He phoned me a few minutes later. "You're lucky you caught me. I'm just going out sailing." I'd forgotten it was a Saturday and he wouldn't be at work. He told me much the same as Ashley had about the labels.

I said, "Does it make any sense to you?"

"Oh, yes, there could be any number of reasons why they would change the packaging and labelling. A change in model designation, a marketing campaign, detail design changes that weren't reflected in the original labelling – you name it."

"So there wouldn't necessarily be anything suspicious about it?"

"Not at all. But you'd need to compare the original labels with the new ones to know exactly what they were doing."

I looked at the picture on my laptop. It was slightly fuzzy because

I'd shot it through a grimy warehouse window. I zoomed in, but the actual labels were just white blobs.

"What about the other pictures – the ones showing stacks of cartons on the floor?"

"Well, it's just a load of product. I can't really tell you anything about it."

I zoomed in on one of them. "You can see the barcodes on these."

"Yes, but I don't know what they mean." He thought for a minute. "Why not email them to Mary Carpenter at Melling Logistics? She might know where the codes fit into the production sequence."

So I attached the images to a message and sent it off to Mary, asking if she had any thoughts about the content. She might not be at work today, so I would probably have to wait until Monday for a response.

Now what? Ashley was preparing to go shopping with Tina in Doncaster, and they'd talked about meeting up with me for lunch. I waved them away and sat on my own in the lounge, thinking over all that had been happening.

In particular, I was wondering again about the cartons that the staff had been relabelling at Ashursts. They appeared to have been delivered by a scruffy white panel van. I'd made a note of the legal owner, and I opened my notebook to find the reference. It was ARC (Leeds) Ltd, trading as Black Cat Deliveries.

I Googled the name, and found an amateurish website for a small company in Leeds offering storage, deliveries and general contracting, whatever that meant. I clicked through to the contact page, and abruptly my eye was drawn to the name of the proprietor: Andy Civet. The surname was the same as that of the driver from Southampton whose truck had been hijacked. It couldn't be a coincidence.

I rang Dave Matthews, who told me I'd interrupted him mowing his lawn. I said, "I didn't think you ever did any gardening. You told me your garden was a permanent wilderness."

He chuckled. "Suzy likes the idea of sitting out in the sun. At the moment the grass is about six feet high."

"She's obviously having a good influence on you."

"So how did you get on with Ernie Bladen? Was my info any use?"

I summarised my encounter with him, and my subsequent success in finding Jenna Melling. He said, "For god's sake, Mike, I told you not to mess with that man. Will you never listen?"

"I know, I know."

"So why are you calling today? Not another favour? I think I'll have to refuse just to protect you from yourself."

"Well, in a way it might be a favour to you."

"That's a first."

I ignored this. "You know the hijacked truck that I asked you about? You found out about the tracking system for me."

"Yep."

"And the driver's name was Roy Civet."

"OK."

"Well I've just found that some product very similar to the stuff that was stolen has probably been delivered to its original destination by a man named Andy Civet. It's consumer electrical goods. Coincidence or what?"

"I don't believe in coincidences." He was silent for a moment. "So this man Roy Civet lets his truck be stolen, and abracadabra, his brother or his second cousin turns up with the stuff at the place where it was already going. So what does that sound like to you?"

"It sounds like fraud. The company claims on the insurance, but also gets the stolen product back, minus a cut for the people who did the heist."

Dave said, "I wonder why the local force didn't pick up on this?"

"Well, the stuff probably wasn't delivered to its destination straight away. It would have been held somewhere else for a while. So if the police didn't already know about some connection between the company and this Andy Civet person, they wouldn't know where to look."

"OK, but what about batch codes and that kind of thing? You'd know more about that kind of thing than I do, but say the original company puts the stolen stuff back into stock. Wouldn't the codes show it up for what it was?"

"I suppose so – but maybe not if someone changed the codes somehow."

"Huh! You've got it all worked out, haven't you? You should write detective novels. Oh, I forgot, you already do."

"Yeah, yeah. I only worked all this out in the last few minutes. I just need corroboration from someone about the codes."

"You seem to have covered all the angles."

"So you agree that it's worth following up?"

"I do. I'll make some calls on Monday."

"You can't do anything before that?"

"Give me a break. Suzy is due here in hour's time. You really want to consign me to her wrath? Anyway, I don't see a big rush here. Can you email me the details? I'll get back to you on Monday."

Almost as soon as I disconnected, the phone buzzed again.

"Mike, it's Mary Carpenter at Melling Logistics. I got your email."

"So you're at work today?"

"Can't seem to stay away."

"And what do you think?"

"Well, I think you might be right. The barcodes on those cartons in your photo seem to follow on in sequence from the latest batch. Can I ask where you got those pictures?"

"I took them myself at Ashursts."

"Oh. So has the stolen consignment been recovered?"

"No, not at all. It's a bit of a mystery how it found its way to Ashursts, but presumably somebody there must have known about it. I'm trying to work out how it happened, and why."

"You've got me intrigued."

"What I wanted to know was this. Would it be possible to change the barcodes on the stolen stuff, and make it appear to be new product from the same supplier?"

She considered that for a moment. "Yes, up to a point. Ashursts could put replacement barcodes on the stuff, and we would just accept it and process it as normal. It doesn't matter to us what the codes are, so long as the customer is happy. The customer in this case being Ashursts."

"You say up to a point?"

"Well, it's not just the packaging that has codes on it. The actual products will usually have codes on them as well – a metal plate, for instance, with a serial number stamped into it. It's often a legal requirement. It would be almost impossible to fake all this. It just wouldn't be worth it. And even if you did, all your subsequent genuine codes would be out of sequence. It would be a logistical nightmare."

"But it would work in the short term, just to keep the supply chain ticking over?"

Almost reluctantly, she said, "I suppose so, yes."

I thanked her and disconnected, then sat there marvelling. I felt as if I'd cracked the lorry hijacking case single-handedly.

Chapter 50

"Mike, it's Jenna. How are you doing?"

I was about to set off for the town centre to meet up with Ashley and Tina. This was the first time I'd been in contact with Jenna since the day after she'd been released from captivity. I didn't know how I would have handled the call if I'd been sitting next to Ashley.

I said, "I'm good. I'm in Doncaster – staying with Ashley's sister."

"Oh, right." I could hear uncharacteristic disappointment in her voice. "I thought maybe you were still up here in Newcastle."

"So how about you?"

"Oh, you know, I'm having my ups and downs. Greg's trying to be nice, but … " She didn't finish.

"Are you back at work?"

"Well, work is home, really. I haven't been over to my dad's office yet, and I'll probably ditch the job with Piers. I'm not saying he was in on the scheme to shut me away, but I'm getting a bad feeling about it."

"I'm not surprised."

She was quiet for a moment, then said, "Do you think Piers will go to prison if the police do find a link to him?"

"I don't know, but it's possible. Kidnapping is a serious crime."

"What a strange thought. I've known him so long. He's a nice guy at heart."

"You're very forgiving."

"Well, if he was involved, he must have been driven to it."

"Maybe he didn't know about it. Ernie Bladen could have set it up entirely on his own."

"I suppose that's true."

I thought about the lorry hijacking. I said, "There's something else. You remember the truck that was hijacked a few months ago? It's looking as if Piers may have organised it himself, so that he could keep the stock but claim on the insurance."

"Are you serious?"

"It's looking that way. You put me on to it yourself, in a way."

"But I never really thought there was anything in it.

"Well, there was. And if the police can prove it, he'll probably be charged with theft or fraud. He might get a prison sentence for that."

"The stupid man. But so typical of him – always punching above his weight, and then floundering around, struggling to make things work the way he wants them." She fell silent, then said, "How come you know so much about all this?"

"Oh, I've been piecing things together, and I have a friend on the force."

"Piecing things together," she repeated. "Huh. I don't know about force, but you're quite a force of nature yourself, in your own way."

"Hardly."

She said nothing for a moment, then, "It doesn't sound too good for Piers, then, does it?"

"Maybe not."

There was another moment's silence, then she said, "I was going to suggest meeting you for lunch."

I simply said, "I'm sorry."

There was a longer pause, then she said, "Me too."

* * *

I drove into Doncaster town centre and found a car park, then made my way to the restaurant where I'd arranged to meet Ashley and Tina. They were both in high spirits, and over lunch they recounted their morning's sightseeing. Then Tina left to do some more shopping, while Ashley and I lingered over a second coffee. It was our first proper conversation since she'd arrived yesterday.

"Andrea Smith isn't so bad when you get to know her better," she said. "She just seems to think the world is against her. You have to prove to her that she's wrong."

"To be fair, she's been very helpful over the Ashurst accounting stuff."

"I think she means well."

Cautiously, I said, "Jenna Melling phoned me this morning."

She raised her eyebrows. "What did she want?"

"Just to hear a friendly voice, I think. She's probably feeling the after-effects of her ordeal. And she's worried about Piers Ashurst. She was seeing him for a while. She thinks he might get banged up if it's proved that he had a hand in the kidnapping."

"And do you think he did?"

"I honestly don't know. But it does look as if he was involved in a lorry hijacking. He might be prosecuted for that." I explained the sequence of events that I'd worked out earlier that morning.

"I thought you'd given up on investigative journalism. Now you're solving two different cases single-handedly. You amaze me sometimes."

"In a good way, I hope?"

"No fishing, thank you very much." She gave me an ironic smile.

I shrugged. "I didn't go looking for all this – it just seemed to happen to me regardless. All I want is for things to go back to the way they were."

"You're not finding life in Cornwall too boring for you, then?"

"You must be joking! Do you think it's exciting living in a motel on the outskirts of Newcastle? Give me Truro any time."

She asked me about the house in Harrogate, and I told her about Angela Crabtree's pleas for me to split the inheritance with her family.

"Do you think you will?"

"I don't know. I feel really sorry for her, but I don't have much sympathy for her husband. It's a tricky one."

"And have you worked out why you were left the house in the first place?"

I told her what I'd learned about my grandmother's connection with the North East. "I'm guessing that she knew this man Roberts, who was Elizabeth Sanderson's father and Philip Crabtree's grandfather. In later years Elizabeth found out about my grandmother, and decided to leave her property to someone in her family line. In other words, me."

"You see? You're a born detective. You missed your vocation."

"I still don't know *why* Elizabeth made the bequest."

"I bet you'll find out."

I asked her about Bob Latimer. "I hardly dare bring it up, but do you think he's likely to keep me on his payroll after all this?"

"I don't know. I do know that when your article was published he was pretty pissed off at you, but since then he seems to have calmed down. I think he's been stressed out, trying to firm up that deal to take on the new high-bay warehousing in Birmingham and Leeds. Now that it's all agreed, he's happier with life."

"Hopefully he might be happier with me, too."

She gave me an appraising look. "But you don't really enjoy working for Latimers, do you? You're just doing it so that your life in Cornwall makes sense."

This wasn't strictly true. The Latimer work was mundane, but in some ways I liked it. It was varied yet predictable, unlike my hand-to-mouth freelance editorial work, and it paid surprisingly well. Currently I couldn't think of anything more appealing. I said, "You don't know what I enjoy."

She gave me a different kind of smile. "I think I do."

Tina returned with an armful of shopping, and we made our way to her car to dump it. Then we strolled round the town centre for a while, arriving at the museum and art gallery just in time for a lightning tour. As we stood staring at one of the exhibits, Ashley's hand brushed mine. It was like an electric charge.

Chapter 51

"They've drawn a blank. No missing stock, no smoking gun."

This message, relayed by Dave just after lunch on Monday, was not what I'd hoped to hear. Phoning me from his car, he said he'd contacted his police counterparts in Sheffield the previous day about the truck hijacking theory. "I should get a life, making these calls on a Sunday."

"What did they say?"

He seemed guarded. "I shouldn't be telling you this, but I suppose you're entitled to know. They sent out a team this morning to take a look at these Ashurst people, but they didn't find anything. Of course, they didn't have a search warrant. They didn't have enough hard evidence to get one. But the boss man, Piers Ashurst, was happy enough to show them around regardless. He said he had nothing to hide."

"Did they know what they were looking for?"

"Oh yes, they already had the consignment details and product codes from Ashursts. It was all in the original report. Ashursts had to provide that kind of thing for insurance purposes.

"But nothing doing?"

"Nope. They also went to see the van company, Black Cat Deliveries, but it was the same story there. No Ashurst product anywhere in sight. This man Andrew Civet doesn't have any kind of criminal record, so he wasn't in their sights."

"But this doesn't prove anything, does it? It could just mean these people have stashed the stolen goods somewhere else."

"True." He made a tetching sound. "If it had been up to me I would have waited until I had more of the facts, and then got a search warrant. Now these people will have gone to ground, and they'll be harder to catch out."

"Do you think Ashursts and Black Cat were tipped off that the police were coming? It seems strange that there was no evidence anywhere."

"I don't see how, but it's one explanation."

"So what now?"

"The local people will keep looking and digging, and see what they come up with."

* * *

I'd assumed Ashley would be returning to Cornwall this morning, but she'd surprised me the previous evening by revealing that she'd been granted up to a whole week off – "so long as I keep on top of my work." That had evidently been the secret plan she'd hinted at when she'd arrived. It was the strongest clue yet that she was ready to rebuild our relationship.

This morning she'd gone into Doncaster with Tina to see her office. They both worked in marketing, but in a very different environments, and Ashley was interested to see how Tina's firm operated. I'd stayed at the flat to try to re-enter my freelance life, such as it was. I had an article on forklift trucks to research, and I was due to do an interview at a transport firm in Sunderland the following day. I'd decided I would drive the hundred miles odd directly from Doncaster; I didn't need to be staying in the locality.

My phone buzzed, and I glanced at the caller ID. It was Mary Carpenter at Mellings.

"Hi Mike, I hope that stuff I told you on Saturday about those product codes was of some use?"

"Definitely."

"Well, I don't know if this means anything or not, but I might have something to add. It's to do with the new warehouse in Leeds. Latimer Logistics have taken a long lease on it."

"Yes, I know about it."

"OK. Well, this morning we received an alert on our computer system saying that some stock from Ashurst Concepts is now in temporary store in this warehouse."

I waited.

"The thing is, it looks to me as if this stock might be part of the missing consignment. Our computer systems aren't properly connected yet, so I can't be absolutely sure. I'm only seeing header codes."

"But they look suspicious, do they?"

"Just in the sense that they don't correspond to Ashursts' forward plan. It's stock that nobody told us about."

I told her this information could be useful. "I'll definitely follow it up."

I disconnected and stared into space. What was going on? Why would Ashursts suddenly transfer stock into a Latimer warehouse? I needed a Latimer perspective, so I rang Jamie Andrews in St Austell, and luckily he picked up at the first attempt.

"It's a matter of convenience," he said. "The high-bay warehouse in Holbeck is empty at the moment. It's going to be used for a new contract, but it won't be full even then. There's spare capacity. If we win the Franchi contract it will be used for that."

"So where do Ashursts fit in?"

"Apparently they've been grumbling to Mellings for weeks that they're overstocked at their factory, and they don't have enough space to store new product. Obviously they're not selling at anything like the rate they expected, but that's another story. So now that the merger is happening and we're all playing happy families, Mellings asked us at Latimers if we had any suggestions, and we said Ashursts could offload some of their stock to our new warehouse." He chuckled. "It's just a handful of pallets. It gives us a chance to play with the semi-automated system before the warehouse is being used in anger."

So Ashursts had shunted a few pallets of product from their own premises to the Latimer warehouse on the other side of Leeds. But were those pallet-loads part of the stolen consignment? If so, this was an audacious way of hiding it – more or less in plain sight. Maybe Piers Ashurst was taking a calculated risk.

I decided I should tell Dave Matthews about this development, but my call went to voicemail. I didn't leave a message; it didn't seem urgent. Then twenty minutes later another call came through.

"Mike, it's Andrea at St Austell. Jamie says you were asking him just now about Ashurst Concepts and the new Latimer warehouse in Holbeck."

"Right."

"Well, I've just had a rather weird phone call with Ashursts. It might be relevant, so I thought you should know about it. I was talking to a girl called Sarah in their accounts department. She took over when they fired that other girl. I was querying something with her, and she had to go and check it with Piers Ashurst. But she said when she got to his office he rushed out, shouting blue murder."

I waited. Clearly there was more.

"She probably wouldn't even have mentioned it, but it involved Latimers directly. She said he'd just found out someone had moved some pallets to our new warehouse on Friday. He was furious about it." She paused. "It can't be a coincidence."

This was a new slant. Whether or not those pallets did contain the stolen goods, apparently Piers hadn't intended to ship them to the new warehouse after all. It had been a mistake. The picture seemed to be changing by the minute.

I started to thank Andrea for the information, but she interrupted. "There's something else. While Sarah was telling me this she was looking out the window, and she said she could see Piers Ashurst and his warehouse foreman jumping into their box van and heading off in a cloud of dust."

It wasn't much of a stretch to deduce that they were heading straight for the new warehouse to collect the offending pallets. If they did, they could be removing a key piece of evidence about the theft.

I rang Dave's phone, but it went to voicemail again. Should I try calling the police in Sheffield who'd handled the original robbery? In theory yes, but in practice I didn't know which police station to call, or which officers to ask for. And I didn't have any police contacts at all in Leeds. How long would it take me before I got the message across to the appropriate people and persuaded them to take me seriously?

The alternative, I realised with some misgiving, was for me to go to Leeds myself.

Chapter 52

Driving north up the A1 towards Leeds, I had a strong sense of *déjà vu*. The previous summer I'd made an hour-long dash across the English midlands after seeing a colleague being driven off at gunpoint. The chase had led to a massive parcel sortation centre, and had ended on its automated carousel system. The gunman had been captured at the bottom of a parcel chute.

This time I was heading for a high-bay warehouse – much taller than the sortation centre, and filled no doubt with racking rather than sorting equipment. Still, the parallels were hard to dismiss. Last year I'd been lucky; the gunman had been determined, but not malevolent. I had no idea how Piers Ashurst would react if I actually had to confront him.

I passed the exits for the villages of Wentbridge and Darrington, and before long the cooling towers of Ferrybridge power station loomed on my right. Then it was up the slip road and on to the westbound M62. I tried calling Dave several times from my dashboard phone mount, but the calls kept going to voicemail.

I'd set off ill-equipped for the task in hand. I had a rough idea how to find the new warehouse, but I didn't have a street address or map coordinates for it, so I hadn't been able to programme the location into my satnav. Forty-five minutes after leaving I took an exit from the M62 in the direction of Holbeck, but from that point I was floundering.

I fumbled my phone out and called Andrea in Cornwall to ask her for the postcode. After a moment she said, "Nobody seems to know it. Do you want me to call you back?" I told her not to worry. I was hoping I would recognise the building when I saw it. I started looking out for tall modern warehousing developments.

For a while I wished I'd let Andrea find the details, but luck guided me in the end. I was passing an industrial park that looked right but was in the wrong place. On a sudden whim I turned into it, and immediately realised I'd found the right location. It wasn't really in Holbeck at all – just somewhere in that general vicinity.

The estate was all gleaming modern warehouses and offices in glass and metallic grey, and the Latimer building was the tallest of them all. Although not brand new, it looked modern and imposing. A large "Latimer Logistics" sign had already been erected next to the entrance.

I pulled up near the gatehouse, peering through the fence for the Ashurst box van. I could see a white vehicle parked at the end of a row of loading bays, but it had no signwriting.

I pulled my phone off the dashboard mount and called Jamie Andrews. The call went to voicemail. Trying to resist panicking, I called Bob Latimer instead. He picked up, and on a muffled line said, "Mike. I'm on the train. What can I do for you?"

"I'm at your new warehouse in Leeds. I think Piers Ashurst might be here, and if so, he's probably trying to remove some pallets of stuff. Can you stop him?"

He reflected on that for a moment. "I don't know, Mike. If it's his own company's product, I may not have a legal right to prevent him taking it away. Why do you want me to?"

At this point I realised I'd never discussed the truck hijacking with Bob. I wasn't even sure if he knew about it. I said, "It's a long story, but the pallets may be part of a stolen consignment."

To his credit he asked nothing more. He simply said, "Leave it with me – but no promises."

He was about to disconnect, but I said, "Just before you go, there's another detail. Can you organise for the people here to let me into this site? I don't think I'll get in on my own say so."

"I'll do my best."

I got out of my car and went over to the gatehouse. A security guard leaned out through the window. "Can I help?"

I told him my name, and said he should expect a call from Bob Latimer or one of his colleagues. Staring impassively at me, he said, "Wait there where you are."

I returned to my car and sat down, dangling my legs over the door sill. Several minutes passed. Finally the security man picked up a phone, listened for a moment, then beckoned me over and wordlessly signed me in. He handed me a badge and passed me a yellow plastic helmet and an orange high-visibility vest. "There's no one inside to give you these. We're on a skeleton staff."

"Fine." I made as if to get into my car.

"Hang on a minute." He lifted the phone again. "Joe, can you come over to the gatehouse? I need you to escort a visitor."

Suppressing a sigh, I said, "Is Piers Ashurst here, do you know?"

"Yes, that's his van over there."

Confirmation, at any rate, that I'd guessed right.

"Can you stop him if he tries to leave?"

He looked at me as if I'd just asked him if he could levitate from the gatehouse by the power of his own will. "What?"

"Can you stop him? Can you keep the gates closed or something?"

"Why would I want to do that?"

"He has no right to remove product from here."

He simply stared at me. "On whose authority would I stop him?"

"Bob Latimer of Latimer Logistics."

He shook his head emphatically. "He didn't say anything about that when I talked to him just now. If Mr Ashurst has the right paperwork I have no right to interfere."

I shook my head in frustration. "Ask Bob Latimer again. He'll probably call you back in a minute anyway."

"Well, if he does I'll take his instructions."

I considered arguing further, then concluded that this was a lost cause. I said, "He *will* ring you." I started to turn to the car. "How do I find Piers Ashurst?"

"Joe will show you."

I went over to my car and leaned on it. A minute passed, then a man of about sixty in a green boiler suit walked over from the main building. The gate swung open and he came up to me. "If you'll give me a lift, I'll show you where to park."

Chapter 53

The modern but empty reception area was built to a human scale. The interior of the warehouse was something else. Joe led me into a cavernous space with a glazed roof suspended some thirty metres above us. A largely empty area stretched far away to my left and right; I saw only a few stacks of timber pallets, along with some moveable conveyors and general clutter. About twenty metres ahead of us the pallet racking began, soaring up to the distant ceiling and arranged in aisles leading away from us. There must have been room for tens of thousands of loaded pallets to be stored here at any one time.

Currently the racking seemed almost entirely empty, but it was difficult to see very far into it. The lighting was limited, and the confusion of metal uprights and diagonals obstructed any clear view.

I said to Joe, "I'm trying to find a visitor – Piers Ashurst."

"Ask him." He pointed to a fork-lift truck that I hadn't noticed until now, poised near the end of an aisle. It looked like a toy alongside the racked area towering over it. A man in an orange high-visibility vest was sitting at the wheel, peering forward down the aisle.

I strode over to him. "Is Piers Ashurst here?"

"Who wants to know?"

"Mike Stanhope. I work for Latimer Logistics. I'm here on behalf of Bob Latimer."

"I wouldn't know anything about that."

"Well, I need to find Piers Ashurst. If he's shifting pallets, he needs to stop."

"Says who?"

"Bob Latimer."

I sensed doubt in his mind. He was clearly out of his comfort zone here, and uncertain of his rights. He said, "He's down that aisle, but I don't think he'll want to be stopped."

This was a narrow-aisle warehouse, meaning that the space between columns of racking was no wider than a fork-lift truck. A special kind of pallet lift was installed in each aisle, running between rails at the foot of the racking to keep it aligned, and swooping up and down in a vertical frame to access pallets on any level. A small glass-sided cabin rose up and down with the pallet forks, allowing the operator to pick the pallets from close range.

In this aisle the lift assembly was currently positioned about three quarters of the way to the far end, and the cab was at a high level as the operator, presumably Piers, selected a pallet from the racking. I turned to the fork-lift driver and shouted, "Can you tell him to stop?"

"Tell him yourself, mate."

So I hurried off down the aisle towards the lifting assembly. I could just make out the side of a man's face up in the glass-sided cabin, and I could see a pallet being slid out of its racking position. As I approached, the face turned my way and I recognised it as Piers. He stared at me for a moment, then turned towards the racking.

I shouted his name, but couldn't be sure if he'd heard me over the hum of electrics and the clunk of machinery. Looking up, I saw the forks push the loaded pallet back into the racking and set it down in position. The forks came out again empty, then the whole tower assembly started moving slowly towards me. An intermittent electronic alarm bleeper sounded.

Should hold my position? Would the system allow the machine to run me down, or would some safety system detect my presence and prevent it? When it was within a few feet of me it came to a stop. Looking up, I saw the forks lunge into the racking again, then start to emerge, this time bearing an empty timber pallet.

It was difficult from where I was standing to see exactly what was happening up there, but the forks pulled back, bringing the pallet more or less clear of the racking, then seemed to swivel, nudging the racking as they did so. They swivelled again, this time to the accompaniment of an echoing crunch of sheering timber. I saw now that the pallet was only just supported on the end of the fork tines, and was wobbling.

Too late, I realised Piers was trying to knock the pallet off the fork and let it drop into the aisle at the point where I was standing. I started to step away, but with a final thrust Piers dislodged the pallet, which started to fall, hitting the racking as it did so with a heavy wooden clatter.

I lunged to the side of the aisle and thrust myself into the ground-level tier of racking, which mercifully was empty. The pallet landed next to me with an explosive crash that echoed round the warehouse.

Instantly I felt a searing pain in my arm, and realised with horror that a large wooden shard had been smashed off the pallet in the impact and had somehow bounced sideways and pierced my shirt, embedding itself in my arm.

Instantly I broke out in a drenching sweat. How bad was the injury? Was my arm broken? Had an artery been pierced?

For a moment there was silence, then I heard the electric hum of the pallet lift. It was moving again, accompanied by its intermittent alarm.

I looked again at the wooden shard. Should I pull it out, or would that be fatal? The instinct to remove it was intense, but I fought to resist it. Then before I'd had a chance to form a view, it fell out of its own accord. Blood immediately oozed through my shirtsleeve from the wound, but not in a torrent. That was something, at any rate. I was dimly aware of the pallet lift clattering and bleeping past me as it headed towards the end of the aisle.

I'd love to say I bravely ignored the wound, but self-preservation was now my priority. What Piers Ashurst got up to seemed a small matter by comparison. Clutching my right arm with my left, I struggled out of the pallet bay and into the aisle. The lift was now at the far end, and I could see the forklift truck picking up a loaded pallet. I started walking towards it, not with any plan to interfere, but merely because I knew no other way out.

Awkwardly I dragged my phone from my pocket and dialled 999. When the call handler answered I asked for an ambulance and the police. Whether or not there was any chance of stopping Piers from leaving the premises, the police needed to know what had happened.

By the time I reached the end of the aisle the forklift truck had pulled away and crossed the empty space beyond it, heading for one of the loading bays. I rounded the corner and headed cautiously in the same direction, conscious that if Piers saw me and decided to attack me again in some way I would be unable to defend myself.

However, he seemed preoccupied with loading the pallet into the waiting box van. The forklift driver placed it delicately on the rear sill of the van, then reversed the forklift truck clear while Piers dragged down the van's roller-shutter rear door and latched it shut. Evidently this had been the last pallet of the consignment. The forklift driver jumped down from his perch and they both climbed into the truck cab. The engine started and it headed away across the yard towards the entrance gate.

Chapter 54

I stood at the loading bay, clutching my arm and watching as the box van reached the gatehouse. Would the gates open or not? I could see the security man leaning out through the window and gesticulating. The gates remained shut.

After a moment the truck's cab door opened and Piers jumped down and strode round the end of the gatehouse, where a couple of steps led up to a metal door. He reached for the door handle and pulled, but the door was apparently locked. Clearly frustrated, he returned to the window on the side. I couldn't hear what he was saying, but his angry tones rang across the yard. Bob Latimer must have phoned through with his instruction not to let the truck leave, and Piers was not a happy man.

He climbed into the truck cab, and I wondered for a moment if he and the driver intended to ram the gates and force their way out. However, before they had a chance to do anything a police car drew up outside and two officers in high-visibility jackets emerged and entered the yard via a pedestrian gate. I breathed a sigh of relief.

The security guard leaned down to speak to them, then they approached the truck. After a moment Piers and his colleague jumped down from the cab. For a few moments they were engaged in a lively conversation with the police, then they were led out through the gate to the police car. Meanwhile Joe, the man in the boiler suit, reversed the truck away from the gate and backed it up to the fence a few metres away.

Presently a second police car and an ambulance arrived at the same time. One of the police officers came to talk to me, and I recounted the events since I'd arrived at the warehouse. Over his shoulder I could see the other officer opening the back of the van and glancing at the contents.

I wanted to take them to the place in the warehouse where the pallet had nearly been dropped on me, but the ambulance crew insisted I should go to the hospital immediately and Joe volunteered to show them the damaged pallet.

* * *

I was seen surprisingly quickly by the emergency department at the hospital in Leeds. They cleaned and bandaged the wound in my arm, telling me it was less serious than it looked. It certainly felt serious enough. It was in the opposite arm to the one that had been kicked at Ernie Bladen's house, so now I ached on both sides.

While I was waiting I phoned Ashley. I insisted I was fine, but told her I was marooned at the hospital without my car. We debated what to do, and in the end she told me she Tina were going to drive over to Leeds together to pick me up and recover my car, saving me the need to drive.

I also phoned Bob Latimer, who was still on a train. I realised now that he was making the long journey from Austell to Newcastle to find out first-hand what had been happening from Chris Melling. I told him the pallet-load had been successfully stopped at the warehouse, and the police would be examining it and considering the implications. The line was poor, so he made little comment. I would have to wait to find out his view of what had happened.

Ashley and Tina finally appeared in the casualty department. Ashley looked alarmed as she walked over, but hid her concern with a grin as she took a seat beside me. Tina stood to one side with a bemused smile on her face.

Ashley said, "I thought you were yearning for the quiet life."

"I was. I am. I just got drawn into something."

"Are you all right?"

"I'll live."

She smiled faintly. "You never told me when we met that I had to expect this kind of thing."

"You don't. This is exceptional. Honestly."

"I'm joking! I'm just glad you're all right."

"More or less, anyway."

They drove me to the Latimer warehouse, where we dropped Ashley off to drive my car over to Doncaster. She insisted that I travel with Tina as a gesture of goodwill.

"You're leading an exciting life," Tina commented as we pulled away.

"Not intentionally. All this came about because I was trying to get back into Latimer Logistics' good books after messing them about."

"And has it worked?"

I gave her a wry look. "I don't know. If so, it's been a painful process."

She laughed. "Is it right that Piers Ashurst faked a robbery? Why would he do that?"

"I think his company's cash reserves were at rock bottom. He misjudged the market and overstocked. Somehow he must have had this idea that he could steal a consignment of product and claim the insurance on it, then feed it back into stock and sell it anyway. In effect, he would have made a hundred per cent profit on it, less a few costs. I suppose he thought the cash injection would buy him some time."

"Insurers can take months to pay out."

"But at least he would know the money was on the way – and he could delay new purchases. Maybe that was enough."

We drove on in silence for a while, then she said, "I looked into that other company that I told you about – the one that sells the Spirit Spiralizer. There was speculation that Piers Ashurst's company might be going to acquire it."

"What did you find out?"

"Well, I don't know if this is true, but I heard that they definitely held talks, and I think I know why."

She waited while we negotiated a motorway junction, then resumed. "You have to look at the history. Ashurst Concepts drummed up a load of publicity when they launched a few years ago, but they've never had much of a high-street presence. A lot of their sales are online, and it's hard to maintain online visibility unless you keep spending heavily on advertising and promotion. If sales were falling, Ashursts may not have been able to afford it." She gave a dry laugh. "They probably found themselves in a vicious spiral, if you'll excuse the pun."

"So how does the Spirit Spiralizer fit in?"

"Ah, well, Wilsons, the people behind that product, had a much better relationship with the retail trade, so their products were highly visible on the high street. I think Piers Ashurst might have decided that if he combined the two operations he would have the best of both worlds."

"But if Ashursts had cash flow problems, how could they afford an acquisition like that?"

"They would have had to borrow massively. It would have been a make-or-break gamble."

I said, "The Spirit people had a load of bad publicity when they were exposed by that TV programme. If Ashursts bought into them just before the shit hit the proverbial, it would have been a disaster for them."

"Maybe they did, and that's what drove Piers Ashurst to desperation."

Chapter 55

I was due to drive a hundred miles north to Sunderland next day to do the rescheduled interview I'd taken on for the logistics magazine, but I had little appetite for the trip. Ashley volunteered to drive me if I wanted to go ahead with it, but I said no. My arm ached and I felt battered.

By the time we got to Doncaster it was too late to contact the company I was due to see, but first thing next morning I phoned the managing director and told him I needed to rearrange our appointment for a second time. Understandably he sounded a little testy about it, but he did commiserate with me over my injury. I said I would write an extra-glowing article by way of apology. We agreed to do the interview on Friday morning.

Postponing the appointment again left space for Ashley to drive me over to Leeds so that I could provide a statement to the police about the events at the warehouse. They had been joined by colleagues from Sheffield who were investigating the lorry hijacking. I explained my theory about the reasons for the hijacking, but they merely said they would consider all leads.

We spent the rest of the day and most of the following day at Tina's flat, catching up with work by remote control. We'd never sat together so long over our computers, but the arrangement worked. Our easy amicability had returned, and neither of us seemed distracted by the other.

Intimacy, however, was still on hold. There was unresolved tension between us, and we were both nervous of making a move too soon. So we skated almost shyly round each other, shocked by every unintended touch. It seemed we were cautiously rebuilding our relationship from scratch.

On the Wednesday afternoon I was phoned from Newcastle by Bob Latimer, who was coming to the end of his flying visit to Melling Logistics.

"Mike, I heard that things worked out all right in Leeds."

"Pretty much. Thanks for intervening when I asked."

"I'm glad I was able to help. We've still got those pallets, and the police are looking at them. I can't believe this man Piers Ashurst would get involved in something as stupid as stealing them."

"I think he must have been desperate."

"I'm just trying to work out with Chris how to deal with this. We have the other issue with Ashursts on top of this – the fact that their accounts seem to have been massaged. You were the one who alerted us to that too. I still don't understand how it happened."

"Well I might have a clue for you. When I was visiting the factory I met a man named Nick. I'm afraid I don't know his surname, but he seemed to be involved in their accounts department. After that I met him again at Salmon Fischer, the company that supervised the due diligence at Ashursts. I get the impression that's where he actually works, which seems a bit odd to me."

"This goes from bad to worse, doesn't it?"

"Sorry to be the bringer of bad news."

Bob was silent for a moment, then said, "You seem to have a remarkable ability to turn up at the right place at the right time. How come you were visiting these Salmon Fischer people, if you don't mind me asking?"

"I don't mind at all, but it's a long story, and it's mostly down to luck. Maybe I could fill you in on the detail when I see you?"

"Fair enough. I'm glad you picked this up, anyway."

On the Thursday Dave Matthews phoned me and filled in some of the gaps left after I'd given my statement in Leeds.

"Mike Stanhope breaks the case wide open," he commented dryly.

"Hardly."

"You'd be surprised. You were the one who made the connection between the hijacked truck driver and the white van man in Leeds. As it turns out, they're cousins, the Civets. The way it's looking, Andy Civet knew Piers Ashurst from way back. He jumped at the chance of earning a quick buck from hijacking the Ashurst load, and arm-twisted his cousin in Southampton to do the necessary."

"But how did Piers know the driver would be up for it?"

"Roy Civet was regular on that run. Piers had got to know him somehow – probably while he was offloading at the warehouse. I suppose when he heard the driver's surname he made the connection with his mate Andy. It's a pretty unusual one. So he hatched the whole scheme, and put it to Andy."

"I got the impression that the driver regretted the whole thing."

"Maybe. He's recently divorced and in debt. I expect he saw this as a way of earning some easy money to get himself back on track. But he had a lot of hassle from the police about it – and now he'll have a lot more."

"So Andy Civet was ferrying the stolen pallets to the Ashurst factory a few at a time, to feed into their normal stock – is that right?"

"Pretty much. He'd got them stashed in an old lockup warehouse half a mile from his depot. The Leeds police have found the rest of the consignment there. The deal was that they would be shipped into the Ashurst factory and relabelled in the evenings, when the daytime staff were at home. Civet got a couple of his mates to come in and do the job."

"It sounds quite an expensive operation, all in all. You wouldn't think there would be much profit for Piers after everyone was paid."

Dave laughed cynically. "You'd be surprised. From what I hear, these spiralizers and coffee makers are top-end models, with a high selling price. That load could have been worth up to half a million – maybe even more. And it was all free money, since the insurers were paying."

"I suppose so. But presumably it was company money, not Piers Ashurst's own money."

"Ah, well, some of these entrepreneurs seem able to make that a very thin line."

I asked if he thought I was right that Piers had never intended to move the stolen pallets into the high-bay Latimer warehouse at Holbeck.

"I'm sure he didn't. I think the intention was to put *some* pallets in that warehouse, but the staff at Ashurts picked the wrong ones while Piers was out. As soon as he realised, he rushed out to fetch them back. They were hard evidence of the fraud, and the last thing he wanted was to put them on public view in someone else's warehouse. That's why he was so keen that you shouldn't stop him removing them."

"So now the police have the evidence that they couldn't find on Monday?"

"Huh. Don't get carried away with your own genius. We're not issuing any medals yet."

* * *

Early on the Friday morning Ashley and I left Tina and Martin's flat and headed off north for Sunderland so that I could do my magazine interview. We found the transport company easily enough on the outskirts of Sunderland, and Ashley came in with me when I was taken to talk to the managing director. He seemed amused at her presence, but I simply told him, "We're combining this trip with a holiday."

He gave me a deadpan look. "I can see that Sunderland would be quite near the top of anyone's holiday list."

At the end of the session we were given a guided tour of the premises. Ashley seemed as interested as I was, and as we wandered among the old-fashioned warehousing and smart blue and white trucks she asked some probing questions. As we drove away she commented, "They could do with a few lessons in marketing and PR. It's all rather 'old school', isn't it?"

"Don't be deceived. They're really profitable. In this business you sometimes don't need to worry too much about image management."

"You're as bad as them! Just don't let Bob Latimer hear you saying that. If he believed it I would be out of a job."

From Sunderland we drove the fifteen miles west to Newcastle. Ashley had decided she wanted to see the city that had held such drama for me in recent weeks, so I'd booked us into the small hotel that Latimers used. It was much more expensive than the motel where I'd been staying, but I'd persuaded myself we were now on holiday. Anyway, Ashley insisted she would share the cost.

She said, "So long as I don't have to meet Jenna or anybody else from the Melling place, I'll be happy enough."

"No chance of that."
It turned out I was wrong.

Chapter 56

I took Ashley on a quick tour of Newcastle city centre next morning. She was impressed with the Georgian architecture, and intrigued when I showed her the street where I believed my grandmother had been filmed.

"But you haven't found out yet how Elizabeth Sanderson knew her?"

"I'm working on it."

We wandered down Grey Street to the Quayside and ordered drinks in the same bar where I'd encountered Jenna and Greg weeks before. We picked a table outside, just as I had last time, and I looked around uneasily, fearing illogically that Jenna would suddenly materialise. Of course she didn't.

As we sat in the sun I thought over recent developments. Piers Ashurst was now in custody, and would presumably be prosecuted for masterminding the truck hijacking. Looked at narrowly, this rather neatly solved a mystery.

However, there was a broader problem for Latimer Logistics. By completing its acquisition of the Melling group, Latimers now owned Ashursts – a failing consumer products supplier whose profitability was in question, and whose founder must be facing a prison sentence. Bad news for Bob Latimer, to put it mildly.

Then there was a question mark over the reason why Ashursts had been incorrectly given a green light in the due diligence process, and there was an even bigger one over Ernie Bladen's apparent involvement in Jenna's kidnapping. I was still convinced that he'd masterminded it to stop her from derailing the acquisition, but from what I'd picked up, there was no hard evidence of this.

The biggest unknown was whether anyone was investigating all this in a coordinated way. Various police forces were involved, but were they talking to each other about it? I wasn't convinced.

* * *

We decided to eat in the hotel restaurant that night, and when we came downstairs from changing, a shock awaited us in the small bar. Chris and Jenna Melling were seated at the counter. Jenna smiled with what looked like genuine pleasure. Chris looked puzzled. "This is a surprise, Mike."

A little awkwardly I said, "Work. Holiday. A bit of both. This is a nice place. It seemed logical for us to book in here."

"A busman's holiday, then." His tone was friendly, but he looked unsettled.

I introduced Ashley. Chris said to her, "We've met you at some of the logistics exhibitions, haven't we?"

"Of course we have, man," Jenna said. "Ashley was the one who came up with the ideas for those wacky Latimer stand designs." She turned to Ashley. "How are you doing?"

Ashley nodded cautiously. "I'm good. I hope you're OK after what happened to you?"

"I'm getting there."

I said to Chris, "What brings you two here on a Saturday night?"

"We're here for our strategy dinner. Did you not hear about it when you were with us?"

I shook my head.

"Most years we round up some of our favourite customers and bring them together for an informal meeting. Just me and them – none of the other directors. We discuss ideas, explore potential synergies – all that good stuff. It's just a handful of people – mostly customers from the North East."

"Sounds a good plan."

"This might be the last one, unless Bob Latimer wants to keep up the tradition." He attempted a conspiratorial chuckle. "To be honest, it's an excuse for some posh nosh. The private dining room here is just the right size, and the food is great."

Turning to Jenna, I said, "I didn't know you were a Melling customer."

She laughed. "I'm not. My dad decided I needed an outing to lift my spirits. It's a chance to do a bit of low-key networking, really."

"It sounds like hard work to me."

"I'll let you know."

I could almost hear Ashley speculating on when that occasion might arise, but before the conversation could go any further a new figure came into the bar: Ernie Bladen. He was dressed smartly in a light brown lounge suit and was wearing a pink tie fastened in a large knot.

Several things happened at once. Jenna drew breath sharply. Chris Melling looked surprised and uncomfortable. Bladen himself stared at me for a moment, then addressed Chris as he walked up.

"Strange company you keep, Christopher. I don't number gossip-mongering journalists among my favourite people." He glared at me as he spoke.

"Mike isn't a gossip-mongering journalist. He works on contract to Latimer Logistics. He's an experienced writer and a friend of mine."

I warmed immediately to this unexpected defence. Calling me a friend was stretching the truth, but hearing it told me a lot.

"Is that so?" Bladen looked at me again. "I must make a note of that."

Chris said, "I wasn't expecting you here tonight, Ernie. Did you not get my message? It's nothing personal, but we cut down the numbers this year."

Bladen seemed unfazed. "Message? No. It's the customer dinner, isn't it? And I'm a customer, am I not?"

"We'll need to get a place set for you." He called the barman over. "Tom, could you get a message to Stephanie in catering? Tell her there will be an extra person at the table tonight."

Jenna was watching all this incredulously, glancing back and forth between Bladen and Melling. She now said to her father, "Are you telling me you're actually going to let this man sit down to dinner with us?"

He shrugged awkwardly. "Well he's here now."

She stood up abruptly. "You can cancel the extra place then. I won't be joining you tonight." She turned to Ashley and me. "Shall we go and sit over there?"

Chris looked ready to protest, but at that moment two middle-aged men walked into the bar and headed over towards us.

"Chris, Ernie, good to see you both."

Amid the greetings, Jenna made her way over to a cluster of chairs on the far side of the room, and Ashley and I followed her. As we sat down Jenna hissed, "I don't know how that man has the face to turn up here – after keeping me a prisoner for nearly a week! The gall of it. And my father sits there and takes it."

I said, "I don't think Chris can have been expecting him. He looked pretty shocked to see him."

"And so he should be!"

Ashley said, "How can Bladen just turn up like this? Isn't he under suspicion for kidnapping Jenna?"

I answered, "Possibly not. From what I picked up, there might not be any hard evidence to connect him with it. He's innocent until proved guilty."

Jenna said, "But my father knows he's in the frame."

"That's probably why he didn't invite him tonight."

"He should be telling him to sod off!"

I said, "What will you do now?"

"I don't know. I'm booked in here for the night, but there's no point in staying now. I might as well call a taxi and head off home."

Ashley said diffidently, "Why don't you join us for a meal? They won't be in the main dining room, so you won't see them."

Under the circumstances her offer was more than generous. Jenna looked between us, hesitating, then said, "No, you're all right. It's a nice offer, but I'd rather not be under the same roof as that man. It looks like you're stuck with him, but you weren't the ones he locked up."

I smiled inwardly. Technically, Bladen might not have locked me up, but I had little enough to thank him for.

"Are you sure?"

"Trust me, I need to leave for my own peace of mind."

Chapter 57

Ashley and I lingered over our meal, talking mostly of our life in Cornwall. She reminded me about our tentative plans for a continental holiday in late August. "There's still time to arrange something."

We were still in the restaurant after the handful of other guests had left, but eventually we wandered out and drifted into the bar. We were the only people in it; there was no sign of the Melling crowd, who were presumably still ensconced in their private room, and the bar itself was unattended. We sat in high-backed armchairs by the window and chatted for a while, then Ashley declared that she was ready to turn in. I said I would give her a few minutes and then join her.

I gazed through the glass doors into the patio, which was dappled with light from the bar. Benign thoughts drifted through my mind. Ashley had been remarkably sanguine in her conversation with Jenna. Chris Melling had been charmingly defensive. Things were looking up.

Then I heard raised voices out in the hall. The swing doors into the bar were thrust open and two people came in, still talking to each other: Ernie Bladen and Chris Melling. Bladen was saying, "It's no good telling me it'll all come out in the wash. What good is that to me?"

Chris said, "It was just a form of words. What I meant was that you'll get your money in the end."

Clearly they hadn't seen me. I had to make up my mind whether to make myself known to them or stay put. They were now standing over by the bar. If I stayed, I had to hope they wouldn't decide to come over to the window.

Bladen said, "That bloody fool Ashurst has got himself arrested for theft, and might get sent down. What you don't seem to understand is that he hasn't paid me my money yet. If they don't let him out, he may not be able to."

"But he might get bail. It's not as if he's committed a violent crime."

"I don't deal in ifs and buts, I deal in certainties. You know that, Chris."

"Well what do you want me to say to you?"

"It's simple. If Piers Ashurst can't give me my money, you'll have to pay it yourself."

"*What?*" There was a moment's silence, then Chris said, "For god's sake, Ernie. Are you serious? That money has already been transferred to Ashursts. You can't expect me to find it all over again. I don't have spare cash like that."

"Even after this Latimer takeover that you're so proud of? You'll be rolling in it, won't you?"

"That's mostly share value, not cash. I can't scrape up that kind of money at a moment's notice. How would I explain it to Sheila? Anyway, why should I? It's ridiculous."

"Don't you tell me what's ridiculous. You know what I'll do if I have to."

He let that undefined threat hang in the air, and for a moment neither of them spoke.

The conversation had now run too far for me to reveal myself. I needed to keep my head down and hope neither of the men would spot me. However, it now occurred to me that I had a unique opportunity – I could record the rest of their conversation. I had no idea what revelations it might yield, but it seemed too good an opportunity to miss. I slid my phone cautiously out of my jacket and launched the recording application, fearful at every step that the phone would emit some sound that would give me away. Thankfully it didn't.

There was a burst of impatient tapping on the bar counter and Bladen's voice called, "Any chance of some service around here?"

No response. After a moment he addressed Chris again. "I don't know what you're so worried about. In the end you can get your money back from Piers Ashurst, can't you?"

Chris sighed. "He's a loose cannon. I can't be sure what he'll do with it. He may be up to his ears in other debts, and use it to pay them off. He may have spent it already."

"Not my problem." There was a pause. "And by the way, you can cancel our BBS invoices for the last two months. We won't be paying any of that."

"What? Do you want to put me out of business?"

"It's not your company any more. You keep telling me that. Lose the money somewhere and let Mr Bloody Latimer deal with it."

Sounding appalled, Chris said, "I can't do that! The company accounts are transparent. I'd never get away with it."

There was a silence, which seemed more threatening than an angry retort would have done. Finally Bladen said quietly, "Then sort this out."

* * *

Bladen muttered, "Where the hell is that barman?" There was another silence, then he said, "Bollocks to this. I'm going to find a place where they pay attention to their customers."

It sounded as if the conversation was closed. Disappointed, I prepared to stop the phone recording, but then Chris spoke again. "You're causing me a lot of grief here, Ernie."

"*I'm* causing *you* grief? That's a good one. You started all this when you introduced me to that pillock Ashurst. I should have known better."

Chris said, "I didn't force you to invest. That was your call. You were happy enough to take advantage when things were going well for him." His voice grew louder as he spoke, and I realised with sudden panic that he was strolling over towards the window. I tried to shrink further into the chair.

Bladen said, "I trusted your judgement – more fool me. I thought you had a proper business head on your shoulders. I never thought you would be led by sentiment."

I could now see Chris out of the corner of my eye, staring through the glass doors into the patio and the darkness beyond. He sighed. "I can't help what you thought, Ernie."

"You shouldn't have been led by that daughter of yours. If it hadn't been for her, you would never have put your money into his company in the first place."

"Leave my daughter out of this." There was indignation in Chris's comment, though it was not as strident as it might have been.

"That's a good one! Her meddling nearly blocked the Latimer deal."

"I could have talked her round. I just needed time to explain things. I mean, good god – holding her for days in that bloody place! What kind of person does that?"

"You should be grateful. Something had to be done."

Chris turned sharply, and as he did so he spotted me in the chair. A shiver ran through me. Would he give me away to Bladen? I held my finger up to my lips and gave him an imploring stare.

He held my gaze for a moment, but I couldn't read his intent. Then he looked over at Bladen and moved out of sight towards him.

"I don't want to hear your justifications," he said angrily.

"There's no need to act high and mighty. I did what was necessary." He laughed humourlessly. "She's a tough one. She seems to have survived perfectly well."

"But what about the long-term damage?"

"Can we skip the psycho-babble? I had to protect my interests – much good that it did me. The bottom line is that I was supposed to get my money when this deal went through, and I haven't. You need to put that right. I'm not going to wait around for it."

There was another pause, then Bladen said, "I don't know what you have to do to get a drink around here. I've had enough of this. I'm going to wake up my driver."

I waited to hear him striding out of the room, but instead there was silence, and I realised he must be calling his driver on his phone.

A ringtone sounded outside the window, and I saw the brief flash of a phone screen coming to life at the corner of the patio. Behind me, Bladen's voice said, "Harry? Wake up. We're leaving now."

Now I saw the faint red glow of a cigarette being flung away. Harry must have been outside all along.

Chapter 58

I heard the doors swing open and shut as Bladen stormed off, but I sensed that Chris was still in the room – presumably waiting for my inevitable questions. I peered cautiously round the back of the chair to make sure we were alone.

"Hello Mike," he said. "You're all right, he's gone."

I slid out of the chair and joined him at the bar – where, surprisingly, the barman now materialised. Chris turned to me, shuffling on to a bar stool. "Join me in a brandy?"

I sat down beside him. "Don't mind if I do."

To the barman he said, "Doubles."

He waited until the drinks appeared, then said, "Could we have some privacy here please?" The barman shrugged and disappeared towards the kitchens.

Chris looked at me appraisingly. "You seem to have a habit of meddling in other people's business – especially mine." But there was no acrimony in his words. If anything, I detected resignation.

"I didn't plan to be in that chair when you came in. It just fell that way."

Chris nodded. "Yes, I'm sure that must happen to you a lot." He looked reflectively at me for a moment. "You're not playing journalist today, are you Mike? I mean, this conversation is purely between friends, am I right?"

"Absolutely. You have my word."

"All right then. I believe you." He took a long sip of brandy. "And you're not going running to Bob Latimer to tell tales out of school?"

I wasn't sure how to answer that. After a moment's thought I said, "You'll have to trust my judgement."

It seemed to satisfy him. He glanced over towards the door through which Bladen had just departed. "That man Ernie Bladen is a miserable bastard. I don't know why I ever thought I could do business with him. He's right – I'm a soft touch."

"How did it start then?"

"Oh, his building supplies firm approached us in the normal way to handle some of its logistics work. Nothing sinister in it. I knew about his dubious personal reputation, but the company itself seemed perfectly kosher, so I thought, why not?"

He stared into his brandy, reflecting. "Back then Jenna was working for me, but she wanted to strike out on her own, and her college friend Piers was just starting up his electrical import business. He got her on board to run his marketing operation, and she recommended him to let us do his fulfilment – to deliver his products to consumers, I mean. It was all very small-scale at that stage, but suddenly the spiralizer took off, and demand shot up." He turned to me. "That's really when things started to go wrong."

I said, "Cash flow problems?"

He nodded. "It's the old story. His company grew too quickly. They didn't have the funds to pay their bills. But the product was sound and the demand was there, so Jenna asked me if I would be willing to buy into the firm, and I said yes."

He waited a moment, but I said nothing, so he resumed. "For a while it solved the problem. Sales kept on increasing. Piers became a bit of a celebrity. I brought him up to Newcastle to one of our strategy meetings, like the one we had tonight, and he met Ernie Bladen. Then the next thing I know, he's hit another cash flow crisis – only this time he doesn't tell me, he gets Ernie Bladen to bail him out. He probably thought I wouldn't say yes a second time."

"But things still didn't work for him?"

"For a while they did, but then everything went wrong again, only this time in a big way. I don't know the details, but for some reason Piers' debt to Bladen shot up. He probably had some scheme to get himself out of the hole he was in, only it didn't work."

I felt I had to give Chris something in return for these confidences. I said, "I think I know what happened with Bladen. I think Piers borrowed more money from him to buy out Wilson Electrics. It would have been a good fit, what with their spiralizer and so on, but then that television programme brought them down. Suddenly their stock was more or less worthless, and Ernie's money was gone."

Chris screwed up his eyes as he listened to this. "Of course. It makes perfect sense. The bloody fool." He thought some more. "But none of this is in the Ashurst accounts."

"I don't think he bought the company through Ashursts. I think it was a private deal, funded by Bladen. It was going to be his escape route after he bailed out of the original company – the one you bought."

"Talk about a tangled bloody web."

As we spoke, the pieces of the puzzle were falling together in my mind. I said, "If Piers had thought for a moment, he might have realised that demand for the spiralizer was already levelling off. People were moving on to the next fad. He was already stuck with excess stock. I don't know how he expected to sell even more of it."

Chris's looked changed to one of curiosity. "You're mighty well informed for a logistics hack."

"I just pick up bits of information here and there. It's more by luck than by diligent research."

"If you say so." He nodded to himself. "Piers is one of life's eternal optimists, but he's also a devious sod. It must have been just after all this happened that he organised that damned lorry hijacking."

"It shows how desperate he was. It's a wonder Bladen ever invested any money with him in the first place."

Chris laughed bitterly. "I suppose even Ernie Bladen has his weak spots. Piers talks the talk very convincingly. You've met him – you know what he's like. I think Bladen was taken in by him, but he soon found out the error of his ways."

"What actually happened?"

"Bladen came to see me one day, and told me Piers was up to his eyes in debt, and there was no way back for him. I wasn't a majority shareholder then, and I hadn't been monitoring his accounts. Anyway Bladen had a scheme up his sleeve to solve the problem. He keeps his ear to the ground, and he'd heard that Latimers were sniffing around, looking at acquiring my company. That was his solution."

I asked him, "How would it have worked?"

"His plan was that I should say yes to the deal, and I should transfer Ashurst Concepts to the Melling pot so that it would be included in the acquisition. At the same time I would buy up the share of Ashursts that I didn't already own, using part of the payoff from Latimers to fund the purchase. It's probably borderline illegal, but it's not uncommon. To cut a long story short, Latimers would acquire Piers' entire company along with Mellings, and Piers would net enough cash from the deal to clear his debt to Bladen.

He put his glass down and stretched. "And that's more or less how it did happen, apart from the bit where Bladen gets his money. Apparently that's still in abeyance."

"And Bob Latimer was happy with all this, was he?"

Chris chuckled dryly. "Being honest, I sort of bounced him into it. He had big plans for the merger, so I was able to slot Ashursts into the deal at the last minute. He didn't want to unwind everything at that stage, so he said he was up for it. Actually I think he was intrigued at the idea of getting into the consumer market. You know what he's like – another of life's optimists."

"And Bladen himself didn't actually own shares in Ashursts?"

"No, it was just a loan."

"What about the due diligence process? How come it didn't show up the fact that Ashursts' finances were all over the place?"

Chris shrugged. "Bladen said Piers had taken care of that, and it seems he was right. Don't ask me how he did it."

I reflected that I probably knew more about this than he did. I said, "Surely the whole thing will come out in the end?"

"Maybe, but many's the slip 'twixt cup and lip, as the saying goes. Ashurst Concepts might still recover, even without Piers. If it does, everyone will be happy. If it doesn't, the sleight of hand will probably disappear in the general fallout. At this stage it's all up in the air."

I sat in silence for a moment. I could see the logic of all this, but something didn't gel. I said, "I don't see why you had to roll over and do what Bladen wanted. You didn't owe him or Piers Ashurst a living.

Why were you prepared to sell out just on his say-so?"

He looked at me sadly. "I was afraid you'd ask that. Bladen has …
leverage, shall we say? He knows things I don't want revealed. That's the
way he operates."

"What things?"

"I'd rather not go into it, if you don't mind."

I nodded dubiously and he cleared his throat. He said, "I was nearly
ready to take a step back already, so in a way this just focused my mind.
I won't come out of it too badly, all in all." He cut himself off. "That is,
I wouldn't have if Piers hadn't got himself arrested. Now Bladen wants
me to pay off his debt myself, in case he doesn't get the money from
Piers. I can't raise enough cash for that."

"So I gather."

Neither of us spoke for a while. Chris had nearly drained his brandy
glass, but mine was still half full. Finally I said, "So Bladen had Jenna
kidnapped to stop her making waves over the takeover. Surely you can't
condone that?"

He was suddenly defensive. "We don't know he did for sure. The
police couldn't find any connection with him."

"But he more or less admitted it just now, when you were talking."

"It could be bluster. It suits him to seem as if he's in control."

I tried to remember exactly what Bladen had said. "It seemed pretty
unequivocal to me."

"Well, you're entitled to your view, Mike."

I thought for a moment. "I recorded the conversation you just had
with him, on my phone. One way or the other, we could probably use
it against him."

"Jesus, Mike!" He looked at me with a panicked expression. "What
if he reveals what he knows about me?"

"He wouldn't if he thought he would be prosecuted as a result. It's a
bargaining counter."

He shook his head. "I don't know. It sounds a dangerous game to
me. People like him are as good as gangsters. Are you prepared to go up
against someone like that?"

"We would need to tread carefully."

"You're damned right we would."

"There's an alternative, of course. You could go public with whatever Bladen has against you. Then he would have no leverage, and we could go to the police with what we have."

He shook his head vehemently. "No way."

"OK, I hear you."

"Good." He looked at me for a long moment, then stood up. "I'm done in. I'm going to bed."

"You're staying over?"

"Yes, it saves a lot of hassle." He started for the door, then turned. "You won't take this any further without talking to me first, will you?"

"It seems wrong to sit on it."

"You need to see the bigger picture – to consider who would be affected if I went public with it. Bear with me on this."

I nodded dubiously, and he said, "Thanks." He breathed in deeply, then said, "I can see that your heart's in the right place, Mike. I know you want to do the right thing."

I wasn't sure how to respond to that. I simply said, "Have a good night."

Ashley was half asleep when I reached our room. She said, "I dreamt you'd gone home with Jenna.".

"Huh! Chris Melling has been baring his soul to me."

"Interesting?"

"Extremely."

She yawned. "Tell me about it tomorrow."

Chapter 59

"I want to see Vindolanda." Ashley looked at me across the breakfast table with a challenge in her eyes. "I've come all this way. It's too good a chance to miss."

I'd read the guide book. Vindolanda was a world famous Roman site some way west of Newcastle. A plethora of day-to-day Roman correspondence and other artefacts had been found there in recent times.

I thought over my conversation last night with Chris Melling. What, if anything, was I supposed to do about it? My presence here with Ashley might have been turning into an impromptu holiday, but the information I'd learned yesterday had plunged me back into the thick of the acquisition saga. I could be picking it up and running with it, yet Chris has made it amply clear that he didn't want me to.

Eventually I would need to tell Bob Latimer as much as I could about the Ashurst situation. It might still not redeem me when it came to future work for him, but I felt I owed him that much. Then again, I couldn't help liking Chris, and I was reluctant to do anything that would pitch me against him.

My main concern was more immediate. Bladen's right-hand man Harry had been out on the patio while I was listening to Chris's conversation with him. Had Harry seen me? I'd been sitting at an angle to the window, and his position had been almost out of sight. Nevertheless, he would only have needed to peer round slightly to see me.

If he had, presumably he would have told Bladen about it, so Bladen would now know that I'd heard the conversation. How would he react? It was hard to believe he would take no action, but I couldn't imagine what he actually would do.

Ashley was looking expectantly at me. "Hello? Vindolanda today? What do you think?"

Her enthusiasm to be a tourist suddenly seemed to put things into perspective. Amid the glorious mundanity of a hotel breakfast it was tempting to treat everything else as a bad dream.

I said, "Thank you."

She smiled, puzzled. "What for?"

I shrugged. "I don't know – for reminding me that there's a world beyond Melling Logistics. I thought I'd got away from all that, and last night was a bit of a shock."

"I know you've had a lot to contend with up here in the north. I don't mean to trivialise the situation."

"You're not. A day out is what we need."

"But you must be wondering about your prospects at Latimer Logistics. Treating this trip as a holiday probably seems a distraction."

"Huh! I was just thinking about that. I *am* wondering, but all I can do is take things a step at a time."

"You could still work from Cornwall even if Bob doesn't give you the job back." It was both a question and a statement, and she was watching me carefully as she spoke.

"I expect so. But we're here now, so let's make the most of it."

She gave me a long look. "So – Vindolanda, then?"

* * *

The sky was overcast, but we were on our own without any urgent obligation. For the first time in weeks I felt almost relaxed. We drove off westwards on the A69, then after a few miles I took the turnoff for Heddon-on-the-Wall, just north of the main road.

Ashley was puzzled. "Where are we going?"

"There's an alternative road west – the Military Road. I read about it when I was killing time in that motel. It follows the route of Hadrian's Wall."

"Sounds good to me."

"The road was only built in the eighteenth century. They used bits of the wall as the foundations."

"Philistines!"

We headed out of the village of Heddon on the Military Road, which was very straight and relatively flat – a two-lane single carriageway with very little traffic. It was bordered by hedgerows and dry stone walls and flanked by open fields. We continued for a few miles, then my eye was drawn to a distant car in my rear-view mirror. I said, "I'm sure that car was behind us before we turned off."

Ashley looked round. "They're probably just tourists, like us."

"Maybe. I'm probably getting paranoid."

"Do you seriously think someone might be following us?"

"Anything is possible." I could feel her quizzical look, so I said, "After you went to bed, Chris and Ernie Bladen came into the bar. They didn't see me, and they started talking about the Latimer takeover. Basically, Bladen more or less admitted responsibility for kidnapping Jenna to stop her upsetting the applecart. And I recorded it all on my phone."

She looked at me in wonder.

I smiled grimly. "Quite." I glanced again at the other car, which was still hanging back at the same distance. "The thing is, just as Bladen was leaving I realised one that one of his people was sitting out on the patio in the dark – and he might have seen me listening to their conversation. If so, Bladen might not be very happy with me."

"Oh, great." She sat up straighter. "That's really great. So he might have sent someone to follow us." She looked through the rear window again. "They're still a long way off. Maybe it's nothing."

"Let's hope so." I turned to her. "Can you find the audio recording on my phone, and email it to Dave Matthews? At the moment I only have the one copy."

Dubiously she said, "I'll try." She fiddled with the phone for a while, then muttered in irritation, "I don't think I'm doing this properly. I obviously don't understand how your phone works."

"Don't worry. Maybe we can stop in a while, and I'll send it myself."

For a while we debated what to do. Could we still treat this trip as a holiday outing, or should we be fleeing an unspecified threat from Ernie Bladen and his men? The situation seemed surreal.

Ashley said, "Maybe we ought to phone the police or something?"

She was still holding my phone, and she swiped the screen impulsively to bring it to life. Abruptly she said, "Shit!" Then, "Fuck fuck fuck!"

"What's the matter?"

"I think I just deleted the audio file. Oh, god! I'm so sorry!"

I felt myself tensing my grip on the wheel, but I tried to stay calm. "Look, don't worry about it. The file might still be there, and if not, it's not the end of the world."

"I'll check, I'll check."

After a moment she said, "I'm sorry, I don't know if it's still there or not."

I took a deep breath before replying. "Never mind."

We continued in silence.

The landscape grew more bleak. We were now surrounded by scrubby moorland in varying shades of green and brown. Long surviving stretches of Hadrian's wall were in view a few hundred metres to our right. Its grey rectangular outline rose and fell with the terrain in an uncompromisingly straight line. A heavy sky hung over the landscape.

"Where are we?" Ashley asked.

I had to admit I didn't know. "I think we might have passed our turnoff. Have you seen signs to Housteads Roman Fort?"

"Yes, ages ago."

"Ah. I'm not concentrating. That's quite near where we want to be."

"Do you think we should turn back?"

I glanced in the mirror. The following car was still there, even though we weren't hurrying and other vehicles had passed us. I said, "That car is still there, but it'll catch us while we're turning."

"But what can he do?"

I said, "Can you get the satnav going on the phone? Then we'll know exactly where we are."

She fiddled with the phone again. "I actually got something to work," she said with irony, then: "We're definitely miles past the road we should have taken."

"Let me see." I took the phone from her and glanced down at it. "Fair enough."

To turn or to continue? I couldn't decide. I could speed up, but the idea of a car chase on this straight and empty road seemed absurd. I decided to turn round and brazen it out with the other car, and I started looking for a lay-by or gateway where I could pull in. Presently I spotted a small break in the flanking wall to our right, and I turned into it. A substantial track stretched away in front of us towards Hadrian's wall, which at this point was a several hundred metres from the road and higher up.

I drove a short way along the track to a point where it widened out slightly, and prepared to make a three-point turn. Then in the driving mirror I saw that the other car had turned on to the track behind us. It hovered ominously near the junction with the road, and I peered nervously at it, trying to identify the driver. I couldn't be sure, but it looked suspiciously like Harry.

Chapter 60

Our way was blocked by a gate thirty or forty metres ahead. There was no other way out. I sat motionless for a moment, unsure what to do, then carefully turned the car round. The other car was still standing near the end of the track. I could only see one face inside.

Ashley looked at it nervously. "What now?"

I glanced around. I felt there should be tourists or fell walkers about, but there was no one else in sight. The other car started moving slowly towards us.

I said, "I'm pretty sure that's Harry, the guy who was on the patio last night."

In a strained voice Ashley said, "What should we do? Should we get out and run?"

How serious was the threat? There were two of us and there was only one of him. Did we need to run, and would we achieve anything if we did? The landscape was open. There was nowhere to hide. Maybe all we were confronting was a conversation. I made a decision and got out of the car, pulling my jacket on. There was a fine mist in the air. I said to Ashley, "Stay there," and closed the door.

The other car stopped short twenty feet from us and the driver climbed out. It was indeed Harry, wearing jeans and a khaki anorak today in place of his pinstripe suit. He called over to me, "Mr Stanhope – please tell your friend to get out of the car."

"Why should I?"

He reached into a side pocket and pulled out a handgun, which he held loosely, almost tauntingly, at his side. "Because I'll shoot you if you don't."

"For Christ's sake!"

It wasn't the first time I'd found myself at gunpoint, but it still sent a violent shiver through me. At first sight it seemed melodramatic almost to the point of absurdity, yet I had to recognise that this was the hard reality of a world I knew little or nothing about. The casual conviction of Harry's tone underlined the threat; I had no doubt that he would do as he said.

I tried to laugh. "You must be having a joke." My fake bravado sounded feeble.

"Don't try me." He walked forward a few paces, watching me carefully all the time. "Tell her to get out of the car NOW!"

Ashley had heard him. She opened the door of her own accord and got out hesitantly, shrugging herself into her anorak.

"Very good. Now let's go for a walk."

"What?"

"Up the hill." He gestured along the track with his gun hand.

"Seriously?"

"And I don't want to see anyone with a phone in their hand. Got it?"

Neither of us replied, and he repeated angrily, "No phones! Hands out of pockets where I can see them. Got it?"

"Got it."

"So go."

Ashley gave me a fearful look, and I nodded. She shook her head in disbelief, slammed the car door shut behind her and set off up the track. I followed, and Harry brought up the rear, his gun half-lowered. Probably at a glance we looked like three fell walkers without their backpacks – not that there was anyone around to see us.

We soon came to the gate, but there was a space at the side where you could walk round it, so we continued towards the wall. By the time we reached it the mist had turned into a persistent drizzle. It was hardly surprising there were no walkers around; they'd checked the weather forecast in advance. The air was very still. The only sound was the faint shush of rain on vegetation.

"That way." Harry pointed to the wall, where rough steps gave access to the top, a couple of metres above us. We scrambled up, and Harry followed us at a discreet distance, pulling the hood of his anorak over his head as he did so. Now he was much more anonymous.

The wall was two or three metres wide and flat-topped, with a grassy footpath running along the centre line. He indicated that we should turn left.

At this point on its route the wall rose quite sharply, following the contours of the terrain up on to an escarpment that dropped away abruptly to the left. As we walked I risked a glance around us. There was still no one else in sight. Every now and then Ashley glanced at me over her shoulder, flashing me a look of alarm and fear. I tried to respond with an encouraging expression, but I had a feeling I wasn't convincing anybody.

I turned round to Harry. "This is pointless. Why do we have to do this?"

He said nothing and waved me on.

After several hundred metres we reached a high point over the escarpment. Harry said, "You can stop here."

I glanced left. The land sloped away vertiginously just beyond the edge of the wall. He said, "Turn round."

Ashley and I stood side by side. Harry glanced around, presumably checking for witnesses, then pointed the gun directly at her. "Move over there." He pointed to the edge of the wall. Her eyes widened and she inched over.

"Further."

She inched further.

"You – step back."

I moved a few paces away from Ashley.

It was time to play our only card. I said, "I don't know what you think you're doing, but whatever it is, it's a waste of time. I recorded Bladen last night in the bar when you were in the garden, and I emailed the file to the police this morning. He admitted to kidnapping Jenna Melling on it. They'll know all about it by now."

This seemed to give him pause. "Recorded it? How?"

"On my phone."

He pondered this. "What police?"

"Does it matter?"

"Is it the Flying Squad, the Canadian Mounties, what?"

"Check the phone if you're so worried."

"I will, but I want to hear it from you. Last chance."

Ashley gasped. Quickly I said, "I sent it to a mate. A detective in London."

"Name?"

"Dave Matthews."

"OK, give me the phone."

I held it out, but he said, "Put it on the ground."

I did so, then stepped back. He walked over cautiously and picked it up, then stabbed at the screen for a few moments, glancing up frequently to make sure we hadn't moved. Finally he said, "There's no email to Dave Matthews this morning or yesterday. There are no emails to anybody since last week. You made it up."

"It must have got deleted."

"Bollocks."

"I sent it from my computer as well."

He looked carefully at me. "No you didn't."

He glanced around again, no doubt to make sure no one was watching, then moved towards Ashley. She gasped again. With horror, I realised he was actually planning to push her over the edge. In desperation I shouted, "Check the audio files!"

He stopped. "What?"

"The original file should still be there." I realised that if he found it he would delete it, but at this point it seemed academic.

He considered this, then lifted my phone again and started thumbing commands into it. As he did so, I inched fractionally closer to him. I was thinking I might be able to rush him. Even if he shot me, maybe I could still bundle him over the edge of the wall.

I could see Ashley looking at me aghast. She was clearly terrified of the threat to her, but also alarmed at what she could see I was doing.

Then, out of the blue, a woman's voice said, "Good morning. Shame about the weather."

All three of us froze, staring across to the far side of the wall. A stout middle-aged woman wearing a cherry-red anorak and light grey jeans was climbing into view, presumably using steps that we couldn't see from where we were standing.

I had only one chance here. I couldn't assume there was strength in numbers; Harry might just as happily push three people off the wall as two. So while he was still looking away I lunged towards him with my arms extended and palms forward, thrusting him towards the edge of the wall as hard as I could. He let go of my phone, which flew sideways and landed in the grass.

People who don't want to be pushed over tend to be surprisingly resilient. Harry stumbled backwards, but immediately tensed and held his ground, raising his gun hand towards me. Before he could level it and fire I lunged at him again, this time committing myself more completely to the effort. Somehow I was able to pin his arms to his sides in a desperate embrace.

He wobbled backwards crazily and clasped my jacket, drawing me with him. For a moment we both teetered on the edge, but I managed to wrench myself away from him, swiping his hands aside. Almost in slow motion he disappeared over the side.

I leaned over the edge and looked down, watching as he hit a grass ledge at the foot of the wall, then bounced off it over the lip of the escarpment and out of sight.

Chapter 61

Looking back, I never doubted that I'd done the right thing. Our lives were on the line, and I'd taken the only action available to me. At the time, however, it took a lot of explaining.

For a start, the woman who'd saved our lives thought I had just shoved an innocent man to almost certain death. Ashley and I stood hugging each other for a moment, but the woman kept on shouting in remonstration as she stared at the spot where Harry had disappeared from view. I probably didn't help matters when I disengaged myself from Ashley and muttered shakily, "Good riddance!"

The woman glanced at me with contempt. "I'm calling the police," she announced.

"Good. But there might not be any signal here." Mention of her phone made me think of mine, and I gathered it up from the grass.

She watched me warily as she made the call. She seemed to have no trouble getting through, and soon she was demanding both police and an ambulance. She was able to describe with pinpoint accuracy where we were.

I looked over the edge of the wall again. How could we get down there to reach Harry and find out his condition? I said to Ashley, "We'd better walk back down and round, and see out how he is."

"What if he's OK and he's still got his gun?"

I shook my head. "I think that's pretty unlikely."

The woman now said, "I don't think you should move until the police get here."

"But that man could be dying. We might be his only hope."

"That didn't seem to worry you a minute ago. How do I know you're not going down to finish him off?"

I didn't know whether to snap at her or laugh at her melodramatic turn of phrase. I said, "Look, you've got this wrong. He was threatening us with a gun, and he was about to push us both over the edge. He probably would have done the same to you. You saved all our lives."

"I didn't see any gun. I think it's up to the police to decide what's been going on here." She straightened her shoulders with an air of authority.

"No it's not. I'm telling you what happened, plain and simple, and now I'm going to see if I can help that man. You must do whatever you have to." I glanced at Ashley. "Do you want to come with me or wait here with this lady? You could put her in the picture if you like."

"I'll come with you."

"OK." I turned to the woman. "If the police come up here, you can tell them where we've gone. We won't leave the site."

"Well, all right."

We ended up half-running all the way back to the point where we'd joined the wall, then striking off across the tall grass and heather at the foot of it. On the way I pulled out my phone, and was relieved to see a faint signal. I called Chris Melling's mobile number, and eventually he picked up.

"Chris – I'm afraid you're going to have to do a rethink on that recording. There's been an incident."

"How do you mean, an incident?"

"Bladen sent one of his men after Ashley and me. He might be dead now, but whether he is or not, we're going to be asked a lot of questions, and we'll have to tell the police what's been going on."

"Jesus Christ, Mike! What have you got yourself into?"

I couldn't think fast and stumble across the wet turf at the same time. I already had it in my mind that we might have to play the recording to the police, but I couldn't focus on the implications. I stopped dead, wiping the rain from my face, and called to Ashley, "Can you hang on just a second?"

She hovered uncertainly and I raised the phone to my ear again. "Look Chris, I'll tell you the full story later. The reason I'm calling is that we might have to play the police that recording. They might not believe what's just happened unless we do."

"I see." There was a sudden coldness in his tone.

"And I'm worried that the recording might make you appear complicit after the event in having Jenna kidnapped. I don't know for sure – I'm no expert. A court might throw the whole thing out, but we can't assume that."

He said nothing, so I added, "There's another aspect. If we do play the recording and Ernie Bladen hears about this, it's possible he might go public with whatever he's holding over you. I don't see what he has to gain, but you never know with people like him. So you might want to do whatever is necessary to square things with whoever is involved."

"Can't you avoid playing it?" I could now hear plangency in his voice.

"I might be able to, but we're in quite a spot here. I may have killed this guy, and I need to be able to explain how it happened."

He muttered, "This is terrible."

I had the sense that he was thinking of his own plight rather than ours, so I said nothing. He said, "Well thanks for contacting me, anyway."

"OK." I disconnected and we headed on across the moorland.

It seemed to take us far longer to reach the point where Harry had gone over the edge than it had up on top of the wall. We had to scramble over dry stone walls and wade through spongy grass. When we got there, we could see no sign of him.

I said to Ashley, "Is this the right place?"

She pointed upward. "It must be." At the top, we could just see the red anorak of the woman who had saved us.

"So what happened to Harry?"

We stared around us. No Harry, and no evidence that he had fallen here. Then Ashley pointed upwards again and shouted, "There!"

The escarpment face was almost vertical and relatively featureless, but about a quarter of the way down from the top I now saw a natural rock shelf. By some miracle Harry had landed on it; we could just make out his prone form in the khaki anorak. He didn't seem to be moving.

I said, "Let's go back to the car. We can't do anything here."

As we walked I called the police again. I said they might need to send out some kind of mountain rescue team. Then I turned to Ashley. "The police are likely to be pretty heavy. They'll probably think I tried to kill that man."

"But he was the one trying to kill us!"

"I know, but you have to look at it from their point of view."

She turned to me as we reached one of the dry stone walls we'd crossed earlier. "We just have to tell them the truth," she said. "With luck they'll realise what a devious bastard this man Bladen is."

A few hundred metres away I saw a police car turning off the main road at the entrance to the track, its blue light flashing. We stayed where we were for a moment, catching our breath and wiping the rain from our faces.

I squatted down with my back to the wall. "It's all very well me telling Chris Melling we might play that recording to the police. We don't even know if it still exists." I pulled out my phone again and rummaged around in the file system. Ashley stooped beside me, watching closely.

I looked up. "It's here! You didn't delete the file after all."

"Thank god for that."

"I'd better send it to Dave now. For all we know, the police might take my phone away from me." Hastily I attached the file to an email and sent it off without comment.

We both stood up. I said, "I like Chris Melling."

"So?"

"Well, if we tell the police about that recording, it'll drop him in it. They'll realise he knows Bladen kidnapped his daughter. It'll probably make him an accessory after the fact, or whatever the legal term is."

"If so, he's brought it on himself. We don't owe him anything."

"I just think it's not my call to bring him down." I watched the police car pull up behind Harry's car. Two officers in high-visibility yellow jackets got out. I turned to Ashley. "I'm not going to lie to the police, but I'll keep it vague if I can, and try not to implicate Chris. I can't tell you what to say, but everything you know about all this is secondhand, so you don't really need to say much at all. Just the facts of what happened today."

"You can take loyalty too far, Mike."

"I know. I'm not going to be silly about it. I'll play it by ear."

"OK. I'll do the same." She gave me an encouraging smile. "You don't need to look so despondent, Mike. I'm not holding this against you."

I laughed. "Thanks for that."

We glanced around, looking for footholds in the dry stone wall, and started to climb over it.

Chapter 62

We were driven to a country police station and questioned separately for several hours. During most of that time I was kept in a tiny interview room containing just a bare table and four chairs.

I tried to tell a straight story in the way I'd described to Ashley, but it was hard to know where to begin and what to include. If I told the police why I thought Bladen wanted to have me killed, it would inevitably implicate Chris Melling. If I didn't reveal enough, Harry's actions would sound like those of a madman. The recording ought to be my get-out-of-jail-free card, almost literally, but disclosing it would mean abandoning my promise to Chris.

Initially the two officers simply let me tell my story. Whether they followed my convoluted logic or not was a moot point. When I was done they started picking over what I'd told them. I could see they were subtly trying to trip me up. At one point I began to think that only my recording would head them off.

Two things helped me. The first was the fact that Harry's gun had been found, corroborating the key point in my story. The second was the news that Harry was alive and apparently not on the critical list – so the threat of a murder charge was off the agenda. A rescue team had lifted him to the top of the escarpment and he'd been taken to a hospital. Initially the police didn't want to tell me anything about his condition, but eventually they thawed a little and told me he'd broken a collarbone and fractured several ribs, but had suffered no apparent internal injuries.

Eventually the officers doing the questioning withdrew, leaving me sitting alone in the interview room. Half an hour ticked by, then forty-five minutes. After an hour and twenty minutes a newcomer entered – a man in his mid-forties with fair hair and very pale eyes. I had the impression he was senior to the other two; he seemed more confident, more comfortable in his own skin. He organised a cup of tea for me, then sat down opposite me and smiled faintly.

"Well, Mr Stanhope. People seem to keep trying to hurl you off high places. Are you working your way through the tourist spots of north-east England?"

I scowled. "Not intentionally."

"And other people try to drop things on you from a great height."

"You're talking about Leeds?"

"Yessir. I've been making some calls. You've been a busy man in the last few weeks."

"I suppose so."

He smiled faintly again. "And you've single-handedly solved a lorry hijacking case for my colleagues in Yorkshire, or so they tell me."

"I wouldn't say that."

"Nor would I, but I get the point."

I looked cautiously at him. Friend or foe? I couldn't decide. He pulled his chair forward, suddenly businesslike. "So you're not the bad guy around here. Let's get that cleared up once and for all. You're off the hook, as of now."

"I'm glad to hear it." But I felt there was more. "What about Harry?"

"Harry Masters? We know all about him. Not a nice man. It was about time someone threw him off a cliff."

"You're kidding me."

He sat back. "You're not going to go quoting me on that, are you? Let's just say I don't think he'll be pressing charges against you."

"Will you be charging *him*? He was about to kill me and my girlfriend."

He looked at me judiciously. "That depends."

"What do you mean?"

"I think you know more than you're saying. You're protecting someone, and I assume it's Christopher Melling."

I said nothing.

"The thing is, Harry's boss is Ernie Bladen, and we've been trying to nail Bladen for years. The trouble is, he always comes up whiter than white. If I've understood the half-baked twaddle you told my colleagues, he's been involved in kidnapping and extortion relating to Christopher Melling's company. If we can get this squared away, you'll have done the world a service."

I looked more carefully at him. His agenda seemed broader than I would have expected at a country police station. As if reading my mind, he said, "I'm part of a special unit. I've come over here from Newcastle. My name's Nick Murray." He handed me a business card.

"So what exactly are you doing here?"

He sat back again. "Ernie Bladen has built up a legitimate business empire, but he just can't drop his old ways. If things don't go the way he wants them to, he doesn't bother about the rule of law, he simply calls out his troops and does whatever he thinks he has to. He's lost sight of the difference between honest trading and extortion – assuming he ever knew it in the first place."

"That certainly fits in with what I know about him."

"So." He looked at me carefully. "Some of his recent investments have gone sour, and we think he's more likely than usual to be putting pressure on people who owe him money. Usually he makes sure he has a hold over people to prevent them talking, but this is just the sort of time when he might get careless – even reckless. So we have to watch for any weaknesses."

"But what can I do?"

"Well, although you might not realise it, you're already helping us on our way. You worked out that Piers Ashurst was behind that lorry hijacking in Yorkshire."

"How does that help you?"

"Ah. The key factor here is that he claims to have been bounced into the theft to help clear a debt that he owed to Bladen."

"That sounds about right."

"Yes, and he's given us a whole list of threats and scare tactics applied to him by Bladen to get his money back. Hearsay, of course, and he'd never even have reported any of it, but now he thinks it might persuade us to treat him more leniently."

"Job done, then?"

"Well, no. We need more, and strange as it may seem, you can help us again. You know and I know that Christopher Melling has got himself mixed up in this, and you need to persuade him to come clean over it."

I said, "Are you offering us some kind of deal here? Are you saying you'll let us go if I help you?"

"Not at all. I'm just suggesting you do some hard thinking. If Bladen doesn't go down, I can't vouch for what Harry's replacement will do to you. Things might not work out so well next time."

* * *

I was reunited with Ashley at the front desk, and a police car took us back to the place where we'd left our own car. When we were finally ready to drive away I said, "Jesus, what a day."

"I've known better."

"Should I be apologising to you?"

"What for? All you've been doing is what you're good at. Chasing things down and working things out. You don't need to be sorry for that."

"I never thought it would end up with someone trying to kill us. You'll probably be traumatised for life."

"No more than you will."

I realised at once that this was a mild feminist rebuke. I said, "Ah – point taken. Well I vow not be traumatised if you'll do the same."

"Deal."

I pulled out on to the road, heading towards Newcastle. Ashley turned to me with an ironic smile.

"So, save Vindolanda for another day?"

Chapter 63

"I need to see Jenna Melling." I looked warily at Ashley over the breakfast table.

"Well tell it like it is, why don't you?"

"I want to ask her something, and I think I need to do it in person."

"Of course you do."

"Her father wants me to think he only found out about the kidnapping after the event. I'm not sure now that I believe him."

She gave that some thought. "But would he really go along with it when it was his own daughter? What kind of father does that?"

"Maybe one who is pushed into a corner."

"Hmm."

"The point is, those people went out of their way to make her comfortable – further than you might expect. I'm wondering if Chris somehow had a hand in it."

"So what do you want to ask her?"

"Let me check something out first, and then you'll see."

She looked doubtful. "It's Monday morning. I should really be making plans to go back to Cornwall. Bob Latimer gave me a lot of leeway to come up here, but I don't want to abuse his good will."

"One more day?"

"I'll give him a call."

After breakfast she rang Latimers, then reported back to me. "I've made a deal. They don't mind me working from Newcastle for a few more days, so long as I go and introduce myself to the Melling team. It's a good idea. They also want me to have a meeting with Mellings' PR firm, Ashby Collins. But that has to be today. Hugh Collins is off on holiday tomorrow."

"Perfect. Their office is very near where Jenna lives, so we can kill two birds with one stone."

I phoned Jenna, and she said she would be happy to see us at her flat later that morning. Then we set off on a circuitous route that would take us north into the Northumberland countryside. Our target was the farm where Jenna had been held captive.

"It's a pretty spot," Ashley said as we turned down the track to the farm.

"You haven't seen the house yet. I don't think anyone's lived there for years. It seems to be slowly crumbling away."

"How strange."

The farmyard was empty, and there was no obvious evidence of the events that had taken place there. As before, everything looked abandoned and neglected. However, the front door was locked, and when I led Ashley round to the back we found that the broken window had been boarded up.

Ashley pointed to a small side-hinged window half-way to the upper floor. It was closed, but not entirely flush with the frame. "I might be able to get that open. D'you want to give me a leg up?"

Despite my battered shoulders I managed to hoist her up, and after a moment she was able to pull the window fully open. "How's that then!" she exclaimed triumphantly.

"Be careful."

She managed to edge her way through on her stomach. I heard a muted clatter as she scrambled to the floor head first. A few moments later there was a reluctant creaking sound as she shoved the kitchen window open beside me.

"Care to join me?"

It was as dark inside as I remembered. I realised I should have brought a torch. I led Ashley through to the main room. She asked me, "What are we looking for?"

"Books. We need to find any room with bookshelves or a bookcase."

We worked our way painstakingly through all the rooms. Most still had dingy furniture in them, but the beds in the two bedrooms were stripped down to their ancient bedsprings. The only books we could find in the entire house were in the front room, where a small row of dog-eared paperbacks sat prominently on a shelf.

We found our way to the storeroom where Jenna had been held. The table and chairs were still there, along with the mattress in the corner. Ashley stared around with a horrified expression on her face. "I can't begin to imagine being shut in here. She's a tough lady, Jenna."

We returned to the kitchen and Ashley brushed her hands together briskly. "What have we learned today then?"

"We've learned that there are no ancient hardbacks in here. Either the kidnappers gave every single one of them to Jenna, which I don't believe, or there never were any in the first place. But there were paperbacks, yet they didn't bother with those."

She shivered. "So can we leave this hell hole please?"

* * *

Jenna welcomed us like old friends. Over coffee we told her about our experiences the previous day.

"You must think the North East is full of mad people," she commented at the end.

"Only some of you."

She gave me a grin that was a little too knowing, and turned to Ashley. "I suppose you heard about those people who tried to chuck Mike off Armstrong Bridge?"

Ashley nodded. "But nobody seems to know if it was connected to your kidnapping or not."

Jenna said, "I think it must have been. I think they were distracting Mike while I was being whisked away."

I said, "I was wondering about those books that you were given in the farmhouse."

"Oh, aye. *The Mill on the Floss*. Did you want a summary of the plot? It's well written but slow. I thought I might post a review of it on Amazon."

Ashley smiled. I said, "I wondered if you told your father which books they gave you?"

"Why do you want to know that?"

I suddenly felt uneasy. I didn't know how to pursue this without making his involvement clear to Jenna. I should have rehearsed this conversation before we arrived. I said, "Humour me."

She looked doubtfully at me, then shrugged. "I didn't tell him any of the titles. I just said they gave me a bunch of Victorian novels to read. I said they seemed old enough to be original editions. Does it matter?"

I did some fast thinking. Jenna had told me the books included *Barchester Towers*, and Chris had also quoted that title to me. Yet from what Jenna had just said, he shouldn't have known any of the names.

I merely said, "Maybe not." I had to put her off the scent somehow. "Did you tell anyone else about them?"

"Only you and my mam. And before you ask, I didn't tell her the titles either."

Ashley said, "Mike! Stop giving the poor woman the third degree."

Jenna said, "It's all right." But she was looking at me curiously.

I decided to launch into something else. "I suppose you heard what happened in Leeds?"

"To Piers? Yes, I know. He really was involved in hijacking that truck. How stupid can you get? He's out on bail now, but I think they're going to prosecute him."

"Did you hear that he tried to drop a pallet on my head?"

It sounded faintly ridiculous as I said it, but she turned to me with concern in her eyes. "I know, Mike. I'm really sorry."

"Why do you say that?"

She looked down. "I'm talking myself into a hole here, aren't I?" She looked up again.

I said, "You contacted him after we spoke on the phone, didn't you? You told him I'd worked out what was going on. That's what made him go flying off to the high-bay warehouse to fetch those pallets out."

"I'm sorry, I'm sorry. I just didn't want to see him in trouble with the police. I know I should have kept out of it, but he's a friend. We've got a history. It seemed wrong to sit here doing nothing." She looked at me in consternation.

"It's all right – I don't blame you. I just wanted to satisfy my curiosity."

"It didn't make any difference in the end, did it? They caught him anyway, so I suppose he's going to get what's coming to him." She sighed. "I'm glad you didn't get hurt."

"Well not much, anyway."

As we prepared to leave, Jenna said, "Those books – you think my father told Ernie Bladen to get them for me, don't you? Or he even provided them himself."

She'd made the connection in spite of my efforts to deflect her. It was hardly surprising. I shrugged awkwardly. "We don't know that. It's one interpretation."

"It would mean he knew what was happening right from the start. But why the hell would he would he go along with it?" She gave me a long look. "I think you know, don't you Mike?"

"Not really. You'll need to talk to your father."

"It's a pretty sad day when your own dad arranges for you to be locked up." She turned to Ashley. "Would *your* dad do that to you?"

Ashley smiled sympathetically without saying anything, and Jenna gave a bleak laugh. "I really will need counselling after this."

* * *

Sitting outside in the car I said to Ashley, "I think I need to talk to Chris Melling again." I took out my phone and called his office, but the receptionist told me he was working at home for the day.

Ashley said, "Now what?"

"I think the best thing is just turn up on his doorstep unannounced. That way he'll have less time to plan what to say."

She stared at me. "You're getting very manipulative in your old age."

I tried to laugh. "I'm getting fed up with being messed around by everybody, that's all. I want to be the one who takes the initiative for once."

She nodded. "But I have to go and see these PR people, Ashby Collins. It's all arranged."

"I could drop you off, then come and pick you up later."

"But I'd like to hear what Chris Melling has to say for himself."

"Maybe if I talk to him man to man he'll be more forthcoming."

"Huh! I suppose that might work. Just make sure you don't leave me stranded here."

Chapter 64

Chris Melling opened his front door to me with a preoccupied frown on his face. He seemed unsurprised to see me.

As we walked through his wood-panelled hall his wife Sheila appeared. She stopped in her tracks for a moment, staring impassively at me, then turned on her heel without speaking and disappeared the way she'd come. Chris waved me into the main lounge and shut the door behind him.

"You saw Jenna this morning."

"I did."

"She rang me. I'm not her favourite person."

"I'm sorry."

"Not your fault. I'm not anybody's favourite person today." He sat down on the sofa with a sigh and waved me towards a chair. "You didn't play the police that recording in the end, did you?"

"No, we managed to talk our way out of it in the end."

He shook his head ruefully. "I should have given you more credit."

"What do you mean?"

"I assumed the police would hear that conversation, and everything would come unstuck. I decided I'd better do what you suggested, and warn the party Ernie Bladen was blackmailing me over. So I did."

"The party?"

"Sheila."

"Oh."

That information hung in the air with all its implications, and for a long time neither of us spoke. Finally Chris cleared his throat.

"It was an affair. With a girl who worked in our marketing department. Woman, I should say. Felicity, her name was. This was years ago. Things between me and Sheila had cooled off, and – well, she was there. And somehow Ernie Bladen found out about it."

"Surely things couldn't have been all that dire? Was it really worth all this grief?"

"It went on for five years, Mike. Five years! You can't shrug off something like that. It's too much of a betrayal."

"All the same … "

"It wasn't the first time, that's the point. There were two others before her. The second time, Sheila told me it would be the last. So this time I was much more careful."

"I'm still not following you. Couldn't you have broken up with Sheila and gone with this other woman?"

He picked at the fabric on the arm of the sofa, looking down at it. Then he looked up at me. "What you don't know is that Sheila's father originally helped me set up Melling Logistics. He invested so that I could buy up a failing firm and turn it round. It wasn't a loan, it was share capital. Sheila inherited his stake when he died, and she ended up the majority shareholder."

"But she's not a director, is she?"

"She's a sleeping partner, shall we say?" He gave an ironic laugh. "Unfortunate term. She's always left me to run things and take all the decisions, but at the end of the day she's always had the option of pulling the plug on me."

"What about the Latimer takeover?"

"Oh, she was happy enough to agree to that. Technically most of the proceeds have gone to her. So if she cuts me off, I'll be walking away from nearly everything I've achieved. I'll end up with just a fraction of the value – and no marriage. What would *you* do?"

"You could have told Jenna about all this."

"No I couldn't." He gave a sign of resignation. "She'll find out anyway now, of course. I told Sheila the whole thing this morning."

There was another silence, then I said, "So what do you think will happen?"

"I don't know. Sheila hasn't said anything, but I know she's furious. I don't blame her. The irony is that after I ended the affair, things were much better between us. Now this."

"Maybe staying with you will seem a better option to her than pulling everything apart, and messing up her own life as well as yours?"

"I'm not going to get my hopes up."

"What about Bladen? If he has no hold on you, you can testify against him."

"I know. But it'll come out that I went along with Jenna's kidnapping, and I might be prosecuted myself."

"I suppose so."

"Even if I'm not, I can't see how Sheila and Jenna can ever forgive me."

"Well Jenna's guessed already."

"I know." He shook his head disconsolately. "Don't get me wrong, Mike, I deserve everything I get. It's the most shameful thing I've ever done. I don't know how I let myself be led along."

As before, I felt sorry for him, yet I still wanted him to know the full implications of his actions. I said, "You realise Bladen tried to have me and Ashley killed to silence us? Killed! That's a bit more radical than kidnapping. I want to see him stopped."

"What can I say, Mike? It's hard to believe this kind of thing can happen."

I reached into my pocket for the card I'd been given by Nick Murray, the detective in charge of the Bladen investigation. "Why not call this man and offer your full cooperation? That's got to count for something. He's after Bladen, not you. I think you'll get a fair hearing from him."

He took the card and glanced at it. "I might do that."

"Let me make a note of the number." I jotted it down in my notebook.

He said, "I wish we'd been working together under happier circumstances, Mike."

"Me too."

* * *

Once I was in my car I phoned the number for Nick Murray that I'd just written down. He answered on the second ring.

"Mr Stanhope, what have you got for me?"

"Chris Melling says he's going to contact you. If he doesn't, this might be a good time for you to contact him – before he thinks the better of it."

"OK, thank you for that."

"Can I ask you something?"

"Go ahead."

"If he tells you he knew about Bladen kidnapping his daughter, is that enough to prosecute Bladen?"

"Not necessarily, but it's a step in the right direction."

"What if I told you there might be a recording of a conversation in which Bladen as good as admits responsibility."

"As good as?"

"Well, you'd have to form a judgement."

"Where did this recording come from?"

"I made it myself a few nights ago, on my phone. Bladen was talking to Chris Melling, and didn't realise I was there."

"I see. Well I'd very much like to hear it. I can't guarantee that it would constitute admissible evidence, but from my point of view every little helps."

There was a moment's silence, then he said, "For what it's worth, Harry Masters might start talking to us. He's very loyal to Bladen, but he might change his tune if he thinks it will save him from prison."

"Can you really contemplate letting him walk away from what he did to us?"

Now he was hesitant. "That woman on the moors didn't really see anything. The only people who can describe the attempted murder are you and your girlfriend – and being brutally honest, you got your retaliation in first. You pushed Harry over the edge before he actually did anything to harm you, so your allegations might not stick."

"Great! How about him marching us up the hill at gunpoint?"

"I know, but you see what I'm saying. Anyway, what matters is that Harry doesn't know how things will play out. At the moment he really believes he could be looking at a prison sentence. So there might be room for some creative negotiation. He knows about a load of past scams involving Bladen. If we play our cards right, his testimony alongside yours and Christopher Melling's should start to add up to a proper case."

"And can you soft-pedal the way you deal with Chris?"

"Don't ask me the impossible. All I can do is try to play fair by him."

Chapter 65

Two phone messages awaited me when I checked my voicemail at the hotel. One was from Dave Mathews.

"I got your email with the audio file attached. Would you care to enlighten me? I get the gist of it, but what are you expecting me to do with it?"

There was a pause, then: "On second thoughts, don't bother to reply to this unless it's urgent. I'm on holiday." A dry laugh. "I'll repeat that: on holiday. Yes, me. At Ripon, if you know where that is. It's where Suzy comes from. So don't call us, we'll call you."

The other message came completely out of left field. A diffident man's voice said, "Hello Mike, it's Eric, from the reading group. Long time no see. I hope life's treating you well?" He waited a moment as if expecting me to reply, then said, "You might think this a bit odd, but a friend of mine in the flat above me wants to get in touch with you. I say friend – more of an acquaintance, really. He's just come out of hospital, so I'm helping him out a bit. Anyway, if you give me a call I can tell you the details."

I'd joined Eric's reading group when I was still living in south London. I was trying to broaden my experience of the literary world. I hadn't seen him in nearly a year.

Ashley was showering in preparation for going out for a meal, so I called Eric's number straight back, and he answered at once. "Mike, it's good to hear you. Sorry for the mysterious message. It seemed too complicated for me to explain it on the hoof."

"That's fine."

"What it is … " He stopped to think. "My neighbour upstairs knows I'm involved with the reading group, and one day he asked me out of the blue if I'd ever heard of an author called Mike Stanhope.

Extraordinary coincidence. Well, of course I told him I knew you personally, which seemed to intrigue him. But then he fell ill, so I didn't hear any more about it. But now he's home from hospital, and he's asked me if I can put him in touch with you."

Suddenly this all made sense. Eric had a flat in the one of the mansion blocks on Prince of Wales Drive in Battersea, south London, and I now remembered that Howard, the elusive brother of Elizabeth Sanderson's partner Derek, also lived on Prince of Wales Drive. Daniella, Elizabeth's colleague at the college in Harrogate, had told me that.

I said, "By any chance is your neighbour's name Howard Salmon?"

"Yes! Do you already know him?"

"Only by name, but I've been wanting to get in touch with him. I'm delighted to hear his health has improved."

"Oh, absolutely. He's very frail, but he's got his speech back, and most of his motor functions are good as well. He's just limping a little. He's been very lucky."

I waited while he read out Howard's phone number and email address for me.

He said, "Changing the subject, I see you went down the self-publishing route in the end. I assume that's how Howard had heard of you." Self-publishing was anathema to Eric, so I'd kept quiet about it, but clearly he'd found out somehow.

"I thought that if I didn't, my book would never see the light of day."

"And how has it worked out for you?"

"Well, I'm not on the best-seller list yet."

He laughed good-naturedly. "I don't mean to pass judgement, Mike. A young man who joined the group a few weeks ago claims to have written an entire novel on his smartphone, just using his thumbs. He thinks self-publishing is the only logical way to go."

I tried to visualise this, but failed. I said, "You amaze me."

He laughed. "Why not remind me of the web link to your novel? I'm not above reading an e-book."

I smiled to myself as I disconnected. I'd always thought Eric pompous, but his heart seemed to be in the right place.

* * *

Ashley wandered out of the bathroom, drying her hair. She was wearing one of the extravagant white bathrobes provided by the hotel. She said, "Who was that on the phone?"

"It was Eric, my reading group man in London. He knows Howard Salmon, the brother of Elizabeth Sanderson's partner Derek. He says Howard is out of hospital, and wants to talk to me."

"Is he the one who might know why Elizabeth left her house to you?"

"That's the man."

"Then ring him. Now!"

I smiled and looked down at my phone, bracing myself to make the call. It could well yield the answers I'd been seeking for many weeks, yet I felt nervous. Mysteries offer infinite explanations, most of them teasingly indistinct; facts reduce them to a single sharply defined reality. I was put in mind of the contrast between viewing horserace contenders at the starting gate and seeing them cross the finishing line. Knowing my connection to Elizabeth might help me decide how to handle my claim on her house, but it would also mark the end of a tantalising pursuit.

I shrugged. I couldn't have it all ways. Life might be a continuum, but there had to be points of progress on it, otherwise everything was just a blur. This appeared to be the time to establish some of those points.

I tapped in Howard's number and waited as it rang out.

Chapter 66

The elderly voice answering the phone sounded stronger than I'd expected. "Howard Salmon."

I said, "My name is Mike Stanhope."

"Ah, Mike, this is very good of you."

Now that we were actually speaking, I wasn't sure how to proceed. I said, "I was sorry to hear you'd been unwell."

"The stroke, yes. It came as quite a shock to me, I can tell you. You think these things only happen to other people. But I seem to have been very lucky."

"I'm glad."

He said, "Norah Stevenson, my brother's old PA, contacted me from Leeds, and told me you wanted to get in touch. I nearly sent a message to your website, but then I remembered that Eric knew you, so I asked him to contact you for me. It seemed more personal that way. I assume this is about Elizabeth, is it?"

"Absolutely. I have a feeling you might be able to explain some things that I don't understand."

"I will if I can. What did Elizabeth tell you exactly?"

"She didn't tell me anything. I hadn't even heard of her until after she died. Then I was told she'd left me her property in her will."

"The foolish girl! I told her to ring you and explain."

"Maybe she would have, given time."

"So are you telling me you still don't know how you're connected to her?"

"Well, I've worked out that it has something to do with my grandmother Emily. I have the impression that she knew Elizabeth's father, Len Roberts. I found that out by pure luck."

"You're absolutely right, but she didn't just know him – she was

Elizabeth's mother."

"So you're saying … "

"Elizabeth was your aunt."

For a moment I said nothing. I was trying to rewind what I knew. Elizabeth was my aunt. That was why she'd decided to leave her estate to me. She fell out with Philip Crabtree and his family, and turned to the nearest alternative – me. Suddenly everything made sense.

Howard said, "Are you still there?"

"Sorry, I'm trying to take this in. How could Emily be Elizabeth's mother?"

"From what I picked up, she met Len Roberts when she was still in her teens, and they had an affair. He was older than her and he was already married, so it was never going to go anywhere, but she didn't know that. It was the old story – she fell pregnant. Her family were appalled, but there was never any question of a termination. In due course Elizabeth was born."

"What happened then?"

"Well, when it came out that Len was married, Emily's parents stepped in. There was no chance of her planning an independent life as a single mother, and they weren't having an illegitimate baby in their household. It simply wasn't on their agenda. These were nice middle-class people, you understand." He spoke with heavy irony. "So a deal was done with the father. At the time it was thought that his wife couldn't conceive, although in fact that wasn't true. She was persuaded to take on Elizabeth as her own child."

"God – that was a big ask."

"I suppose it cut two ways. She had to face up to her husband's infidelity, but on the upside, she got a baby out of it without the hassle of adoption – a baby who was actually her husband's natural child. Presumably pragmatism won out."

"But what a sad thing for Emily."

"That's for sure. I don't know what she was expecting to happen with Leonard, but you can be sure it wasn't that. First she loses the boyfriend, then she loses the child. A terrible start in life. But not so sad for Lizzie. She always said her father was a good man, and her adoptive mother treated her well. It was a nurturing home, as they would probably call it these days."

I was still catching up. I said, "If none of this had happened, Emily would never have left Newcastle and married my grandfather, and I wouldn't be here now."

He laughed. "Yes, I suppose that's right. It's the silver lining."

I said, "How do you know all this?"

"Oh, I just picked it up over the years. Elizabeth got the true story from her father after his wife died, and she told most of it to my brother Derek. Then after he died we became very close, and she told me the rest."

"Do you know what happened to my grandmother?"

"Not really. Lizzie found out that she left home and moved away as soon as she was ready to face the world, and as far as I know she never went back. I think Lizzie tried to contact her eventually, but by then it was too late."

"That fits in with what I know."

"Actually, Elizabeth left you a clue in her adopted surname – Sanderson." Howard chuckled. "But it seems you didn't latch on to it."

"What do you mean?"

"Elizabeth was very independent – never wanted to be married, for instance, although Derek would have been delighted to marry her. When she found out the true story of her parentage, she decided to drop the Roberts surname, and she took on her mother's maiden name instead. It *is* Sanderson, isn't it? I'm surprised you didn't recognise it."

"Huh!" I thought about this. "Now you mention it, I have a feeling you're right. It's one of those things you hear as a child and immediately forget. Her father must have been pretty upset when she told him about this."

"I wouldn't know about that, but he must have been accustomed to her independent spirit. He probably wasn't surprised."

"I wish I'd known her."

"So do I."

* * *

I thought this would be the end of the conversation, but then Howard said, "What happened about the final will, if you don't mind me asking? Are you still included in it?"

"I'm not sure I follow. The only will I know about leaves more or less everything to me."

"Ah, that's interesting. I'm pretty sure Elizabeth was going to write another will. We discussed it by email. I would look it up, but my machine's not switched on at the moment."

"Could you explain a bit further?"

"Sorry, yes. We discussed her will a lot in her last few months. She became quite obsessed with it. She told me all about her plan to leave everything to you, but then she had another change of heart." He broke off. "Do you know about Elizabeth's niece, Maggie Crabtree?"

"Yes. I was told that Elizabeth fell out with her."

"She did. Lizzie was very volatile, and tended to change her mind about people very quickly. She got fed up with Maggie's waywardness, but towards the end of her life she came to the conclusion that she was being too harsh. She decided to revise her will yet again, and include Maggie in it."

Cautiously, I said, "Just Maggie, or Maggie and others?"

"That I don't know. But it sounds as if that will has disappeared, and I suppose it's not really in your interest to find it."

"Please don't judge me. If it exists, it ought to be honoured."

"I'm glad to hear you say that."

"Where might it be? Would it be lodged with different solicitors?"

"I shouldn't think so. Lizzie liked to keep that kind of thing close. If her existing solicitors don't have it, it's more likely to be in her house."

"In that case Philip Crabtree has very probably found it and destroyed it."

"Ah, so you've got the measure of Philip then. An arrogant shit, if you'll pardon my language."

I thought I'd better not comment on that. I said, "Was there anywhere to hide the will that he wouldn't know about?"

"Curiously enough, yes. If the will exists at all, I know exactly the place. It will be in the hidden drawer."

We seemed to be moving into *Secret Seven* territory. I said, "What?"

"There's an old Victorian desk in Elizabeth's house that came from my family home. Derek and I used to be fascinated by it, and he kept it when our father died. Elizabeth ended up using it all the time. I wouldn't have had any space for it in my flat … "

"And there's a secret drawer?"

"Indeed there is. You have to release a latch under the desktop, and then you slide the whole top towards you. The secret drawer opens at the back. It's not what you'd call secure, but you have to know about it or you wouldn't go looking for it. I don't suppose Philip Crabtree does."

"It sounds as if I'd better go and see it for myself."

Chapter 67

Our hotel seemed surprisingly flexible about making and breaking bookings. It must have been the Melling Logistics effect. We packed our belongings next morning and I booked us into a motel on the outskirts of Harrogate. It would be the first leg of our return trip to Cornwall.

However, there was unfinished business to attend to in Newcastle first. Ashley's deal with Bob Latimer for staying on here required her to go over to Mellings and introduce herself to the team there, and she was still committed to doing it. When we phoned them she was told that Chris Melling wasn't at work, but Greg Atkins would be happy to see her in his place.

He greeted us amiably enough in the reception area. As we walked upstairs he said quietly to me, "I'm sorry I gave you all that grief over Jenna. I shouldn't have jumped to conclusions."

"It doesn't matter. I'm glad she came out of it all right."

Greg took Ashley on the same guided tour that Chris had given me. I opted to wait in the small office I'd shared with Andrea and Jamie, and I opened my laptop. Something was nagging at my consciousness, and I had a feeling the computer would provide the key.

It took me less than five minutes to work out what I was looking for. Weeks ago Jamie Andrews had sent me the photograph of Ernie Bladen that he'd taken at Newcastle racecourse, and that image also included Philip Crabtree. At the time, seeing Philip there had alerted me to the possibility that he might be a gambler, but I hadn't considered the likelihood that the two men knew each other. I'd assumed they'd simply been caught in the same frame.

This time I peered at the picture more carefully. Were they together? Were they conversing with each other? It was hard to tell. Bladen was frowning towards the camera; Philip was looking away in another direction. It was a long-focus shot, so the distances were foreshortened. I couldn't even work out how close the two men were standing to each other.

Angela, Philip's wife, could probably tell me. I just needed to catch her on her own.

* * *

"Mike," Angela said in answer to my phone call, "it seems a long time since that day we met up in town."

I was relieved. She seemed willing to speak to me, which suggested that Philip wasn't around. I said, "Before you ask, I'm still trying to work out how to handle the inheritance."

"Fair enough."

"How are things with you?"

"No better, to be honest. Philip is at his wits' end. We could really use that money."

I'd vowed to myself not to be arm-twisted over Elizabeth's will, yet there was a poignancy in Angela's predicament that I found oddly affecting. I heard myself saying, "I'm not unsympathetic." I knew this was a weasely evasion, but it seemed to be the best I could come up with.

She said, "That's good to hear, Mike."

"I don't want to get your hopes up."

"I know."

I waited a moment. "Could I ask you something about Philip?"

"What is it?"

"You told me he's a gambler. I just wondered what sort of mess he's into. Do you know much of the detail?"

"It's private bets. He's got himself involved with a gambling circle run by a racehorse owner. These people are very unforgiving."

On a whim, I said, "By any chance, does the name Ernie Bladen strike any chords with you?"

"Yes it does! That's the man I'm talking about."

For a moment I couldn't think of anything to say. I couldn't believe this coincidence. Wherever I went and whatever I did in the North

East, Ernie Bladen's name kept coming up. Until now it had never occurred to me that there could be any link between Melling Logistics and the house I'd been left by Elizabeth Sanderson, yet here was the evidence.

Angela was still speaking. "What a nasty piece of work. He came to our house one day … " She tailed off.

"What happened?"

"To be honest with you, I couldn't believe what I was hearing. Phil had told me this guy was head of a public company, and yet he sounded like the worst kind of playground bully. He really had me frightened."

"He actually threatened you?"

"It wasn't so much what he said as the way he said it. You should have seen the look on his face."

"Hopefully he hasn't actually done you any harm?"

"Not up to now, but how are we supposed to live our lives with someone like that breathing down our necks?"

I hesitated before speaking again. "I feel you should know that I've found something out. Something that finally makes sense of Elizabeth's will."

"What is it?" She sounded wary.

"I was related to her. She was my aunt."

"Seriously? How do you make that out?"

"It's a long story. Philip might know some of it – you could ask him. Her mother was my grandmother, that's the connection. Her father was Len Roberts, and he and his wife brought her up. My grandmother went on to marry someone else and start her own family – and here I am."

"My god." I sensed that she was weighing up the implications. "So does this make you feel less willing to split the estate?"

I didn't really know the answer to that. I said, "Not necessarily."

"Well, I suppose that's something."

I asked if she could give me an address for Philip's sister Maggie in Consett. She said, "Why, are you planning to write to her?"

"No, I thought I might go and see her."

"What for?"

I wasn't sure. I said, "To satisfy my curiosity, I suppose."

"Well, you're welcome to try. She probably won't give you the time of day."

I asked her not to let Maggie know I'd expressed interest. She said, "Don't worry, I have no desire to speak to the woman."

* * *

Ashley and Greg returned from their walk round the premises, and he asked us if we'd like to go out for lunch with him. We said no, making the excuse that we had a long trip to make. We sat chatting with him for a while in the office, then slid away.

As we drove south across the Tyne on the A1, Ashley commented, "He's a strange one, Greg Atkins."

"In what way?"

"Well, he was happy enough to show me everything that was happening at Mellings, but he didn't seem at all interested in anything to do with Latimer Logistics. He didn't ask how we do things, for instance, or how I thought the Melling setup compared with ours. It was as if he was giving a tour to a member of the public."

"I've never been able to make him out. He seemed hostile to me as soon as I turned up here, but I never did work out why. I think it's just his way."

"Well I wouldn't want him on my team."

"He seems to think he's involved with Jenna Melling, but to hear Jenna talk about him, you'd think they were just passing acquaintances."

"Why does that not surprise me?"

I took the first exit from the A1 south of the Tyne, and headed off in a south-westerly direction through the suburbs. Ashley said, "Where are we going? I thought it was next stop Harrogate."

"Sorry, I forgot to mention. Brief diversion to Consett on the way. It's not far."

Chapter 68

Half an hour later we were driving through Consett's low-rise central area. The town's economy had taken a massive hit in the 1980s with the collapse of the steel industry, but it was clear that efforts had been made to revive it, with some success.

Maggie lived in a terrace of small redbrick Victorian houses with front doors that opened directly on to the street. The surrounding houses had been smartened and modernised, but Maggie's seemed largely untouched. With a glance at Ashley, I knocked on the door.

It was opened by a thin woman in her late thirties with short dark hair. She was smartly dressed in jeans and a cream top.

I said, "Maggie Crabtree?"

"Who's asking?" She had a more pronounced Geordie accent than Angela.

"I'm Mike Stanhope." Now that I was here, I was nervous. I tried to summon up my most friendly and unthreatening manner. "I'm sorry to descend on you out of the blue. I just wanted to make contact while I was in the area." I gave her a gimcrack smile. "I'm your cousin, more or less."

"You what?" A look of disbelief spread over her face. "So why have I never heard of you?" She was still holding the door part-open, perhaps ready to slam it shut if she disliked what we had to say.

"It's a long story, but the connection is your aunt, Elizabeth Sanderson. I found out lately that she was also my aunt. I never knew her, but when she died she left me her property in her will. It's all properly documented. The first I heard about it was when I was contacted by her solicitors in Newcastle."

She listened to this with eyes wide. Finally she said, "Well aren't you the lucky one?" She glanced between me and Ashley. "So what are you doing here? Have you come to gloat or something?"

"Absolutely not! Look, could we come in and talk more?" I turned to Ashley and introduced her.

Maggie said, "How do I know this is true, and not some scam?"

"Ask Angela if you like. She's the one who gave us your address. I spoke to her on the phone this morning. Just give her a call."

"You know Angela?"

"Yes, I've been in touch with her and her husband about this."

"Right." She nodded. "Well we're not exactly on speaking terms."

"That's up to you. Anyway, we don't want anything from you. I'm just trying to work out how come Elizabeth left me her estate instead of you and your brother."

"No secret in my case. We fell out. She was always trying to tell me what to do. I didn't match up to her idea of how a young lady should live her life." She was mocking the way Elizabeth might have spoken. She stared belligerently at me.

"Well could we come in? It would be better to talk about this inside." As I spoke, Ashley gave her a winning smile.

She gave us a long look, then said, "All right, you might as well." She stood aside and waved us past her into a small front room.

* * *

The room was well decorated and homely. "All the front rooms in the other houses along here were knocked through years ago," she commented as we sat down. "This one escaped."

She sat opposite us and asked me more about my own life and my connection to Elizabeth. Gradually she seemed to come to terms with what I was telling her.

She said, "You probably want to know how come I'm here in Consett while my rich brother is living in a posh house in Hexham? Simple. I shacked up with a guy called Danny, and this was his house – or his parents' house, actually. They died a long time ago, and now Danny's gone as well. I haven't seen him for four years." She gave me an ironic smile. "But here I still am."

"But you're doing all right for yourself?"

She shrugged. "I don't see what business it is of yours, but yes, I make my way. I manage a charity shop in town. And before you ask, I get paid a proper salary for it." She watched us as we took that in. "You're lucky you caught me. Today's my day off."

I nodded, and she said, "I suppose you were expecting me to be an alcoholic no-hoper? That's how Philip and Angela like to see me. It means they don't have to associate with me."

"And you have a son?"

"Yes I do. They probably told you he's disabled, but that's bollocks as well." She didn't elaborate. "He's at school now." She glanced at her watch.

"So you don't actually own this house?"

"No I don't, but I've been paying the bills on it for years."

I nodded. I couldn't think of anything else to ask, and I allowed my eyes to range over the framed photographs on the mantelpiece: a younger Maggie, a shaven-headed man and a small boy.

"So what are you really doing here?" she said. "You didn't need to come and find me. What's your angle?"

"It's hard to explain." I glanced at Ashley, who smiled encouragingly. "I have the impression that Elizabeth kept changing her mind about who to leave her money to. For some reason she ended up choosing me, and I felt I should get to know the other people who were in the frame."

"In the frame." She considered the phrase. "Well you could certainly include Phil in that, I suppose. From what I hear he was dancing around her for months, getting into her good books. He wanted to make sure he was under her nose when she was deciding how to hand on her worldly goods. I know I shouldn't diss my own brother, but he's never done me any favours."

"I see."

"But I wasn't in the frame, as you put it. I never expected my auntie to leave me anything. Why should she? We hadn't spoken for years. She gave up on me." She gave an ironic shrug. "It would have been nice if she'd had a bit more faith."

* * *

"Maggie seems a nice person," Ashley said as we drove away.

"She's obviously worked hard to sort out her life. Philip and Angela just don't want to accept it."

"Is Angela as awful as she makes out?"

"No, not at all. I like her. She's making the best of her life, just like Maggie. But Philip is a weak-minded bully. You met him in the house in Harrogate – you know what he's like."

"So what was this visit all about? Are you thinking of handing over some of your inheritance to Maggie?"

"Well, if there really is a later will, she might get it anyway. I suppose I just wanted to know whether I should be fighting in her corner."

"I think you've got your answer."

Chapter 69

On the way down the A1 I noticed a sign for Ripon. I'd heard the name mentioned somewhere recently, and after a moment I realised it was the place where Dave Matthews had said he was on holiday. I turned to Ashley and pointed at the sign.

"Perhaps we should drop in on Dave and have a reunion," I suggested.

"What, and invade his first holiday in ten years? He wouldn't thank you."

I laughed. "I'm not serious."

It was early evening when we reached Harrogate, but the sun was still shining. I said, "Let's go and have a look at Elizabeth's house before we check in at the motel."

"How are you expecting to get in? I don't suppose we'll find a convenient window for me to climb through this time, and even if we did, the neighbours might have something to say about it."

"I don't know. Maybe we can arm-twist Rosemary next door. I'll just feel happier knowing that all's well."

As we approached the house it became obvious that getting inside was the least of our problems. A white box van was parked in front of it, and two men were manhandling a cupboard into the back. Apparently Philip was shifting Elizabeth's antique furniture out.

I pulled over and parked a few doors short of the house on the opposite side of the road, and for a couple of minutes Ashley and I sat watching. Another cupboard followed the first one into the van, then two chairs. The larger of the two men doing the removal job was unmistakably Philip Crabtree. I didn't know the smaller one, though he seemed vaguely familiar. Both were dressed in jeans and T-shirts.

I said, "We've got to do something. Some of this stuff is quite valuable, and if they bring that desk out and take it away, we'll never get to find out what's hidden in it, if anything. He'll store it away somewhere where we can't get at it."

"Should we call the police? Would they do anything about it?"

"I don't know. By the time we've explained everything, who knows what will happen?"

"So what then?"

"Well, there *is* another option … "

Ashley looked at me. "You're not thinking what I think you're thinking?"

I gave her a sheepish look in return. "Ripon was only ten or fifteen miles back along the road. He could be here in half an hour."

"That's if he feels like coming. Would you? And if he picks up the call."

The phone rang out seven times. I was preparing a message in my head when Dave answered in person. "Mike, we're just getting ready to go out for dinner. What is it, mate?"

"I'm really sorry to trouble you, Dave, but I could use some backup. We're in Harrogate, and you're only about half an hour away from here."

There was a long pause, then he said, "Tell me you're joking."

I took a deep breath. "I've inherited a house here from a distant relative, but her nephew thinks he should have got it. He's here now, stripping the furniture out of it. I don't know how I can stop him."

All this must have been news to Dave, but to give him credit he seemed to assimilate it remarkably quickly. However, he merely said, "It sounds like a civil matter to me. What do you expect me to do about it?"

"He's a volatile man. If I interfere, he could be violent. And he's got a mate with him."

"Call the police then."

"Will they stop him?"

"Well, you could argue that it's plain and simple theft."

"But how long do you think it will take me to convince them of that?"

"Pass on that one." There was an even longer pause, then Dave said, "And you reckon you're only half an hour away from me?"

"Something like that, if you're in Ripon."

"Yes, we're in Ripon." He sighed deeply. "Give me the address and postcode."

* * *

We continued to watch. The two men brought out more chairs, then an antique glass-fronted cabinet. I said to Ashley, "What if they finish up and leave before Dave gets here?"

"I doubt if they will. This kind of job takes time."

"All the same, maybe I should go over and slow them down."

"For goodness sake, Mike! You know what that man's like."

"I was thinking I could put my phone in recording mode. It worked pretty well up in Newcastle, so why not here? He might condemn himself out of his own mouth."

"But that's not going to help you if they decide to beat you up!"

"It won't happen." I was probably trying to convince myself as much as Ashley, but merely speaking the words seemed to give me confidence. I pulled out my phone and started the recording app, then put the phone in my jacket pocket and shrugged my arms into the sleeves. I started to open the door. "Keep your head down, so they don't know you're with me if they see the car."

"For god's sake be careful!"

I walked cautiously over towards the house. Both men were inside when I reached it, so I walked up the short path to the front door and into the hall. I nearly collided Philip Crabtree coming down the stairs. He was looking behind him and calling up to his companion. Turning and confronting me, he stopped I his tracks. "Christ! You gave me a start." Then he realised who I was and approached me indignantly. "What the hell are you doing here, Stanhope? I told you to stay away from this house."

"What, and leave you to rob me of everything in it?"

"Bollocks to that! It was never yours in the first place."

Instead of answering, I pushed past him into the main lounge. I was relieved to see that the big Victorian desk was still in place by the window. I said, "There's a new will. Elizabeth leaves everything to Maggie."

He stopped short, staring at me. "Is there bollocks! If there was, why would you care? It makes no difference to you whether the money goes to Maggie or me."

"Maggie might not want all her furniture shipped out of here."

"So what's it to you?" He thought for a moment. "Where did this new will come from, anyway? How come nobody told me about it?"

I said, "Elizabeth hid it in the house where you wouldn't find it."

As soon as I said this I regretted it. I had given him information needlessly. I could have said the will had been found somewhere else. But I couldn't unsay it now.

"Hid it? What are you talking about?" He turned to the hall door and shouted, "Des, can you get yourself down here please!" He turned to me. "So where did she hide this new will then? I turned this place over from top to bottom, and I never saw anything like that."

"You can't have been looking in the right place."

Suddenly a calculating look spread over his face. "You haven't got it, have you? Otherwise what are you doing here? Not looking after my sister's inheritance, that's for sure. You've come here to pick it up, haven't you? You probably want to tear it to shreds and make certain the inheritance still goes to you. So come on, where is it?"

Chapter 70

I shook my head, hoping I looked convincing. "I found the new will the last time I was here. It's with the solicitors now."

"And nobody's taken the trouble to inform me about it? I don't think so. Where is it?"

His companion now appeared in the doorway – a man in his early twenties with close-cut light hair and a grey T-shirt. Philip turned to him. "Des – can you sort out our friend, please?"

Suddenly Des was inches away from me, pointing a knife at my waist. He raised his free hand and pushed me backwards – a slight, insolent shove – staring straight into my eyes as he did so. I had no option but to step back, and he pushed me repeatedly until I was forced to sit down abruptly on an upright chair.

Philip said, "OK, so what makes you so sure there's another will?"

"Elizabeth told Howard Salmon about it."

"Fucking Howard." He thought about that. "And does he have a copy of it?"

"Yes he does."

"No he doesn't. You're a useless liar, Stanhope." He looked around. "Are you here on your own?"

I nodded.

He turned to his companion. "Keep him there. I'm going outside to check."

He disappeared for a couple of minutes, then came back into the room. "OK, so you're on your own."

I breathed a quiet sigh of relief. Either he hadn't recognised my car, or Ashley had somehow managed to make herself invisible in the passenger seat.

He turned to his companion again. "What are we going to do, Des?"

Des, still standing next to my chair, cast a glance at me, then said, "This is your show, Phil. I only came here to do a bit of humping."

I gave him a silent vote of thanks, but then Phil completely changed my opinion of him. He said to Des, "That didn't bother you last time." Glancing up at Des, I realised where I recognised him from. I was sure he was one of the two men who had tried to throw me off Armstrong Bridge. He hadn't seemed averse to killing me then, so why should he be now?

Des said tersely, "This is different. Broad daylight, someone's house. Forget it."

Philip stared at him, his eyes burning with frustration. Then he said, "Just keep him where he is." He pulled out his phone, half-turned and placed a call.

"Ah, hello, is Mr Bladen there please?" There was a pause, then: "Sorry Ernie, I didn't recognise your voice." Another pause. "Well, you know you said to call you if things got tricky with the inheritance thing … "

I could hear traces of an irritable response from the other end of the call. Phil eventually said, "I know, I know, but I'm thinking on my feet here. I'm looking at the guy who's supposed to inherit the house. He's giving me grief about some missing will, but basically *he's* the obstacle here. He needs persuading, and it looks as if I'm on my own here."

Another pause, then: "I don't know, Ernie. I just thought you might have some ideas. This guy Stanhope is constantly meddling … " He broke off, interrupted by a sharp question from the other end, then said, "Yes, Mike Stanhope. That's right. You know him?" More indignant comment from the other end, then Philip said, "Bloody hell, what a small world." He listened for a moment. "Well then. This is your chance to put him right about that."

He listened some more, then said, "What, you personally? But that could take you hours … " Then: "Oh, I see. OK. Well it's near the centre of Harrogate." He gave Bladen the address. "I'll see you in half an hour then."

He disconnected. "He's coming down from his place in the Dales." Des said, "Who is?"

"Someone who will know how to sort this out."

* * *

Philip said, "I'm going to put some more stuff in the van. We can't all sit around here." He glanced at Des. "But you'll need to stay here and watch him."

"Don't be too long then." Des turned to me. "Get up slowly, and go and sit in that armchair."

I did as I was bidden, realising as I sat down why he'd moved me. The chair was deep and yielding. It would be difficult for me to stand up from it in a hurry. Des drew the upright chair forward and sat down obliquely in front of me.

I was thinking fast. Hopefully Dave Matthews was on his way here from Ripon, and might arrive any minute. But now it seemed that Ernie Bladen was also on his way here. Who would arrive first? Would they arrive at the same time? What would happen if they did?

In fact Dave turned up first. I heard raised voices in the street, then there were footfalls in the hallway and Dave appeared in the doorway, dressed in a jacket and smart trousers. He was followed closely by Philip.

Des lowered the knife as soon as he heard Dave's approach, but I said, "Watch out Dave, this guy has a knife."

Des stood up briskly, apparently in fight-or-flight mode. Dave said calmly, "That's OK. Let's all just have a nice chat."

Philip said, "Who the fuck are you?"

Dave half-turned. His bulk dwarfed Philip. He said, "Just consider me a friend."

Des said, "He's a cop. Sticks out a mile."

Philip said, "*Are* you?"

"I told you, I'm a friend."

Des said, "Bollocks! I've had enough of this." He started to move towards the doorway, and Dave stepped half a pace back to let him pass. I stood up and said, "You're not going to let him go, are you?"

Dave turned to me. "What exactly do you expect me to do about it?"

Des strode past him and out of the house. Dave turned to Philip. "I'd advise you not to follow him."

I reached into my pocket and pulled out my phone. "They've just been discussing doing away with me. I've got it all recorded." I held the phone out towards them.

"Have they now?" He turned to Philip. "Your name please?"

"Philip Crabtree.

"Well I suggest you sit down now, Mr Crabtree, while there are still some chairs around here to sit on."

I said, "Dave, this isn't the end of it. Ernie Bladen is on his way here now, and could show up at any minute. You know who Bladen is?"

"Obviously." He shot me an ironic look, then turned to Philip. "And what will Mr Bladen be doing when he gets here?"

"No comment."

Dave looked at him with amusement. "Very good. I like that." He waved Philip towards the upright chair vacated by Des, and Philip sat down gingerly.

I said quickly, "I've been having all kinds of trouble with Ernie Bladen up in Newcastle. His right-hand man kicked the shit out of me, and then the same man tried to kill Ashley and me. It was all at Bladen's instigation, but he usually keeps out of it himself. If he turns up here, it will be a rare thing." I turned to Philip. "Mr Crabtree doesn't work for him, he just owes him money."

Dave listened to this carefully, then turned to Philip. "What I'm getting from my friend over here, Mr Crabtree, is that we have enough evidence to prove a serious embarrassment to you. Now you can side with Mr Bladen when he gets here, and dig a deeper hole for yourself, or you can do yourself a favour and leave him to us."

"I'm not saying or doing anything without speaking to a lawyer first."

Dave gave him an ironic stare. "I don't know where you're expecting to whistle up a lawyer from, but in any case nobody has said you're under arrest. I'm not here in an official capacity, I'm just trying to help out."

"Of course you are."

Dave straightened. "You need to make a decision here. Are you going to side with Bladen, and probably go down with him, or step away from this?"

"What do you think will happen to me if Bladen thinks I've given him up to you?"

"It's your call."

Chapter 71

Dave told me to sit back down in the armchair, then he got Philip to move the upright chair to a different, more commanding position, and told him to sit down again on it. It felt a bit like watching a director dressing a film set for the next scene.

He asked me, "Is your phone still recording?"

I checked, then slipped the phone into my pocket.

Dave himself swung the door back and forth on its hinges for a moment, and tried standing in a position immediately behind it. Apparently satisfied, he stepped out. "Now we wait."

Minutes ticked past. Dave perched on the edge of the desk, glancing at his watch. I said, "Sorry about your dinner."

"It'll keep."

Finally we heard footsteps on the doorstep and a man's voice called, "Philip?" Dave stood up quickly and stepped over to his position behind the door. He signalled to Philip to acknowledge the call.

"In here!"

Bladen appeared in the doorway. Although he wasn't a big man, his stocky form seemed to fill it. Incongruously he was wearing a beanie hat pulled down low over his forehead, and a dark jacket with the collar turned up. He took in the tableau of me in the armchair and Philip apparently sitting on guard over me.

Philip said, "Ernie. I didn't recognise you for a minute."

"Too many CCTV cameras in an area like this." He turned his collar down. "So what the fuck have you been me getting into?"

Philip pointed towards me with his thumb. "He says he can block the inheritance process. If I don't get my money, you won't get yours. It's as simple as that."

"And for this you drag me out here in person? You've got some cheek."

Philip shrugged. "I thought … I assumed you had people to deal with this kind of thing. I didn't realise when I called you that you'd come here yourself."

"My best man is out of action." Bladen turned to me. "And this interfering bastard is responsible." He eyed me malevolently. "I don't know what I have to do to get you off my back."

I tried to shrug, but wasn't convinced that I'd pulled it off. Bladen was a chilling presence, and even the knowledge Dave was waiting behind the door didn't entirely cancel out the threat in his voice.

He said, "Harry will make a better job of it next time."

I said nothing, and he turned to Philip. "So what exactly are you expecting me to do here?"

Philip was under-rehearsed. It was a wonder he'd improvised this far, but we hadn't had the chance to discuss a proper plan. Involuntarily he glanced towards the door where Dave was hidden, presumably looking in vain for some sort of cue.

Bladen was too quick-thinking for him. He saw Philip's look, half-turned to the door, then took hold of the knob and thrust it open violently. There was a muffled cry from Dave, who stumbled forward with his hand on his head. As he did so, Bladen slipped a handgun from his side pocket and waved it in front of him. I thought: not again.

Bladen shouted, "What the fuck have I got into here? Who else have you got hiding under the table?" He gave Dave a shove. "You, go and sit there." He pointed to the only other chair left in the room, and Dave reluctantly sat down. "And everybody, I want to see your hands at all times. If I see anyone with a mobile phone, I'll shoot them. Understood?"

Before anyone could speak, a voice from the hall called, "Ernie? Are you there?"

"In here, Neville. You took your time."

A tall man in his fifties appeared behind Bladen. He was wearing a hoodie, which gave him an incongruously youthful look, but he now shoved it back to reveal a long face and vigorous dark hair thrusting upwards from his scalp. He said, "Well don't thank me for putting myself out."

Bladen said nothing, and the newcomer asked, "How's it looking?"

"Bit of a problem here."

"So what's the plan?"

"We need to decide what to do with these people." He sighed. "Christ knows how many CCTV cameras there are out there. This is Neighbourhood Watchville. We need to be creative."

The newcomer said, "A fire, do you think?"

Philip shouted, "You're not going to burn this house down? You'll never get your money if you do."

Bladen turned furiously on him. "Forget the money, you stupid man. You've well and truly fucked things up here with your whingeing incompetence, and now I have to put them right."

Philip blanched at this, perhaps finally comprehending the nastiness of what was happening. It was no doubt also dawning on him that he might become a victim, not a beneficiary, of whatever Bladen had in mind.

Bladen said, "A fire's no good. If there are cameras, they'll have seen us coming in."

Neville said, "They wouldn't recognise us."

"No, but they would wonder what happened to us. It wouldn't work."

Philip said quickly, "There's a lane out the back, at the end of the garden. You could leave that way."

Bladen glanced out of the window. "Fancy that. I wouldn't have thought of that." He turned to Neville. "Why don't you go and find your way round the back in your van?"

In some ways the idea of leaving via the back garden was appealing. In the open air, and spread out, some of us at least might be able to escape Bladen's clutches. But if we failed, there was no telling where these two would take us or what would happen to us after that.

I wondered what had happened to Ashley. Had she seen Dave arrive, closely followed by Bladen and his mate Neville? If so, she must realise things were getting out of hand. With luck she might have called the police, but on the other hand she might think Dave was police enough.

* * *

Neville headed off out to the street to collect his van. Bladen now had to contend with the fact that he was on his own, holding three people at gunpoint. He seemed to realise he needed a more secure position and shifted sideways, moving away from the doorway so that his back was against the wall.

Dave, recovering from being hit by the door, now spoke to Bladen for the first time. "I'm a policeman. Did you realise that? You can't just make me disappear and expect there will be no consequences."

Bladen glared at him but said nothing.

Dave went on, "You're a businessman. You understand risk. Have you weighed all this up properly? At the moment you can still walk away from this, but if you do any harm to any of us, you're permanently fucked. You won't come back from this."

"So you're all about to go home and say nothing, are you? I don't think so."

"We could discuss the options."

"Options? I don't deal in options."

I sensed that Dave's true purpose was to unnerve Bladen, and felt I should join in. I said, "He doesn't. I've heard him say that before."

Bladen switched his gaze to me, but at that moment Philip chose to stand up and start to walk over to the door.

Bladen turned abruptly to face him. "Where do you think you're going?"

"I need to lock my van and shut the front door." I admired his bravado, though his shaky voice rather undermined it.

"Sit down, Philip. Nobody is going anywhere until I say so."

"This is ridiculous. How is any of this going to benefit anybody?" He took another step towards the door.

Bladen turned further, following his movements. "I'm warning you. This is not a joke." He pointed his gun directly at Philip.

I had no burning desire to intervene on Philip's behalf, but for some reason something snapped in my head at this point, and without any conscious thought I started to lunge forward out of my chair. However, the ancient armchair chair was so low and softly-sprung that I underestimated the effort it would take to get out of it, and fell back ignominiously into a sitting position.

That misjudgement probably saved my life. Bladen sensed the movement, swivelled round and fired his gun impulsively in my direction. The sound was deafening. However, because I'd failed to stand up, his shot went high.

He lowered the gun, now pointing it straight at me, but I'll never know if he would have fired again because he never got the chance. A voice from outside the rear window shouted, "Armed police! Put down your weapons. NOW!"

Through the window I saw several blue-clad figures crouching with automatic weapons pointed at the house. Bladen gave a small sigh, stooped and placed his gun carefully on the floor.

Chapter 72

"So Maggie doesn't get the house after all. It still goes to Mike." Ashley smiled at Dave over her beer, then turned to me. "That's right, isn't it?"

I said, "Technically speaking, yes."

We were sitting with Dave and Suzy in an olde worlde pub in Ripon – an attractive period-built town (technically a city, Suzy had told me) on the edge of the Yorkshire Dales. Suzy was a pretty, slightly-built woman in her early forties with angular, lived-in features and dyed blonde hair fashioned in a dated-looking chop cut. Her bright, spiky personality matched her appearance. "What does that mean?" she asked.

I needed to decide how much to say. On the face of it, Elizabeth's new will was exactly as expected. In it, she left more or less everything to Maggie. But the will wasn't signed. From a legal point of view it was valueless. The issue in my mind was whether or not I should pay any attention to it.

It still seemed a miracle that I was in possession of it at all. In the brief moment before the police had surged into Elizabeth's house the previous night, I'd edged over to the desk, groping under it for the lever that would release the hidden compartment. Amazingly, I'd found it at once, and was able to slide the desktop a few inches towards me, revealing a small oblong recess across the back. In it was a small bunch of folded A4 sheets, and I'd snatched them and slid them into my pocket.

Once the police had entered, the evening had unfolded with relentless predictability. At first there was a lot of shouting and a great deal of tension, then finally we were all taken to a police station in separate cars. There we were questioned individually for hours – an experience which, as far as I was concerned, seemed to be turning into a regular occurrence. I tried to feel philosophical about it, though the strain of repeatedly telling the same story to an implacable audience was exhausting.

Finally the three of us had been released, and we'd arranged to meet up in Ripon at lunchtime the following day.

I looked round the table. Everyone was waiting to hear my thoughts on Elizabeth's will. I said, "Legally, it looks as if the house will go to me, but it's obvious that Elizabeth, my relative, was all over the place about what she really wanted. One minute she left everything to me, the next minute she switched it all to her niece. And at one stage she also wanted it to go to Philip, her nephew. I feel I have to mediate, and decide on the fairest solution."

Suzy said, "But the law is the law. If everything goes to you, you should take it and be thankful."

I couldn't help smiling. Her vigorous practicality was refreshing. Yet I wasn't convinced it was the right answer. I turned to Ashley. "Actually I'm wondering about splitting the value three ways: Maggie, Philip and me."

"Then you would be playing into the hands of that horrible man Philip."

"But I feel sorry for his wife and kids. It doesn't seem fair that his reckless gambling and bullying should have deprived them of the money just when they really need it."

"Huh! That's taking generosity to a fault, if you ask me. That man tried to have you killed! In any case, how do you know he won't gamble the money away at the first opportunity?"

"Well, he won't be able to if he goes to prison over any of this. Anyway, maybe I can pay the money directly to his wife. Or I could talk to him first, and impose some conditions. I could tell him I might remember certain things more clearly if he steps out of line."

Dave said, "I don't want to hear this, Mike. If you deliberately misremember something, you could be accused of perverting the course of justice. Seriously."

I nodded, chastened. "OK, but you get the gist."

"Just be careful. I've already been bending over backwards to help you. Don't drop me in the shit over this."

"I know, I know."

I'd hoped that Dave's police background might have helped Ashley and me during the questioning last night, but he'd told me that initially he'd been under just as much scrutiny as everyone else.

"The clincher was that Ernie Bladen was implicated. They knew the hunt was on for him, and once they realised they'd got him on firearms offences, they started looking more favourably on you."

I asked what had happened to Phil Crabtree.

"I don't know, but I imagine they'll have let him go for the time being. He may not have committed any crime, although he was putting himself up for being complicit in one. They might prefer to see him as a witness against Bladen."

"But it's obvious to me now that he organised for those two bastards to throw me off Armstrong Bridge."

"Where's the evidence?"

"Well, I more or less recognised one of them last night at the house."

"More or less? I don't think that cuts it, Mike."

I shrugged.

He said, "Maybe they only intended to frighten you. They were interrupted, so we'll probably never get the chance to find out."

"Whose side are you on?

"I'm just trying to be realistic. Anyway, they're not likely to try it again."

I said nothing to this. Maybe Dave was right. It upset me to think that would-be killers might on the loose, but there was little point in fretting over it.

Dave turned to Ashley. "What exactly happened to you at the house last night after Mr Hero went in on his own?"

"To begin with I just kept out of sight. I saw you arrive, but I was too far away to speak to you. I nearly followed you over to the house, but then another man turned up with a woolly hat covering most of his face, so I hung back. It must have been Ernie Bladen, but from where I was sitting I didn't recognise him. I've only met him once, and I had no reason to think he would be turning up in Harrogate."

I said, "So you didn't feel you should intervene?"

"What could I do? I didn't like the look of him, but I didn't really know what was going on inside. I thought I might mess things up if I barged in."

"What changed your mind?"

"Well, time passed and no one came out, and I started to worry. Then another man arrived, wearing a hoodie. I felt that the odds were swinging the wrong way."

"And somehow you managed to call out the armed police."

She shrugged. "There was something odd about the way the first man walked, believe it or not, and I suddenly realised it reminded me of Ernie Bladen. He kind of struts, as if he's trying to look taller than he really is. I couldn't imagine what he would be doing at the house, but I thought maybe he'd somehow followed us all the way from Newcastle. Anyway, I felt that if it *was* Ernie Bladen, he couldn't be up to any good, so I'd better do something radical. Having him *and* Philip on your case wasn't going to be doing you any favours."

"What did you tell the police?"

"I said I'd seen a man go into the house with a gun in his hand. I didn't think they'd take the situation seriously otherwise."

I looked admiringly at her. She hadn't in fact seen any gun, but she knew Bladen and his people weren't above using one, so she'd taken a chance. If she'd been proved wrong, she might have had some very tough explaining to do.

* * *

As we made our way out of the pub I pulled Dave aside.

"I'm sorry I dragged you into all this. It wasn't fair on you."

He gave a deep laugh. "One day you'll stop meddling in things that aren't your affair – things you can't finish on you own. But the day you do, you'll stop being the Mike Stanhope we know and love."

"Yeah, yeah."

He held the door open for me. "Sorry, was that a thank-you? It didn't sound much like one to me." We stepped out into the sunshine and he gave me a friendly shove as we crossed the car park.

I said, "I paid for the lunch. What more do you want?"

"Being left alone to enjoy my holiday would be nice."

I stopped and turned to him. "I owe you. You know that. I don't know what else I can say. How I can ever repay you?"

He swatted away the words with a wave of his arm. "OK, OK, that'll do. No need to get carried away."

I reached for my car keys. "I like Suzy."

"So do I." He chuckled. "I'm not so sure what I think of her parents though. They live in a village north of here. Very traditional. She says they would have given us separate bedrooms if we'd stayed with them. That's why we're in a hotel here in Ripon."

Ashley and I waved Dave and Suzy away from the car park.

"She's great," Ashley commented with a smile. "She's just what Dave needs."

"I must say I've never seen him looking so cheerful."

Still smiling, she said, "So can we go home now, please?"

Chapter 73

Cornwall felt like another country. Maybe it was just the lack of stress after I'd experienced so much of it in the north. My flat still didn't seem like home exactly, but it was certainly a refuge, and I was glad to settle into it. Ashley stayed over with me on our first night, reinforcing the sense of convivial calm.

Bob Latimer seemed to have stopped taking my calls again, so for the rest of the week I kept away from the Latimer Logistics offices. In any case I had other things to do. There were bills to pay; I had to write the article about the firm we'd visited in Sunderland; and I needed to make a start on the forklift truck article I'd agreed to write on that day when I was engaged on my stake-out.

It seemed I still had a working life of sorts in Cornwall, with or without Latimers.

I phoned the solicitors in Newcastle about Elizabeth's will. I told the partner, David Smythe, that I'd found a new will post-dating the one leaving everything to me, but it wasn't signed.

"Basically it has no validity," he said. "There have been a few special cases in recent years where courts have taken a different view, but in these circumstances I think that would be highly unlikely."

"But there's nothing to stop me taking account of what it says, is there?"

"Nothing at all. You can do what you like with your own assets. Just let the probate run its course, and then when you've taken possession of the estate, redistribute the assets as you see fit. You might end up paying more tax than you would have if you'd only inherited part of the estate, but you can't bring an invalid will to life just to reduce your tax liability."

Dave Matthews called me from Ripon. "I just thought you'd like to know we've got your furniture back in your house. But I can't say it's all in the right rooms. We just bunged it wherever we could find a space for it on the ground floor."

On the day after the events in Harrogate I'd phoned the local police and pointed out that a load of furniture – in effect *my* furniture – was sitting in a van outside the house. I wanted to know what we could do about it. They said the house couldn't be disturbed until they'd finished their examination of it.

Dave had saved the day. He'd kept in touch with the police, and now that the way was clear, he and Suzy had shifted the furniture into the house.

"As usual, I don't know how to thank you," I said.

"As usual."

I asked him if Philip Crabtree had been released by the police.

"Oh, yes, they let him go that same night. I knew they would. Next day he went home to Newcastle. But that doesn't mean they've finished with him. We'll have to see how things go."

"And he just left the rental van in Harrogate?"

"They told him he would be committing a crime if he drove away with the furniture, but evidently he decided it wasn't his job to offload it. In a way his hands were tied. They will have made it clear to him that it wouldn't help his position to interfere any further with the house or its contents."

"So he ends up with a big van rental bill."

"That's his lookout. At least he left all the keys behind."

I asked about Bladen. He said they'd kept him in custody overnight, but now he too had been released pending further action.

"What does that mean?"

"It means he's likely to be arrested any day. The team in Newcastle will be busy getting their ducks in a row.

"So in the meantime, should we be worried for our safety?"

"Probably not. They're watching him closely, and he'll know that."

"What about Neville, Bladen's mate?"

"He's a local villain from Leeds. They've been talking to him, but I don't know what case they'll bring against him, if any. It probably depends how deeply he's been involved in Bladen's other affairs in the past."

* * *

Now that I knew Philip Crabtree was back in circulation, I was dubious about phoning his wife again. Finally I plucked up the courage.

She answered in a subdued voice. "Oh, hello Mike. I'm amazed you're calling me after everything that's been going on."

"Is Philip there now?"

"He's just taken the kids out to the shops. That's got to be a first."

"Have the police told him he's going to be charged with anything?"

"Not exactly. I think they want him as a witness against Ernie Bladen. He thinks his life has ended either way." She was quiet for a moment. "I suppose it won't count for much, but I'm really sorry for what happened in Harrogate. Philip can be very foolish sometimes. I try to tell him, but … he doesn't always listen."

"I appreciate the thought."

"Just so long as you know."

I waited a moment, then said, "I thought I should tell you that I will definitely be inheriting Elizabeth's estate."

"Well that's no surprise. That's what Phil was worried about all along."

"She wrote a final will leaving everything to Maggie – but she didn't sign it, so legally speaking it doesn't carry any weight."

After a pause, Angela said, "Well fancy that."

"I wanted to put something to you. I'm willing to consider sharing the estate three ways – you, Maggie and me. But only if your share goes to you and not Philip."

"Seriously?" A sudden spark of hope.

"No promises. It just seems the fairest outcome. But Philip has given me a lot of grief, so I don't see why he should benefit."

"I know he has, Mike, I know." I could hear her mind whirring. "The trouble is, Philip has debts. Even if Ernie Bladen is in prison, he will expect them to be paid.

I drew a deep breath. "Do you know how much?"

"Maybe forty or fifty thousand."

"Oh." I couldn't see any way round this. I said, "Well, I suppose I wouldn't be able to stop you using the money as you see fit. But it has to be your call."

"What if I set up some kind of trust or something, and you paid the money into that?"

"I don't know what that actually means – do you?"

"No!" She gave an edgy laugh. "But I could find out. We could talk again."

I waited a moment. "But it's no good if Philip beats the money out of you. How can we avoid that?"

There was a longer silence this time. Finally she said, "He's not a bad man, Mike. He's a child at heart, with an inferiority complex."

"So there's no chance you'll be splitting up?"

"Why no! This is a time when we need to stick together."

"OK, well he just he needs to be clear that you won't get the money if he gives you any grief over it. I mean that. Maybe it should be paid in instalments?"

"Whatever you think, Mike. It's your call."

I said, "Look, it won't be a fortune. It might just help you pay the mortgage for a year or two."

"That's what we need. If Philip comes through this, he can get another job, and we can start paying our way. *I* can get a job. We'll survive."

"OK then. I'll get back to you when I've got my head round this."

"I don't know what to say, Mike. Thank you."

Chapter 74

A late summer sun was shining as I drove over to St Austell on the following Monday morning. The landscape had altered subtly since the last time I made this trip. The cow parsley along the roadside had died back, the foliage on the trees was heavier, and the crops had matured and changed colour. It was intriguing to think I was noticing these things. Maybe it meant I'd started to feel part of the area without even realising it.

I'd left some notes and other bits and pieces in the office I used at Latimers, and since my work for the company appeared to be on hold, I felt I should take possession of them. I was also hoping that if I encountered Bob Latimer while I was on the premises he might be willing to talk to me.

It worked. He put his head round the office door. "Mike, good to see you. Would you like to come and have a word when you've finished here?"

He was seated behind his desk when I knocked. He waved me over to the visitor's chair. "The Melling acquisition has turned into a right cockup, hasn't it?" Yet he didn't look especially upset.

Cautiously I said, "I don't know. Has it?"

"In some ways." He swung his chair into the upright position. "This conversation is confidential – are we agreed?"

"Of course."

"The problem is, when you started working for us I thought I could take your discretion for granted. It's not much good if I have to keep checking with you that it still applies."

"You don't. I've learned my lesson." I gave him what I hoped was an earnest look.

"OK, Mike, well let's not get into that now. So long as I know we're off the record in this conversation."

I nodded.

"The thing is, we seem to owe you a debt of gratitude, and I want to give credit where it's due. You spotted the anomalies at Ashurst Concepts, and you found out that Piers Ashurst was behind that lorry theft."

"But I didn't work things out until it was too late to stop the acquisition going forward."

"True enough, but at least you were on the case when nobody else was. The due diligence process was a complete fiasco."

"Have you found out exactly what happened?"

"Well, our London people subcontracted the audit on Ashurst Concepts to a local accountancy firm in Leeds, Salmon Fischer, and one of their team was in cahoots with Piers Ashurst – a man called Nick Weller. You flagged up a lot of this for us yourself."

"But I don't know the details."

He nodded. "OK, well it seems that this Nick Weller had been moonlighting for Piers on Ashursts' accounts for more than a year. Piers' own head of accounts was a complete idiot – his uncle, apparently – so Weller took control in all but name. Then we started talking to Mellings about the acquisition, and Chris Melling threw Ashursts into the mix. But that was around the time demand for Piers' products had taken a dive. Piers realised the deal could fall apart if Ashursts appeared to be a basket case, so he persuaded Nick Weller to start faking Ashursts' accounts to make them look more profitable than they really were."

"Hence the double accounting that Andrea spotted."

"Exactly. Of course, this should have shown up in the due diligence report, but because Weller happened to work for the very firm doing the due diligence, he was able to fake the report as well."

"Talk about a conflict of interests."

Bob gave an ironic laugh.

I said, "I wonder what hold Piers had over Nick Weller?"

"I don't know. These people seem to operate in a world I know nothing about. It might just have been a case of inducements."

"But surely Weller couldn't have got away with it in the long run?

Someone in his own firm would have spotted it eventually – or your finance director would have."

"You'd think so, wouldn't you? But obviously he thought he could." Bob ran his hands through his hair. "And I suppose you could argue that he did. The takeover went through, after all." He laughed dryly. "He didn't reckon on someone like you sticking their nose in."

"But since I did, you must have reported all this to Weller's company?"

"I certainly have. In fact I got a lot of this stuff from them. Apparently even Weller was dubious when he was asked to fudge the invoices for that stolen consignment, and make it look like a new delivery."

"So he had some scruples, then."

"But it didn't stop him carrying on with what he was doing."

"What's happened to him now?"

"Oh, I think he's out on his ear. But I still wouldn't want to work with that accounting firm again. I've warned our London people about them."

I thought of Norah Stevenson, the kindly woman who had worked for Derek Salmon and had been so helpful to me. I said, "One bad apple ... "

"Maybe so. I can only leave them to decide."

I said, "What will happen to Ashurst Concepts now?"

"Well, I've got a team going through their real accounts with a fine-tooth comb. Once we get the full story, we'll decide what to do. Piers will be voted off the board, and if there's anything left to salvage, we'll either put the company on the market or just keep running it ourselves. But between you and me, I suspect we may have to close it down and take the hit."

"Not a very good start to the acquisition."

Bob gave me a surprisingly disarming smile. "No it's not, but I've no one but myself to blame for that. I shouldn't have let Chris Melling arm-twist me into including Ashursts in the deal. I thought it sounded fun, but I'll know better next time."

"Can you sue the firm in charge of the due diligence process?"

"Maybe. I'm talking to our solicitors about that. But it might be more trouble than it's worth."

"What about Melling Logistics?"

"It's is a good company. It's a shame Chris Melling has painted himself into a corner, but the business itself is sound. They've got some valuable contracts, and there are some excellent people up in Newcastle. The acquisition is still a very good move for us, even after all that's happened."

"Will you still honour the contract with BBS, Ernie Bladen's company?"

"I don't see why not. It's an arms-length operation. I can't blame them for the corrupt man at the top of the tree. Basically Bladen acquired an existing business and renamed it, and most of the original people are still in place."

"Where does Chris Melling himself stand in all this?"

Bob frowned. "To be honest Mike, I don't know. I always thought he was a good man. That whole company has his stamp on it. He was supposed to work a year's run-out contract for us, with the option of an extension, but I hear he might be facing charges over this kidnapping episode, so I don't know."

The conversation seemed to be coming to an end, so I prepared to leave. I said, "Thank you for being so frank over all this, Bob. I appreciate it."

"I think you've earned the right."

Tentatively I said, "To be honest, I was hoping some of this might cancel out my indiscretion over that news story I wrote."

I couldn't read the look that came to Bob's face. He said, "I see your reasoning, but it's a matter of trust. Your article could have done a lot of damage to us. Happily it doesn't seem to have, but I can't simply wipe the slate."

"I see that."

He gave me a long look. Inconsequentially, he said, "I'm very fond of Ashley."

"So am I."

"She's good for us."

"I know. She's good for me, too."

He said nothing for a moment, then: "We'll discontinue your

ongoing arrangement with us, Mike, but we'll contact you if we want individual jobs done – text for a new brochure, say, or a one-off press release here and there, that kind of thing. That's the best I can offer you at the moment."

It sounded feeble, but the goodwill gesture was impossible to ignore.

"I can't argue with that."

Chapter 75

I nearly collided with Ashley in the corridor. She was looking preoccupied.

I said, "What's the matter?"

"Arrggh! I've just come out of a meeting with the sales team, and it looks like we might have lost the Franchi contract after all."

"What? It wasn't because of my article, was it?"

She looked blank for a moment. "Oh, no, nothing like that. Another contractor has put in a better bid – some new outfit that no one has even heard of."

"Is it a lost cause?"

"It's on a knife edge." She frowned. "What I don't get is why Gary is taking it so philosophically. He seems to have adopted a 'win some, lose some' approach to it. The other sales staff are much more annoyed."

"Sorry, who is Gary?"

"Oh, he's Gareth Hobbs, our sales manager. We'd all been calling him Gareth, but he put us right the other day."

"And is this contract his baby?"

"Well, no, as a matter of fact he hasn't been involved directly with it. The negotiations started way before he joined. All the same, you'd expect better of him than a 'not invented here' attitude."

She asked me if I'd talked to Bob Latimer, and I gave her the salient points of the conversation I'd just had with him.

"So you're not exactly out, but you're not exactly in?"

"Something like that."

"On the whole it's probably a good result."

"I suppose you're right."

"I'd better get on." She gave me a bright smile. "See you later."

She headed off to the marketing department, and I went back to my little office. After the conversation I'd had with Bob I wasn't sure whether to remove all my belongings or leave them there.

I sat down at my diminutive desk and drummed my fingers on the surface. Something about what Ashley had just told me was bugging me, and after a moment I realised it was her mention of the name Gary. I'd heard some reference to another Gary recently, and it seemed an odd coincidence. But where?

It took me a moment, but finally I got it. I heard that name when I was sitting in Jenna's flat in Newcastle on the night she was kidnapped. A man left a message on her answering machine, and I was sure he announced himself as Gary. Could it be the same Gary?

I thought about this. I was pretty sure Gareth Hobbs had made several trips to Newcastle with Bob Latimer during the talks about the acquisition, so he could easily have met Jenna Melling while he was there. Or maybe he knew her already, and they'd renewed their acquaintance.

What had the Gary on the phone said in his message? It was too long ago for me to remember clearly, but I was pretty sure he'd mentioned someone called Greg. Presumably this had to be Greg Atkins. So if I was right, Gary, Greg and Jenna all knew each other, and had apparently been discussing something. What could that possibly be?

I took out my phone and rang Ashley's number.

"Mike, this is such a surprise!"

"I didn't want to come into your office and talk in front of other people."

"OK. So … ?"

"I wondered if you could introduce me to Gareth Hobbs. Gary. I've never met him properly, so you could just say something about wanting to get us together while I'm here in the office."

"I won't ask why."

"I'll tell you later."

"OK, I'll come up and take you over. He's based next door."

* * *

Gary Hobbs was a good-looking man in his mid-thirties with short light-coloured hair and tanned features. He looked like someone you'd see on the cover of a sporting magazine. He had the easy affability of a born salesman, and he greeted me with a confident handshake.

"I've seen you around the place, Mike, and I know about the work you do for us here. I don't know why our paths have never crossed before."

I managed to make small talk with him for a couple of minutes. I simply wanted to hear him speak, and see if his voice reminded me of the one I'd heard on Jenna's phone. The answer was a qualified yes. I couldn't remember the phone voice clearly, but I was pretty sure there were correspondences.

As we were about to break up I got round to the one question I wanted to ask. "As a matter of curiosity, where did you work before you joined Latimer Logistics?"

"I was with Edgeley Stevens Logistics. I was sales manager, working out of their head office in Stoke-on-Trent."

"A good company."

"I thought so." He gave me his full-force salesman's smile. "I learned a lot there."

Ashley and I had to cross a yard to get back to the main Latimer offices from the new block where Gary worked. Once we were outside she said, "What was all that about?"

"I'm not sure. I've got a feeling he's in touch with some of the people at Melling Logistics – specifically Jenna Melling and Greg Atkins. I was wondering why."

"We're taking Mellings over, in case you hadn't noticed. He's probably just been building bridges."

"It seemed a bit more furtive than that."

"What did?"

I stopped and looked at her. "I'll tell you later, if that's OK. I want to sound someone out first."

She gave me a half-smile. "Well don't go putting anyone's back up."

"I'll try not to."

I sat down at the desk again. A theory was beginning to form in my mind, and I was wondering how to test it out. The key question was this: what would Gary, Jenna and Greg be likely to be discussing? And the only answer I could think of was one thing: logistics.

I took my phone out and put it on the desk, planning what to say, then I pulled up a number from my contact list and pressed the green button.

Chapter 76

"Mike? Long time no speak. How are things?"

Freddie was a Yorkshireman of Asian descent. I'd known him slightly for years, and followed his career path through several transport and logistics companies. He was now a line manager at Edgeley Stevens Logistics in Stoke-on-Trent. He knew me as a journalist, and I was hoping he hadn't picked up on my connection with Latimer Logistics.

"Not bad, thanks," I said. "You?"

"Life is good. We've got a great team here and some brilliant resources. I've never had so much fun."

"I'm glad to hear it."

"I heard you pulled up your roots and headed west. Is that true?"

I answered cautiously, "It is. I'm living in Cornwall."

"And that's convenient for your work, is it?"

"No, but there are compensations."

"Yes, I heard you paired up with that marketing lady from Latimer Logistics – what was her name? We used to see her at some of the trade shows."

"Ashley Renwick. The word gets around then."

"You know how it is."

Thankfully he said no more about Latimers, and his tone switched to professional mode. "So what can I do for you, Mike?"

As casually as I could manage, I said, "This Franchi operation – I was wondering how it's going to work? Purely on a non-attributable basis, of course."

"You know about that, do you? You're very quick off the mark."

I gave an inward whoop. It seemed I'd struck lucky. But I had to keep my tone low-key. I said, "Oh, you know, you just hear things."

"I'm sure you do." He seemed to think for a moment, but not for long. "To be honest, Mike, there's not a lot I could tell you even if I wanted to. It's all been negotiated above me. All I know is that if it goes ahead we'll need to take on new warehouse space. I've already got it earmarked. And of course we'll need to increase the fleet."

"You must have some more specific plans than that?"

"Course we have, Mike. The people upstairs have worked things out to the nth degree. But as I say, I can't tell you the details."

"Fair enough, point taken." Now came the big question – but it had to sound like a throw-away. "And just to be clear, Edgeley Stevens isn't the lead contractor – is that right?"

"Yeah, officially the deal has been negotiated by one of these fourth-party logistics outfits. You know, the kind who don't have any assets of their own, just an office somewhere. They buy in everything from real-world companies like ours."

I tried one last bluff. "I thought so. What was the name of the company again?" I pretended to rack my brains.

He laughed. "Good try, Mike. I can't seem to bring it to mind either. But when it all goes live, I'm sure you'll be the first to know."

* * *

I stared unseeing at the glass partition wall opposite me. Just when I thought I'd unearthed enough intrigue to last me half a lifetime, I seemed to have discovered some more.

I now knew that an unspecified assetless logistics company had put in a bid to take on the Franchi contract, and had arranged to subcontract the work to Edgeley Stevens, Gary Hobbs' former employer. I didn't know the name of the company, but I was willing to bet that the whole thing had been concocted by Gary in association with Jenna and Greg. They'd presumably pooled their knowledge about the negotiations between Franchi and the Latimer group, and put in a lower bid.

I wasn't sure how I should feel about this. In some ways I had to admire their gall, but I also felt angered by their bare-faced disloyalty. Jenna had gone behind her father's back, and Hobbs had taken advantage of Bob Latimer's confidence in him. What they were doing probably wasn't illegal, but it seemed resoundingly unethical.

Then again, who was I to be self-righteous? A few weeks ago I'd picked up some confidential information about this very contract, and published it in a news article. We were all using information gained through privilege to feather our own nests. It wasn't a very comfortable thought.

I wasn't clear if the rival contract bid could be deflected at this stage. I knew that executives like Hobbs sometimes signed confidentiality agreements with their employers, and if he'd done so with Latimers, he must have flouted it. Latimers could presumably take legal action against him.

In reality that kind of thing seldom happened. It was messy, and there was always a risk that the sour-grapes aspect would taint the company taking the action. Sometimes the mere threat of it would frighten away the rival bid, but I wasn't sure how resolute Latimers would be about it.

In a corner of my mind I felt let down by Jenna. From the day I'd met her I'd known she was ambitious, but I'd persuaded myself that behind her hard-boiled exterior beat a heart of gold. Conceitedly, I'd felt that somehow I'd managed to recognise and tease out her gentler qualities. Perhaps so, but evidently none of this had been enough to deter her from unrepentant scheming.

I smiled grimly to myself. If my father had been party to having me kidnapped in order to keep me quiet about something, I probably wouldn't have felt much loyalty towards him. I could hardly blame Jenna for feeling like that about Chris Melling. Yet she must have embarked on this scheme long ago. She was already prepared to betray Melling Logistics well before she knew what he was up to.

I wondered what to do. I could report what I'd discovered to Bob Latimer, hoping it would help restore me to his good books, or I could keep quiet and let matters take their course. If the rival bid for the contract was a done deal, telling Bob about it might not help matters. In due course Gary Hobbs would resign from Latimers and Jenna and Greg would resign from Mellings, and life would go on.

But it might not be a done deal. There might still be time to stop it. Surely I owed it to myself to try to do something about it?

* * *

The clincher came that evening when I told Ashley what I'd found out. She'd arranged to come round to my flat, and she sat on my sofa, staring at me in indignation.

"I *knew* there was a reason why I hated Jenna."

"It's not just her – it's all three of them."

"I know, and one thing's for sure. When Bob Latimer hears about this he'll hit them all with legal action for breach of confidentiality. He's done it before."

"Really?"

"Yes, something like this happened around the time I first joined the firm. I don't remember the details, but I know he hates disloyalty more than anything else. It's a miracle he's kept you on board after that article you wrote. If it was anybody else, he'd have dumped you straight away, but I know he appreciates all the good stuff you've done for him."

"Surely if he takes legal action he'll antagonise the Franchi people and lose all hope of winning the contract for Latimers?"

"That's probably true, but I think he'd rather cut his losses with them than allow himself to be shafted by his own employees. Someone needs to tell them that."

Chapter 77

Jenna answered her phone next morning at the second ring. "Mike, I wasn't sure if we'd be speaking again."

"Why not? We've been through a lot together. It gives us a permanent bond."

She laughed. "Is that what you reckon?"

"So what's been happening up there in the north?"

"Well, my mum hasn't thrown my dad out yet. I suppose that's one good thing."

"But he's not back at work?"

"Not yet. It depends if he can resolve things at home, I think."

"What about the police? Are they taking action against him?"

"I don't know. It's all a bit vague. It's Ernie Bladen they really want, so I think my dad's hoping they'll treat him as a side issue."

"You're on speaking terms with him, then?"

"No way. My mum told me that."

"Do you think you'll be able to make things up with him eventually?"

She took a while to answer, then said quietly, "I don't know."

I waited for a moment, wondering how to introduce the Franchi contract. Into the blank space Jenna said, "I heard you had a run-in with our Mr Bladen down in Harrogate."

"Yeah, it was a complete coincidence. He was owed money by a distant relative of mine. Long story, but he turned up there with a gun, hoping to make sure he got his way. The cops showed up just in time."

"My god! What an exciting life you lead, Mike Stanhope."

"Not by choice."

"Ah, you'd miss it."

Her friendly manner made my task more difficult. Then she gave me an opening. "So what made you ring me this morning? It wasn't to ask how I am."

"Yes it was – partly. But I also wanted to ask you about the Franchi contract."

Immediately she sounded more guarded. "What about it?"

"Look, I may as well tell you I know about your arrangement with Greg and Gary. I know about the Edgeley Stevens involvement."

"Bloody hell, Mike." She was silent for a moment. "You really do keep your ear to the ground, don't you?

"Sometimes."

She fell silent again, and said nothing for so long that I started wondering if she'd been cut off. Finally she said, "I suppose you think I'm being disloyal."

"Well, you probably don't feel much loyalty to Mellings after what your dad did, but you must have started talks with the Franchi people a good while ago. Didn't it seem a bit unethical to you at the time?"

"No it didn't! Not really."

"So what then?"

She seemed to think about this, then apparently decided she had nothing to lose by coming clean. "I got chatting to Gary and Greg in the pub one day, and we all reckoned we could run the Franchi operation better than Mellings or Latimers would. Gary said it would have been a breeze if he'd still been working at Edgeley Stevens. But working independently, we could do it even better. Edgeleys would provide the warehousing and core services, but we would run the thing, and we could choose which carriers to use for the home deliveries. Everyone would win."

"Except Latimers and Mellings."

"Yeah, well, it just seemed that a great big opportunity was being dangled in front of our faces."

"So when you told me you were worried that your income was under pressure, in reality you knew you would be making big money through this contract. You were just spinning me a hard luck story."

"No! That's not fair. I didn't know for sure that we'd win the contract. It might all have come to nothing. It still might not work out."

"Right. Well I feel I should tell you that it *won't* work out. Your best advice is to withdraw now, and avoid any fallout later."

"Why should we? We don't have to do anything on your say-so. You're just an onlooker here." Her voice was rising in pitch with her indignation. "I don't mean to be rude, Mike, but you know fuck all about this."

I sighed. I'd known she would take this badly. After a moment I pressed on. "I'm trying to save you embarrassment later. If you go ahead with this, Bob Latimer will take legal action against Gary and Greg, and probably against you as well. Your bid will be totally derailed." I was improvising a lot of this, but it seemed to reflect what Ashley had told me.

"I don't see why. Even if a load of poxy writs come flying in, we can still get the contract under way. These are just details."

"But think about it. How do you imagine the Franchi people will view the situation once they know there are legal issues? They'll be worried that the contract with you might be compromised. If it is, they could be left with no logistics company on board. Can you seriously imagine them going ahead on that basis?"

"For god's sake, Mike, this is just smoke and mirrors."

"It's a matter of perception, that's the point."

She thought for a moment. "But if Latimers really did take action against us, you surely don't think Franchi would give the contract to them instead? They would blame Latimers for all this crap."

"You're probably right. What's more like to happen is that Edgeley Stevens will negotiate a new contract with Franchi in their own right, and everyone else will lose out."

That seemed to give her food for thought, so I pressed on, "The real question is, who stands to lose more if you press on with this – Latimers or your little team? Latimers would still have all their other work. You would have nothing but legal hassle and a tarnished reputation – and that's even before you started trading."

"Fuck you, Mike. Fuck this." She disconnected.

* * *

Half an hour later my phone buzzed on the table. It was Jenna calling me back.

"Sorry, Mike, I got a bit carried away before."

"Apology accepted."

"It was just a bit of a shock, finding that you knew all about this."

"I didn't have to warn you. I could have kept quiet."

"I know. I see that. I was blaming the messenger, wasn't I?"

"Sort of."

She took a long breath. "I'll have to talk to the guys. They might say they want to carry on regardless."

"That's up to them, but personally I think it would be a really bad idea."

"Gary's got an office set up – in Gloucester. He's recruited two staff already to hold the fort there. He's had some investment from a couple of sleeping partners, and he's got bank guarantees set up – all the good stuff you need if you're going to convince clients you're a sound business. It's going to cost him if he decides to back out now."

"All the same, he might as well do that. I honestly don't see him winning the Franchi deal, and I would guess he's going to lose his job with Latimers either way. But he can try to build up this new company, and pitch for other contracts. You could still work with him."

She gave a sad laugh. "What – with no customers and no income?"

"Wasn't that how you started out with Ashurst Concepts?"

"Not really. I got a proper fee from them right from day one. I've got bills to pay, Mike. Living on a shoestring isn't me, is it?"

"If you say so."

Reflectively, she said, "I really thought at one point that I might stay on at Mellings and work with the marketing team at Latimers. But Ashley's never going to wear that, is she?"

"Probably not."

"I like her. She's a nice person."

"Thank you for that."

Hesitantly she said, "I'm sorry I kept you in the dark about the

Franchi project, Mike. I would have loved to tell you all about it when I first met you, but you were on the wrong side. There was no way I could say anything."

It sounded sincere. I said, "I can see that."

"In another life … "

Chapter 78

Hello Mike

Write the next book! Stop overthinking it and worrying about where it's all going. Just do it! Have a bit of confidence in yourself.

I know it's easy for me to shout encouragement from the sidelines, but life is short – I should know. You have the time and you have the ability. These are gifts, and you should make use of them. You might not get the chance later on.

I expect you're surprised to have received this letter, but I don't want to send it to you until the time is right – and I don't know how to set up an email or a blog post so that it will be delivered in the future. So I'm having to resort to good old snail mail.

The fact that you're reading this note will mean that I am no more, as they say. I'm going to ask my solicitor to send it out for me. I suppose all this will come as a surprise to you, and if it does I can only apologise. It didn't seem relevant to mention my condition to you. It would have coloured the comments you posted, and I didn't want delicacy, I wanted honesty. I think that's what we've had.

I'm leaving you my collection of books. Sorry! I was going to hand them on to an old friend, but she'll never read any of them, and you might. But it doesn't matter if you don't. The mere thought that you'll have them gives me pleasure, and if they widen your horizons a bit, it's all to the good. I realise the future is digital, and I wish I could be there to see how it evolves, but I hope you'll agree that there's still room in our lives for the printed word too.

I just wanted to say that it's been a delight to exchange ideas with you over the past year. I only wish I'd made contact before. I knew who you were a long time ago, but until lately it never occurred to me to get in touch. I suppose discovering our shared interest in writing made the difference.

If you haven't already worked out or been told who I am, my name is Elizabeth Sanderson (but you can call me Liz – much good that it will do you). Your grandmother, Emily Sanderson, was my birth mother, so that makes me your aunt. She was only a teenager when I was born, and my father was married to someone else, so she gave me up to live with his family. Maybe in her shoes I would have done the same thing. I'm not complaining. I had a very happy childhood.

So that's why I tracked you down, but it's not why I've kept up the contact. I like to think our exchanges have been purely those of like-minded people with a common interest, and I hope you feel the same.

I could feel tears at the back of my eyes as I read this letter. The first time I glanced through it I felt I must have stepped into a parallel universe. How could this woman be claiming to know me when we'd never even met? The second time, everything was clear. We'd met online.

Specifically, she'd been an active contributor to a writers' forum that I'd joined several years before. Initially I'd commented on postings by a variety of other people, but gradually I'd lost interest. In the end I really only followed this one member, a woman who (unlike me) posted under a pseudonym.

I'd sensed that she was involved in a serious way with the literary world, but she also had a penchant for popular fiction, and we'd shared an enthusiasm for mysteries and thrillers. At the same time we'd railed at the flaws and inexactitudes of other would-be writers, indulging ourselves in the kind ranting that is usually reserved for old friends.

It felt as if we had been.

The letter had been clipped to the back of the new will leaving everything to Maggie, and like the will it was unsigned. I'd missed it when I'd found the sheaf of documents in that hidden compartment of Elizabeth's desk, but now, six weeks later, I'd spotted it for the first time. Obviously she'd intended to sign them both and hand them to her solicitor, but it had never happened.

She must have researched my family and tracked me down, then made contact with me anonymously through the forum when she found out I had aspirations to becoming a novelist. I remembered her postings clearly; they'd contained a mixture of wry wit and erudition – quite different in tone from some of the other, often scolding comments that my postings seemed to provoke. I'd suspected that she was older than me, but it hadn't struck me that she might be in her seventies. Her comments had had an ageless brightness about them.

I smiled to myself at the mention of her books. Her official will left everything to me, including the books – all those bookcases full of them – so I'd ended up inheriting them along with everything else. I'd already wondered briefly what to do with them. Now I felt an obligation to treat them with respect.

* * *

Probate had now been granted, so I was officially the owner of a house in Harrogate. However, I'd decided to stick to my plan to split the value three ways. I was already in touch with an estate agent about putting the house on the market.

Maggie had been nonplussed when I'd contacted her to tell her about my intentions. I asked her if she might use her share of the money as down payment on a house or flat in some other town. "No way!" she'd exclaimed. "Consett is where I live, and it's where I'm stopping."

Angela had told me she was looking into possible ways I could pay her share into an account that Philip could never access. I knew this was bound to create tension in their household, but all I could hope was that the outcome would be better for them than if there had been no payment.

So far, she told me, Philip hadn't been charged by the police with any offence, so it might be that he'd escaped that fate. However, he was almost certain to be called as a witness in Ernie Bladen's trial for extortion, fraud, and possibly attempted murder. He had to hope that Bladen had run out of associates willing to exert intimidation on his behalf.

I, too, was likely to be called as a witness in that trial – a prospect that scarcely filled me with joy. I would be glad to see Bladen brought to justice, but I'd never before had to put my head above the parapet in a situation that would make me so exposed. One piece of encouragement had come from Dave, who told me, "Even other gangland people don't like Bladen. They think he's too erratic and indiscriminate. So he may have run out of favours to call in." I couldn't judge if this was true, but it made me feel a little more secure.

Chris Melling was another man facing possible court action, but from what I'd heard, he had not so far been charged with anything. No doubt he was being lined up as another witness in the Bladen trial.

Ashley told me he hadn't returned to work so far, but her colleagues had been in touch with him informally to help ease the transition of his company to Latimer ownership. He was still living at home, she said, so despite his fears, his wife hadn't thrown him out. "In fact he gave one of his film shows to some neighbours the other day, so it can't all be doom and gloom."

Chapter 79

I glanced at the wall clock: ten forty-five in the morning. The supermarket was ten minutes' drive away. I could be there and back in half an hour. I gathered up my keys and headed out to the car.

A kind of routine had re-established itself. I spent most nights with Ashley at her flat, then returned to my own place the following morning and worked there during the day. However, tonight Ashley was going out with some girl friends from the office, so I would be staying at home for once. But I'd neglected to re-stock my larder, and this morning I'd found myself staring into an empty fridge. It was an excuse to break off from the article I was trying to write.

I drove down a few short streets to the point where my small estate joined the main road towards the town centre, but then I remembered I'd left my laptop lid open with several applications still running. I knew from bitter experience that in the absence of any interaction from me, its fan would start to race and it might eventually shut itself down, trashing any work I hadn't saved.

Annoyed with myself, I made a hasty three-point turn and drove back to my apartment block. A grocery delivery van had already taken my parking place, so I had to continue several vehicle lengths past it before pulling in. I strode impatiently back towards the entrance.

There was a low wall surrounding the block. I vaulted over it and approached the front door diagonally across the small lawn. At least my flat was on the ground floor, so I had no stairs to climb. Then out of the corner of my eye I thought I sensed some slight movement behind my front window. I stopped in my tracks.

Had I imagined it? Was I becoming paranoid? Probably, but after everything that had happened to me lately I wasn't taking any chances. I stepped a couple of paces back, then approached the building at right angles, keeping out of direct line of sight of the window.

Reaching the wall, I inched my way along it and peered warily round the edge of the window. It was difficult at first to see past the reflections, but the figure of a man on my sofa was unmistakable. He was leaning forward, typing on my laptop. How convenient, I reflected ironically, that I'd left it switched on and running for his benefit.

I recoiled, thinking fast. How had he got in? The answer, unfortunately, was all too clear. I'd left the front door to my flat unlocked. So stupid. The main door to the building had its own lock, but often it failed to close properly. Whoever this was, I might as well have put up a sign inviting him in.

The fact that he'd already settled himself at my computer suggested he'd been watching me, and must have entered as soon as I'd left. He wouldn't have expected me to come back so soon after driving away. That made this more than a random intrusion.

My first instinct was to barge in and stop him before he did any serious damage, but then I thought again. My laptop was a cheap one, and all my important stuff was backed up in the cloud. Disrupting the computer could certainly inconvenience me, but that was probably all, whereas confronting the intruder in the confines of my lounge could be a dangerous strategy.

Instead, I reached for my phone to call the police, but then I hesitated again. I could video this man on my phone; then if he escaped before the police arrived, I would still have evidence. My recent voice recordings had served me well, so why not try the same trick again?

I switched my phone to video mode and peered cautiously through the corner of the window again. The man was still typing. He was wearing a woollen hat that partly disguised his features, but I had a strong sense that he was Neville, the man who had turned up in Harrogate to help Ernie Bladen. I set the video app running and raised the phone to the window.

Ten or fifteen seconds passed. I prepared to end the recording and make the call to the police. Then I heard a sudden shout from behind me. "What do you think you're doing, mate?"

I jerked my head round to see a middle-aged man standing on the pavement beyond the flanking wall. "Are you some kind of pervert?" he demanded.

Foolishly I looked back into the room. The man had straightened and was staring over at the window, and our eyes briefly met. He'd probably also seen my phone making the recording. I was sure now that it was in fact Neville.

He pushed the coffee table away, stood up and strode quickly out of sight towards the hall door. In three or four seconds he could be emerging from the building.

I backed away from the window. Would he simply flee, or would he come after me and try to take my phone from me? I didn't fancy my chances in a fight with him, but this was broad daylight and there was a witness. Surely I must be safe enough? I stepped half-way across the lawn, then stopped. I would stand my ground.

Sure enough, the front door to the block burst open and the man came storming out. He'd pulled his woollen hat down over his face so that it looked like a balaclava, which gave him the benefit of fierce anonymity. He strode quickly towards me.

"Give me the phone!"

I didn't know what to do. I hated the thought of backing down, but I had no idea how to defend myself. This man could do me serious damage, and I'd already had enough of that in recent weeks. Anger alone wasn't going to protect me.

I glanced over at the passer-by, who had started to walk away and was hovering at the end of the property. "Call the police!" I shouted to him. He looked uncertain; a moment ago he'd thought I was a peeping tom, and he seemed to be struggling to adjust his perception.

The man ignored him and stepped up close to me. He had broad shoulders and was a couple of inches taller than me. It was no contest. He said, "I want that phone NOW! I won't ask you again."

I felt a surge of resentment. I knew I wasn't going to give up my phone, and evidently that meant I had to take another beating. I was back in the school playground, and he was the bully no one could challenge.

Almost unconsciously I started to brace myself, thinking wildly that

I would throw the first punch. He anticipated the move and simply shoved me brusquely away. "Be your age! Just give me the phone."

"Why should I?"

"Because you're a wuss." He stepped forward and shoved me again. This time I nearly stumbled over backwards. "Give it to me before I get really angry."

"Stop it!"

We both looked round. The call had come from the passer-by, who was staring over at us, open-mouthed. I was surprised; I'd already dismissed him as someone who wouldn't get involved.

We were close to the low boundary wall now, and during that brief interruption I decided there was no ignominy in flight. I turned, stepped away and vaulted over the wall. The man immediately followed, but I was now a couple of paces ahead of him. I sprinted off in the direction of my car.

And tripped over.

My toe had stubbed the edge of an uneven paving slab. I lunged forward, scuffing my knees and scraping my palms painfully on the ground, and came to a stop just short of where my car was parked.

The man walked up and stood over me, and without hesitation kicked me in the shoulder. I tried to roll away, but immediately I slid over the edge of the kerb and into the gutter.

From some distance away the passer-by's tentative voice called, "What on earth is going on?" The man turned and shouted, "If you know what's good for you mate, fuck off and mind your own business. NOW!" He had a deep, resonant voice, and his warning seemed to do the trick. There was no further protest from that quarter.

He turned back to me. "Phone please."

Chapter 80

I stared up, my heart racing. I heard myself saying, "Or what?"

I was too slow to squirm out of the way. Another angry kick landed on my shoulder. The man shouted, "Give it to me, you pathetic creep!"

The next blow marked an escalation. He caught me in the middle of the wound I'd received in that warehouse in Leeds, when Piers Ashurst had dropped a timber pallet on me. The damage had been healing nicely, but now a sharp pain was shooting up and down my arm. I couldn't withstand much more of this.

An engine started up somewhere nearby, and I heard the sound of a vehicle pulling away. The delivery van quickly came into my peripheral vision, presumably off to its next call. Then, miraculously, it came to a halt adjacent to us. From inside the cab a man's voice called, "Are you all right, mate?"

My attacker paused and looked up at the van, and I took the opportunity to roll over and struggle into a kneeling position. He seemed to be inhibited by the presence of a second witness, and while he hesitated I managed to stand up shakily and make my way round the front of the van. From there I continued across the road, thinking I might try to disappear into a front garden opposite.

At the other side I paused and glanced back. The man had followed me round the front of the van and was starting to lunge across the road after me, but at that point things happened very fast. There was a fleeting cry, then a cyclist barrelled directly into him at high speed. I was aware of an anguished yell, a muffled groan and an ugly scraping sound. The man was spun round and flung to the ground, while the cyclist went scudding sideways along the road. He ended up at the kerbside in a tangle of fluorescent vest, legs and wheels.

* * *

Waiting amid the flurry of ambulances and police cars, I spotted a USB pen drive in the middle of the road, presumably lying where the man had dropped it. I was reluctant to put my fingerprints on it, but I was also determined that he shouldn't reclaim it himself, so I kicked it under a parked car.

Neville, now unmasked and clearly identifiable, was in fact unconscious, and looked incapable of reclaiming anything. The cyclist was conscious, but had apparently broken an arm. When I was sure Neville wasn't going to be able to pick up the USB stick I drew one of the policemen's attention to it. He bagged it carefully and took it away with him.

Eventually I seemed to have convinced everyone that I was relatively unharmed and was the victim, not an assailant, and I was allowed to retreat to my flat. Then later in the day the police returned and took away my laptop computer, aiming to find out what Neville had been doing to it or with it.

Next day Ashley lent me her old laptop, which at least restored some semblance of normality to my life, but it didn't feel anything like normal. I was looking over my shoulder every time I went outside. It seemed Neville was no longer a threat, but who else might be lying in wait? I'd somehow assumed that Cornwall represented a safe haven. Now I knew it wasn't.

It took a couple more days before I got the full story from Nick Murray, the detective leading the Bladen investigation. I hadn't heard anything from him since returning to Cornwall, but out of the blue he phoned me.

"You had a lucky break," he told me.

"How so?"

"Your friend Neville Hurst was copying some very nasty pictures on to your laptop. Child porn, serious hardcore, that kind of thing. Stuff that would have made you look a very bad person."

"Jesus."

"He'd already copied at least a hundred images when you turned up, and he was in the process of deleting them."

"Deleting them?"

"So that you wouldn't realise anything was wrong. The first you would have known about it would have been a visit from the police. A forensic examination would almost certainly have recovered at least some of the images. In short, you would have been in the shit."

For a moment I couldn't summon up any coherent reaction to this. The nightmare quality of what Nick was telling me was only gradually sinking in. Finally I said, "Thank god I interrupted him."

"It might not have come to that. You would have received a threatening message first – an untraceable email or phone call. 'Keep quiet at the trial, or your good name will be trashed.' But you wouldn't have known what to look for, so you couldn't have done anything about it. Basically, you would have been nobbled."

"Right." I reflected on that for a moment. "But what if I'd refused?"

"A tip-off to the police. Your reputation would have gone out the window, and your evidence would have been called into question." He paused. "They would have won either way."

"Unbelievable."

"Internet blackmail is an increasing problem, unfortunately. It's the world we live in."

It was a chilling thought. I'd grown up before the era of internet bullying, but I had no doubts about how damaging it could be. My good name could have been damaged for life. The power of the media was almost limitless. Suddenly the world seemed a much more fragile and dangerous place.

"And Ernie Bladen was definitely behind this?" I asked.

"There's no question in my mind, though we don't have any hard evidence yet."

"So should I be preparing myself for more of the same?"

"I seriously doubt it. For one thing, Bladen is running out of favours to call in. Hurst was one of the last of his gangland associates with any loyalty to him, and he's out of the picture now."

"I'm glad to hear it."

"More to the point, they've shot their bolt with the internet stuff. It won't work again. If there's anyone left in Bladen's camp, they know we'll be watching their every move now, so there's probably not much more they can do."

I laughed humourlessly. "I hope that's true."

* * *

In the event, Nick Murray was proved right. The attack on my computer turned out to be Ernie Bladen's last hurrah. A few weeks later I travelled to Newcastle for his trial, and in the witness box I faithfully recounted what I knew. As I'd suspected, I was just one among many witnesses Bladen had evidently failed to frighten off, and my part seemed to be over before it had begun.

After testifying I wandered through the court's circulating area. Dave had been called as a witness too, but somehow we'd ended up attending on different days. I was staying on my own in a hotel in the city centre, and I was ready to return there for the night. However, on my way out I spotted Jenna Melling. I was tempted to avoid her, but she caught my eye and came over.

"I hope they lock him up and throw away the key," she said vehemently, but she followed this with a winning smile. "How's life in Cornwall, Mike? Are you happy to be home again?"

"Very," I said with emphasis. "I'm thinking of putting all this in a book."

She looked carefully at me to see if I was joking. I gave her what I hoped was an inscrutable smile.

She told me Piers Ashurst had been found guilty of theft at his own trial in Leeds. "He's waiting to be sentenced, and they think it will be custodial."

"I'm sorry."

"If he survives it he'll bounce back. You watch."

"And your father … ?"

"They've dropped all charges against him. I'm not making a fuss, and apparently Bladen is saying nothing. There's insufficient evidence."

"But you haven't made it up with him?"

"Give me a break."

We made our way over to the exit. The modern court building fronted directly on to the Quayside, and a chilly wind was gusting over the water. Standing at the top of the steps, Jenna said, "Fancy a quick drink?"

I looked at her for a moment. "Probably best not."

Chapter 81

The sun gave an unexpected intensity to the seascape at Land's End. I stood in silent wonder for a moment, then turned to Ashley.

"I'm glad we came."

Initially she'd been sceptical about my proposal to visit this spot, which was a good hour's drive from Truro. I'd persisted. I'd never been here before, and I told her I couldn't consider myself a true Cornishman until I had.

"You can't call yourself a Cornishman anyway, but it's charming to think you'd like to."

She'd warned me that I would be disappointed. "There's nothing there – just a café and a signpost to New York. I think you'll find it's about three thousand miles away."

I could see what she meant about the area, but on a day like this even the scrubby grass and the rocky outcrops were bursting with colour. The cliffs were doing their best to seem imposing, and the sea was a deep shade of blue. High clouds were moving rapidly across the sky.

After all that had been happening in my life in recent months, I'd woken on that Saturday morning with an urge to stand back and regain some kind of perspective. Suddenly the idea of visiting Land's End had come to me. Here I could literally look at my world from the periphery.

"Is it working?" Ashley asked cautiously.

I screwed my eyes up as I stared into the sun. "I think so. It's good to be standing on the edge."

She smiled. "Better than living on the edge, I should think."

I laughed.

"I encouraged you to go to Newcastle," she said. "I actually encouraged you. I can't believe it now. I bet you wish you hadn't listened to me."

"It wasn't your fault. You didn't know all those things would happen. It seemed such a simple assignment."

"I should have known your urge to investigate everything would get you into trouble."

"I'm not very good at it, that's part of my problem. I can be careless and impulsive. And we know the result."

"But you survived. We both survived."

We gazed at the landscape for a moment. Ashley said, "At least the trial is over, and we can move on from that."

I nodded. The expected guilty verdict had come in. I'd lost track of all the crimes Bladen was accused of, but the bottom line was that he'd been sentenced to eight years.

I watched as the breeze whipped Ashley's dark hair around her face. I still felt privileged that she'd let me back into her life. I made a silent vow to ensure she had no reason to eject me from it again.

I said, "Without the income from Latimers, I'm only just covering my bills."

"At least the money from Elizabeth's house will keep you going for a while."

"Not forever though. And anyway, I should save it for something more worthwhile."

"Do you wish now that you'd kept all of it?"

It was a fair question, but there was only one answer. "I couldn't have. I couldn't have lived with myself, feeling that people who'd known Elizabeth all their lives were missing out simply because she lost patience with them at a terrible time in her life."

"Perhaps you shouldn't have gone to such lengths to meet them. They became a lot more than just names on a piece of paper."

"I'm not sorry, though." I looked away again across the water. "But I do want to pay my way in my life in Cornwall."

"Bob Latimer will relent in the end – you watch. You just have to hang in."

She might be right. He'd certainly seemed grateful when I revealed the scheme to steal the Franchi contract from under his nose. But it hadn't so far prompted him to restore my previous part-time contract with the company, and in truth I wasn't sure how far I wanted to revive the former arrangement.

Gary's new firm had pulled out of the Franchi contract bid, leaving Latimers to clinch the deal. It was due to go live some time in the next few weeks. Gary himself had resigned from Latimers, and Greg Atkins had left Mellings at the same time. I'd heard that the two of them were now touting for logistics business together.

I wasn't sure if Jenna was playing any part in this, but I suspected not. I had the impression she'd stayed on in Newcastle and was trying to rebuild her marketing business from there.

I said, "It's a shame that I can't report on all the stuff that's been going on. Some of it's confidential, and in any case, if I went public with any of it I would burn my boats with Latimers forever."

"Maybe after the dust settles … ?"

"Maybe. Or I could fictionalise it all, and put it into a book."

She smiled. "Do you think you will?"

"I don't know. Elizabeth seemed to think I should persevere with the novel writing. Maybe I should take note, and put more of my energies into that."

"It's amazing to think you were in touch with her all that time without knowing it."

"I know. I miss her even though I hardly knew her."

"When you think about it, you spent ages digging into my past, and you ended up discovering a half-sister I didn't know I had. Now you've found a new relative in your own family. Don't you think that's weird?"

"There's a kind of symmetry to it, I suppose."

We both looked out over the sea for a moment, then she said quietly, "I'm sorry I misjudged you over Jenna."

"You don't need to apologise for anything. I should have played things differently. I'm not as wise as I think I am."

"That sounds like a line from a song."

"It probably is."

She gave me a wry look and brushed her hair away from her face. "So you're happy to be here in Cornwall, and you're going to stay?"

I probably looked surprised. "Why are you saying that? Was there any doubt?"

"Oh, you know, I just wondered." She smiled uncertainly at me.

"What else would I do?"

"I don't know."

"Why would I possibly want to leave?"

Epilogue

1948

Northumberland Street was thronging with lunchtime shoppers, drawn there no doubt by the summer sunshine as much as by any great desire to spend hard-earned cash. She threaded her way urgently among them, anxious not to be late. He had only limited time to spare, and she was determined not to waste any of it.

Past Fenwicks' department store, past the Northern Goldsmiths clock, she finally slowed down as she reached the Odeon cinema, where she paused, waiting.

He was from across the river, from that strange other world that centred on Gateshead. She'd been over there in her time, of course. Who hadn't? There were enough bridges across the Tyne, after all. But on those rare occasions she'd usually been on the way to somewhere further afield. The idea of actually visiting the town and its hinterland, of lingering to absorb their alien qualities, had never occurred to her.

Now she wondered what it was like over there. He himself seemed perfectly normal – he watched the same films as she did, spoke with more or less the same accent. Perhaps civilisation didn't end at the Tyne Bridge after all.

She shook her head. These were childish thoughts, and this wasn't a day to be childish. There were places in Newcastle she'd never visited (and some she would never want to visit). Gateshead was just more of the same.

They were going to the pictures. Not to the extravagant picture palace behind her, but to the little News Theatre across the road. But now she felt a sudden wave of apprehension. There was something faintly decadent about the idea of sitting in the dark while the sun was shining outside. It was a denial of the life still going on in the world beyond.

She shrugged off her concern. She'd been taken to the News Theatre in the daytime by her mother, so why should today be any different? It was an opportunity to spend time alone with the person she most wanted to be with – to allow the darkness to envelop them, to exult in the simple ecstasy of touch.

A tram clattered past. The familiar box shape with its rounded ends was reassuring. Trams like this had often carried her home from the city centre. The sight of this one made her feel less exposed here – less detached from the comfortable ordinariness of her everyday life. Not that she wanted to focus on that. A different, more exciting future beckoned, and today was part of it.

And here he was, looking overdressed in his dark uniform, but beaming as he caught sight of her. A thrill ran through her.

"You got away then?" he asked.

"Of course I did."

He took her hand. "Shall we go in then?"

She nodded and they turned to cross the road, but he held out an arm in warning. A vehicle was approaching – a small open truck with two people standing at tripods in the back. They were filming the scene – one facing forward, the other to the side.

Her face broke into a smile.

If you liked Deficit of Diligence, please review it!

Thank you for buying and reading *Deficit of Diligence*. If you enjoyed it, could you do me the great favour of writing a review on the Amazon/Kindle web site? Positive reviews play an enormous part in spreading the word to new readers. Use links below to find the book on Amazon and write your review there. Thank you!

UK book page: https://www.amazon.co.uk/dp/B01N0PRFV0
US book page: https://www.amazon.com/dp/B01N0PRFV0

Have you read Alternative Outcome yet?

Alternative Outcome is where the Mike Stanhope story starts. Even though you've now read the sequel, you'll still be fascinated with the tortuous path Mike has to tread before *Deficit of Diligence* begins, and the romantic story behind it.

Other books by Peter Rowlands

Alternative Outcome (Mike Stanhope Mysteries Book 1)
Available now as an e-book and in paperback

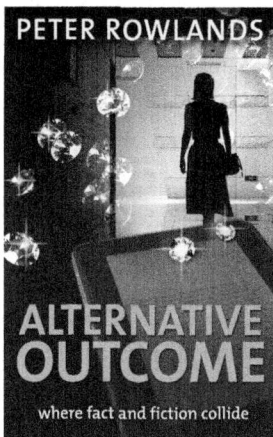

Mike Stanhope, divorced and disillusioned with his job in journalism, hopes to switch his life to a new tack by self-publishing a mystery novel based on a true story. But someone is after him, and the pressure is mounting.

Could his pursuer be the subject of an investigative article Mike once wrote? Could there be a link to Mike's attempts to track down a girl he knew as a child – the memory of whom he hijacked for his novel? Or might there be some deeper connection to his book?

As Mike struggles to keep his life on an even keel and tries to grasp at the chance of a new relationship, fact and fiction start to intertwine.

UK book page: www.amazon.co.uk/dp/B01CK1XVHK
US book page: www.amazon.com/dp/B01CK1XVHK

Mike Stanhope Mysteries Book 3

Publication spring 2017

The prospect of ghost-writing an autobiography for a top executive appeals to journalist Mike Stanhope. He can use the money, and he knows the man's business background well. What could possibly go wrong?

But Alan Treadwell is a tough taskmaster, imposing tight deadlines and taking a demanding slant on the way his book should be tackled. Soon Mike is wondering if he's bitten off more than he can chew. It doesn't help when he starts finding out things about the great man that he'd rather not know – things, moreover, that someone would prefer to keep quiet.

Meanwhile, Mike's hard-won relationship with his girlfriend is on edge, and his repeated absences aren't helping. Before he knows it he's juggling his precarious home life with the increasing distractions of his job, and lunging towards a crisis on all fronts.

Escape Sequence (standalone novel)
In preparation

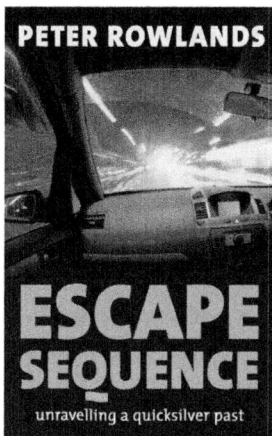

Who is he? He can't remember. All he knows is that he's driving north, perhaps fleeing something. He starts to piece his past together, yet feels like an observer in his own life. Struggling to take control of his complex relationships and responsibilities, he fends off increasingly aggressive threats as he tries to find out what happened to him.

Author's note and acknowledgements

This book has given me the opportunity to celebrate Newcastle past and present. I've tried to be faithful to my knowledge and memories of the area, for which I have great fondness, so the geography and the specific locations are as correct as I can make them.

There are just a few instances where I've moved or slightly reinvented real places, but in most cases I haven't named these. It's also worth pointing out that there's no motel on the A69 in the position where I've placed mine, and as far as I know there's no police station near Armstrong Bridge. And because of spending cuts, country police stations in the Tynedale area are now few and far between, so mine probably amounts to wishful thinking.

I've also taken some liberties with the geography of Hadrian's Wall (or "the Roman wall", as we locals used to call it), mainly by shifting some aspects of the terrain eastwards to make them reachable within the context of the action.

The Tyneside Cinema is real and is thriving, and it was indeed referred to as "the News Theatre" in the past. The Odeon was real too, and the building was still standing when I wrote this book, though it had been unused for fourteen years. Sadly its days appeared to be numbered.

I haven't seriously attempted to reproduce the Geordie accent in quoted speech. It would have been easy enough to throw in many more of the unusual pronunciations and vernacular words, but to those who know the accent I feel this would have seemed patronising, and to those who don't it would probably have been an obstacle to understanding.

I owe a debt of gratitude to many friends and colleagues for their support and encouragement during the preparation of this book. In particular, my thanks go to Stewart and Sue for reading the draft and giving me such positive feedback, to Ros for helping to build my confidence in the benefits of marketing, to Mel for continuing to take me seriously, and above all to Helen for encouraging me to press ahead with the book, and then reading and re-reading it and discussing it with me endlessly.

Thanks are also due to people too numerous to mention for their encouraging responses to my first book, *Alternative Outcome*. I'd always thought of myself as a novelist in waiting, but it's been immensely rewarding to hear that thought echoed by people who seem to be enjoying what I'm writing.

About the author

Peter Rowlands was born in Newcastle upon Tyne, but has lived almost all his adult life in London. He edited and contributed to transport and logistics magazines for many years. *Deficit of Diligence* is his second published novel, and the sequel to *Alternative Outcome*, which is also available on Amazon.

Printed in Great Britain
by Amazon

57693879R00212